ACCLAIM FOR R.M. DOYON'S

UPCOUNTRY

"Doyon's talent lies in portraying everyday people...who are all trying in their own ways to survive in the face of prejudice and pain...a dynamic read...peppered with dramatic events that move along at a good pace."

— IndieReader.com

"What a great read! I can always tell that I like a book when I find myself mentally casting the characters into a movie version. Doyon delivered on this front. Bring on the next!"

— Eileen Chadnick, Toronto, ON

"A very heart-warming and touching story, with a cinematic feel that could be iconic. The core of the story is brilliant...Doyon did a good job with its emotional journey. He nailed it!"

— GuysCanRead, Dallas, TX

"An ending that will bring tears to every reader's eyes. This novel gets Five Beautiful Carousels with Five White Horses!"

— Fran Lewis Reviews, New York

"Doyon's characters come alive!"

— Books and Pals Reviews

"A dysfunctional family sits down for a Thanksgiving dinner after years of sorrow and separation. Hold on tight because once readers get to the part when the dishes are being cleared, they will not be able to put it down. This is the type of novel which begs to be read in one sitting."

— Kathryn Cunningham, Richmond, VA

THOU TORTUREST ME

A NOVEL

R.M. DOYON

Open Kimono Books

Copyright © 2013 R. M. Doyon

ISBN: 1484108256
ISBN-13: 9781484108253

Library of Congress Control Number: 2013907616
CreateSpace Independent Publishing Platform
North Charleston, South Carolina

Cover design:
Julie S. Tremblay
www.jtandco.ca

This book is dedicated to the people who populate an extraordinary piece of geography that is upstate New York—and to all my friends and family that hail from a special Canadian town named Kirkland Lake.

And to Shelley…for your talent, imagination and love.

THOU TORTUREST ME

A NOVEL

BY R.M. DOYON

A PROLOGUE

THE FOLLOWER WATCHED the scene unfold in the wild grasses high above the waters of the big lake. Careful not to utter a single sound—the thicket under the intruder's feet was bone dry, the result of a rainless, late-summer heat wave—a closer look was required. No, it was more than that; there was an overwhelming desire to inch closer.

But to be exposed, now, was the last thing the intruder wanted. So, quietly and stealthily, a move was made, and in seconds, the evidence was clear. There was no doubt about it. Amid faint sounds of laughter, giggles even, under once cloudy skies that fortuitously opened to reveal a full white moon on the horizon, the couple ahead was about to engage.

Words were spoken. But a gust of wind arising from the direction of the Adirondacks made it nearly impossible for the intruder to understand what was being said, particularly those coming from the pretty girl. The man's reply was succinct, however; it was clear, and one that inflamed the trespasser the most.

"You are the most beautiful girl I've ever seen," he said rapturously.

Then it happened. As the silvery waters behind them created a silhouette of sorts, in effect two lissome figures becoming one, the couples' lips met and soon their bodies were obvious with excitement. A blanket appeared and they were horizontal. And, within moments, all clothes were forsaken.

Another utterance from the young woman could be heard, and it too was shocking. "I've wanted you ever since we first met..." she purred, almost prompting the follower to gasp audibly at the betrayal being committed on this warm night. Still, the intruder would wait. For minutes, for many, many minutes the coupling continued, much to the chagrin of the extra pair of eyes in the woods.

After what seemed to be an interminable length of time, the young two-some completed their task, donned their clothes and were bidding each other good-bye. There was a last kiss, with a promise of more, and moments later the young man disappeared into the darkness.

He was gone.

The young woman, however, lingered high above the rocks, enjoying the mesmeric sounds of the lapping waters below. From her perch against the moon-light, she could see a series of rock formations, aged and foreboding, perhaps fifteen feet below her feet. She had visited this very spot many times over the years, but rarely stopped to savor the sight. Tonight she would. Quietly she sat at cliff's edge, one hand softly caressing a necklace containing a single stone.

She was deep in thought, satiated, and at peace.

Happy.

The intruder, still surreptitiously only yards away, was witnessing it all, especially the signs, faint as they were, of a smile crossing the attractive woman's full face.

"I've been watching you."

The follower's words jolted the young woman from her thoughts. Quickly she whipped her head around and, pushing with both hands, rose to her feet. A look of fear enveloped her. But her reaction soon changed to anger at the loss of her privacy. She and her lover had been so alone, or so she thought. She was wrong and now she felt violated.

"What are you...doing here?" she demanded, her inquiry turning to accusation.

The brightness of the night was sufficient to illuminate the intruder's face, and immediately, the young woman saw a level of ferocity that she had never observed in anyone before. Their eyes, steely locked on each other's, became so intense that she failed to notice an object in the follower's hand.

"I've seen everything," the intruder announced.

"That's sick!" the girl cried. "I'm leaving..."

Fearing she would escape, the follower grabbed the girl from behind, and once again, they were eye to eye.

"No, you're not."

ONE

JOSHUA TROYER WATCHED HELPLESSLY as his big Belgian Bay, a beast of Goliathan proportions at nearly seventeen hands, snapped its reins like a twig and bolted across the stubbled remains of his hayfield toward the busy county road.

Damn, he cursed. That horse was always giving him trouble, and this morning he knew he was pushing his luck. Those leather straps should have been replaced, but his work load today was so full that he had failed to address the problem at the barn. Now he was paying the price and Joshua was more upset with himself than with the damned horse.

Temper was at least fifty yards away, and the space between him and an older, less impatient Belgian named Sorrel, was growing. It was not even noon and yet it was scorching hot. He didn't have the time for such nonsense. Sweat had formed in rivulets across his forehead, so much so that the young farmer had unfastened the top three buttons of his dark blue shirt. Sometimes he would remove his upper garments completely. Both acts were forbidden, Joshua knew, but his younger brothers would never turn him in.

"Elijah," he barked to his twelve-year-old brother in his native Pennsylvania Dutch, "make sure Sorrel doesn't get any ideas!" Then he turned his attention towards Levi, a second sibling who was about a year younger and who stood atop the mammoth wagon.

"Stay there and don't move!"

From the corner of his eye, Joshua could see Temper defiantly enjoying his freedom. The handsome stallion, a strong, spirited steed with a lustrous, copper-colored coat, a flaxen mane and a narrow patch of white fur down his narrow nose, was a sight to see. The hard-muscled animal—seemingly weightless though it could tip any scale at more than a ton—pranced near the edge of the road. Temper's right ear, deformed at birth and bent forward as if it was winking at its owner, fluttered with excitement. *'Come and get me, if you can,'* the young animal seemed to tease.

Joshua's father, Menno, had purchased the year-old Belgian from a carpenter near Heuvelton as a prospective wedding present for his son only weeks before, hoping that the younger man, the strongest, fittest member of their large family, could impose his will on the four-legged rebel. Damn, Joshua cursed again, but out of earshot of his brothers. He realized it was improper for him to demonstrate anger, let alone introduce inappropriate language to a couple of impressionable youngsters. But why hadn't he fixed the *damn* reins?

His workday had started poorly, and again he knew why. He had tossed and turned all night and this morning he was paying for it. He hadn't slept well the previous night either, and for a number of nights since last Sunday. That was when he asked Rachel, his sister sixteen months his junior, to approach a girl from a neighboring farm. To enquire about her availability.

He and the girl had been observing each other curiously for months. Joshua thought their first encounter was at *Rumspringa,* a running around period with their peers, when they were still teenagers. But Rachel had corrected him, as was a sister's prerogative. They had met at a pig-butchering frolic last fall, Rachel insisted, and Joshua was in no position to argue. Either way, the girl had made an impression upon him. How profound an impression he did not know.

Menno had wondered, too, when his son would make a decision concerning the rest of his life. Joshua was twenty-one now, an age when most Amish men would leave the family farm and set out on their own. "The boy needs to choose a mate," Joshua overheard Menno telling his wife Sarah the week before. The pressure was on. As the eldest of their thirteen children, it was expected.

Since their move from Ohio nearly ten years before, they had lived and worked the family farm near Morgantown, New York. Attracted by inexpensive land, though hardly as rich as the soil near Millersburg, a hamlet about sixty miles southwest of Akron, Menno had made the decision to move to northwestern New York. They had followed many of their brothers and sisters to this part of the state and now their order numbered in the thousands. They had settled within sight of Remington Pond, a large body of water some twenty miles in length that emptied, like most lakes in the shadows of the Adirondacks, into a rayless and winding river named the Oswegatchie, a moniker derived from the Mohawks who ruled the land centuries before.

For the most part, Morgan County had been hospitable to the Troyers, notwithstanding its barren, rocky soils and its sometimes inhospitable weather during seeding time. Ohio's weather conditions would never have been confused with those of Georgia or South Carolina. But New York's growing season for hay and corn, the dual staples, was adequate for their needs. Here they could cultivate berries of all kinds, sweet corn and apples to sell to the English, along with basketry and quilts. Theirs was a life of subsistence but spiritually rewarding.

The sparsely populated, even bleak, countryside of Morgan County made sense to Menno. He uprooted his growing brood, then only half the size of what it was today, and made the journey north, carving a new life in New York's tough environs. And at forty-one, Menno Troyer was not finished breeding. When a neighboring farmer suggested, good-naturedly, that Menno could use a hobby "to keep him away from the old lady," the Amish man replied that the best way to attract good labor was to "make them." Hard to argue with that logic, the neighbor conceded.

Now, however, Joshua was wracked with doubt, especially as he witnessed the lives of his younger English neighbors and their carefree ways. The clothes they wore. The automobiles they drove. What would it be like, he wondered, to sit behind the wheel of one of those powerful Ford or Chevrolet trucks, with their big rubber tires and their lusty, cacophonous engines? How many times had he watched as their vehicles thundered past his fields, their laughter indicative of a frivolous yet convivial life.

But these destructive pangs of envy would have to be banished from his mind. He would go about his business, and that business was to settle down. At service on Sunday, with Rachel as his matchmaker, Joshua had noticed her again. The girl's name was Hannah Zook, and this time he discovered the courage to approach her. Would she like to ride with him after Sunday singing? Yes, she replied quickly, and their *bundling* would go forth. By evening, the two found themselves lying side by side on her bed, fully dressed, talking quietly. Though frowned upon by some elders as immoral, it had become a common practice among the young people. They would get to know each other.

Joshua quickly felt Hannah's sheepish diffidence towards him, remaining nearly mute and answering his questions only with shrugs and one-word answers. From her responses, lean as they were, he discovered that—unlike him—she was native to Morgan County, since the Zooks had been one of the first young families to arrive here, mostly as carpenters and millers and farmers.

A year younger, she was tall and strong, much more so than most girls her age. Though a pair of round, dark unblinking eyes were her most appealing feature, he was struck immediately by her pale, almost tallowy skin. It reminded Joshua of a freshly-plucked chicken ready for the cooking pot. And, yet, a complete picture of her appearance was almost impossible to decipher, since as the hour approached midnight, she still had not removed a black bonnet that smothered her hair, the color of which remained a mystery to the young farmer. That first bundling felt like an eternity to Joshua, but he sensed Hannah Zook *could* be a worthy mate.

If he was prepared to make such a decision.

Now edging closer to Temper, Joshua realized his active brain and sleepless nights had exacted a price. He had to corral this cagey, taunting animal—and now. Temper needed to know who was in charge. He reached down behind the buckboard's seat for a makeshift lasso that he had always kept aboard his wagon. Now was the time to bring this horse to justice.

Slowly, he approached the colossal beast as it grazed quietly on the high grasses beside the paved road. Over the course of his five or six minutes of stolen freedom, a couple of cars had ventured by, moderating their speeds only slightly at the site of the Belgian on the loose. Joshua surveyed the situation and decided he had one chance of roping Temper and returning him to the wagon. Better make it good, he thought.

As Temper raised his head, Joshua pounced. Expertly, he threw the lasso around the Belgian's head, and pulled tightly on the rope. He worried that the big horse would revolt and pull him down the road or, worse, attempt a foray into the nearby thicket. He was in luck. Temper seemed to realize the jig was up and succumbed to the young farmer's orders to stay put.

From behind, Joshua could hear another motor vehicle approaching from the west. Glancing over his shoulder, he noticed that it was one of those open cars with its vinyl top down. They called them convertibles. Though a rarity, he had seen them before, driven by tourists travelling through the county. As the black polished automobile was arriving, now only about forty yards away, Joshua could see its occupants. In the front, two young men were engaged in conversation; in the rear, deeply set, was a woman stylishly dressed in white with dark glasses and shiny green jewelry around her neck. Typical English, he assumed. Too much money and nothing better to do.

Temper became agitated once again. Still clutching the rope around the horse's head, Joshua gathered the remnants of the shattered reins and pulled violently on both. The horse bucked against its impending servitude. It seemed to know what was coming next as both master and servant went face to face, perhaps only ten or twelve inches away. Then, with one wild, forceful swing, Joshua struck the horse on the side of the head with his fist. Temper winced in pain. That blow was followed by yet another. And another, as the horse let out a series of clearly audible whimpers.

"You big bastard," he now screamed in English, "if you don't do what I want you to do, I'll sell you to the plant!"

Just then, the driver of the car honked his horn, prompting Joshua to turn his head briefly towards the vehicle. The horse, spooked by the proximity of the fresh noises, reacted as well. It began to buck again, jerking its large snout sideways, colliding hard with the young farmer's head and tossing Joshua's straw hat to the ground. Without missing a beat, Joshua slapped the horse once again. This time, the horse settled as the convertible came to a halt beside the road.

"That's the trick, Troyer, get that big dumb shit under control," the driver bellowed. "Show him who's boss!"

"You're not helping much," Joshua replied meekly, his back to the threesome in the car. Though embarrassed by being caught in the act, he would show no weakness. He knew what the English thought about the Amish. They confused discipline with cruelty.

From the back seat, the young woman watched and listened in silence. She had just witnessed the kind of punishment that many of the residents around the county had talked about for years, but she'd never seen firsthand. And she didn't like what she saw.

Then, as he tightened the lasso around Temper's neck, Joshua turned to face the vehicle. In an instant, they became spellbound by each other; she by the clarity of his beaming, emerald-green eyes set above a pair of pronounced and deeply tanned cheekbones and anchored by a strong, decisive chin; he by an alluringly beautiful face surrounded by long and silken strawberry blonde hair, combed back pony-style. To her, his handsome face, chiseled and square, was likely the product of long summer hours in the fields. His hat still resting in the grasses, she could see that his thick, bowler-cut hair was the color of rich brown topsoil.

The Amish she had seen as they hawked their baskets or fruit or baked goods from their buggies at the Wal-Mart parking lot were diminutive in stature. Most of the men were lucky to make it to five foot six, and sported wooly, unkempt beards. But this guy's different, she thought. He was tall, perhaps exceeding six feet with broad shoulders, and very unlike any she had ever seen before. Another moment or two passed. Their mutual stares had not gone unnoticed by the man behind the wheel.

"Hello?" the driver asked. "I'm still here. You remember me, Troyer?"

Joshua returned his attention to the front seat. He nodded, though he could not remember the man's name. Brad or Chad, something like that. He seemed a couple years his senior, but couldn't tell for sure since he was wearing shaded glasses. The Amish farmer stole a glance at the man in the passenger side of the front seat, who appeared bored with the entire exchange, saying nothing. No introductions were offered.

"Yes, I remember you...from that camp over on the Pond," Joshua replied, his head nodding in the direction of the big lake. "I did some work at a couple of places over there this summer, clearing brush and building fences. Delivered some wood, too."

"Yeah, we've been fixing up the old compound all summer and, well, that's why we're here," the driver said. "Can you bring a load of hardwood over today? None of that shitty pine, either. It's too soft and burns too fast. We're having a couple of Labor Day parties this weekend, and you know how we like our bonfires." A slight grin emerged from the driver's lips. Joshua had seen that look on the English many times before.

Sensing that his horse was again growing perturbed, Joshua wrenched the reins tight once again. "Temper!" he admonished. "Enough!"

The woman in the back seat spoke up.

"Your horse's name is Temper?" she asked.

"Yes," was all he could reply.

"Appropriate name for an appropriate owner," she mused. "Maybe we should call you that too."

The passenger in the front seat snickered.

This flustered the young farmer. "It was my horse's name when we bought him," he said, not sure if her question justified an answer. Now he addressed the driver again, quickly changing the subject.

"I can deliver a load of ash and maple. After supper?"

"Sure. How much?"

"Would forty dollars be all right?" Joshua asked.

"For a cord?"

"Yes. And stacked where you want it."

"It'll be dry, right? Wet wood's useless to us."

"Yes, it's been in the sun all summer," Joshua said.

"Okay, that'll work, Troyer...but don't be late. We have some serious celebratin' to do."

Joshua nodded once again. Ignoring the man in the passenger seat, he locked eyes again with the woman in the back seat. She smiled, knowing that she'd made her point.

In a flash, their vehicle was gone.

Joshua cursed a fourth time.

TWO□

PERCHED ATOP HIS RIDER MOWER, Hubie Schumacher removed his khaki-colored Safari hat and mopped his brow with the sleeve of his shirt. God, it's September and we're still having hot friggin' days, he muttered to himself. Glancing at his digital watch, it read nine-forty-nine. He released a deep sigh. It's time, he thought.

"Hey Griz!" He yelled across the lawn toward a large sugar maple under which a chocolate brown Labrador retriever was sleeping. Who said the dog days were restricted to August? The canine's ears perked up, but his master's greeting failed to elicit much more than that.

"Is it time for a brew?" Hubie cupped his ear, playfully. "What'd you say? Sure, why not? It's gotta be ten o'clock somewhere, right?"

With that, the elderly man climbed from his tractor and began the hundred-foot trudge towards his open garage. His gait was difficult now, what with the accident and all. It was a year ago spring that he was thrown from the tractor on a wet and hilly section of his property, the John Deere landing on top of him, crushing his left ankle so badly that it required two titanium pins and nearly ten weeks in a cast.

Wasn't his fault, he had thundered to his VFW pals two days later. Wasn't even drinking. No, the damned accelerator had jammed, revving the contraption at exactly the wrong moment. He was lucky not to have cut his goddamned leg off. If it hadn't been for the Amish kid who had witnessed the fall, he might have been under that machine for hours since Dee was in Watertown on business.

Hubie was nearly seventy now and walked with a limp similar to the one that had bedeviled his son-in-law, Denny, even before the son of a bitch married his daughter. The kid broke his leg running from his mother's crazy, gun-toting boyfriend only hours after he practically demolished the opposing quarterback in the regional finals. So bad was the break that it kiboshed a promising pro career, and Denny never got over it. Didn't matter now, though. The son of a bitch was dead.

Hubie's injury never stopped him from drinking beer, though. His favorite brew, for as long as he could remember, was Labatt's Blue—the Canadian import—but last year Dee had talked him into its lighter, less caloric version. He'd made the transition after his doctor, a fellow Army veteran, had suggested rather bluntly that he had to lose about thirty pounds from his six-foot frame and a good way to start might be to cut back on his beer. All right, Doc, Hubie agreed. I'll do what you say. Light beer was his idea of compromise.

Despite his age, he still didn't look too bad, he thought. Unlike his younger brother, John, who shaved his head Kojak-bald to appeal to younger women, Hubie's hair was surprisingly thick and wavy and polar white. A few years ago, vainly, he decided he would return his hair color to its former hue, a dirty blonde, by experimenting with a bottle of Grecian Formula he bought from Kinney's. But that was a disaster. Turned his hair the color of an overripe lemon about to fall from the tree. He never heard the end of it from his VFW pals.

His sister Barbara and her husband, Roger were expected anytime now from Pennsylvania. To his regret, he hadn't seen much of her over the years, and it might have been due to their differences in age, though that was not the only thing that separated them. For as long as he could remember, their political opinions were miles apart. Miles? More like light years. Barbara was a bloviating, dyed-in-the-union-wool liberal with a short fuse; he, on the other hand, was the calm cool voice of common sense—by his own admission.

Bred over four decades in conservative northwestern New York, his views, he figured, were considered mainstream across the country, especially now that the new president and Congress were doing their best to bankrupt the country. Of course Jane, one of his twin daughters, would have something to say about the current mess they were in—if she were here. He knew she would heap the blame on the previous occupant in the White House for putting two tax cuts and a couple of wars on the country's AMEX card. God that kid of his liked to argue.

Still, he was looking forward to seeing his baby sister and her husband again. Roger Cahill was a good guy, though he didn't say a whole hell of a lot any more. But how could he manage to get a word in around Barbara anyway? She had spent the last fifteen years as the mouthpiece for that steelworkers union in Pittsburgh, organizing voter campaigns for candidates running for Congress, the Senate and every dog-catching position in western Pennsylvania.

She even managed to get more than ten thousand union suckers out for a rally during the last primary for Wendell Foley, Jane's old boss and the governor of New York who early polls indicated would be the Democrats' choice for president. Hubie had met Foley, albeit under terrible circumstances, and the governor had impressed him to the point that he voted Democrat in the primary. Not that he ever fessed up; that would have been an act of treason punishable by lynching in the eyes of his euchre-playing pals down at the hall. A Reagan Republican like him? Never would he venture to the *dark* side. And so he kept it to himself, mostly. That was three years ago, and a bit premature as it turned out. Nobody predicted, certainly not a shocked and disappointed Foley, that that junior senator from Illinois, the one with the big ears, would sweep the country by storm a year later.

Hubie entered the garage and grabbed a beer from a well-stocked refrigerator. A regular fridge, too, not one of those miniatures they had at roadside inns, the kind of place in which he stayed when he scored tickets to an Orange game down in Syracuse. As he popped the tab and began retracing his steps to his tractor, he glanced at the two-story house next door. It belonged to his daughter, Joanne, but now it sat empty. Its back stoop was sloping badly, its patio boards rotten. The paint around the windows, which Denny had neglected for years as he drank himself into daily stupors while chasing skirts, was in worse shape than ever. A sad sight, Hubie concluded, but not uncommon either, in these parts.

Nothing he could do about it. Now living in the Adirondacks, Joanne had asked her father to keep an eye on the decrepit house while she made up her mind about its future. If it was up to him, he'd slap a for-sale sign out front and take the first offer on the table. Maybe a new owner would fix it up. Then he wouldn't have to cringe every time he looked across the yard. But it wasn't his decision.

The retired postmaster placed his beer in the rider's convenient cup holder and was about to fire up the aging tractor when he glanced down the road. A team of horses, pulling an overflowing buckboard, was arriving. It was led by a familiar young man for whom Hubie had a soft spot. These kids worked hard for everything they had, unlike the shiftless boors who overstayed their welcome at the Paddle or Swigs every night. No one has a work ethic worth a damn anymore, he thought. But this kid and his brothers knew what hard work was. Leaving his tractor behind, Hubie sauntered over to greet the young men.

"Good morning, young Troyers," Hubie said warmly, glancing as well at the younger boys sitting on their hay.

"Mr. Schumacher, good day," Joshua said, tipping his straw hat. "How's your ankle?"

"Getting better, Josh. Can't complain." Hubie's memory returned to that morning in May when the tractor overturned, trapping him underneath. The pain was so acute, so piercing, that he felt as though he would pass out. Out of nowhere arrived the brawny Troyer kid, returning the Deere to its upright position and freeing the elderly man in seconds. Then he raced to a neighbor's house and asked him to call an ambulance.

"Still need that cedar fence built behind the garage, Mr. Schumacher?"

Hubie nodded. He had angered some of his contractor friends by spiriting work to the Amish, but he didn't care. The Amish were more dependable and, besides, loyalty was a two-way street.

"When can you start?"

"My brothers and I will start peeling the posts," Joshua said, "because the cedar bark has to be removed to give them a long life, sir. When we're finished with the corn, we can come over. Will that work? A couple of weeks?"

Hubie glanced up at the younger siblings, Elijah and Levi, though he couldn't tell them apart.

"Hi boys," he waved, eliciting only a smile from both. It was Joshua's role to interact with the English.

"Great, but stop calling me 'sir', Josh."

"Whatever you say...*sir*," Joshua replied, returning the affection.

"All right, get that wagon outta here. I've got to finish this job before my sister gets here. And don't forget to put a few diapers on those horses of yours. You wouldn't believe the bitching and moaning I hear about you guys around town."

Joshua threw his friend a smile as he whipped the reins to his team and soon was rolling down the road.

Good kids, Hubie thought, as he returned to his tractor, downing the last dregs of his first beer. He was making the last sweep of his acre-sized lawn when a lumbering Cadillac Escalade, deep maroon in color, pulled into the long gravel driveway. Greeting them with a wave, he powered his machine in their direction. Barbara was the first to emerge from their vehicle, with Roger moving slowly behind her.

Maybe because of their ages, he had never acknowledged it before, but there was no doubt that his sister was still a very beautiful woman. At fifty-six or fifty-seven—he couldn't remember what year she was born—Barbara could have passed for a woman at least ten years younger. Slender and fit, she carried herself gracefully, even sensually, up the driveway. When he would arrive home on leave, he had recalled her as a teenager with long, beatnik-styled hair, parted down the middle, sometimes braided. Like the flower child she thought she was. She wore her hair three-quarter length now, slightly above her shoulders and stylishly colored a rich dark-brown with reddish-blonde streaks. A stunning contrast to what she looked like a couple of years ago, he thought. After her battle with cancer.

For a fleeting moment, he was taken aback. Perhaps it was his imagination, but his sister eerily resembled his late wife, Donna. It had been more than a decade since Donna had died from another hideous form of the disease, in her case, ovaries. Sometimes he thought his family was cursed.

Roger was another story. Eleven years her senior, Barbara's second husband had been in poor health for a number of years. Originally, she had told Hubie that Roger was suffering from an early onset of Alzheimer's. That diagnosis had changed to some sort of encephalopathy, apparently caused by a faulty thyroid that produced memory loss, a lack of concentration, and that kind of thing. Hell, Hubie had thought, doesn't every guy our age have those problems? He figured he had just described half the male population of Morgantown.

Whippet-thin with narrow shoulders, Roger was never a formidable man. But now he looked gaunt, almost emaciated. His hair, which was the color of beach sand during his twenties, was now thinning visibly and had turned a dirty white. His trademark Harris tweed jacket, itself a cliché with its obligatory elbow patches, symbolized what he was: an erudite, doctorate-carrying classics professor at Carnegie Mellon with a penchant for everything from Jane Eyre and Jane Austen to Shakespeare, Chaucer, Dickens and Defoe.

Derisively, he loved to discuss with graduate students the demerits, as he labeled them, of such American giants as Hemingway, Faulkner, Updike and Sinclair. But, secretly, he envied and admired their greatness. Indeed, Americana often crept into his lectures; his one wish being able to travel back in time and play poker with Harpo Marx and Ring Lardner at the Algonquin Round Table. He reveled often in the quickness of one of the Algonquin's most infamous participants, Dorothy Parker, who when challenged to create a sentence including horticulture, famously remarked, 'you can lead a horticulture but you can't make her think!' Clearly, Roger was born in the wrong era.

Now, Roger appeared to be failing. It was sad, Hubie thought, since he had always preferred this guy over Barbara's first husband, whatever the guy's name was, he was that insignificant. Thank God that that loser decided to bolt the scene very early in their marriage. It had hurt Barbara at the time but she was better off without him. Watching his sister dote on her stricken husband, waiting patiently for him to catch up, warmed his heart. It was clear they were still very much in love.

"Welcome back to God's country, little sister." He opened his arms broadly, awaiting her embrace with a kiss on both cheeks, European style. She did this to annoy him, he thought, but he'd let it go. Hubie turned to greet his brother-in-law, holding out a firm hand for Roger to shake. "Good to see you again, Rog."

"Same here, Hubert," Roger replied, using his brother-in-law's formal name much in the same way as Dee always did.

Hubie turned to address his sister. "Have a good trip?"

"Yeah...uneventful," she replied. "Pittsburgh is too far to drive in one day, so we broke it up with an overnight in Syracuse. Five hundred miles was enough for me."

"Well, I seem to remember a trip you took by yourself to the Left Coast in search of the Promised Land. But you were too late... the druggies and other bums had all left by the time you got there."

Barbara smiled weakly. She wouldn't let him get away with a comment like that.

"I'm still waiting, Hubert," she replied with a vicious grin, "for that wonderful day when you can open your mind a mile wide. As an optimist, I know that day is coming. After all, Joanne told me that you met a big-named Democrat when he was running for president and that the two of you got along famously. Convinced you to vote for him, she said. You might say it was your personal conversion on the Road to Damascus!"

"The one in Pennsylvania or Virginia?" Hubie retorted. "Heard of them. Never been to either."

"Don't be coy," she replied. "You know what I mean."

It was his turn to smile. "Me vote for a Democrat? It gets colder than hell up here but the landscape isn't completely frozen over. Besides, this is New York and downstate is crawling with Democrats and he didn't need my vote."

Barbara decided to change the subject.

"So, how are you, Hubert?"

"Well, I'm still above ground, if that's what you're asking, Barb," he replied.

"That's what I'm asking."

It was then that Barbara noticed the beer can in the cup holder. She too glanced at her watch, which appeared to Hubie as one of those overpriced Bulgari's or Gucci's or whatever. One of those fancy Italian jobs. That was his sister, a classic silver-spooned socialist.

"Two hours *before* noon...what took you so long?"

That put her brother on the defensive.

"It's hotter 'n hell out, or haven't you noticed? Driving that fancy, air-conditioned Caddy all the way from Pittsburgh?"

She patted him on his protruding beer gut and almost let the comment go unanswered. Then she decided to give him one last shot. With an exaggerated hand gesture to create an even larger girth, Barbara replied, "You remember what Dad used to say? You keep this up and soon you're gonna need a pecker scope!"

He let out a laugh. He hadn't forgotten just how earthy and unfiltered Barbara could be. Must be all that time she spent with steel workers.

"Duly noted, oh smart-assed sister of mine," he said, pointing to his package below the belt. "But not needed, yet. I might be old but still okay in that department."

Now it was Barbara's turn to frown.

"Definitely too much information!"

"You brought it up. So, how're you?"

"I'm fine. Clean as a whistle but have to admit that it scared the living hell out of me. You *do* remember that I had breast cancer, don't you?"

"Not really," he replied with a grin. "I didn't even know you had breasts."

Even Barbara saw the humor in that remark, and laughed. He's still quick on his feet, she thought.

Barbara allowed her eyes to survey her brother's property. Unlike the house across the yard—she knew that was still Jo's place—Hubert's homestead was in good shape. A couple of years ago, he had installed vinyl siding, Cape Cod-blue in color, replacing its former tiled exterior. Its expansive, wrap-around porch with a series of red-white-and-blue Adirondack chairs was the home's most appealing feature, and she could imagine her brother and the lovely and articulate Dee enjoying late summer nights together. Nearby stood a flag pole but Old Glory drooped quietly in the breeze-less, humid air. At the side, an oversized garage was still the center of his universe, housing his vehicles, his guns, his beer. Next to the garage rested a rusting snowplow blade, prompting Barbara to recall her brother's lifelong affinity for a part of the country that gets hammered relentlessly by the snows from Lake Ontario. If nothing else, it gave him a reason to get his ass out of bed every frigid winter morning. Hubert's a lot of things, she thought, but he's not lazy.

Still, his property hadn't changed that much in the forty years since he had moved north with his reluctant bride, pregnant with twins, after his discharge from the Army. He had completed one tour of Vietnam and was likely heading back for another when he met Donna at some off-base saloon. Much to Donna's chagrin, she found herself expecting just when her plan to graduate from SUNY Cortland was about to become reality, with medical school in her sights. She had done the Catholic thing, married the Army man, and before she knew it, they were living in Morgantown where he could walk to his job at the Post Office.

"Well, we're glad you're here," Hubie said. "I was just over at the Pond yesterday. The old shacks are looking good."

Barbara nodded. Hubie was referring to the work her son Brad had completed this summer. She and Roger bought the properties a decade before with a plan to spend their retirement years closer to her brother. But they hadn't used the places much, opting to rent them out to fishers hauling bass boats from cities to the south. They had considered selling the camps but decided against it when their daughter, Ria, chose to attend university in the area.

Now that Ria had graduated from teacher's college and luckily found a job at an elementary school in Gouverneur, it was their plan to spend an extended long weekend with her before she had to enter the real world. Barbara had had no worries about Ria's future, but was concerned about her son. Though intelligent with considerable street savvy, Brad was a rudderless, often angry young man in search of the next good time.

To have both her children in the same spot was an achievement in itself, however, a victory over geography, since she had seen little of either of them lately. Both had left Pittsburgh after high school and, with the exception of their first summers following their freshman years, never returned home. Her friends said she and Roger should be celebrating; how many kids *never* leave home? Even in their thirties and beyond. She guessed it was a tribute to the independence they had instilled in their offspring. Rare for this generation.

Emerging from the back yard was a tall and slender woman carrying garden tools. She was Dolores Killian, or nicknamed Dee to her family and friends. With spiked, silvery hair, Dee at sixty-eight was attractive and intelligent, and someone who was liked at the point of introduction. Though she once owned a home of her own only six or seven blocks away, the widowed Dee had been Hubie's live-in friend for nearly two years now, having been a couple for more than six. She valued her freedom to come and go, but when Hubie asked her to stay permanently, she had accepted. Surprising even herself.

"Greetings, Pennsylvania people," Dee said, exchanging hugs with the couple.

"Does he suspect anything we're up to?" Barbara asked, whispering in Dee's ear.

Dee smiled and shook her head.

"Good. I've been thinking about my speech all week," Barbara said out of earshot of her brother.

Before Dee could respond, a flashy, horn-honking black Saab convertible pulled into the Schumacher driveway. A broad look of excitement flashed across Barbara's face.

"There they are now!"

THREE

SHERIFF BRIAN BOYCHUK of Morgan County had been in a foul mood all day and it wasn't even noon. So much so that he felt the need to escape the office for an hour or two to rid his mind of the inordinate amount of crap he and his deputies were forced to deal with regularly. The best medicine was to watch his Court House office disappear in the rear view mirror of his Tahoe cruiser. Never did he consider himself much of an office cop, anyway, preferring to check out everything for himself.

Of course, as he left the parking lot and exited on to Prospect, his mind returned to the antics of last night. It being the Thursday night of the last long weekend of summer, he knew there would be trouble—and he was right. Maybe it was due to the balmy nighttime temperatures that barely dropped below seventy degrees, unusually warm but not uncommon for northern New York at this time of year. It was more like the Labor Day weekends of old when every moron across the county decided to raise big-time shit.

First there was that Cobb kid—well, more of a twenty-six-year-old punk with the emotional maturity of a preteen—who decided to get piss drunk again and get behind the wheel of his Dodge Ram. His blood alcohol content wasn't just borderline at zero eight; no, he had registered a tidy twenty-two when the deputies found him weaving to and fro on a road that paralleled the Oswegatchie. Not surprising for Mickey Cobb, especially if you glanced at your watch; it was only two o'clock in the afternoon. He must have been at Swigs for hours. His third offense in twenty-four months, too; he'll do some time in the county lock-up.

Then there was the case of old Warner J. Conway, over in Esker Mills, about fifteen miles from town. What was he now? Seventy-five? Maybe even seventy-eight? The old reprobate got himself liquored up, had an ugly spat with the wife and took his short-barreled, Winchester 30-30 out for target practice. Trouble was, his targets were paint cans sitting on fence posts as cars drove by his double-wide. Damned near hit a vehicle or two. Now the sheriff's deputies were processing charges of reckless endangerment and illegal discharge of a dangerous weapon against the irascible old man. Not the first time, either.

To top them all off, his office got a call at three this morning from a hysterical young woman who complained that her boyfriend, some lowlife from over on County Road 10, backhanded her in the face while she was driving. After she slammed on the brakes, straddling the yellow lines, her beloved stole her keys and threw them onto the roof of the Grange Hall. This guy's going to court on charges of petty larceny and harassment. Never ends.

Boychuk had known he wanted to be a cop since he was a teenager. Originally he had envisioned higher ambitions, possibly joining the FBI or even the Secret Service. But that would have required a college education and, though he was a solid student at Morgantown High, his decision was governed by impatience. At eighteen, he had wanted his police career to start yesterday and, when he discovered that the county sheriff's office was recruiting, he signed up. After serving as a deputy for more than fifteen years, Boychuk decided that it was a good time to go for the top job. A take-charge guy, he surveyed the electoral scene and asked himself, 'why not'? He was as qualified as any.

For a guy pushing six-three and scaling two-twenty, with a balding pate, a thick brown moustache and a protuberant jaw, he looked like he would have been more at home policing the Rio Grande than the big northern county straddling the St. Lawrence Valley. Not many of his eighty thousand constituents dared to mess with him, though he knew it took more brains than brawn to succeed in this business. So, five years ago he threw his 'smokey' into the ring and was elected. Leading a small, efficient department, he quickly became so damned good at it that he expected to sail to reelection next year.

Now as he drove through the center of town, he was happy that the town was relatively peaceful today. At one time, Morgantown offered solace to hundreds, if not thousands, of migrant miners and loggers. Gypsies, even, as they moved into the area to scratch out a living in a pre-Depression era. Today, it was just a hamlet of a few thousand, mostly aging souls, living out their lives in just another of the many towns and villages in northern New York that Albany forgot—and voter-rich Manhattan ignored.

Unlike its neighbors, Morgantown had long lost the lottery of prosperity. Towns like Canton and Potsdam could boast of having a couple of the best colleges in the northeast, enjoying large payrolls and upscale neighborhoods. Throw in once-sleepy Watertown to the south, too; it now had money. But not because of any new-found industry. If it wasn't for the big Army base that deployed its 10th Mountaineers regularly to Iraq and Afghanistan, there wouldn't be an economy there at all. Wars create jobs. The Pentagon was one big employment agency.

His cruiser was now rolling slowly through the outskirts of town, past the boarded-up paper mill, its multitude of windows pock-marked, shattered and victimized over the decades by bored, rock-throwing teenagers. Across the road, a thoroughfare that resembled more an asphalt quilt than a paved highway, its potholes requiring constant patching, stood a company that once manufactured shades and blinds. Like the old mill, this low-level, brown-brick edifice ached with abandonment, its parking lot overgrown by pokeweed and Asiatic dayflower, its roof sagging badly.

Next to it rested yet another sad reminder of happier days. This place once built filters, transformers, chokes and coils in an electron-ics industry for which America was famous. This factory had been important; its hundreds of skilled employees toiling proudly within its confines. Now it was gone, and Boychuk knew why. Just the other day he had read about a company in Shanghai—one company with nearly a million workers—was assembling most of the fancy cellphones designed in Silicon Valley and sold around the globe. Its workers putting in twelve-hour days and longer, slaving for peanuts.

Boychuk pointed his Tahoe down the main drag. It too had seen better days but, if anything, at least to his voters, he had to remain optimistic. He had made his life here and he would be damned if he would not stay positive. And besides, even in the last twenty-four months or so, he had seen a renaissance in the old town. Albany, broke and battered, had been working overtime to close prisons across the state. Reluctantly, the governor granted Morgantown a reprieve; its facility would remain open for business, so to speak. A few hundred guard jobs—they used to be called 'screws' but no longer—had been saved and, as sheriff, he'd do his best to keep it filled. Then just last week it was reported the big slaughterhouse over on Route 37, which had been closed nearly three years now, was set to reopen, along with a dairy that shuttered its doors last year. It was bought by some huge cooperative down near Buffalo, and its CEO said it too would reopen. So, things were looking up, or so thought the forty-three-year-old sheriff.

Of course, nothing changed the behavior of some his constituents. He'd always have his share of hell-raisers, shit disturbers and ne'er-do-wells. He smiled to himself at that last description; he'd always liked to call them that. But he always faced the facts; after all, Boychuk had *applied* for this job. He had asked voters to make him sheriff. No one put a gun to his head, or at least not recently.

Boychuk now aimed his SUV in the direction of River Road. Soon, he'd be passing the Paddle Inn and the drinking hole that his old pal Denny Lowry used to frequent. Of course, he was just being facetious since Denny was never a friend. They had been teammates on their high school football team—the Morgantown Marauders—but that was as far it went. No, it was because Denny was once Joanne Schumacher's husband, and a guy who had regularly caused trouble. More than once his office had been called by neighbors reporting loud screaming noises and breaking dishes.

The Lowry wars, one-sided battles for sure, usually commenced when Denny had absorbed about eight or ten beers at the Paddle, and another six-pack in his septic pumping truck as he travelled the back roads. But the result was always the same. If he managed to make it home, after skanking around with every barfly who'd have him, Denny would walk into the house he was sharing with Joanne and kick the hell out of her. But that ended a few years back.

Boychuk sighed plaintively as he passed by the Paddle. Since bars could legally open for business at eight every morning, it was no surprise to see a few Silverados and F-Series trucks already outside. Maybe he should stop and pay them a visit? Just be friendly, let them know he was around? Drinking drivers just love it when cops walk in.

But not today. He'd leave it to his deputies, who would probably get called to the bar later tonight. Probably because a fight would break out, or some drunk would back his truck into a pole, resulting in yet another DUI arrest. The sheriff decided to head over to the Pond before circling back to the courthouse. His police radio had been silent. No one was looking for him. Maybe he'd grab a bite of lunch at Bart's, a lakeside diner that catered to the hundreds of bass fishermen from around the state who made Remington Pond their angling paradise. The big tournament was in a few weeks.

He was passing a cluster of Amish farms on Route 58 when his BlackBerry rang, and its screen read *MAKENNA CALLING*. In an instant, the dour mood that corralled him since leaving the office disappeared. A smile crossed his face. It was his *daughter* on the phone! Hopefully from the road, hopefully with an update about her voyage north for the long weekend.

Her plan was to leave northern Virginia early this morning, stay a day or two at Hubie's and then proceed northwards to Plattsburgh. The trip would encompass hours of driving, possibly eight or more, but what's a distance like that to a twenty-three-year-old? Or was she already twenty-four? All he remembered was that her birthday landed in March—of that he was positive. Though he was lousy with birthdays and anniversaries, that was no excuse. He should know this, especially since it was the *one* day of the year that should have been engrained in his mind.

Pushing the hands-free button for his cellphone, Boychuk activated a technology that he hadn't a clue as to how it worked. His deputy, Jimmy McKelvie, had configured it for him.

"Ken!" he bellowed. He enjoyed using the nickname that her friends had given her years ago; it offered him a stronger, emotional link to the young woman.

"Goooood morning, Brian!" she said, her voice bouncing from the dashboard of his SUV. Since they had met for the first time more than three years ago, Makenna's use of his formal name was understood. For two decades the only 'dad' she knew was part of a loving couple who had adopted her as an infant in Lake Placid and raised her in Plattsburgh. But after discovering the shocking truth—she was still angry at her parents for not informing her about her real mother, a teenaged runaway—Makenna had decided she would get to know Boychuk better. She would give him a chance, and for that he was grateful. To him, their relationship was at times tentative but was growing with each passing month, despite her being a full day's drive away in Virginia. Unfortunately, Susan—his wife of more than ten years—hadn't yet bought into the concept, and wasn't likely to do so. He and Susan had been having their problems well before Makenna had arrived on the scene. But he was damned if his wife would stop him from seeing his daughter.

"You must have hit the road early," he said.

"Yes, making good time today. I'm on eighty-one and just passed Binghamton."

"Well, I hope you haven't got that phone of yours up to your ear," he lectured. "After all, a smart girl like you has to be keeping up with technology."

Makenna laughed. "You mean Bluetooth?"

"Yeah…I guess that's what they call it."

"I'm surprised you've even heard of it!"

"Of course…or at least my deputies have," he replied, momentarily on the defensive. "I'm not the Luddite you think I am."

"No?" she asked. "I just thought a guy whose most advanced piece of electronics was still a VCR might not have it figured out!"

It was Boychuk's turn to laugh. "Going straight to the Schumachers?"

"Yeah…want me to call when I get closer to town?"

"No need. I'll meet you there later. Now you can hang up and drive carefully."

She agreed, and ended their brief conversation. In much better spirits, Boychuk continued the short drive towards his favorite diner. He would enjoy his lunch.

FOUR

HER PONY-STYLED BLONDE HAIR dancing excitedly, Ria Cahill climbed from the rear of the Swedish-built ragtop and ran in the direction of her parents. She was followed by her brother Brad, but the third passenger in the Saab lingered behind, maintaining a healthy distance from the other two. It had been nearly four months since Barbara and Roger had travelled north to attend Ria's graduation from St. Lawrence University, and they were looking forward to this reunion. As Roger looked on, his elated wife stood there with open arms to greet her daughter. A moment later, Brad joined his sister.

"So good to see you again, we've missed you," Barbara said.

"Us too," Ria beamed. "Aren't you glad we ordered good weather for you? Brad's been over to the Pond and the cottages are all set up."

Dee was watching the scene unfold with enthusiasm. It had reminded her of her own two children when they were their age. Ria was a very captivating young woman, perhaps five foot six or more, with the build of the tri-athlete she was. Not super-model stunning but clearly a girl who turned heads easily, especially as she flashed a pair of brilliant eyes that resembled robin's eggs. Now standing next to her mother, it was clear that Ria also inherited Barbara's radiant smile and earthily attractive poise. She was definitely a looker, Dee thought, and if her dedication to fitness continued, could grow more attractive as she aged.

Brad, on the other hand, was a study in contrast. At twenty-four, nearly three years older than Ria, her half-brother was a rubbery-faced young man who stood two or three inches above six feet. His wooly, ash-colored hair, already thinning at the forehead and unkempt everywhere else, gave Brad the look of a pubescent teenager who was waiting for the day he would attain adulthood. The rest of his body was ample and round and indicative of an even beefier future if he wasn't careful. Only in his twenties, Dee thought, and already over-weight, despite a summer spent in construction. But she knew that many of the men who hammer nails all day often spend their nights at places like the Paddle.

Hubert had told her about Barbara's first husband, the one who had deserted his sister when the boy was about eighteen months old. She arrived home to hear him declare that he was no longer willing to serve as her husband. Moreover, as he duly informed Barbara, he didn't want to be a father, either. Fortunately for Barbara, a career woman forced into single parenthood by her early thirties, she met Roger in the studio of the local NPR affiliate and within six months, they were married. Not long after that, Ria had arrived. A year later, Roger had made it official; Brad became a Cahill.

Barbara, enjoying the presence of both of her offspring, now looked over their shoulders at the young man leaning against the hood of the Saab about twenty feet away. His arms were crossed as if he was impatiently awaiting introduction. Ria noticed as well, and spoke up.

"Mom, Dad, I'm sorry, but in all the excitement I forgot about Nick," she said, signaling to the young man to join them. Reluctantly, the man approached the family gathered in the driveway. Hubie, re-turning from his garage, was also approaching the group, his hands carrying several cans of beer.

"This is my friend, Nick Wells," she said, her head jockeying like a tennis fan between the young man and her parents. "Nick," she said, gesturing towards her parents, "…my mom and dad. And, of course, you've already met my uncle Hubert, and his friend, Dee."

Roger was the first to extend his hand to the younger man.

"Nice to meet you, Nick," he said, who was joined by his wife in greeting their daughter's friend.

"My pleasure," the young man replied. Offering his hand to Barbara, he was quick with a compliment. "Mrs. Cahill...I've heard a good deal about you."

"Some of it might even be factual," Barbara said, smiling.

"All very good, I can assure you," he replied, a grin of his own emerging.

Barbara stole a quick glance in her daughter's direction, for confirmation. This young man has some charm, she thought.

Hubie could see his sister's mind heading into overdrive, attempting to size up the younger man. Nick was a bit shorter than Brad but more powerfully built, his shoulders and arms rippling, the result of hours of bodybuilding. His platinum blonde hair was cut military short, almost shaved, his sculpted chin sporting what appeared to be the pale tufts of a new goatee.

When Hubie first met the man, he guessed Nick could have been Army. But Nick quickly disabused him of that notion. "The military's not for me," he had barked one day. "Not gonna be like one of those jarheads from Drum who're lucky—*lucky!*—if they pull down four-hundred a week." That was his response, at least until Brad was able to whisper in his ear that his uncle was a veteran and that he'd better shut the hell up if he knew what was good for him.

The weather was truly equatorial yet, unlike the other youthful adults dressed in summer attire, Nick was dressed in blue jeans, Birkenstock sandals and a black trucker's T-shirt, complete with a tan fedora, its tip raised skywards Bruno Mars style. A pair of aviator Ray-Bans prevented the group from seeing his steel gray eyes. He was a good-looking young man, but Hubie wondered what message was he trying to deliver? Cool ass dude? Or was he just overplaying his cards? Maybe both.

Ria continued, "Nick and I met at a hockey game last winter. He was working for his uncle, a contractor, and well..." Shrugging, as if to say things were working out, her voice trailed off.

"Oh, construction?" Roger asked, his voice deflating. He had hoped that his daughter might have been hanging with a graduate student from Dartmouth or Yale. No such luck.

The young man didn't hesitate for a moment.

"Uh, yeah...I wasn't cut out for the college scene, much to the dismay of my dad," Nick said. "He's a judge downstate and wanted me to, you know, go to law school and follow in his footsteps. But I told him, 'no thanks.' I wanted to work for myself."

"A judge? What court?" Roger countered.

"Not sure," Wells replied. "Never paid that much attention."

Barbara decided to enter the conversation.

"Work for yourself? Starting your own company, you mean?"

"Yeah, my uncle's company is up in Malone, you know, near the border? I've worked with him, and he's taught me a lot."

"I know the town," Roger replied. "Is that where you're from? Malone?"

"Only if you're a golfer or a prisoner!" he said with a smirk. "No, I grew up in Dutchess County north of the city, near Poughkeepsie. Always wanted to be on my own."

Hubie interrupted. "Construction's a tough racket around here, Nick. Not much money being splashed around."

But Nick was prepared for the debate.

"Who says I'll stay around here?" he replied flatly. "Besides, college to me, other than keeping my old ma—" He stopped short. "—my *dad* off my back, was never in the cards. The only way you can learn is by doing. You don't learn anything in college—"

"Hey!" Ria interrupted him.

Nick immediately became contrite, but he continued.

"I didn't mean it that way, *babe*," he replied, quickly. His smile in her direction looked like an appeal for forgiveness.

Brad listened with amusement.

"That didn't take you long to suck up," he said.

Nick flashed his friend a scowl, which was not lost on Barbara. He resumed his thesis.

"What I meant was...*real* life is the best education you can get, and I intend to get on with life. You never make any money in this world unless you sign the checks."

There was something about him that set Barbara off. Maybe it was his calm, confident demeanor, betraying a sense of impatience or unease with older adults. His 'babe' comment towards her daughter rang phony, or at the very least, gratuitous and condescending. Working with union workers for the past decade and a half, the vast majority of them being men, she had become a keen observer of the male ego. She could spot a shithead in less than three minutes, she had often boasted, and with considerable accuracy. Now, her radar was working. There was a fine line between confidence and cockiness, and maybe this guy was crossing it? Not sure, she thought; she would probe Ria later to determine the extent of this relationship. Or maybe she'd ask Hubert. He'd know.

Having moved to the wraparound porch from the heat of the driveway, their brief reunion was going well, as parents and children updated each other on the events of a summer now winding down. Hubie had made another trip to the garage for reinforcements, as Dee brought out sandwiches, cheese curds from the Amish dairy and other hors d'oeuvres. She suggested that a glass of champagne might be in order to celebrate the occasion, and to no surprise, Barbara had accepted.

Roger, the academic, turned his attention to his son. To an enquiring father, Brad told the group that, yes, his job renovating cottages was fine, and it paid the rent. And no, he would not return to college.

"I've got enough work to last me to November," he declared, a grin appearing. "After that, I'm going moose hunting. And after that, maybe the Keys. Beaching it for the winter sounds rather... enticing."

Roger frowned.

"You could enroll for the winter term, son."

"Not gonna happen, Dad. Me getting a piece of paper right now would not make a lot of difference in my life."

Inhaling deeply, his disappointment showing, Roger decided that he would address the subject later when he could get Brad alone. Now he turned his attention to his daughter.

"When will you be able to move into that apartment in Gouverneur, honey?" Roger asked.

"In two weeks, Dad," she replied. "The landlord is doing some painting and cleaning and so we're gonna stay at the cottage until the fifteenth."

This exchange caught the attention of her mother.

"We're...as in 'we are'?" she asked. "Who's we? Have you found a roommate?"

Hubie peered over at Dee who grimaced slightly. Both had seen a good deal of Barbara's kids this summer and were privy to their plans. In an instant, Ria seemed a bit flustered. She had wanted to break the news to her mother privately.

"Me and...Nick, Mom," she said, her voice tentative. "We've decided to move in together. I'll be able to walk to my school and Nick feels he can commute to his jobs wherever they are."

Nick piped up.

"Gouverneur is close to everything I want to do," he added.

Hubie rolled his eyes. Maybe now's not the time to speak, kid, he thought. Now's the time to keep your mouth shut. He glanced at his sister and watched as her expression turned to angst. She had received the answer to her earlier question.

Or at least *an* answer.

They weren't just acquaintances.

FIVE

HANNAH ZOOK WAS PLACING the last row of wicker baskets on makeshift shelves, with a simple '4 sale' sign implanted in the gravel, when she saw Joshua and his younger brothers approaching with their wagon. She allowed herself a smile. There was a more direct route to his farmhouse but she suspected—or at least hoped—that he had opted for this circuit instead.

Soon her mother would join her under the century-old oak beside the road. It was the only spot of shade around and they would need it today, one of the warmest of the summer. As with other such sales they had held nearly every day over the past two months, their work was long and tiring—and sometimes not profitable. Customers would slow their fancy vehicles to a crawl, perusing their wares through open windows, sometimes stopping, sometimes buying. But this was a holiday weekend for the English, and the two women hoped there would be tourists using this route to the river, the nearby Pond or points east, such as the Adirondacks. It was expected that a few would stop and admire their handiwork. As Mama often said, 'the English come for more than our baskets, Hannah…they're here to stare at us. We're not like them."

Hannah was ready to leave the family farm. She was prepared for the next stage of her life; having reached two full decades of age, it was time to take charge of her own kitchen, a fine garden and establish a bed with a husband. A man she could call her own. That was her duty. To continue the traditions of her church, her community, her family.

From the moment that Joshua had signaled his intentions, Hannah had become another woman. Their bundling last weekend was exquisite; he was polite and gentlemanly, everything she'd hoped he would be. Many of her friends her age were already married, and were with one child or more. Now it was her time and she'd never felt such joy. He was the answer to her prayers. So handsome, so strong, she couldn't be happier. But the wait—likely more than two months, until the harvest was complete—would be excruciating. Once they were *published*, once their engagement was announced, it would be official. But until then, late October at the earliest, how would she cope?

Hannah knew her blessed event would be just grand. But she wondered how her friends would react. Would they be happy for her, or more likely, envious? After all, she had landed Joshua Troyer, probably the best suitor available in their church. Others more devious, however, would have some fun, she feared. Why, she had heard of things that she'd hoped wouldn't happen to Joshua and her. One involved a cousin over in the next county—a male cousin, she recalled—who had deliberately placed a harness on backwards on the future groom's own horse! Then immediately after church, they teased the couple mercilessly as they rode together in his new buggy. Of course, the *vilest* trick possible was the one that Hannah feared the most: the placing of an overripe onion under their bed on the night of their marriage. That smell could permeate their room for days! They said it was just fun, but she did not agree.

As Joshua and his team approached, Hannah let her imagination run wild in anticipation, not just for his foray past their farm but for her wedding. Theirs would be a *Hinglefleisch* frolic, a veritable chicken feast, since her father and the boys would be slaughtering chickens all the previous day, enough to feed hundreds of church and family folk.

Though Hannah knew she would have to keep their upcoming nuptials a secret for two more months, she wondered just how she would do that. Impossible, she thought! Everyone would figure it out. *They would know just by the celery!* She and Mama had been growing patches of it all summer, perhaps in anticipation that Mr. Troyer would signal his interest. After all, she was nearing twenty-one-years and her mother assumed that Hannah would capture a suitor—soon. And it was a given the vegetable would play a big part in her wedding; they would use it in their stuffing, and in their creamed soups, and even to decorate their homes, like flowers in a vase. They would carve it into pieces and offer them to their families and friends as 'appetizers', as the English liked to call them. Oh, the rumors that would create! She was so excited!

Hannah snapped from her daydream. Was she getting ahead of herself? Today was Friday and she didn't know if he would want to bundle again after Sunday service. Why hadn't he tried to kiss her last time? Hannah was certain that Joshua—she decided she would just call him Papa when their blessed union occurred!—would ask her again this Sunday. And, if he did, this time she vowed to remove her outer dress. This time she would put on her best courting dress; nothing suggestive, certainly, and *nothing* low cut or sheer. And no cottons made with those wild colors worn by the foolish English. Those people like to flaunt their yellows, pinks—or God forbid—whites!

Her baskets were now on display, and her '4 sale' sign was prominent. The 's' in the word sale had been inverted and appeared almost like the numeral '2', but she was oblivious to the minor error. English, after all, was her second language. Now Hannah noticed the wagon was only a few yards away and wondered if the young man would stop this time to say hello. The other day, he simply slowed his team and tipped his cap. She knew their church frowned upon any outward signs of affection. That would violate the *Ordnung*, the rules, and the elders—maybe even the Bishop himself—would admonish her father.

Right now, however, Hannah did not care about rules. These periodic, unexpected visits by Mr. Troyer were exhilarating, the highlight of her day, indeed her week. There he was at the reins, standing tall on the buckboard as his brothers sat atop the hay. Seconds later, Joshua pulled the team to a halt in front of her display of goods.

"Good day, Miss Zook," he said in his native tongue. Though he preferred speaking English as often as possible, it was the proper thing to do.

"Mr. Troyer," Hannah nodded. "A hot one again today, isn't it?"

"Yes, and my horses have not cooperated either," he said, gesturing toward Temper, now firmly in place as the strongest of the team. "The smaller one is obedient, at least. The big one here...well, he has a mind of his own."

"That's too bad," she said, as a hint of a smile crept upon her plump face, her large, brown eyes locked on his, hoping that Joshua would signal his interest in her again. Surely he would ask her if he could join her again on Sunday, would he not? She certainly did not want to spend these brief moments with the man of her choice discussing horses!

But Joshua remained stoic, almost distant. "Yes, it was bad," he repeated and, with a courteous tip of his straw hat, he issued a command to his team, signaling his departure.

"Good day, Miss Zook," was all he had to say. He did not hear her polite good-bye. Nor did he notice the look of puzzlement and disappointment on her face.

SIX

NO SOONER HAD RIA AND THE YOUNG MEN returned to Brad's convertible and departed Hubie's house for their cottages on Remington Pond when a glistening, gunmetal-gray Mercedes pulled into the driveway. The last time that Makenna Monteith had set foot in Morgantown, it was one of the coldest days that January in upstate New York could deliver. That was more than three years ago—almost four now—and the circumstances were not pleasant. But time always found a way to heal most pain, and she had hoped this reunion with the Schumachers would be a good one. Still, doubts remained; she had never met the extended clan. How would she be received?

Having spent nearly four years at Clarkson and the previous eighteen or so further north along the shores of Lake Champlain, Makenna was used to what an upcountry winter could offer. Good and bad. The terrain surrounding Potsdam, depressed and dreary as it seemed, was the price she paid for a good education. Her respite, therefore, was a weekly commute to Lake Placid, some ninety minutes to the east. It was there that she'd stay with her friend, Kelly, put in a shift or two at one of the village's toniest ski stores, and schedule a few runs over on Whiteface when time permitted. There was always snow on the Olympic mountain by Thanksgiving, humanly made, but snow nevertheless.

Growing up near Lake Champlain with superior grades, she could have opted for a full ride at one of the Ivy League schools to the south. But Clarkson had beckoned, its environmental program being one of the best, but inevitably her parents were disappointed.

Princeton was not to be; the world was going green and Clarkson was her choice.

But that plan changed over the course of a few weeks around the holidays during her final year. First it was that bizarre encounter with a strange woman one Thanksgiving weekend at her ski store. Then came an even stranger phone call from the same woman about six weeks later. The woman had shared a secret with her, and ten days after that, when she gently tapped the shoulder of the sheriff of Morgan County, her life changed forever.

Now, as she was waving warmly to Hubie and Dee on the porch, an enormous SUV bearing the insignia of Morgan County pulled in behind the Mercedes. The uniformed sheriff quickly put his car into park and stepped out, wiping his brow with his sleeve before placing his brimmed police hat across a slightly balding crown. Approaching her car, Boychuk peered with affection at his striking young daughter. Inordinately taller than most her age, perhaps five-nine and fit, her dark mahogany hair was now coruscating past her shoulders, landing softly over a halter-topped sun dress. Her cheekbones, conspicuous and dazzling, were evocative of her mother's at that age, Boychuk figured. It was as if time stood still.

But was Susan right? Was he just trying to resurrect the memory of a long lost love, as she had charged? Tilting heavily on a bottle of Pinot Grigio one night last month, his wife had leveled another serious charge: this "clone," as she labeled Makenna dismissively, meant he was living in the past. It took everything in his power to suppress a retort that night, and for many nights since.

Genetically, however, the evidence was there; they looked the same, walked and talked the same and, as he surmised all too well today, Makenna displayed hints of a sassiness reminiscent of another beautiful woman from a different time. Place them side by side, at the same age, and they could pass for twins. But Susan's accusations were preposterous, and he told her so. Put yourself in my place, he had demanded. What would you have done? Susan couldn't answer that question.

"So, this is Makenna," a smiling Barbara announced as they arrived. "Now I know what all the excitement was about."

A N HOUR OR SO PASSED pleasantly on the expansive porch. As Hubie gazed down Seward Avenue towards the Oswegatchie, now free of the swarms of mosquitoes, black flies, deer flies and other locusts that populate the murky river in spring, he couldn't help but recall just how events, some tragic, others uplifting, had changed his life.

"So, Boychuk here tells us that you've changed your plans?" Hubie asked, as Makenna sipped a glass of iced tea.

"Yes, so to speak, Mr. Schumach—"

"Call me Hubie, please," he interrupted. With a grin, he glanced in the direction of Dee and his sister, he added, "Nearly everyone does."

The bond between Dee and Barbara was strong and determined; he knew he was facing a relentless, two-front war this weekend. Maybe he would call a couple of the boys and go fishing, or at least sneak off to the VFW tomorrow when they weren't looking.

"You were saying?"

She told her story.

Her plans had been set, she said. Europe, Norway to be specific, was where she would pursue a Master's degree. There were few schools better for advanced environmental studies than in a city called Trondheim, and she was considering such a move. And why not? Norway was years ahead of the rest of the world in its commitment to green technologies. Besides, as she'd chided her friend Kelly, who had never ventured out of New York State, the skiing there was terrific. But she had changed her mind.

"I'm studying forensics now," she replied. "I loved the idea of green...but after getting to know Brian a little bit, and understanding what he did, I started investigating other careers. So, forensics seemed very interesting. The science and the math of it all...the methodologies, which brought out the engineer in me."

Now the assembled group could see, first hand, the true passion in the young woman.

"I liked the intellectual curiosity of it all," she continued. "High-level detective work to me was very appealing...and when you think about it, criminals are so vastly outmatched by the technologies of today. And so I just wanted to be part of something important. That's how I found myself at GW—George Washington University. At their Virginia campus, actually. That's where the forensics school is located."

Listening to this woman speak, Hubie couldn't help but appreciate the irony of it all. Imagine what Jane would think about this? Maths and sciences were certainly not his daughter's forte. Bored her to tears, in fact. And police work? Of all the people in his life, who pushed back against authority more than his daughter? Jane had vilified the Vietnam War, and his role in it. She had abhorred guns and what they stood for. Only to resort to their use when faced with violence.

"You could be the star of CSI Morgantown!" a chuckling Hubie said with a wide grin. During the long winter nights, after he'd return from plowing driveways and parking lots, or spreading rock salt and sand, he would spend his time in front of the tube, watching re-runs. The CSI shows were all over the channels and so he tuned in. He liked the original Vegas version with that bossy, clever redhead in charge. Its New York City knockoff, the one that starred Lieutenant Dan from *Forrest Gump*, wasn't bad either. But he never much cared for the Florida version with that actor, David what's-his-name, who spent the entire show with his hands on his hips, his head angled just right, while sporting pricy Georgio Armani shades, trying way too hard to be cool as he bombed around the Intercoastal in a cigarette boat.

Not much else on television these days, he thought, other than the constant boner ads, showing some good-looking couple in their forties having problems south of the belt buckle. Never an issue for him, even with the way his ticker had started acting up. But if it weren't for drug companies, the networks would go broke. Those commercials are all the same, he thought; the first twenty seconds of the ad tells you they've created some miracle cure for the ailment of the day, and then spend their remaining time warning that if you take their damned pills, you're going to die. Not just television, either; the radio said today that Botox, the wrinkle filler, had to settle a six-hundred million dollar lawsuit for claiming it stops migraines. Drug companies have no soul; they would make any claim to make a buck.

The odd time, masochistically, he'd catch a Syracuse football game on the tube. That hapless bunch kept getting smoked by second-rate colleges. Officially, Dee leaned towards the higher-brow networks such as PBS and A&E, and was known to have only National Public Radio programmed in her car. Hubie long suspected, however, that she secretly watched the so-called reality programs when he was out plowing snow. Shows like *Survivor* or *The Bachelorette* or one of those *Real Housewives* of—well, name a town and the networks brought them to you!—were trash. But these shows proliferated. They were cheap to produce, garnered big fat ratings, proving that the television industry never went broke overestimating the intelligence of its audiences. That pundit who said these people were famous for being famous was right. Celebrity worship had taken over America.

Letting out a laugh, Makenna took it all in stride. "If only it was that glamorous," she said. "Hollywood likes its brainiacs solving crimes in such sophisticated ways, always guessing right the first time, knowing all the answers and catching the crooks. Conveniently, too, in less than an hour. In truth, it's just old-fashioned police work.

You know, most crimes are solved on the simplest of evidence. Common sense stuff."

She continued her story. Her longer-term interests lay in white-collar crime by those who used information technology to bilk or harm innocent people. Maybe, she said, she could land a job at the CIA or the FBI and specialize in forensic terrorism.

"Very fascinating work," she continued, "everything from civil disputes and medical malpractice to employee misconduct—"

Barbara interrupted her.

"Employee misconduct?" The indignant labor union activist in her was now emerging. She was getting worked up. "Everybody goes after the poor slobs who pay their bills and play by the rules. What about *corporate* misconduct? Have you noticed no one's gone to jail over this Wall Street mess? Not one! All those phony mortgages they sold and re-sold? The average CEO makes four hundred times the salary of the average worker, for Christ sake!"

Hubie released a sigh. Not here an hour and she's already on her soap box, he thought. Barbara noticed her brother rolling his eyes.

"Well, it's true, Hubert," she insisted. "It's been two years since Lehman Brothers went down, and the only guy they nailed was that king of the Ponzi schemes, and even he wouldn't have been caught unless the financial system hadn't nearly collapsed around him."

"As Reagan would have said, 'there you go again,'" Hubie chided. "You're sounding more like Jimmy Carter every day. This country always bounces back."

"Famous last words, my brother, but we're in a mess. Because of the previous guy and his gang of cronies, nobody was watching the till. Never mind a recession. I was worried we'd be heading into another damned depression! And don't get me started on Reagan!"

Boychuk decided to enter the fray.

"Well, Ken, we could use your talents around here," he said, slipping into a backwoods accent for some fun. "You know, I've had to bring in more than my share of gomers for tippin' cows and poachin' deer."

Hubie jumped in again, flicking an eyebrow in the direction of Joanne's house next door, the scene of an event that went well beyond a deer shot out of season.

"You had your hands full over there, pal," he said.

The older man could never erase that memory, one that found him trudging through several inches of new snow, entering his daughter's home in church-like stillness, discovering the broken glass on the floor amid fallen pictures and overturned dining room chairs.

"We didn't need forensics to figure out that case, Hubie," the sheriff replied. "It was cut-dried-and-*fried* from the beginning."

Boychuk glanced over at Makenna, who was squirming in her chair, obviously uncomfortable with the discussion and where it was leading. She, too, knew that that was the night when justice was delivered. But as disturbing as it was, Makenna was strangely grateful for the events that had unfolded. Otherwise, she might have never discovered the truth.

Dee recognized the awkwardness of the conversation, and decided to take another approach. "Life's certainly been a whirlwind for you, Makenna. Hasn't it?"

Makenna nodded. "But in a good way, mostly, Dee." She pointed to her Mercedes in the driveway. "That was the second nicest gift I've ever received. Joanne was wonderful about it."

"Jo's always been an SUV lady," Dee said. "Just too fancy for her style. I remember the day she told me she wanted to give it to you. She wanted you to have something of your mother's that was very special..."

Makenna nodded with a smile. "I never imagined that I'd be driving a car like that! The timing was good, too, since my old Honda clunker was on its last legs."

Barbara was listening intently to the conversation. She, too, was mostly an absentee aunt to Hubie's girls over the years, and well into their teens. That she never saw eye to eye with his shrewish wife was true. And she never bought into the notion that Hubie had shattered Donna's dreams. It was a weak argument, Barbara thought; Donna had had options and didn't take one of them, including a return to college. Just excuses from a woman with low self-esteem. Now watching the young woman in action, Barbara knew Makenna was the best thing to have happened to Hubert in years.

"You said the car was the second nicest gift?" Barbara said. "So, your number one?"

Makenna, smiling in acknowledgement, glanced at Boychuk. He threw his daughter a wink.

SEVEN

HAVING DISPENSED with his load of hay, and leaving the younger ones behind, Joshua saddled his wagon with firewood and was pushing his team toward Remington Pond. It was dusk in the north country and the young farmer knew his return home would be well after dark. Prudently, he had placed two kerosene lanterns aboard, which would serve as taillights for him and his horses. He dreaded the three-mile journey to the Pond tonight; too many English in their fast cars had been careless, colliding with buggies and wagons, sometimes killing their horses. Or worse, the drivers.

It was a warm windless night. Already, the dominant sugar maples had joined forces with stands of white birch, and the odd mountain ash, to signal the looming arrival of autumn. Menno had warned the family about the coming equinox. Daylight was disappearing; their work days were shorter. They had to work faster and more efficiently, since their corn crops, turning yellow-brown in color, were sending them a message.

In the distance, stretching for miles, he could see the blackened images of the large silent lake. It was quite a sight, and a welcomed one at that. For if it wasn't for Remington Pond and its scenic beauty, this section of the county wouldn't have much to offer. In fact, a good deal of the big county was depressing, even bleak. Certainly not like Ohio, Joshua thought, with its prosperous rolling hills and valleys and rivers and rich black soil. Not even close.

As Temper and Sorrel lumbered along the road, a series of seedy, bedraggled aluminum trailers came into view, single-wides mostly, their yards littered with refuse. At one, an abandoned ringer-washer lay next to an ancient refrigerator, its doors removed to prevent children from locking themselves in. No thought, apparently, was given to take the dead fridge to the dump. Across the way, the rusted-out shell of a school bus rested on blocks, its wheels and windows missing, with weeds growing healthily through its former chassis. On the porch sat a gruesomely obese woman with long salt-and-pepper hair tied at the back with an elastic band. She had a cigarette in one hand and a fly swatter in the other, and she was barking orders to a litter of youngsters running rampant across the property. Her husband, Joshua figured, must fix and sell old lawn mowers, since there were at least forty machines in sight.

Overhead, a murder of crows—numbering more than twenty—sat menacingly in the towering oaks, squawking loudly with impatience as the wagon approached their dinner, the remains of a blood-spattered raccoon not far ahead. Moments later, four large barking dogs greeted their arrival, snarling and teasing his team. Be careful hounds, he thought, Temper's in a foul mood and if allowed his freedom you will be sorry. After nipping at the horses' heels for a few yards, they wisely retreated. Often, when he was alone, or when he toiled in the fields as he had done today, he sometimes wondered what another life would be like. Maybe go to college. Learn architecture. Or maybe just venture further east, towards the Adirondacks, especially as a passenger—or better still, as the driver—of one of those fancy, furious automobiles. But it was just a dream. It wouldn't come true.

His mind now wandered back to the brief encounter he had had with Hannah that afternoon. Why he had detoured past her farm today, he didn't know. What purpose did he have in mind? She had smiled nicely in his direction, and had welcomed his arrival, even as they both knew they were breaking church rules. Six days of the week were for family and work; only on the seventh could such activities take place. But his mind was beset with doubt. He didn't know what he wanted to do, though he was well aware that his duty was to choose a mate, to buy his own farm and...to breed.

It was a busy Friday night on a long weekend, and pickups and SUVs hauling shiny bass boats with outsized outboard motors were racing down the county road. The speed limit on this thoroughfare was a nominal fifty-five, but Joshua knew vehicles were travelling much faster tonight. Already, one driver had signaled his dissatisfaction with his slow-moving wagon, leaning heavily on his horn and screaming profanity as he sped by. His command of the English language was good; he knew their meaning.

Fifteen minutes later, he reached his destination, turning his team down a country lane bordered on both sides by tall, healthy cedars, their boughs so close together they looked like they were joining hands about ten feet off the ground. Pulling on the reins, Joshua cleared the arbors successfully, and immediately he was struck by the number of vehicles parked along the lower road, maybe as many as fifteen, occupying nearly every space imaginable. As Joshua had expected, the slick black convertible from earlier today was there, its top still down, awarded a prime spot befitting its position as the collection's trophy car.

His team turned the corner and was greeted by a lawn half the size of his hay field. Flanked by clusters of mature oaks, black spruce and pine, an assortment of dwellings, garages, sheds and boat barns butted against a picturesque horseshoe-shaped bay. Some of the cottages had been recently built, or renovated, and in his opinion were bland monuments to sparse resources and even sparser creativity. Simple boxes or rectangles resting on slabs of concrete. Where was the stylishness that he had witnessed in the Ohio Valley? There, homes had majestic porches and attractive dormers with handsome spires and real shutters. At night, by candlelight, he read books on design and construction that he borrowed secretly from the library in town. He could do better, he thought.

Another group of dwellings were not cottages at all, but year-round, modular homes that were transported in two sections and assembled on site, a practice common for northern New York. Jutting towards the lake, on a rocky point, stood a series of quaint, two-bedroom camps with mismatched roofs and haphazardly-built additions. They had stood the test of time for generations, their manicured lawns littered with Adirondack chairs, picnic tables and the odd stone fireplace. This was how the English spent their summers.

Instantly, Joshua was bombarded by the sounds of loud, pulsating music, interrupted only by bursts of shouting and laughter, though he couldn't make out what was being said. There had to be at least forty revelers here. They were his peers, at least in age. Some of the men were shirtless, wearing only bathing trunks while others were dressed in T-shirts and shorts. Over to the side, where a net was set up, a number of female partiers, scantily clad in what the English called 'bikinis', were spiking a large white ball back and forth, producing more laughter. For a few moments, Joshua's eyes were glued to the game the young women were playing. No one would ever witness such a spectacle on Amish farms. But the young Amish farmer continued to glare.

Then he turned his attention to the lake's shore and a small beach leading to the water. Another group of celebrants was assembling an enormous mound of what appeared to be discarded boards and other refuse from a recent renovation. From behind a large shed, a young man emerged carrying a blue plastic container, likely kerosene, Joshua guessed. After dousing the stack with the clear liquid fuel, another man flicked a lighted cigarette on the woodpile. Loud cheers went up as an enormous fire roared to life.

Beyond the inferno and near the rocky point, a long, narrow dock held together by rusted iron stanchions extended into the lake. A pontoon boat, complete with a Bimini-styled top and laden down with at least another ten young people, was cruising towards the wharf. One of them jumped from the boat and was now fastening it to the dock. He recognized her; she was the girl in the back seat of that convertible earlier today.

The arrival of the horse-driven wagon with the tall, oddly-dressed man at the reins created a stir among the crowd. Soon, a group approached the wagon as if it was the first time they had set eyes on such a sight. Leading the way was the Cahill man, quickly followed by other curious celebrants armed with cell phones, their camera lights flashing one-by-one as they positioned themselves near the team. Temper, the larger and least temperate of the beasts, became unsettled, bucking and snorting with excitement. Joshua was not amused. Sorry he had agreed to the transaction, he quickly decided to unload his cargo and leave the property. Pulling on the reins, he turned a pair of steely eyes in the man's direction.

"No pictures!" he hissed, his eyes darting between those of the young Cahill man and the guilty parties. "You're scaring my horses!"

Brad, sensing the urgency of the situation, quickly took charge. He knew how the Amish had resisted any form of photography.

"Guys, put your goddamned cells away!" he barked, his facial expression slowly transforming into a grin. "Or Troyer here will turn this friggin' wagon around we'll be shit out of luck for firewood by nine o'clock. And we don't want that, do we? We got ourselves a long weekend ahead." It worked. The crowd backed off, and a sense of relief came over Joshua. Scanning his eyes towards the edge of property, he spotted a small, nearly depleted woodpile.

"Do you want me to stack this wood over there, Chad?" he asked, pointing to the pile.

"It's *Brad*, not Chad, Troyer," he replied.

"Well, then you can call me Joshua," the young farmer said. It was his turn to demand a level of respect.

Brad, nodding, signaled a truce—of sorts. There was no doubt, however, who would remain in charge.

"Deal," he said, smiling. "How about pulling that team of yours over to the shed, and maybe I can get a couple of the boys to put their beers down long enough to help you."

"No…that's not required," Joshua replied. "I can do this by myself, and leave you and your friends to your party."

Brad shrugged, pulling out a thick wad of cash from his pocket, an act not lost on the young Amish farmer. He selected a couple of twenties and handed them to the farmer. "Suit yourself, Troy—" Grinning again, he quickly corrected himself. "—I mean, Josh."

Their curiosity satiated, most of the partiers had moved on, leaving the Amish farmer to complete his appointed task. From his vantage point across the compound, Joshua watched as the woman and the goateed man from the convertible made their way up the embankment, stopping by the fire to chat with friends. Then the man walked to a cooler and selected a beer as the woman continued across the lawn towards a young couple working a large stone barbeque, smoke billowing upward as what Joshua suspected was meat sizzling on the grill.

Working quickly, his back to the ongoing celebration, Joshua was almost finished when he heard a voice from behind. Startled, he turned around to find the girl standing there. Like the others, she was dressed in one of those bikini bathing suits, but had covered herself with an oversized T-shirt that read 'SLU Athletics'. He had heard about that university in Canton, and another in neighboring Potsdam and how good they were, often wondering what it would be like to attend college. A baseball cap now covered her long hair, which was still tied in a ponytail. But she had removed her shaded glasses and Joshua could see the color of her eyes; pale blue, beaming and quick.

"Hello, again," she said, simply.

In a courteous fashion, Joshua removed his hat to reveal his mushroom-cut of dark brown hair, now beaded with sweat from the late summer day. She could see that his shirt was open several buttons below the collar, displaying a hairless, tanned chest. He had obviously spent time in the sun, shirtless, she surmised, and wondered if this was allowed. Probably not.

"Good evening, ma'am," he replied, politely.

"Ma'am?" she said with a laugh. "No one other than the nine-year-olds in my fourth-grade class ever called me that before." Without extending her hand, perhaps unsure if there was a protocol involved, she introduced herself.

"My name's Ria...Ria Cahill." She pointed across the compound and towards the barbeque where her brother was engaging playfully with Nick and about a half-dozen others. The taller man had a paper plate in his hand and was waiting for one of the young women to fill it. "I'm Brad's sister."

"I sensed that..." Joshua replied, nodding in the direction of the parked cars at the entrance to the property. "When I saw you in that car today."

"I know your last name's Troyer," she said. "My brother called you that today. But do you have a first name?"

"It's Joshua," he replied, a moment of awkwardness briefly coming over him. He was not used to such attention from anyone, including Hannah. Ria turned her focus to Joshua's horses, now standing in quiet docility nearby. She walked to Temper's side and began stroking his mane.

"I notice that Temper has cooled down a bit," she said, quickly adding, "Now, have you?"

Her comment made Joshua blush with embarrassment, unlocking his eyes from hers and returning to his work. Ria suspected her attempt at sarcasm would be met with silence, but decided to stick to her guns, awaiting his answer.

For a few moments, he continued his work. But then he turned, faced the young woman and addressed her.

"You saw me strike my horse," he replied. "And now you question my own temper. But what you English don't understand is that our horses need to obey us. We depend on them, and Temper—"

Ria interrupted him. "We *English*? Is that what you call us?" She knew the answer to her question; she had spent the last four years in the midst of one of New York's largest Amish settlements.

"Yes," he said. "We are *not* English. We are *not* part of your life. I began learning your language at about five years, but mostly we use our own tongue...a German tongue. And what we do with our horses is our business. Not yours."

She nodded, but only to appear polite. She was sure that animal rights activists would argue that statement, but she decided not to pursue it. The Amish farmer had bested her.

"That's true," she conceded. "It is your business...but that doesn't mean I have to like it."

She returned her attention to Temper, gently stroking his chestnut-colored snout with the flash of white fur down its center. Then with a free hand she began to caress his bent and deformed ear. This calmed the large animal.

"Good boy, beautiful boy..."

Ria turned to address the young Amish farmer. "I love horses, and Temper's a wonderful animal...and I guess I'd never seen anything like that before. I do understand that you need to make him work for you. I just question your methods."

For a moment, Joshua remained silent, taking in her criticism. Then he returned his attention to his wagon, removing the last few pieces of firewood.

"You're entitled to your views, and I am mine," he replied. "I'll finish my work and leave you be."

But Ria, still patting the big animal's mane, attempted to make amends.

"I would have thought that Amish horses had names like Hans or Fritz," she said with a grin. It was an attempt to get a rise out of Joshua, but he didn't bite. "But Temper...it's a great name for a handsome horse!"

"Thank you," he replied. Their eyes met again.

Tilting her head towards the party behind them, she asked, "Would you like to join us?"

EIGHT

NINETY MINUTES LATER, the Morgan County sheriff's cruiser weaved its way down the narrow lane towards the Cahill camps. The first indications that a boisterous party was in progress were the thumping sounds of rap music coming from the direction of the fire. If he could hear that music from the highway, neighbors in the surrounding bay were in for a treat. Still, it was not even eleven o'clock. Don't some of the ponders remember they were young once? He personally recalled the many parties—one in particular, when he graduated from high school—that went deep into the night, and nobody complained.

That Hubie's niece and nephew were hosting such a bash was reason enough for him to check it out personally, maybe issue a warning before it got out of hand. Knowing Brad and his pals, there was a good chance of that happening. Earlier this summer, though he hadn't mentioned it to Hubie, his office received a call about some kids firing buckshot at jerrycans of kerosene at some secluded beach. The mastermind was clearly Brad, leading a band of thrill-seekers getting their kicks at exploding balls of fire. By the time his deputies had arrived, however, the fires were out and nobody was around. Still, Boychuk knew the culprit and that was why he decided to take the call tonight himself. Nephew or no nephew to Hubie, Brad might need a lecture.

"What the hell?" he heard himself saying out loud, as his SUV's headlights beamed in the direction of a large Amish wagon and the team of horses. Though he was still at least fifty yards away, Boychuk realized instantly that something was out of sync. As he drove nearer, he counted at least two dozen partiers bumping and grinding to music thundering from four box speakers set up on the edge of the lawn. Enjoying likely the last nice weekend of the season.

At the shore, a bonfire was raging, leaping six feet or higher. Another group of celebrants had lodged themselves firmly to a series of makeshift benches consisting of two-by-twelve spruce planks resting on cinderblocks. It was at the center of one bench that the sheriff spotted Joshua Troyer, Menno's eldest kid, whom Hubie had spoken about so fondly. Boychuk knew that young Troyer was due to set out on his own; he had even recommended to Menno that the young man look into a couple of farms the sheriff knew were for sale on the other side of Plager Junction.

Beer in hand, Joshua's blue work shirt was unbuttoned and his chest was bare. If he had worn his customary straw hat, it was nowhere in sight. His black suspenders, no longer affixed to his shoulders, dangled like broken guide wires by his sides. Next to him sat a laughing Ria Cahill, she too lifting a beer to her lips. On his opposite side, another young lady had slung her arm over the Amish farmer's shoulders and was stroking his bowler-styled hair. Then Ria leaned over as if to whisper something in his ear and a broad smile splashed across his chiseled face. Trash drunk, Boychuk concluded.

But where was the instigator here, he wondered. Scanning the gathering one more time, Boychuk spotted him. Brad was standing by the coolers, next to that Wells kid who Barbara seemed to have had misgivings about earlier. Nick was his name, and both he and Brad appeared upset at something, pointing in the direction of the Amish man. Reading Nick's lips, Boychuk figured that Joshua was clearly an uninvited guest.

It was then that Brad noticed the authoritative figure of the Morgan County sheriff in their midst. He was joined now by one of his deputies whose cruiser was parked behind the sheriff's Tahoe. A look of dismay came over Brad; it was as if a large raincloud had thundered overhead. He motioned for someone to turn the music down and ventured over to where the police officers were standing.

"Evenin', Brad," the sheriff said sternly. "Looks like you and your gang are having a good loud time tonight."

"Just lettin' off a little steam, Sheriff, after a long summer's work," Brad replied, slurring his words slightly. "Are we in trouble? No one here's under twenty-one."

"It's the noise, Brad," Boychuk said. "If you don't reduce the decibels on those boom boxes, and by a lot, you will be. You're keeping everyone in this cove awake...so don't make me shut you down."

As Nick sidled up, and was listening to the conversation, Boychuk decided to weigh in on the subject of their unorthodox guest. Amish parents had experienced misbehaving children, suffering the 'temptations' as offered by their English peers. There had been stories of drinking, carousing, even unwed pregnancies. The Ohio Amish now populating his county gave their 'youngies', as they called them, the opportunity at seventeen to experience a bigger world outside their farms. Some sects, mostly in Pennsylvania, had even allowed their kids to buy cameras, radios—even cars—to rid the evil English spirits from their systems.

By the time they were twenty-one, however, activity of that sort was supposed to be left behind. They were expected to dedicate themselves to God's will, and most did. Menno had called it something like *Gelassenheit*, which apparently meant that his kid would have to yield to their church; it would rule their lives, their entire future.

"I see you've invited one of our horse-drawn friends to your party," Boychuk said, his eyes pointing in Joshua's direction. But before Brad could reply, Nick decided to chime in.

"Well, he wasn't asked by me or Brad," he barked. Beer in hand, he was still dressed in his black T-shirt and jeans, his fedora tilted to one side. "The fuckin' guy shows up with his firewood, and the next thing we know, he's sitting on the bench by the fire, drinking our beer."

"With Ria and her friend, too, I see," Boychuk added.

"Yeah, it's a goddamned freak show!" Nick barked.

The sheriff had heard and seen enough. He whispered a few words in his deputy's ear, and then looked in the direction of the party.

"Well, you'll have to deal with it," the sheriff said. "I'm not getting involved. But keep the sound down—"

Brad interrupted him.

"Is there a noise ordinance here, Sheriff?"

"No, just *my* ordinance, Brad. If we get another complaint, party's over. Understand?"

Brad shrugged in agreement. He had made his point.

"One more thing, Brad. You don't have that shotgun of yours anywhere around here, do you?"

"No, sir,"

"Not in your car?"

"Nope."

"Then where is it?"

"It's locked away," he lied, pointing to the cottage.

"Good, it better stay there tonight. I don't want a repeat of what you and your friends did over on Crystal Beach a while back."

"And what was that Sheriff?" Now Brad, fortified by beer, was challenging the police officer.

"Don't be cute with me, Brad, you know what I'm talking about. Just do yourself a favor and lower the noise. Curb some of that drinking before it gets out of control." The sheriff, who was an inch or two taller than Cahill, glared steely into Brad's eyes.

"If we have to come back here tonight, you won't like it, I can assure you."

IT WAS LATE, VERY LATE, when Joshua guided his wagon down the long, dusty road leading to his parents' farm. He was still dizzy on his feet. Though he remembered glancing at that girl's wristwatch—the greenish-blue one that matched the color of that stone around her neck—he knew that it had been time to leave. Daylight was only hours away and there was no doubt he would pay a big price for his actions tonight. For now, however, his only hope was to dislodge the team and slip into bed unnoticed. Maybe Papa won't wake. It was a tall order.

That girl!

She was all he could think about as he led the horses to the barn. Her name was not a church name like his sister's—or Hannah's, for that matter. But a different one. She informed him that her real name was a bit longer. Ria…short for Maria. Yes, he remembered that now. Against his better judgment, he had accepted her invitation and the next thing he knew he was drinking alcohol by the fire. Sitting next to him all night, laughing and singing those English songs, she on one side and another friend, a girl named Natasha, on the other. Natasha kept touching him on the back of his neck, massaging him, putting her fingers through his hair. It was Ria, however, who had cast some sort of spell over him.

"Damn!" he said out loud.

As Temper took noisily to his stall, upset by having to work late, Joshua staggered once again. His tongue now encircling his lower lip, he could taste the blood. His memory was returning; it was *all* coming back to him now. Was it only an hour ago that it all occurred? After he had announced it was time to leave? He remembered Ria saying that she would walk him to his team, immediately locking arms with the young farmer to stabilize his wobbly legs, laughing drunkenly as he staggered some more.

It was a moment frozen in darkness, the only light emanating from the distant bonfire. Leaping to her toes, impulsively she made her move. Her lips met his. It was an act that lasted only seconds but for Joshua, a lifetime. He was shocked. Euphoric! This was new to him, so new…yet so soft and moist and appealing. The alcohol was one intoxicant, the kiss another. Then she reopened her sparkling blue eyes, the best players of a broad affectionate smile. No words

were spoken. Not yet at least. But he knew what she was commu-
nicating. She was granting him permission. This was all right. This
was okay.

Finally, she spoke.

"Be careful on your way home," she purred. "Maybe we'll meet
again..." It was an image burning in his memory.

Then from nowhere emerged the man he had seen on the passenger side of Brad's convertible. Joshua remembered his name as
well. It was Nick, and he was her brother's friend. Or more than that,
maybe.

"It's about time you got the hell outta here," the man had said,
belligerently. He too was drunk with alcohol after a night around
the campfire. "You don't belong here, Amish boy! Take your filthy
horses—they've been *shitting* here all night—and get the fuck out!"

All Joshua remembered now were screams coming from Ria.

"Nick!" she cried. "Go back to the fire and leave him alone!"
Quickly she searched for Brad, and spotted him about ten yards away.
He had been watching the incident unfold.

"Brad, do something about Nick, will you?"

Now she could see Nick's fierce gray eyes filling with rage as he
attempted to get between herself and Joshua. She tried to intervene.

"You two were getting pretty cozy tonight," he shouted, pushing
her hands away.

"Nick, I'm just making sure that Josh gets on his wagon so he
can go home," she pleaded. "Nothing more than that."

"So, it's 'Josh', huh? You and *Josh*. How quaint."

"It was nothing," she repeated. Now she was wondering if Nick
had seen the kiss. Maybe he had. "We were just having fun."

"Not the way I saw it," he replied.

"Nick, get real...you don't think I'd have a thing for an Amish
guy?"

"That's what it looked like to me, Ria!"

"Oh, bull shit!" she said. She reached for his arm as if to lead him away from the Amish wagon. "We're just drunk. Why don't we head back to the fire?"

But Nick had other plans. Pushing Ria away, he marched closer to Joshua, who was gathering the reins to his horses. Joshua was a taller man than Nick, but Nick, the bodybuilder with Popeye limbs, outweighed the farmer by at least twenty pounds. In a sudden move, he ripped Joshua away from his team and, with a lightning right hook that would make a prizefighter envious, landed his fist on the Amish man's lower lip. The force of the blow sent Joshua crashing into Temper's enormous torso and then to the ground, his brimmed hat a victim as well. The Belgian, snorting loudly, became startled and the wagon began to move. Sorrel, acting in unison with his larger comrade, followed suit and became restless.

Ria screamed again. She grabbed Nick's shirt and began to pull him away from Joshua. Seconds later, Brad arrived on the scene but he was too late to prevent the damage inflicted on the young farmer. Joshua, clearly in pain and startled by the violence, retrieved his hat and pulled himself up. The horses had settled.

"I'm leaving," he announced. "You won't see me again."

"Good fuckin' thing, Troyer," Nick said, attempting to free himself from Brad's grip. Ria, her eyes filling with tears, pleaded with her brother to alleviate the situation.

"Brad, please, get Nick out of here!"

Then she turned towards Joshua. His lip was now welling up, a trickle of blood growing larger. Reaching into the back pocket of her shorts, she removed a tissue and began dabbing the wound. But Joshua pushed her away before scrambling aboard his wagon, glancing at Ria one last time.

Her moist, caring eyes told the story. She was sorry.

And then he was gone.

Now, as he toiled in his barn to the light of a lone lantern, Joshua was hoping that Temper for once would *not* live up to his name. That he would go quietly to his stall. But the large, excitable horse had other ideas. He began to bray as if he was still prepared for action, despite having trotted over paved roads for nearly three miles in the dead of night. Once again, Joshua knew he would have to exert his will over the animal. Holding tightly to the reins as he backed the horse into the stall, Joshua grabbed Temper by the snout and squeezed hard. The horse, attempting to pull himself back, winced in pain.

"Bastard!" he bellowed, his native tongue assuming control.

From behind, Joshua heard a sound and jolted his head around. At the entrance to the barn was the silhouette of a diminutive man in his early forties. It was his father. Joshua had no idea how long he had been there.

Now the older man was close enough to see the swollen lower lip, and to smell his son's breath. They locked eyes.

"Go sleep off your errant ways," Menno ordered. "We'll speak at sunrise."

He turned and walked from the barn.

NINE

AS MORNING ARRIVED over the big lake, Ria donned a pair of cross-trainers, a racer's tank-top, shorts and her baseball cap and was off for her daily run. Her route, normally an eight-mile slog that led her down the county highway, crossing Bidgood Road and winding around a long, horseshoe loop known as the Dobie Trail, would normally take her less than seventy-five minutes, depending on the pace she set and what she did the night before. Today, she thought, this will be painful.

This morning she decided to alter her routine slightly to pay a visit to her parents who had stayed the night at her uncle's place in Morgantown. She also wanted to put some time and space between her and Nick, especially after the spectacle he had created the night before. He had been remorseful, vowing that it would never happen again, and had issued an apology, of sorts. In one breath, he had told her he was sorry; in another, he blamed her.

"What can I say, Ria? You do this to me," she now recalled him saying later, a broad grin splashed across his face. But she wouldn't forget it. She had left him at the fire and spent the night on the couch.

Now, as she discovered her rhythm in the early morning heat, her pace steadily increasing, the only sounds heard were a pair of Nike LunarGlides, turquoise in color, slapping the weathered asphalt road. She had to break these new shoes in fast, she thought, or she'd pay the price later.

In moments, she found herself passing the old general store, now boarded-up and infirm as flowering pokeweed, some of which were reaching five feet in height, sprouted from the concrete base of its dormant gas pumps. This sight saddened her, for it was all too common in this poverty-strewn spot of northern New York. It was especially poignant since she'd decided to build a teaching career here. Her SLU friends had encouraged her to join them in nearby Vermont or New Hampshire, states whose economies had fared better in this never-ending recession. She had said no. She had grown to love this part of New York and wanted to stay, much to their chagrin and that of her mother.

As a teenager, she remembered this store; it had been a vibrant meeting place for boaters, anglers and old gossips that summered on the Pond. For the longest time, it was called Jensen's. Then it became Fowler's for a few years before it was finally sold to a couple of Iranian immigrants who simply named it the PondSide Grocery, an innocuous handle that camouflaged their heritage after nine-eleven. Not that Iran had anything to do with Ground Zero or the Pentagon or that field in Pennsylvania. But its owners feared the 'Ponders', as locals called themselves, wouldn't know the difference and boycott their store. Or worse, maybe one of them would put a match to it after midnight.

The PondSide had suffered the fate of many of the establishments—the bait shops, the antique stores, the beer joints—that once populated the area. They too had been driven into bankruptcy by job losses and escalating property taxes. The cash-deprived Persians knew their investment was lost. Their shelves empty, they began treating their waning number of customers with contempt. Making matters worse, no more than two hundred yards away, a rival general store had flourished. Its clerks actually smiled once in a while, its pizza and chicken wing deals growing in popularity. The neighbors had won the battle of the Pond.

Ria had loved these fast-paced runs. Throughout spring, and blessed with a surprisingly dry summer, she had trained vigorously, perhaps too hard and too often in Nick's opinion. There was a triathlon in Burlington in a few weeks and she wasn't going to miss that. The pool at SLU had been useful, but she knew she'd have to master the dark choppy waters of the Pond and, later, an even larger, more treacherous Lake Champlain if she was to succeed.

But she would prevail.

Her coach for the past year, Margaret, was a fifty-something, unmarried physiology prof who Ria felt at times was hitting on her. The elder woman was as gruff and sadistic as any Marine drill instructor. Like the one she once was. But Margaret was always right. Stop fighting the water, Ria! You need to get over this, she ordered, you need to get that two hundred meter down pat, without tiring yourself. Balance that stroke! Stop wasting energy. You need...you need...you *need*...

By race day, Ria realized she would have to complete a swim program four times the length of any pool. Jesus! It was the same with cycling, and Margaret's voice continued to haunt her. Focus on your cadence, change gears often, keep that cadence at ninety-plus. This will make your run after the bike feel better. You have to rid yourself of the brick, she'd nag. You don't want your legs feeling like friggin' bricks when your run follows the bike. That way your transition will be smooth, efficient and achievable. God, what a bitch! But Margaret was always right.

Now she was finding her pulse, her dark-blue Oakley's and her Pirates cap protecting her from the blazing sun. Her mind shifted from Military Maggie to the events of the last twenty-four hours. The reunion with her mom and dad was lovely and, though her outspoken mother lacked a filter and never failed to tell Ria what was on her mind, she was looking forward to spending some time with both of them this weekend.

The day on the pontoon barge, tunes-a-blaring and endless beers, had been their last hurrah. Soon, she and her college friends would face the real world. Soon she would find herself standing in front of about twenty-four primary schoolers, eyes wide open, some even eagerly awaiting knowledge and guidance.

But it was the first and last encounters of yesterday that now occupied her mind. Her chance meeting of Joshua by the side of the road, witnessing his treatment of a beautiful yet testy horse, was unforgettable. Though his actions were disturbing, his explanations were acceptable, strangely. His horses, she realized, were central to his life's calling, a means to an end. They needed to behave.

It wasn't his treatment of Temper, however, that affected her so indelibly. No, it was the innocence of his soft emerald eyes that was most attractive. Why she had asked him—on a whim—to join their party she didn't know. Why he accepted her invitation was an even greater mystery. Never in a gazillion years had she figured he would have stayed. But he did. He *stayed*...and he *enjoyed* himself. Then she had walked him back to his team, they staggered, they laughed, they...

Her run continued, and just as she was about to pick up the pace, she came upon an Amish farm ahead. Speak of the devil, she thought, though she knew that was the wrong choice of words. This wasn't Joshua's place; she knew his farm was located on the other side of town, closer to her uncle's house. As she approached, she could see a couple of women setting up a roadside stand.

At first, Ria figured they were selling baked goods, such as pies and breads, and perhaps preserves. Such stands were common across the county. Her friends, however, had warned her about the cleanliness of the ingredients that went into them. "Don't buy Amish pies or pastry," they admonished. "Don't you see how these people live?" But upon closer look, she realized this couple—dressed in full smocks—was not selling food but attractive wicker baskets and quilts instead. She decided to stop.

"Good morning," Ria said warmly. "Nice day again today, isn't it?"

The younger Amish woman mumbled something under her breath, a reply that was incomprehensible to Ria but one that caused her mother to frown visibly in her daughter's direction.

"Yes, it is another *fine* day, miss," the mother said with a stilted smile, an apology of sorts. A curious way to deal with customers, Ria thought, glancing in the younger woman's direction. She was about her age, Ria determined, but taller and heavier. Her round full face of porcelain-colored flesh was squeezed into a black bonnet fastened tightly under her chin. As Ria returned her focus to the display, she felt the younger woman's scrutiny. She was now judging *me*, Ria thought, as if to say *'I am not like you.'*

"You do very nice work," Ria complimented, as she surveyed the assortment of baskets and blankets. She now wished she had brought her wallet. Her mom would have liked one of the baskets.

"Thank you," the older woman said. Again, the younger one remained mute.

"I don't have any money with me, but are you going to be here later today, or tomorrow?"

"Yes, we'll be here all weekend, or at least I will be, miss," she now offered. "My daughter has to travel over to another farm but one of us will be here."

"Good, thank you," Ria replied. "I'll come back."

She glanced quickly at the younger one again, and the two locked eyes. No further words were spoken.

As she resumed her run down the gently sloping road and around the corner, she wondered about their lifestyle. How could they live as though it was 1875? Yes, their lives were lived devoutly, but why such a choice? She knew she was truly ignorant of their customs, their beliefs—even their history. But life was hard enough these days. Why make it tougher?

That prompted myriad questions: what the hell had she done with Joshua? Was this just a fleeting infatuation, a night of playfulness accentuated by alcohol? Or was it more than that? Surely there couldn't be a future with this man, or any man like him. *A future?* Hell, there was scarcely a present! For all she knew, Joshua had probably forgotten, or dismissed, their embrace last night. He was drunk, after all.

Of course, there had been other boys in her life. At parties in the basement of their Pittsburgh side-split when her parents were not home. Followed by episodes in cars that resulted in more than fogged-up windows. But she always considered herself a *good* girl, she rationalized. Certainly not as bad as some of those bitches in high school, the slutty chicks who boffed every kid who ever winked at them. But there had been boys. Some were all right; others easily forgotten. And some were downright awful.

Like her first. As a starry-eyed high school sophomore, she met a freshman from Cleveland State who had returned home for Christmas. Justin was his name, he was four years her senior, and he was beautiful. And quickly she had granted him permission to make her a woman, officially, with all its plasmatic and painful consequences. Trouble was she overheard the braggart boasting about his conquest the next day. He took pride, he laughed, in going balls-deep with the hot Cahill chick, learning that she had been his number one target for months, much like a farmer eyeing a prize heifer at the State Fair.

He had told his friends that he had to have her.

He had succeeded.

By the time she enrolled at St. Lawrence, her mission was different. It was to pony up at least a three-point-eight GPA, obtain her teaching credentials with a Masters in mind while exploring levels of athleticism that gave her more satisfying highs. Let her girlfriends back in Pennsylvania attend state schools and get their 'MRS' degrees; that wasn't for her. She was there for a purpose, and that was to excel.

Still, at SLU, she hadn't exactly been a nun. There were three or four guys who treated her nicely, one of whom taught her a great deal about coital communion. His name was Sean, and he was a gorgeously polite hockey player from some place up in the Canadian sticks called Larder Lake. Presenting her with a beautiful pendant on her birthday before Christmas, he had mentioned the M-word for the first time and she had given his invitation a good deal of consideration. His desire was to play professional, travelling from one rink to another in northern Europe. But while the prospect of foreign travel seemed exotic, she wasn't crazy about becoming a puck bunny and, besides, at twenty-one, she wasn't ready to get married. She told him she wanted to stay here and teach. Stung by rejection, and after a river of tears, he flew off to Sweden and was out of her life forever. For weeks, she felt she had made a major mistake. But then, on the rebound, she met Nick.

Nick!

Now he was good. But why she fell for him was the question of her time. Well, she knew the answer. He too was beautiful. And different. Very different...and *damned* good!

With streams of sweat now staining her Pirates cap, she approached her uncle's house. Ria could see her parents relaxing in their high-back chairs, sipping cups of morning coffee. Dee was placing a large tray of what appeared to be croissants, cheese and fruit in front of them as Hubie walked up the steps from the direction of his garage.

Sitting next to her parents was a brunette about her age, perhaps a bit older. Ria had heard that she'd had some sort of mystery cousin, some drop-dead gorgeous chick who was Uncle Hubie's long-lost granddaughter. Moreover, she was somehow related to his pal, the county sheriff. All of this was *so* soap opera-like, even scandalous, she'd told her mother with a laugh over the phone last week. Her mother, who'd had a knack for rooting out the truth, said she'd enlighten her later. You don't know the *half* of it, Barbara had hinted.

"Good morning," Barbara said, as her daughter bounded up the steps to the porch. "How are you feeling today? We heard you guys had quite the bash last night."

"We had more than a little fun," she admitted, turning her attention to Roger who was sitting there with his coffee. "Dad, you look good today!" He simply smiled at the compliment. Ria adored her father, but was worried sick about him. His health wasn't improving.

Barbara turned her attention towards the brunette sitting across from her.

"Ria, I want to introduce you to someone. Meet Makenna Monteith...she's a cousin of yours. Well, technically, your second cousin."

"Hi...nice to meet you, Makenna," Ria said, offering her hand. Her mother's description of Makenna didn't do justice to this woman. Not that Ria had met Jane Schumacher in real life. But she had seen pictures of her. Google had delivered voluminous amounts of information and hundreds of photos of the former journalist turned political aide over the past few years. Hers was a story that even Hollywood would be hard-pressed to match.

"Please, call me Ken," Makenna said. "All my friends do."

Makenna pointed to an exquisite, oval-shaped stone around Ria's neck. About the size of a quarter, the turquoise gem was set against rare Tibetan silver with black, jagged arterial lines bursting brilliantly in the morning sun.

"That is so original," she said.

"Thanks, I love it too," Ria replied.

"Where did you get it?"

"Um...a friend at college gave it to me on my birthday, last December. My birthstone, actually."

"It's beautiful," Makenna added.

"I agree," Dee added. "The way the silver frames the turquoise compliments your eyes, dear."

"Thank you, Dee...what a nice thing to say."

Barbara decided to enter the conversation.

"You know what Shakespeare once said about turquoise?" she offered. "From *The Merchant of Venice*?" In dramatic fashion, she threw her head back as if she was a star on the stage at Stratford herself. *"Out upon her! It was my turquoise!"* Now she was growing more theatrical. *"I would not have given it for a wilderness of monkeys!"*

It was now Hubie's turn. "We've always known you've been *more* fun than a barrel of monkeys."

As his wife shot Hubie a glance, rolling her eyes, Roger decided to contribute a few words.

"Truth be told, it has been called *The Precious Stone of Persia* for a reason," he said. "Shylock had other names for it but I'll leave it to my lovely wife to quote the Bard. After all, she dabbled in English at Syracuse...when she wasn't hell-bent on journalism." He smiled affectionately in his wife's direction. "How can I *not* adore a woman who can quote Shakespeare?"

With a smile, Barbara returned her husband's love.

"We went to New York in July where we saw Michael Corleone himself, starring in the *Merchant*. Pacino was astounding!" She pointed to Ria's turquoise gem. "That's why, honey, I was able to quote the man's words on the beauty of turquoise...dating back four hundred years!"

This piqued Makenna's interest.

"My friends and I were in New York last year, and took in a performance under the stars. What a wonderful setting. Central Park in summer."

"Oh," Barbara said. "What did you see?"

"Anne Hathaway in *Twelfth Night*."

"Not a big fan of that actress—everything she does is over the top—but I always wanted to see that play," Barbara replied, glancing at her husband. "Roger, we have to find out what's playing in New York next summer."

"Or Canada, Barb," he replied. "Their Stratford isn't far from Pittsburgh."

"How about the two of you joining us as well?" Barbara asked Dee.

"Would love to, Barb, but you'd have to consult your brother here."

Hubie's face turned to a mild frown.

"Not my pitcher of beer, sister," he admitted.

"Yeah, forgot that, Hubert," Barbara replied. "Nitro glycerin couldn't dislodge you from this house, let alone this town." Allowing herself a smile, she added. "And since I've never been one to preach—"

"—no pulpiteer in you at all…" Hubie countered.

"Not at all," she smiled, "but as I was saying, why wouldn't you want to travel, experience things? Open your mind to this big bold world of ours? Take this lovely lady somewhere, like Europe."

"We went to Buffalo this year," he deadpanned.

"I rest my case," his sister replied.

Makenna turned her attention again to the young triathlete.

"Your mom tells me you're in training for an event in Vermont soon?" Mackenna asked. "Now that's impressive."

"Yeah, or crazy," Ria replied. "I probably didn't do myself any favors last night, either. Brad's in worse shape." She smiled. "He said this morning that he felt like an '84 Escort…runnin' rough."

All but Barbara shared the humor.

"That's my son," she sighed. "Always running…from something."

"Do you run, too?" Ria asked.

"Not to the extent of your dedication," Makenna replied. "Just to keep my legs in shape for the slopes. I'd like to get back to Whiteface again this winter but, since I'm graduating in January, I have to find a job. A real job, that is. My parents in Plattsburgh have told me that more than once."

"You're in Washington, now, right?"

Makenna nodded. "Across the river, actually, in Virginia. I hear you spent four years at SLU?"

Ria nodded.

"I went to Clarkson," Makenna said. "All this time we were next door and didn't know it? Maybe we saw each other at games?"

"Strange how things come about," Ria said.

Barbara weighed in once again.

"You know, the sheriff was here earlier. He told us he was called to your party last night. You guys were a bit noisy, he says."

That took Ria by surprise. To hear that the cops had arrived at their party, and not know about it was unsettling. But she wasn't about to admit that she had failed to witness their presence.

"Brad's boom boxes, I'm afraid," she grimaced. "Too much beer, too…"

"Brian also told us that some young Amish man was there too," Barbara offered. "Didn't know they went in for that, myself."

Ria hesitated. Her mother knew more than she was letting on.

"Yes, a guy named Joshua…I think. Delivered some wood."

It was Hubie's turn to speak.

"Know him well…a nice kid," he said. "Not a kid, I guess. He's over twenty now, I think. Helped me out a lot over the past couple of years." Hubie pointed to his still-damaged right ankle. "Saved me, in fact. Picked the machine up by himself and then called the paramedics."

"No kidding!" Ria said, her interest warming. "Never heard that story, Uncle Hubie."

"Yeah, if he hadn't done that, I don't know if I'd be walking to-day on this leg. Hell, they might've had to saw the goddamned thing off!" Then he tilted his head in the direction of the wooded area at the rear of his property. "He's building me a fence over there this fall. With his little brothers."

"Nice," Ria said.

"Didn't think they drank alcohol, though," Roger said. "Our Lancaster Amish are more liberal, if that's the correct term, but I've never heard of them ever consorting with us, especially."

"Our Amish here are members of an order that dates back centu-ries," Hubie replied. "Very strict. They don't allow their kids much running room, though I've heard some wild stories about some of their kids going AWOL with booze at times. Tell you the truth, I wasn't a bit surprised that Joshua was involved. Especially after what Brian said."

This piqued Ria's interest again.

"Why do you say that, Uncle Hubie?"

"Just my impression, Ria. Just think he's not a very content young man. He's a dreamer…who might want more outta life than his order can deliver." He shrugged his shoulders. "But I don't know. Might be wrong."

Dee, who was following the conversation, decided to weigh in.

"Would you like to join us for breakfast, dear?"

"No, thank you, Dee. I have to get back to my run or my trainer, who's a drill sergeant, won't be happy…especially since we might have partied a bit too much last night. Right, Mom?"

Before Barbara got the opportunity to reply, Ria turned in Makenna's direction once again.

"So nice to meet you," she said. "Will I see you later at the Pond? Maybe we can have a chat."

"Absolutely," Makenna replied. "Or maybe we could run together sometime this weekend, as well?"

"Yeah, that would be great," Ria replied. Moments later, bidding everyone good-bye, and as quickly as her arrival had been, she bounded down the steps and disappeared up the street.

TEN

SIX FAST HOURS after his head hit the pillow, Joshua was leading his team towards his fields. To his dismay, his morning arrived much too early, and once again, he knew it would be another long tough day of work. True to his word, Menno rose at dawn and immediately awoke his wayward son, telling him he would meet him in the barn in fifteen minutes. Joshua had thought his moment of reckoning might have been delayed, or better still, ignored if he had enlisted his brothers for another day's harvest. No such luck. The elder Troyer had dispatched the youngsters for other chores and directed Joshua to park his wagon at the entrance of the barn.

"Your behavior last night," Menno began, "was inexcusable. I can find few words to describe my disappointment. Mama's as well." He searched his son's face for any sign of remorse that may have told him that last night was just an aberration and that it would not happen again. But there was none. Instead, the young man simply lowered his head, kicking the dust under his feet, seemingly prepared to accept his penance.

"Well, what do you say for yourself?" Menno was determined to get to the root of the story. His friends, the church elders from surrounding communities, would label Joshua a sinner. Joshua could face the *Bann*, ex-communication in other words, for committing such acts. Or worse, the *Meidung*, or as the English would understand, a total shunning. Rebellious children, unaccepting of the truth, had departed, never to return again, and Menno was determined never to have that happen to a member of his family.

"Not much, Papa," Joshua said.

"That is all you can say?"

"Yes."

"Well, that is unsatisfactory," his father said, sullenly. "You are of age now, Joshua. An adult. I don't understand, my son. Since you were five or six years, you have had many relations with the English—selling wood, hay, berries, corn—and this has never happened. I expected this when you were younger. But now?"

Still no response. Menno would delve further.

"Or is it something else? Or...are we talking about *someone* else?"

Joshua was caught off guard by his father's last question. He had expected an interrogation about his consumption of alcohol and his arrival home well after midnight. But he was unprepared for the final query. His father was intelligent; he was wise in the vagaries of life, having uprooted his family from one part of the country to another. But he had brought them here for reasons in addition to cheap land; Ohio had offered one too many temptations for his young family.

Immediately, Menno knew he had shaken his son; it was written all over Joshua's face. There was more to his nighttime thrills at the Pond than he was letting on. His son had not just consumed English beer.

"I speak the truth, do I not?" he now asked. "There is a *woman* involved. Am I not right?"

Joshua's continued silence was all the confirmation his disconsolate father required. A drunken night among his English neighbors was inappropriate enough, behavior that could be dismissed as a careless, even juvenile, excursion into adulthood. He had seen situations like these before in the church; it was not the first time that alcohol had swayed its youthful members. But the introduction of a romantic partner, from the community of English, was dangerous. It meant his son would be lost forever. Now Menno was consumed with rage.

"Tell me it is *not* true!" he bellowed. This jolted Joshua from his silence.

"I cannot, Papa!"

It was then that Menno noticed his son's injured face. Though Joshua had wiped all traces of blood from his swollen lip, it had remained engorged and now it was obvious to Menno that his son had been involved in more than drinking. There was more to this story than possible romance.

"What happened here," the older Troyer demanded, nearly touching his son's injury. Joshua snapped his head away.

"It's nothing," he replied.

"Nothing! You have wounds on your face, and you say it is nothing? Stop lying to me."

But lie he would. Joshua would not reveal that an English man had struck him last night. Members of their church, their order, abhorred violence; it was a tradition that dated through the centuries. If beset by harm, their sect always faced a difficult choice: suffer the consequences or move away.

"I fell to the ground last night," he said, meekly. "It was the alcohol."

Menno, now glaring at his son, was not buying it.

"Your version of the truth, if it is the truth, troubles me, Joshua," he said, his voice a mere whisper. "Go to the fields. Your brothers will follow."

As Joshua turned away, resuming his tasks ahead, his father had one last admonition for him.

"Son, end it now...or I will end it for you!"

Still stunned by Menno's dictate, the muscular young farmer had obeyed his father's orders and was now busily working one of the far corners of their fields. He and his brothers would gather their last forage of hay, creating as many as a hundred or more pyramids of straw, most exceeding twelve feet in height. The English employed their mechanized thrashers, tossing enormous, plastic-wrapped bales of hay high into the air as if they were giant marshmallows. At times, he had envied their access to modernity. But he knew his lot in life. He would build a village, row upon row of conically shaped stacks that to outsiders resembled more the historic habitats of the native Plains people than sustenance for livestock.

In the distance, the reflections of the morning sun bounced from Remington Pond, and once again Joshua felt his heart racing. It was not from the sweat of his brow, or his labor. No, it was his recollection of the events from the night before. He allowed himself a smile. He had never had such an experience and it gave him pleasure.

Jumping from the wagon, he was about to toss his pitchfork aside for a drink of water when he heard the sounds of footfalls behind him. Startled, he turned to discover Ria standing there.

In stillness, a tentative half-smile lighted up her face.

"Hello, again," was all she said.

ELEVEN

THE ROAR OF THE HIGH-TORQUE EVINRUDE, two hundred and fifty horses strong, shattered the silence of the bay and the sleek bass boat pulled away from its lift. Brad had risen late, about two hours past his plan, but he was determined to get some fishing in before the festivities would reignite later in the day.

Conditions were perfect. Though it was a Saturday and the weather was willing, there were surprisingly few boaters on the big lake. Its warm black waters were as smooth as slate. Now behind the wheel, he noticed only a few fellow fishers had violated its tranquility. They were far across the Pond, by Sylvanite Island, and were now using their electric motors to avoid scaring their prey. That was a good spot, Brad admitted. Not just for bass, either. There were schools of yellow perch, walleye, muskellunge and crappie available for the opportunist in him.

He knew he should've moved sooner, at dawn preferably. But he was too goddamned hung over to rise that early. No matter; he knew this lake. He knew it better than anyone else. He had his secret places and was now revving the engine to full throttle en route to the best of them, gracefully skimming the waters at more than sixty miles per hour towards his destination.

Eat. Sleep. Fish. That was the motto adopted by every lunker on this lake, and others like it. But that logo was incomplete; if he was designing the T-shirts, he'd add a couple more descriptors: '*Drink. Screw.*' Brad allowed himself an audible laugh. He was one witty guy.

Today, he was alone in his boat. But not by choice, since he had informed both Natasha and Nick that his broad-hulled Skeeter, in shining red metallic, would depart its pier this morning for a few hours on the Pond. Maybe bring a few beers, and some snacks, and relax. He had especially hoped that Natasha, his sister's friend from Rome, would join him. And Nick, too, he supposed. But Nick was missing in action; as usual, Houdini was nowhere to be found.

Another education major at SLU, Natasha was an astonishing beauty who stood out like the former high school cheerleader that she was. Her ink-black curly hair and round dark eyes were enough to push Brad's libido into overdrive. Throw in a perfect nose and an even more delicate mouth, not to mention a great rack, and she was bitchin'. When he first met her at an SLU football game last fall, Brad thought she was Lebanese or Italian. Some place swarthy. But when Ria introduced them, she fired off her last name so fast that he hadn't caught it. All he knew was that she was Greek. Constantinidies or Constantinou, or some fucking thing like that.

Whatever. He didn't care what her name was, nor did it matter that the chick was thick as a plank. Going to college didn't mean you were smart. It only meant Daddy, some hotshot carpet dealer back home, could afford her hefty tuition. Brad could predict her future: a boring teaching job followed by a marriage to some loans manager at the bank, or the local chiropractor, or maybe even snag the attention of a real estate lawyer. Didn't matter. Soon, she would pop out four or five biters, followed by richer and richer meals and a gargantuan ass. As the Greeks would say: *Opa!*

But after all that horseshit with the sheriff, not to mention his sister's decision to invite Troyer—of all guys—to join their party, Brad knew his chances with Natasha would crater. Nick wasn't helping either. Wells had watched as the girls fondled that farmer all night by the fire and, in angst, his temper boiled over. The jackass just had to give Josh a poke and put a damper on what should have been a promising night. Ever the optimist, however, he knew there was always a silver lining. There would be future opportunities.

Where Nick was now was anyone's guess. The guy just disappears without explanation. When Brad finally climbed out of bed,

Natasha, she too nursing a hangover, was in the La-Z-Boy—sipping coffee. Of course, he knew where Ria likely was. On another run. God, why? Far too much work. And for what?

"No idea," was all Natasha could say when Brad asked about Nick's whereabouts. "He was gone when I got up. Have you checked the tents?"

"No, but I'll look around," he replied. "Will I see you later?"

"I'm not going anywhere," she beamed.

He had returned her smile with a wink. As he walked through the compound towards his boat, Brad surveyed the scene. At least a dozen of their friends had spent the night in tents on the edge of the property, and few were stirring. Women wearing only shorts and T-shirts clutched their mugs of coffee with both hands; the guys, their hair askew, their heads aching, were scratching their balls.

The big bonfire, fed by Troyer's hardwoods, was still smoldering. The makeshift benches were still in place, and behind them, clear evidence of the night's carnage. Beer cans and other empties were strewn about. Next to the barbeque were three large garbage cans, now filled with the refuse of a successful feast. Good times all around, he thought. But as he had ventured towards his boat, he had barked orders to clean the place up. The last thing he needed was his mother ragging on his ass.

Now Brad had arrived at his secret fishing spot on the Pond, a weedy passage that was so shallow the Evinrude's stainless-steel prop might stir up its muddy bottom or, if he wasn't careful, hit a birch log just below the surface. As he raised the trim on the motor, he glanced across the waters. Those dumb sons of bitches just didn't know how many times this inlet could cough up some beauties. No catch and release for him either. Everything was a keeper. Screw the conservation cops.

Reaching into a cooler for the first beer of the day, his mind wandered back to the arrival of the sheriff and his flunkies. Goddamned neighbors of ours will bitch us out about everything. Not that he was entirely surprised to see Boychuk there last night. They had been carrying on pretty good. Still, what time was it when the cops arrived? Eleven o'clock? Maybe earlier? Chill the fuck out, he thought. And what was all that shit about his shotgun? Thanks for the lecture, Sheriff. Made me sound like a friggin' redneck whose idea of kicks was to blast everything in sight.

He smiled again.

Maybe the old cop had a point.

Plunking himself down on the fisher's chair, he reached into his breast pocket, pulled out a joint and lit up. Some of Quebec's finest hydroponics. Those frogs know how to grow good weed. His dealer, a slippery, pointy-nosed little dickwad by the name of Reggie Garçon, regularly brought garbage bags of this shit across the St. Lawrence aboard his party barge, often in plain sight of the border boys. Good buds, clean, stem-free, and the crop's ready in twelve weeks, the greasy Garçon had told him. He had shown Brad a picture once. Quite the elaborate operation. He cut the engine and was now firing up the electric motor on the Skeeter's bow for a troll through the weeds. One or two casts later, he got his first bite. Goddamn, this is a good spot.

And so was the compound. If Natasha, or Tasha or whatever the fuck she wanted to be called didn't work out, maybe someone else would? He found himself smiling once again.

It was going to be good day...and night.

TWELVE

NERVOUSLY SHUFFLING HER FEET, Ria stood next to Joshua's hay wagon and awaited his reaction. From her uncle's house, she had taken a shortcut through a neighbor's field, across the flat, dry stones of a parched Murdock Creek, and past a clump of thicket filled with youthful oaks and middle-aged pine. She knew this route. She had navigated it before, hopscotching through the high brush and fallow fields, many of which had been abandoned years before as local farmers renounced their land for other pursuits.

Normally, Ria had watched for snakes and other gruesome creatures that lurked in the high, yellowed grasses. But today, as she leapt over a rotting, crumbling hemlock that had fallen victim to an ice storm, she brushed up against a nest swarming with bees or hornets. Instantly, the angry insects gave chase, and one or more landed on one of her bare legs. Letting out a loud squeal, she picked up her pace, thinking she could outrun the damn things.

It was a good thing her workout was nearing an end. Soon, Nick and the rest of the party would be wondering where she'd gone. But her mission was clear. She needed to see Joshua again, if for no other reason than to clear the air about last night. And there was no way she'd pay a visit to his family's farm.

Joshua locked eyes with the young athlete. She had removed her Pirates cap and was massaging its visor with both hands. Her satiny hair was now pulled back by a beaded crochet tieback and her Oakleys, perched on the cusp of her perspiring forehead, allowed her bright blue eyes to sparkle in the morning sun. She was fit and strong, Joshua thought. And so pleasing to the eye.

"I wanted to see you today," she said. "To apologize..."

He had been leaning on his pitchfork, but now resumed the task at hand. There was just too much work to do, and Papa was right. He had no business with the English, or their ways. Last night was a big mistake.

"There is no need for...sorry," he replied from over his shoulder, now tossing forkfuls of hay to the top of the wagon.

Ria sensed his reluctance to talk and was not surprised, since she knew she was putting him on the spot. His diffidence was one of his most appealing traits. This guy was so different. So unlike the other men who had entered her life since arriving at SLU. Not just because he was Amish, although that was a factor, but also because he was polite and sensitive. So definitely *not* an alpha male. They had met. They had argued. They had laughed. And they had *connected*. But was this a bad idea? Probably, but no one was going to find out, no matter where it would lead. She pressed ahead.

"Josh, please, stop working for a minute, okay?" she pleaded. "I need to apologize for Nick's behavior. My brother, too, but Nick especially. He was being an asshole...and I'm so sorry he hit you. I hope you can forgive me."

As he turned once again to face her, Ria noticed that his swollen lip had turned a dark blue color. It was less pronounced than last night but cause for contrition nevertheless.

"Oh my God," she cried, "he did a real job on you." She reached toward his mouth only to have her hand pushed gently away by the young Amish farmer.

"Please, Ria, there is no need for your sympathy," he replied. He felt it necessary to end this situation immediately. He must show respect for his father and his admonishment. He needed to get on with his life, minus the intrusions by the English. Especially those of this young woman.

"It wasn't your fault, what happened at your party," he added. "It was my fault. I should not have stayed."

It was then that he noticed a series of red welts the size of golf balls on Ria's leg and, immediately, knew their source.

"Have you been through those woods?" he asked, pointing in the direction of the deep underbrush at the edge of his property.

"It was the quickest route from my uncle's," she replied, "and I just got stung by bees or something. They were buzzing all around me."

"I can help you," he said, pitching several forks of hay beside the wagon to create a soft bed. "Please sit down."

Reaching up to the wagon's bench for his container of water, he removed its lid and poured several ounces. Then, scooping up a handful of soil, he began to mix it with the water to create a mudpack and before Ria had the opportunity to object, he was applying the mud to the growing contusions.

"This will eliminate some of the swelling and itch," he said, authoritatively. "It's not one of your fancy potions that you might find in one of your drugstores, but the soil has strong healing powers. Do you know if you're allergic to bees or hornets?"

Ria shook her head.

"But this is kinda gross," she now said, unsure that he'd catch her drift. But he had, keeping his hand filled with mud over the infected skin. Now he would have some fun.

"*Dieses ist grob!*"

She gave her head a shake. "What did you just say?"

"Just repeating what you said," he replied, smiling.

"*Grob* means gross in Pennsylvania Dutch?"

"More like German," he replied.

"Maybe I should have majored in German...so I could speak with you in your own language?"

He nodded. "I'd recommend it. You English would benefit if you came to know us better."

"There you are again with that 'English' stuff," she said. "You can speak the language better..." She searched for a comparison. "... than my brother!"

Continuing his treatment, he looked up with smiling eyes. "You were probably the victim of a yellowjacket. They're dormant at this time of the year and soon they will die. But they like to feast on humans and our refuse, especially if you disturb their nests. We have known about yellowjackets since Ohio. They were discovered there first and as a youngster, I was victimized many times. They are bold, and aggressive and you provoked them—"

Ria interrupted him. "Provoked? I didn't do a damn thing. All I was doing was cutting through the woods to the field."

Joshua smiled.

"Did a large group of them chase you once you were stung?"

"Yes," she admitted.

"You see, yellowjackets are very communal. They stick together. If one is threatened, their friends come to their rescue. They are like your armies and will pursue you if provoked."

"*My* armies?" she asked.

"Yes," he replied. "They're not mine. Your wars are not mine."

"Hey, you're just as much of an American as I am!"

Josh paused for a moment.

"We do not believe in military service. We stay away from wars."

Ria remained unconvinced.

"You don't defend yourselves either, do you?" she asked. "Was that why you didn't react when Nick hit you?"

"We do not believe in violence, Ria."

Sensing that this was all he would say on the matter, she watched as Joshua grabbed another handful of soil and began to construct a new mud pack, replacing the first.

"How did you learn all this?" she asked.

"I am not a college graduate like you, Ria, but we do know things. We are not as primitive as you may think."

"Did I call you primitive?" she demanded. "God!"

Joshua looked up and smiled.

"We learn a lot at a very early age," he said, articulating his words slowly. "The English language first, of course. Then we learn mathematics, geography. I am very interested in architecture…buildings, homes. And history too. I read history. Your big lake? Remington Pond? Surely you know it was named after the famous painter and sculptor?"

Ria interrupted.

"Frederic Remington? Yes, he was born in the town where…you know, where I went to school?"

"Yes, that's what I'm talking about. This county is very interesting to me. Very dynamic. Is that the English word I am searching for?"

She shrugged her approval. He continued.

"The Onondaga, the local Indians, they lived much like we do today. They were here first. They lived off the land. Part of the Iroquois nation, working with the Jesuits and the fur traders, over at the mouth of the river. They sided with the British during the revolution but, like us, they were eventually forced to become American…"

As his voice trailed away, Ria watched in newfound admiration. That he had helped her uncle survive his tractor accident was a revelation. This man had integrity. He was clearly intelligent and learned as well, displaying interests that she never would have guessed, though that was due mainly to ignorance on her part. Like everyone else, she had never paid much attention to people like him, preferring to perpetuate a stereotype built upon their backward, traditional ways. Observing Joshua now, she realized it was a grossly inaccurate one. *Grob!*

He continued to apply his medicine, his eyes lingering on hers for no more than a moment at a time. Their silence stretched further. He knew he was making an impression, but the memory of this morning's confrontation with his father returned and, removing his mud-caked hand from her leg, wiping it against his trousers, he rose up and again retrieved his pitchfork.

"Rub that mud in its place for a little while," he said. "It will remove the poisons. Now I must return to my duties and you should probably leave me to them. Please go back to the lake and your life there."

Ria was surprised by the brush off she was receiving. Ignoring his orders, she began cleaning some of the mud from her wound and rose from the ground, in protest.

But before she could speak, Joshua interrupted her.

"I remember what you said last night…I was there. I drank your beer but I remember."

She looked puzzled.

"What do you mean? We said a lot of things last night…by the fire, and when you were leaving."

"You said to that man…Nick? That I was 'nothing' to you—"

"—I didn't mean that!"

"I also heard you say, 'get real'…that you would never have anything to do with 'an Amish guy'. That's what you said." He had confronted her with her own words. It was a moment of truth.

"I—I was only trying to calm Nick down. Get him to stop punching you! I didn't mean—"

It was Joshua's turn to interrupt.

"I think you did, Ria…"

Rather than face her again, he returned to his work.

"We are from different worlds," he said in a hushed tone, "and you know that as much as I do."

"Are we, Joshua?"

"Yes…"

"Look at me," she commanded. As his eyes slowly met hers, she continued, "All right. I'll leave you alone…if that's what you truly want."

"I want that," he replied softly.

Just then, Joshua heard the distinctive sounds of another buck-board arriving over the paved road about a hundred yards away. Instantly, he knew it was Menno coming to check on him. He be-came flustered. The trust and respect he enjoyed with his father had suffered a serious blow. But it would be shattered completely if he was found here with this English girl. Ria, looking over his shoulder, noticed the source of his fear.

"Your father, right?"

"Yes," he said, nervously.

"Okay, I'd better leave."

"Yes, that would be wise..."

Quickly she moved behind Joshua's hay wagon in an effort to remain unseen by Menno. Grabbing him by his soiled, sweat-stained shirt, she pulled him close to her.

"But I have to say something first," she said, "because I don't think you're telling me the truth. You see, I don't believe it when you say you want me to leave. Maybe you just can't admit it. That you might—just might—want me in your life." Her eyes were glued to his, searching for confirmation.

Now their youthful faces were only inches away. With two fin-gers, she made an affectionate kissing motion and pressed them gen-tly to his injured lips.

"Don't forget me, okay?"

She turned slowly and began to walk through the fields to the thicket, content in the belief that Joshua was watching her every step of the way.

THIRTEEN

HUBIE POINTED HIS TRUCK down the long cedar lane and immediately he knew something was up. Cars were lined on both sides and in the distance, near the lake, he could see RVs parked behind a series of tents. The arrival of Barbara and Roger yesterday was the first clue. That he couldn't find a single fellow caster for some fishing today was another. But the kicker was the presence of a huge, white-topped party tent now set up on the lawn. And under it was a stage where he recognized two of his favorite people.

Turning towards Dee, Hubie smiled. "You crafty thing, you," he said. "You planned all of this, didn't you?"

She returned his smile.

"Well, I had some help, Hubert," she replied. "Some very active co-conspirators."

He placed his truck in park, draped his arms over the wheel and sat motionless for a moment, gazing across the yard. Then he noticed a banner, perhaps a ten-footer, proclaiming 'Happy 70, Hubie!' It was spread across the top of the large pavilion and festooned in red-white-and-blue aluminum foil letters. Puncturing the lawn below were a dozen miniature American flags, fluttering in the gentle breeze.

The elderly couple exited their truck and walked towards the gathering. They were greeted immediately by a couple of regulars from the VFW who had assembled near the bar. They were, like him, comrades from the big Army base to the south when it was still known as Camp Drum. Dwindling in numbers now, they were the aging and often denigrated combatants in the nation's dumbest war. Or at least Vietnam held that distinction until the fiascos of this century.

Nine years ago, Afghanistan was a worthy cause, he'd railed often over a beer at the post. Bastards, he had barked. We could have mopped up those cave-dwellers in short order if the U.S. hadn't gotten bogged down in Iraq. Better to fight 'em over there than on our own streets was the mantra of the war-mongering crowd back then—and he had agreed. But age and circumstance had tempered his views of late; buckets of blood and untold treasure had been spilled in the rice paddies of Vietnam, and now more was being lost in the mountains and deserts and caves. And for what? The paper said today that that corrupt Afghani president, no real ally, had offered a jail pardon to a rape victim *if* she agreed to marry her attacker. How do we go to war for people who wouldn't know the difference between the thirteenth century and the twenty-first? Still, he was pleased to see his Army pals here. A feeling of satisfaction overcame him, though he was never one to seek attention.

On the opposite side of the compound, he spied his nephew. The kid was at the horseshoe pits, engaged in a spirited game with a trio of friends. Beer in hand, Brad looped a cast-iron shoe—twice the size of a real horse's boot—through the air, landing it with a steely thud in a pit of sand around a stake some forty feet away. A ringer! That set off a series of high-fives and cheers from Brad and his partner, who might have been one of the tent squatters that Boychuk had told them about the previous night. Brad, unfortunately, was all present tense; tomorrow was too far in the future for Barbara's kid to think about.

Hubie returned his focus to the stage, where a playful scene was quietly unfolding. There he could see the lead singer laughing with a man as he tuned his guitar. Another bass guitar leaned against a tent pole with no apparent owner in sight. At their left stood a keyboard, and behind it, a set of Yamaha drums. Four stands of microphones awaited the vocal sounds of what promised to be a concert under the stars, aided by a weatherman who continued to cooperate. A cold front from Canada was expected soon but it hadn't yet arrived.

The singer, a slender woman in her early forties, was his daughter. Less than four years ago Joanne was a defeated and disheveled woman, living a life of loneliness, fear and desperation. Her hair then was bottle-blonde, spaghetti-like, stretching half way down her back, often tied haphazardly with a simple elastic band. Four years ago, her kind and gentle face, sculpted by generous genes, had waned, the result of too much stress and far too many smokes. Her clothes came from the racks at the Salvation Army store, since they were all she could afford after her husband pilfered her paycheck from her cashier's job at Turnbull's, the town's sole hardware store.

Today, however, a different picture had emerged. Today she was stylishly dressed in a mint-green silk blouse over a pair of tightly shaped, snow-white capris. A pair of pricy Okabashi sandals from Nordstrom's of San Francisco adorned her pedicured feet. Her once sinewy hair, shorn in honor of her stricken twin sister during that sorrowful Christmas season, was now cut shoulder-length and the color of a soft amber ale. A pair of large gold hoops dangled loosely from her ears, supported by a matching necklace containing a single pearl.

The lead guitarist was Matt Booker. A man of medium build, perhaps only an inch taller than Joanne at five-nine, Booker was forty-two now. When he and Hubie first met, his hair had been wavy black and had covered his ears; today it was cut shorter and brushed back, Springsteen-style, showing specs of gray at the temples. As the weekend musician he once was, he would sport a black headband and show off a couple of visible tattoos. Now Matt could pass for any businessman from the nearby foothills, which he was until this past spring when he and Joanne had decided to hit the road on a fulltime basis, doing what they had preferred to do. Their group, *The Never Say Never Blues Band*, was booking venues throughout northern New York, New England and Canada. They weren't getting rich but they were happy.

Joanne looked up from the stage and noticed the arrival of her father and his live-in partner. A broad smile emerged across her face. Tapping Matt's shoulder, and pointing in the direction of the elderly couple, she bounded from the platform and ran towards them, throwing her arms around the birthday boy.

"Surprise!" she shouted at her father. "We pulled it off, didn't we Dee?"

"More or less, Jo," the elder woman replied. "Your father is loath to admit it but I think we surprised him. Barbara just told him they were coming to see their kids, and he bought it."

Hubie piped in.

"I had my suspicions."

Hubie pointed to the banner above the tent. "That might've been a giveaway, too. Tell you the truth, never did give a damn for birthdays. Just another day, I've always said."

"Ah, you don't believe that, Dad," Joanne replied. "Everyone secretly wants their friends and family to remember their birthdays. So, you're not fooling me."

He looked around the compound.

"Brent and Tracy here?" He was referring to his grandson, an only child that she and the now-dead Denny had created and the primary reason she married Denny out of high school. But Brent proved that he could ditch his father's legacy through education, first at Syracuse and then a graduate degree from Cornell.

"Sorry Dad, but no, they couldn't get away. Just too busy in Monterrey this time of year. The hotel business, especially where they are, is round-the-clock. But he did tell me to tell you that you should switch your allegiance this year from the Sabres to San Jose. The Sharks are the team to beat, so he says."

Hubie grinned.

"Took him no time at all to become a Californian, didn't it?" he retorted. "What do they know about hockey? Last time I checked, ice doesn't form under palm trees. How's he doing?"

"He and Tracy like the big surf, Dad," she replied. "They're west coasters. It's beautiful out there."

"Been there once, when I was in the Army, but for the life of me don't understand the appeal," Hubie countered.

"Dad, they're young!" she argued.

"Won't hold that against them," he smiled. "But, hey, I thought you were going to be in Kingston all weekend and that the earliest we'd expected to see you was going to be Monday or Tuesday, on your way back to the hills?"

Grinning, Joanne simply shrugged.

"I lied. That gig was last week. Thursday and Friday, we were at the Opera House down in Clayton, but nothing was gonna keep us from your birthday and playing a few tunes for you. God knows the Schumachers have done far too little partying over the years. Don't you agree?"

Hubie nodded. Theirs had been a divided family. But he couldn't foist all of the blame on his late wife. He had accepted his share of their dysfunction. Rather than attending a soccer or softball game, as *real* fathers would have done, he'd grabbed his tackle box instead. His lack of involvement, he had recognized, had contributed to Jane's decision to abandon the family. And to his shame, he had never made an effort to bring her back, since his punishment would have resulted in eternal damnation at home. In cowardice, or at least convenience, it was a decision he had regretted for a long time.

But there was more to his sordid past and he knew it.

Now he was seeing Jane again. A painful flashback had begun. She was in her hospital bed and was making her return, angrily denouncing him.

"Why didn't you do *something*, Dad?" she bellowed, her accusations ringing in his ears. Jane was making reference to the abuse that Denny had heaped on Joanne for years. Though Hubie had had his suspicions, he did nothing about it. "It's between me and Denny," Joanne had always told him and, in other words, butt out. She had been too proud to ask for help. And so he did nothing, an admission of gross parental negligence if there ever was one.

Jane, however, had been blunt.

Not good enough, she said.

"You've lived next door to them for years! You must have seen something, because it was going on for so goddamned long!"

His answers were lame and, as he came to admit later, were never satisfactory to him either. He had failed his daughters.

Now as Matt approached, Hubie snapped from his daydream. The two men clasped hands heartily and exchanged hugs. Booker's entry into his daughter's life, and the circumstances around it, was an incredible stroke of luck—a Godsend if there ever was one—since he'd never seen Joanne this elated.

"Happy birthday, Hubie," Booker said, giving him a hug.

"Thanks, Matt," he replied. "That is if anyone should cheer about turning seventy."

"Only numbers, my friend…only numbers," the guitarist said, turning his attention to Joanne.

"The natives are getting restless, Jo," Booker said, with a smile as she answered a call on her cell. "Seems they want to hear a few tunes."

"One minute, Booker," she replied. "Speak of the devil!"

She handed her father her phone. It was Brent on the line, calling from California. Instantly a broad smile swept over his face. Joanne, too, beamed. It's all right now, she thought.

"WAS HE THAT SURPRISED or was it just a bad acting job?" Barbara asked Dee as the band ended its last set. Two hours before, Joanne had officially welcomed the partiers, perhaps a hundred strong, and their band entertained the crowd with a gentle mix of country rock and blues.

"Hard to say, Barb," Dee replied. "But you know your brother. He's no fool. But once I got him to come, which was a feat unto itself, I know that he admired our treachery. Loved your speech, by the way."

"Thanks, Dee," she replied. "You wouldn't believe all the crap that guy did to me when I was a kid. Teased me till I'd cry. He was sadistic."

"Older brothers, Barb," Dee replied. "That's their job…to torture their younger sisters. But that ghost story was very funny." The older woman was referring to an episode when Barb was about seven. Hubie would lie await outside his sister's window until she was nearly asleep and then start moaning like a living corpse.

"Not at the time, though," Barb said, smiling. "Cruel, cruel man!"

Of course she didn't mean it. With a garage replete with guns of every caliber, her brother always tried to project a gruff, steely image. All a ruse, she had long felt. Inside, he was a pushover.

"I'm still pissed that John and Samantha wouldn't make the effort to show up," Barbara shrugged. Their remaining Schumacher sibling, a central Illinois attorney, and his latest bride, his fourth, declined Barbara's invitation to celebrate. "Like Hubert, he wouldn't budge from that place of his in Normal. Appropriate name for a town with Schumachers in it, don't you think?"

"Maybe," Dee conceded.

"You've met Johnny, haven't you?"

"Hubert and I dropped in on them on our way back from seeing my grandkids in Milwaukee last year," Dee replied. "Let me say this…he's an interesting guy, and not at all like Hubert, or yourself, for that matter." That was vintage Dee; diplomatic, never disparaging, always circumspect in her words.

"If we didn't have the same DNA, nobody would guess we were related," Barbara replied. "But that Johnny, he is something. Never could keep his zipper up. So it's no surprise that he'd wind up with a woman who is two years younger than his oldest daughter! Guess Sam's keeping him too poor to retire. What does she do? Teach *Zumba* to fat mid-western women all day? Now, that would be a sight. But having another family at his age? He's sixty-seven! Thinks he'll live forever but that ain't gonna happen. He should've been here."

Now Barbara could see her brother standing, as expected, by the coolers. He was with Brian Boychuk, who was out of uniform, and next to him Makenna, radiant in another summer sun dress. The retired postmaster seemed to be enjoying himself. Suddenly, he let out a huge belly laugh, and that pleased her. Though she never wished demise on anyone, and a premature one at that, Barbara the atheist thanked God her brother's misery ended with Donna's death from ovarian cancer at fifty-one. Why he hadn't just packed up and left before that, Barbara never could understand, especially after Jane had bailed. Complacency? Probably. Or the fear of being alone? Men cannot live alone, she concluded.

Barbara continued to survey the grounds. Predictably the young people, now mostly bare-footed and dressed in shorts and T-shirts, were winning the battle of stamina as the 'antiques', as Brad called them, slowly made their exit from the Pond. But not before Brad bitched to her about Roger's edict on music. "Can't we find a few tunes from this freaken century?" he demanded.

At the end of the bench stood Nick. His shirt had disappeared and now he was playing to his strengths. Even from this distance, Barbara could see a number of bizarre-looking tattoos across his muscular upper torso, including an coal-black tarantula with a bright red streak across its shell. A very bizarre yet very creative three-dimensional piece of art. So menacingly real, the deadly insect appeared to be crawling slowly across his shoulder blade, ready to pounce on its next prey.

Compared to his appearance the day before, he was now wearing a pair of white denim shorts that stretched below his knees. If his mission was to display his tanned and sculptured physique, it was working; a number of the grads, all female, were hanging on his every word. One of them was playfully stroking his scrawny, billygoat-like beard.

His fedora from yesterday was missing, too, replaced by a red-and-white polka dot bandana that was tied tightly around his Marine-cut scalp. An alarming image suddenly entered her mind; Nick was a dead ringer for that boyish actor in *Platoon*, Martin Sheen's kid who played a scary sociopath for Oliver Stone. All Nick needed was a pair of khaki pants, an AK-47, a jug of Jack Daniels and a little dirt rubbed across his torso and the image would have been complete.

Nick was sidling up to a young woman who was now pouring a bottle of vodka into a large pitcher containing lemons, limes, cranberry juice and ice. Immediately Barbara recalled her bartending days in Pittsburgh, just after her first husband had departed. She was building a whole mess of 'train wrecks', a drink whose principal purpose was to get you shitfaced, fast. Soon a tray of shooter glasses appeared and the boozy barrage continued. It was going to be another one of those nights, she thought. Such is the culture of alcohol amongst today's youth, she winced, a precursor to serious trouble down the road for more than a few of them if some form of moderation wasn't adopted. We drank at their ages, too. *Heavily.* But not like this.

She scanned the group in search of Brad and found him near the boathouse. Dressed in a sleeveless white T-shirt and a black bathing suit, Brad was sucking on a thick cigar, a Cuban, of course that had been smuggled in from Canada. The putrid appendage was sandwiched so tightly in his teeth that he resembled a forties Hollywood mogul supervising his latest Cagney movie. He was holding a plastic cup filled with a dark liquid, likely whiskey and Coke, since beer was much too slow an intoxicant for her lad. Like Nick, Brad was in a playful discussion with an olive-skinned beauty with dark curls and rich brown eyes. Ria had introduced Barbara to the young girl. Natasha, her name was, Barbara now remembered.

Now Barbara turned her attention back to the bonfire where she noticed her daughter rising from a bench. Ria was moving towards one of the coolers at the edge of the property, near the barbecues, when Nick intervened. The elder woman watched as he approached Ria, exchanging a few words. Then he began caressing her necklace, closing his fist around the stone as if his actions would pull her closer to him. As he bent down to kiss her, Ria pulled back, turning her head in apparent defiance, removing his hands from the gem. There was friction there, Barbara thought. No doubt about it. A look of fury in his eyes told the story. Throwing his hands in the air in evident frustration, he uttered a few more words, probably laced with expletives if she read his lips correctly. Ria simply waved him away and proceeded towards the coolers.

Barbara allowed a few moments to transpire before approaching her daughter, who was now standing alone, seemingly lost in her thoughts.

"Hi, honey. Are you having a good time?"

Jolted from her daydream, Ria turned at the sound of her mother's voice.

"Yeah, it's a great time, Mom," she said. "I didn't know Joanne's band was sooo good…and that *she* was such a great singer!"

Barbara nodded in agreement. "Seems she's been playing the piano since she was about eight years old, too," she said. "But Denny, so cultured and supportive as he was, didn't encourage her much and so she'd always had to play behind his back."

Ria now pointed to her uncle thanking his friends as they were leaving. "He seemed surprised, too. Nice work, mother."

"Thank you. Heaven knows my brother needs some fun in his life."

Barbara decided to change the subject.

"So I'm waiting for you to tell me more about Mr. Wells," Barbara said. "After all, we spoke on the phone just last Wednesday and there was no mention of a serious roommate."

Ria knew this moment would arrive, but she was still dreading it.

"Mother, don't go jumping to conclusions," she replied.

"Well, give me one reason why I shouldn't? You haven't told me much about him, or your intentions. Moving in with a guy is a big decision, in my opinion."

Ria frowned, a look that wasn't lost on her mother.

"Nick's just going to be my roommate, Mother. He's a nice guy when you get to know him, and we get along fine."

"Do you? I just watched you two a few minutes ago and there didn't seem to be a lot of affection there."

"Ah, Mother, you never miss a beat, do you?"

"Always been a keen observer of human kind, Ria. But it's one thing to have a roommate. It's an altogether different thing when you're sleeping next to a man—"

Ria interrupted her again. "Mother!"

"Sorry I asked," Barbara replied. Well, not *that* sorry, she thought.

For the moment, Barbara would let this line of conversation lapse. But she'd had serious doubts about the guy. It wasn't just their introduction yesterday that had disturbed her. More like his demeanor. An unhealthy mix of arrogance and anger.

Earlier, without Nick's knowledge, she had come up from behind him as he was having a conversation with another of his friends. She couldn't catch enough of the exchange to make a definitive judgment but one sentence or two certainly was cause for dismay. Something like 'when are these old fuckin' crocks going to guzzle their last Manhattans and go home?'

"So, what do you know about this guy?" she now asked her daughter. Barbara, the parent, was going to get to the bottom of it. "Something about him is just not right."

Ria continued to show her exasperation with her mother. She was in no mood to discuss Nick, especially after what had transpired over the last twenty-four hours, and especially if her mother knew about Nick's attack on Joshua. She'd have a stroke.

"Mom, why don't we just drop this for tonight, and enjoy Uncle Hubie's day?"

"Fine with me. We're here all weekend, and I'll be all ears…as you might expect me to be." She smiled in her daughter's direction, signaling a truce had been signed—for now.

But as Barbara now knew, things weren't fine. Though she and her daughter had never been distant, they never offered up false images of intimacy, either. Parents had to be goddamned parents, she had opined often. Not bosom buddies sharing teenaged secrets, texting to and fro about boys, jealousies and other assorted nonsense. Sadly, she knew of such people. How pathetic was that? Never one to be shy, she'd often castigate a colleague or acquaintance who'd hover like a flying saucer over their kids, seeking love and affection in all the wrong places. A healthy mutual respect was paramount in any parent-child relationship. They had had many warmer times, intelligent and even intellectual connections. Barbara knew she and Ria could sit down and talk when the time came.

Not tonight, however, and perhaps not this weekend, Barbara now thought. Ria had become uncommunicative, even embarrassed about her apparent post-college nesting plans. It was disconcerting.

Wistful and worried, the elder Cahill watched as Ria walked away and joined the rest of her group by the fire, its flames offering one dimensional visages of youthful jocularity. Then she watched as her daughter spoke briefly with Natasha before reaching for a nearby wheel barrow, disappearing into the darkness towards the wood pile on the edge of the property.

Barbara turned away in search of her husband. She spotted him at the far end of the lawn, near their cottage, next to Hubert. It was time to get him to bed, she concluded, and walked off in his direction.

FOURTEEN

AN HOUR PAST DAYBREAK, Brian Boychuk was shaken from a deep sleep by the ringing of his bedside phone. Normally, he'd lift the receiver after the first or second ring but not this morning. After returning from Hubie's party at the Pond, he had discovered that Susan had cut short her trip to Syracuse. She was waiting for him, ostensibly to revive her complaints. The next thing he realized it was well after midnight.

Boychuk had asked Susan to join him, even for a brief appearance to extend a few good wishes to his old friend. He was *their* old friend, too, he thought, since Hubie had known the tall, buxom redhead before she and Boychuk were married. But Susan had begged off, declaring that he had known for weeks that she and her sister had tickets to a Keith Urban concert at the State Fair. That, of course, was Susan's stated excuse for skipping the Schumacher family event. Her real contentions—'or bugs up her ass' as he'd mutter from time to time—were two-fold. Not only was it a Schumacher party, which was bad enough given his obsession with that bunch, but its latest recruit—Makenna Monteith—would be in attendance. Susan wouldn't come right out and admit it but the beautiful young woman, a spitting image of her husband's former flame, was living proof of his past.

Two weeks before, he and Susan had spent a couple of days in Stowe, celebrating their tenth anniversary. He would have preferred Lake Placid for its Olympic delights and rugged beauty, but Susan had nixed that idea. No way in hell, she said. Too much history there. Celebrated? That was much too inaccurate a word, since from the moment they had met, at some county reception, theirs had been a relationship borne more of lust than like, before morphing into one of convenience.

He was a busy cop. She was a school board superintendent and both were leading hectic lives. No children had emerged. But how could they have considered kids, the sheriff wondered sadly? He and Susan were like freighters passing in the night. Coming close, oh so close, yet still safely apart. Often, Boychuk had felt their childless relationship had been a mixed blessing. They were active professional people. Of course, he'd had pangs of envy when he'd seen other couples enjoying their kids. Many times he had thought he would have made a decent father. He realized early in their marriage, however, that Susan wasn't the motherly type. Hadn't they discussed children before they got married? He had thought so.

They had booked a suite that weekend at one of the nicest hotels in the Green Mountains, only to realize their careers always seemed to take priority. Ever glued to her laptop, Susan became obsessed with making a few final touches to the board's long-range strategic plan. For his part, Boychuk discovered he couldn't ignore his BlackBerry, or perhaps maybe he consulted it just to keep him company. Their dinner, at some foo-foo French joint, had been an obligatory affair. He'd had the boeuf bourguignon, in punishingly decadent gravy, while she nibbled simply on a Lyonnais quiche.

The eatery had a sommelier that went on and on about wines he had never heard of, which was probably the game plan cooked up by the snooty waiter. He was some refugee from Aix-en-Province, it turned out, in his late sixties, squat, moustachioed and nearly bald. He was dressed in a requisite white jacket over black dress pants.

"You must try some of *ze* best wines from *my* region," he implored. "Les Grenache, les Cinsaut...quelques Tibouren! Right here," pausing for effect, "in Vermont—of all places!" The green mountain state's name, naturally, was pronounced *Verre-mo*. "Ze varietals," the smug connoisseur of the grape added, "can be savored, if properly cultivated…and *en France*, they are! *Jamais mes amis!* Never pass up un très bon Grenache!"

So they didn't and, as it turned out, it was the highlight of their tenth anniversary night in the mountains. It must have been, since he couldn't remember any memorable points in their conversation. Did they actually talk to each other? Or was their night just a fog? What *was* memorable was their failure to consummate the tenth year of their union. They had fallen fast asleep upon returning to the hotel.

Now, as sunlight streamed through their bedroom window, he glanced at the empty bed beside him. Habitually, no matter how much she drank the night before, Susan rose at dawn and was likely in her study on her computer. It was coming back to him. After dropping Makenna off at Hubie's, he'd returned home to find a surly Susan ready for battle. Pouring himself a couple of fingers of Belvedere on the rocks, he had groaned, dreading the looming confrontation. Here we go again, he had thought. What do you do with a woman who was jealous of a ghost?

His bedside phone rang for a third and fourth time before he picked it up. His mood soured once again. Only the office called him this early on a Sunday morning. This better be good.

"Boychuk," was all he growled into the receiver.

"Sheriff, it's Jimmy."

"What's up?" There was no time for small talk at this time of the day.

"You'd better get down to the Pond."

"Why, what happened?"

"There's been an incident at the Cahill cottages. A serious one. We're up on the bluff above the lake. You know the spot. I think you'd better get here right away."

Twenty minutes later, after a quick shower and once again in full uniform, Boychuk arrived at the trail that encircled Remington Pond. The soft gray-blue haze that had blanketed the region for the past ten days was now history, and in its place, cooler weather had arrived, reducing temperatures to the high forties. A far cry from last week's reign of heat and humidity.

Immediately, he saw two of his deputies' SUVs, gumballs flashing, parked on the road leading to the top of a rising cliff overlooking the water. Behind them was a Morgan County ambulance, its rear doors wide open, awaiting the arrival of its latest patron. A short distance away, at the edge of the grassy ledge, the sheriff could see the paramedics rolling a stretcher towards the vehicle.

Off to the side, members of the Cahill family stood anxiously, pain evident on their faces. There was Barbara, dressed only in a housecoat, pajamas, and slippers. Next to her, slumped and sagged, his face now an ashen gray, was Roger. He was adorned in a pair of tan pants, a buttoned-down shirt and loafers. Before Roger's arrival Friday, Hubie had told Boychuk about his brother-in-law's diminished health, and he had agreed with the retired postmaster's diagnosis. Now, the learned professor looked even more haggard and drawn.

Even from this distance, perhaps ten yards or so, Boychuk could see a look of deep concern, even anger, on Barbara's face as she followed every movement of the stretcher. Hubie had told Boychuk about his sarcastic and hopelessly liberal sister. "But nobody messes with her, Brian, she's crazy smart," the elder Schumacher had said. Now as he gazed in her direction, the sheriff knew that was true.

Next to them was Brad. Bare-footed, his hair misshapen from the night before, he was wearing only a tattered and torn navy-blue bathing suit and sweat shirt, providing Boychuk with a clear view to the young man's growing girth. He looked like he was still drunk. At his side was the young woman whom he'd recognized as one of Ria's friends by the fire the other night. She was sobbing uncontrollably. There was no sign of the other guy, Nick something.

Jimmy met his boss at the ambulance and together they scanned the unfolding scene. In an instant, as he approached the stretcher, Boychuk's heart skipped a beat. His fears were realized. Lying inert and unconscious on the flat rolling bed was Ria, a blanket covering her athletic body to the top of her shoulders. The paramedics had wrapped her head entirely in high-absorbent gauze bandages. Normally, these bandages were bleached hospital white but this morning they were blood red. Her eye lids were closed. Only a portion of her tanned and appealing face could be seen. A series of scratches were evident across her chin and another contusion could be seen above her left eyebrow. The paramedics paused a moment before loading the stretcher into the emergency vehicle.

"What've we got here, Trish?" Boychuk knew the chief attendant; she was a stocky single woman in her mid-thirties, thick at the waist with a butch haircut.

"Young woman in early twenties, Sheriff," the veteran EMT replied, pointing to the rock formations past the grasses towards the water. "She was discovered down there. Banged up…"

"Critical?

Trish nodded. "She's lost a lot of blood."

"You taking her to Hargreaves?" he asked, a reference to the closest critical care facility in the county.

"For now, yes, but judging from the damage to her skull, I think she'll have to be sent down to Syracuse. I'm not sure she'll make it, but right now, she's stable. Her vitals are satisfactory. Her parents told me she's a triathlete. Good thing."

"Okay, thanks," he said. "Get her out of here fast. One of my guys will accompany you to the hospital. But…do what you can to keep her alive."

"Will do, Sheriff."

As the paramedics loaded Ria aboard their emergency vehicle, Boychuk drew a deep breath. So much for the mundane, he thought, the routine DUIs, the shitty little bar fights and all the petty domestic squabbles. So much for old jackasses like Warner J. Conway, and codgers like him who get their kicks by firing their Winchesters at passing cars.

This situation was serious, perhaps grave.

And once again, it was personal.

He knew he was about to be bombarded by Barbara and her family about answers to this incident. All eyes now were on him. But business came first, and he gathered his deputies together. Holding his hand high in the family's direction, indicating that he'd speak with them soon, he summoned his chief deputy to his side.

"Okay, Jimmy, what happened?" Boychuk watched as his deputy retrieved his notebook.

"Not entirely certain yet, Sheriff. The victim's name is Ria Cahill...but I'm sure you already know that. We got a call just after dawn from that girl over there." He pointed to the simpering young woman cuddled closely to Brad.

"Her name is Natasha Constantinou. Not sure if I'm pronouncing her name right but she was Ms. Cahill's roommate in college, and was at that party we dropped into on Friday night."

"I remember her," Boychuk added. "I saw her again last night too. At Hubie's bash."

Jimmy continued, "Well, it seems Ms. Natasha and the rest of the gang got pissed drunk, again, and discovered that Ria was missing in action. The last time Natasha saw her was at the fire. Shooters were being passed around, and then more and more beers and, eventually, most of their bunch staggered off to bed. Natasha says she woke up to take a pee and couldn't find Ria anywhere." Jimmy checked his notes once again. "She couldn't locate the victim's boyfriend either—some guy named Nick Wells."

Boychuk interrupted his deputy again.

"He was the guy bitching us out on Friday night, remember? About that Amish kid who had crashed their party. Grabbing all the attention from the girls."

"Right, I remember him now, Sheriff," Jimmy said.

"Where the hell is he now?"

"Don't know Sheriff."

"Okay, we'll have to find him. But, go on."

"Well, seems Natasha grabbed a flashlight and began looking all over the place for Ria. She told me she checked the woodpile and the beach over on the other side of the bay. All over the property. She thought maybe Ria had passed out too, since she was well into the sauce. So, she went back and woke up Brad and the two of them started looking. They were about to give up when they decided to come up here to the bluff. By that time, the sun was coming up, and that's when they saw Ms. Cahill at the bottom of the cliff, on the rocks. That was when Natasha called us from her cell—these kids go nowhere without their cells. And when we got here…"

The Morgan County Sheriff now took charge.

"Okay, let's seal everything off and check this out."

"Right, I've alerted forensics. They should be here any minute now."

"Good. Get Rob over to the hospital, too and have him speak with the staff, and I'll get over there too. They'll have to work up a kit. My priority—hell, my hope—is that kid'll survive. But they'll have to do a few swabs…and check for fibers, hair, the works. I'm gonna speak with the family."

Jimmy interjected once again.

"Okay, Sheriff, but before you do that, there's one more thing. See that over there?" He pointed to a small birch log approximately two feet in length and a diameter of about three inches. It was resting next to some high grass near the edge of the cliff.

"Yeah, what about it?"

Now grimacing, Jimmy continued.

"Haven't touched it yet but it's clear there are blood stains on it, Brian. We don't think she got those injuries from just falling on the rocks."

FIFTEEN

A S THE THUNDERING HELICOPTER, navy blue with a
New York State Police insignia on its side, lifted effortlessly
from the hospital pad, Boychuk pointed his cruiser to the opposite
side of town. The paramedic's diagnosis was correct; Ria Cahill's injuries were far too severe for Morgantown's health center, and its limited, acute-care capabilities to handle.

Not that the eighty-seven bed W.W. Hargreaves Memorial
Hospital, named in honor of one of the area's mining magnates, was
a mere clinic. The facility was fully capable of dealing with many
medical emergencies, including ruptured appendices and gall blad-
der explosions. But serious mishaps, such as knifings or shootings,
required special skills. In Ria's case, this was a serious injury; she
needed a brain trauma specialist.

It wasn't easy, though. When Jimmy told him the region's sole
medevac helicopter had been summoned to Herkimer and was un-
available, the Morgan County sheriff had called in a marker. His old
pal from Saranac Lake, a head trooper named Roland Bouchard, had
come to his rescue and ordered the state chopper over to Morgan
County. Those twin Rolls-Royce engines would power poor Ria to
Syracuse in less than forty minutes.

Boychuk's meeting with the Cahills, lasting only a couple of
minutes, was a difficult one. Consoling loved ones was the toughest
part of his job but Boychuk had read the moods of Barbara and Roger
correctly. His was one of sullenness and shock; Barbara's demeanor,
on the other hand, was one of anger. Brad stood there as well, open-
mouthed, saying nothing. His eyes told the sheriff that he shared

his mother's views. Natasha, her sobs in abeyance, was listening attentively.

"Are you telling me, Sheriff, that this was an accident?" Barbara had demanded. "My daughter's an athlete for God's sake! How could she fall down that goddamned cliff?"

Boychuk was circumspect in his reply. There was no way he'd reveal any of the early evidence before him.

"We're not sure of anything right now, Barb," he said. "My forensics team will be here in a few minutes and we'll be looking at everything. But from all accounts, that party last night was another boozy affair. For all we know, maybe she wandered off, trying to sober up, and lost her bearings. It was a dark night. We haven't found any sign of a flashlight, at least not yet. We'll search the area thoroughly today."

But Barbara wasn't buying Boychuk's explanation. As with Brad, she worried about her daughter's alcohol consumption. Hell, Brad's affinity for anything irresponsible was well known. She'd always said he was twenty-four going on sixteen and had often hoped he'd show some signs of adulthood someday. Now in Ria's case, the difference between her and Brad was night and day. That she would venture into the darkness, seemingly trying to sober up, didn't make sense. She certainly wasn't drunk when Barbara last saw her but who knew how long she'd been here on this cliff? Or on the rocks below.

"That's not good enough, Sheriff," she said. "I smell a rat here."

Brad decided to end his silence. "Yeah, a big friggin' rat, that's for sure!"

Barbara shot her son a disapproving glance. She'd handle this situation, a look not missed by Boychuk.

"I understand your concern, Barb," he said. "We'll do everything we can to find out what happened here last night. I'm not ruling out anything. Let's just hope that the doctors can fix her up. My paramedics have told me she is one strong, young gal."

Boychuk's words to Hubie's sister reverberated through his mind as he pulled his SUV into the retired postmaster's driveway, thinking it was yet another tragedy to haunt the Schumacher family. Sitting on the edge of one of his Adirondack chairs, leaving no doubt his sister had called, Hubie offered what the sheriff thought was a perfunctory, almost mechanical, wave. Even from his car, perhaps twenty yards away, Boychuk could see that his old friend was now morose and absorbed, likely wondering what the hell he and his family had done to deserve such grief. Of course, he knew Hubie had blamed himself for the events across his yard. So, now, this incident involving his niece was, again, too close to home.

As he emerged from his cruiser, Boychuk watched as the older man arose with difficulty from his chair. Rocking to and fro, it seemed that it took three attempts, indicating just how his friend of twenty-five years had aged over the last few years. The accident on his lawn tractor last year had set him back as well. Then, from the front door came Makenna. She was pulling her travel bag, and Boychuk remembered her plans to visit her parents in Plattsburgh before returning to Virginia. Grim-faced like her grandfather, she descended the steps and met him at the edge of the driveway.

"We heard," was all she could say.

"Yeah, not good. We choppered her down south about twenty minutes ago."

"What do you think?" she asked.

"I think you might want to delay your trip north."

SEETHING WITH FURY, Brad stormed across the grounds of a Cahill family compound still in the process of waking up. He knew the Sheriff and his deputies would not be far behind and Brad wanted to begin his own investigation.

Like his mother, Brad didn't believe the sheriff's initial explanation for his sister's injuries. Sure, Ria was probably as wasted as the rest of them, but she was always in control, annoyingly so. Not only that, she'd been coming here for years and knew every inch of the landscape; there was no way she could have fallen over that cliff. But why was she there anyway? Why the hell had she ventured nearly five hundred yards from the camps in the middle of the night?

Dumb shit Boychuk said it was a dark night but even Brad—pissed or sober—knew that the cloud-filled skies had cleared, offering a full moon and stars and yet another reason to believe Ria never would have fallen onto those rocks. Goddamned if he was going to let this one go anytime soon.

Entering the compound, Brad stopped and gazed across the property. Not many signs of life. Only a few hours ago their party had been in full force, essentially picking up where they had left off the night before, despite his mother's warning to keep the festivities to a dull roar. To his right rested the stage where his cousin and her friends had entertained the local troops. But he noticed his uncle's American flags that had surrounded the stage had become detached and uprooted and were now strewn across the lawn. Good thing the old man wasn't here, Brad thought.

A few hours ago, the bonfire had soared well into the night. But now only a few dying embers remained, a plume or two of gray smoke drifting skywards. Brad allowed himself some satisfaction; he and two others had doused its flames by emptying their beer-filled bladders into the inferno to roars of both delight and disgust. Then, he and Natasha stumbled back to one of the outer tents for some extracurricular fun. That all ended, of course, when Natasha flashed that light in his eyes. Freaking out.

Now ignorant of the crisis that had hit their circle, only a handful of partiers were coming alive. At the door of the largest RV, coffee in hand, was one of Ria's friends whose name he'd forgotten. She was wearing blue jeans and a hoodie, signifying the change in temperature overnight. Beyond her, at the tents near the water, a couple of the boys were moving about, slowly.

"Bitches are still comatose," Brad muttered to himself as he approached hoodie girl, a freckled-faced alumnus from Potsdam State and another education major. Everyone wants to be a teacher these days. Not a bad gig, he concluded. Get every summer off.

"Fuck is everyone?" he asked. It sounded more like an accusation than a question, the intensity in his eyes telling the story.

"Jesus...good morning to you, too, Brad," the girl replied. "Still in the sack, I'm guessing. I'm shocked you're even up. What time is it?"

"I dunno, around eight, I think. Doesn't fuckin' matter. Don't see Wells. Any idea where he is?"

"Nope. Haven't seen him since around midnight," she replied. "Both him and Ria. I just assumed they tucked themselves in early last night."

"Well, I've got to find the son of a bitch."

"Ouch. I don't like that look on your face. What's going on, Brad?"

But Brad, impatient with the lack of information, simply dismissed her with a hand gesture and was on the move again. That he wasn't quite sure about Wells was an understatement. They had met last winter in Canton when his sister introduced them and they had hit it off, even to the point that Brad had offered Nick a job for the summer renovating the Cahill camps. Wells was good with his hands. In more ways than one, he guessed, after seeing him with Ria.

However, Brad had seen firsthand how Wells would explode with rage, and it was discomforting to say the least. Not that Brad figured he himself was a model for anger management. Far from it. More and more people were beginning to piss him off these days, and Brad wasn't one to stand for much. But Wells, he was another matter.

With still no signs of life emanating from the young squatters, Brad marched past the last of the canvas dwellings listening for any sounds that would resemble Wells' voice. At each tent, he unzipped the flaps enough to peer in without disturbing them. Not that he gave a damn about waking any of them, mind you. All were wrapped up tightly in their sleeping bags or makeshift blankets, sleeping off the celebration.

At the last tent, the smallest since it held at most two people, he stopped for a brief moment to listen. Hearing nothing, he reached for its opening and rolled down its zipper. Inside was a young woman who Brad recognized as Naomi, another of Ria's house mates from college. Slightly older than the rest, her hair was a spiky reddish-orange color with streaks of flaming pink woven through it. When they met, he had ignored her weird hairdo but had been struck by a pair of sparkling eyes when she smiled. She had other attributes as well, including a magnificent, rock-hard ass.

Unfortunately, as soon as she had opened her mouth, a high-pitched accent emerged and one that only upstaters could own. Only they could turn a simple word like 'camp' into two syllables, roughly coming out like '*kee-amp*'. Another lamentable feature was her Chelsea Clinton-sized nose, which he predicted would be fixed at a later date. Still, he wouldn't have been surprised if one the boys had taken a run at her last night in the dark. They all look the same in the dark.

Now as he peered inside the tent, Brad saw Naomi sleeping on an inflated air mattress. There was a man beside her, with a sleeping bag barely reaching their waists. His face was pointed away from the tent's entrance. In an instant, Brad's heart sank. The son of a bitch was already sleeping around on his sister!

Suddenly aware of his intrusion, Naomi let out a scream.

"Brad! What the hell are you doing?" she demanded, grabbing the sleeping bag to cover herself up. "Get the hell out of here!" The sound of the scream awoke her night-time partner who turned suddenly in Brad's direction to see what all the excitement was about.

Just then, before he could identify Naomi's bedside mate, he felt a tap on his shoulder. From behind, it was Nick. Given the frosty arrival of an early New York autumn, he was dressed in blue jeans and a T-shirt. Where his Birkenstocks were from the day before was a mystery.

"*Ant*-hill, what's happenin' man?" he said with a growing grin. "I hear you've been lookin' for me."

SIXTEEN

THE STATE FORENSICS TEAM, three members in total, had arrived and had joined Boychuk's deputies scouring the cliffs high above the Pond. Knowing that Jimmy's men might do more harm than good, Boychuk had restricted his staff to the perimeter until the Troopers had arrived. Boychuk would need the state's help in gathering evidence but they had to know that he was personally supervising this investigation.

As he and Makenna approached the scene, Boychuk knew the arrival of the brisk, northwest winds would play havoc with the ubiquitous stands of cedars, their dying fronds shedding heavily across a wide area. There would be no rain today, and that was a good thing. But the abrupt change in weather could masque the critical subtleties of any breaking case. They would need to know what happened here—and quick.

He knew, also, that bringing his daughter to a crime scene might cause some raised eyebrows, a sentiment shared by Makenna. To the young Virginia grad student, the state's experts were clearly qualified; they might resent any intrusion by some ivory tower amateur. However, Boychuk had dismissed her fears. A fresh pair of eyes on an emerging crime scene was always welcome and besides, she knew more about advanced forensics at this stage of her career than most of his deputies.

Boychuk was more concerned with the evidence he already had in hand. There was no way he could keep news about the bloody log quiet, especially from Barbara. Of course, she was right; Ria was a finely-tuned athlete and knew the area as well as anyone. The likelihood of her falling down that cliff was next to nil.

"How'd it go at the hospital?" Jimmy asked.

"Not good," Boychuk replied.

"Bouchard to the rescue?"

"Yeah. The Cahills are on their way to Syracuse now but there's little they can do. Where's Brad?"

"He and the girl who called it in returned to their camps."

"Okay, I'll want to talk to him and his drinking pals, especially that kid Wells. You and Bill start taking depositions from everyone at the party. Don't let anyone go home before they talk. I want to know every recollection of what happened…as accurate as that can be, given all the boozing that was going on. Everything, especially if any of them disappeared for a while around eleven. That seems to be the key time here."

"Will do, Sheriff."

"One more thing. Barbara witnessed something last night that she shared with me, and it'll be something we'll look into."

"What?" Jimmy asked.

"I'll brief you later, but for now what have you got?"

"Well, I'll let the technician give you a full report, or at least what they've found so far." The deputy introduced him to the sheriff and his daughter.

Andrew Webster was a barrel-chested man in his late thirties with prematurely graying hair protruding from under a cap emblazoned with the state's police insignia. He was a former Army infantryman turned trooper turned sleuth. Boychuk thought he was dressed too casually for this assignment, wearing only beige Dockers and a black golf shirt. He looked like he had just interrupted Webster's tee time, the kind of guy who didn't appreciate getting rousted from bed on a Sunday morning—or on a long weekend for that matter. He should know better. Criminals don't work bankers' hours.

"Thanks for getting here so soon," the sheriff said. He introduced Makenna to the technician, quickly mentioning that his daughter was studying at one of the nation's top forensics schools. From the skeptical look in the technician's eyes, Makenna began to regret accepting her father's invitation.

"No problem, Sheriff," the technician replied. He was all business.

Still wearing rubber gloves, the forensics man proceeded with his brief, starting with the blood-stained birch log that had been inspected and bagged as evidence. He told Boychuk they had dusted the log for prints, but figured they may be of very little value.

"Let me show you something else." He was referring to a section of high grass near the cliff.

"See how that appears to have been matted down? We think that one or more persons had been lying down, since it looks as though some sort of blanket was spread."

This aroused Boychuk's curiosity.

"Are you suggesting what I think you're suggesting?" the Sheriff asked. "That young Ria may have been having some fun with someone up here?"

"I don't know that yet, Sheriff, since there's no evidence of semen anywhere, let alone a prophylactic...that is, if kids their age even use them." In mild embarrassment, the investigator glanced sheepishly at Makenna for a moment, who remained detached. But why was she here? Was this the sheriff's idea of 'bring-your-kid-to-work day?' Webster had heard that Boychuk always did things his way and if the voters didn't like it, they could throw him out.

The technician continued. "We found a few fibers which we'll process in the lab."

"Well, if there was a blanket, I'd like to see it," the sheriff mused.

"That would be helpful. Maybe we'd find some fluids too." He turned and addressed the sheriff. "Do you want to know what we think?"

"By all means," Boychuk replied, in a tone that sounded more sarcastic than he had intended.

"Okay. We figure that at least two people were on this cliff last night, and likely a third given a few partials that we've discovered—footprints, that is. And, Sheriff, when I say footprints, I mean exactly that…five toes, arch, heel—the works. No shoes at all. So, that means that Miss Cahill, her friend and possible assailant were likely bare-footed."

Boychuk's curiosity was again aroused.

"Bare feet?"

"Yup."

"Evidence of a horse, too."

Boychuk interrupted him.

"A horse?"

"Yes," he said, pointing to the edge of the clearing. "And let me say there's some very clear evidence of that…if you get my drift."

Boychuk nodded. He allowed the technician to continue.

"Anyway, at least two people arrived here, placed a blanket on the ground, and were on it for a while. I have no idea what they did, but they laid down on a blanket, enough so to make the imprint they created. Then, after they finished doing what they were doing, we found at least one print walking back to where the horse was tied up." Webster pointed in the direction away from the Cahill compound.

"We think the chick—excuse me, the victim—then proceeded in the direction of the camps but didn't get very far." He pointed to the edge of the cliff. "This is where we think she met up with someone, judging from a number of footprints clumped together in the soil. Not much to work with, but they were close in proximity, indicating that an altercation—"

"—a fight, Andy?" Boychuk interrupted, opting to use a more familiar version of the man's name, though they had just met. "How do you know?"

"We think so because we found a bit of blood on the grasses."

"Blood," Boychuk mused. "Has to be Ria Cahill's right?"

"We'll test it with the blood on the log," Webster replied. He threw off a look of impatience at all the interruptions.

"As I was saying, there was an altercation. Perhaps some pushing back and forth just before she was struck in the head and either fell, or was pushed off the cliff. Maybe the blunt force of the log was enough to propel her backwards, we don't know. But judging from the amount of blood on that piece of birch, it was a good swing, and I tell you, it could've knocked you or me off our feet. Then we found one set of prints leading away from the scene."

Boychuk paused for a moment before continuing.

"Interesting," he said. "Maybe one or more of the Cahill girl's friends had ventured up here from the party? Most of them appeared to be barefooted..." His voice trailed off.

Makenna, speaking for the first time, interjected.

"Or they were Amish?" she said. "Mr. Webster said a horse was nearby."

"Or Amish, right," the sheriff replied. "Our other bare-footed friends. But that doesn't make much sense, unless young Ria met up with..." Again, he stopped his train of thought. He had seen Ria and her friends at the fire with Joshua Troyer.

Webster spoke up. "Well, there are a lot of Amish around here. And in addition to the cow pies we found in the thicket, there were hoof prints down the hill." Webster pointed in the direction of the Cahill camps. "Buggy tracks too, from steel or iron wheels. No signs of rubber."

"They don't believe in rubber tires," Boychuk replied. "And some people want them to put *Depends* on their geriatric horses!"

Webster's eyes squinted with surprise.

"I kid you not," Boychuk continued. "You'll document what you found?"

"Already done, Sheriff," Webster said, triumphantly. "We'll get you the photos."

Boychuk walked to the edge of the cliff and surveyed the rocks below. He'd venture down at a later date. He spoke up again.

"So far, not much in this case makes much sense, Webster," he said. "If we can believe your theory that Ria was likely here with a lover, and you may be right, who was the third one in? Was there someone watching it all and decided to act? Who the hell wanted to see a nice girl like Ria Cahill hurt…or worse, dead?"

"I don't know, Sheriff," the investigator said. "That's your job to figure out. All I know is that the wind picked up over the past couple of hours and may have hampered other evidence."

Boychuk let out an enormous sigh before asking one last, critical question.

"Yeah, that's a problem. We'll be talking to the doctors about her injuries. But in your opinion, Webster—"

Testily, the investigator interrupted him.

"Name's *Andrew*, Sheriff."

Boychuk reeled and turned. A sensitive Sunday golfer. But he knew he'd have to work with this guy on this case.

"My apologies," he said. "So…*Andrew*, do you think Ria was unconscious at the time of her fall, or did that birch log make her lose her balance? In other words, had there not been a cliff here, could she have been in a better position to recover from the blow?"

The investigator reflected on the question before answering. He removed his cap, revealing a dark-red, Gorbachev-like birthmark across a bulbous dome that was encircled by only strands of buttery gray hair. It caught Boychuk off guard. Couldn't they fix things like that these days? People get drunk, run off to tattoo parlors only to regret their decision and remove the blights on their bodies later. Surely they could fix a birthmark.

"Hard to say, Sheriff. But judging from the amount of blood on the log and the blood that we found down on those rocks, there is no question that her fall was more serious than the blow, though I'm no expert on concussions. You'll have to ask the docs that."

As Boychuk walked the forensics officer towards the police vehicles, Makenna stayed behind. Other than her one interjection, she
had said nothing while her father led the way. But it was clear she
had other things on her mind and began scouring the spot where the
punishing blow was struck. She knew the team had likely searched
this ground with a fine-toothed comb, but maybe they missed something. The last thing she wanted to do was to embarrass the state's
forensics team.

There it was. A remnant of familiarity that most women would
recognize instantly. Bending down, peering in the direction of the
battered brush, she noticed a tiny, circular-shaped object, perhaps
only a fraction of the size of a dime. If it wasn't for a ray of sunshine
that broke through the early morning cloud cover only seconds before, it might have gone undiscovered.

Then, she looked up and noticed that Boychuk had been watching her from a distance, and waved him over. A few moments later,
he arrived back at the scene.

"What's up, Ken?" he asked.

Pointing to the small, glittering object, she said: "See that?"

SEVENTEEN

THIRTY MINUTES LATER, after dropping Makenna at the Schumacher homestead, Boychuk found himself once again at the wheel of his cruiser driving over a dusty Bidgood Road towards the Troyer farm. Her detection of that tiny piece of white gold had to be part of Ria's necklace, a simple clasp that connected the chain carrying her distinctive turquoise stone. Yet, it was only a clasp. Where was the chain and, more importantly, where was the gem? Was it ripped violently from her neck during a scuffle and thrown into the dark, weed-infested waters of Remington Pond? If it was, chances of its retrieval were not good.

Boychuk was not relishing his looming encounter with Menno Troyer. Though not close, he and Menno were on a first-name basis and sometimes they could be as jocular as men of a similar age can be. Last year, Menno and a couple of his sons, including Joshua, had delivered a custom-made storage shed to Boychuk's property, the former ranch home of his late father. The officer always liked to help the hard-working Amish, often coercing his neighbors into buying sweet corn, blueberries and quilts delivered personally by the farmer's young daughters. It was a relationship built on respect. But today might be a different story.

As he made the turn down Bidgood Road, the sheriff couldn't help but see Benji Hoggarth ambling slowly towards his farmhouse, his mutt Molson, an aging chow husky mix, following loyally behind. The dog's probably more nimble than his owner, at least this morning, he thought. Old Molson was a much loved canine, but an itinerant one at that, often found wandering miles from his master's property, a single-wide trailer with a sagging aluminum roof and a crumbling front porch.

Only two years younger, Benji was built like a fireplug whose beard was so thick that he probably had to shave twice a day. So he didn't bother. He practiced carpentry when he could find work but spent most of his summers contracting himself out to farmers at harvesting time. But whether it was haying or hammering, Benji found it difficult to find his way to work on Fridays. That was because 'Twenty-Five-Cent Thursdays' at Swigs was too good to pass up, Swigs being a watering hole down near the Pond that offered patrons a superb deal on hot wings and cheap beer.

The bender must have continued last night, Boychuk now thought, as he watched Hoggarth trundling towards his mailbox by the road. There was no name identifying Benji's residency; just a hand-painted word, spelling 'M-A-L-E', which Boychuk guessed had nothing to do with the man's gender. That brought another smile to the cop's face. He loved the characters that populated this county.

Beeping his horn and offering a wave, Boychuk continued his drive and soon the Troyer farm came into view and, immediately, a sense of dread overcame him. There before him were more than two dozen buggies, raven black, its owners now congregated on benches in the front yard. The Amish didn't have churches per se. It was an edict from their God, their New Testament, telling followers not to 'dwell in temples made with hands.' Instead they met every other Sunday at one of the families' homes and, unfortunately for Boychuk, today was the Troyers' turn to host their day-long observances, visitations and prayer. The last thing he needed, though, was an entire Amish community witnessing his arrival on such serious matter. But in his line of work, Sunday was just another day.

Parking his SUV at the end of the driveway, contemplating his next move, he could see a strapping young lad walking towards the horses, his assigned task being the care of the animals. Only males were nominated and chosen to lead the Sunday services, Menno had told him. Though no formal training was involved, their sect democratically ordained a bishop—a *Voelliger-Diener* or minister with full powers—who served as the titular head of their church district. The service would begin with women to one side, men to another, most seated on backless benches imported bi-weekly to the chosen home. Older members got a reprieve; this last generation would be afforded more comfortable chairs. Then a large meal would be prepared by the women, with male adults eating first, followed by women and small children. The older children, the teenagers, ate last. Menno and his wife, as hosts, would provide a meal consisting of cold meats, cheese, pickles, homemade breads and dessert. It could have been a scene right out of the nineteenth century.

Unlike his many visits before, Boychuk could see that the Troyer farm had been thoroughly scrubbed for the big event. Normally, the house was by modern standards a shambles, its outer buildings fairing no better. But today the Troyers had spruced the property up. Gone were the chickens, cats and several rail-thin dogs that typically ran across the property with abandon. Gone too was Menno's prized sow and her eleven piglets that had clamored competitively for an unequal number of teats. Looking around now, Boychuk assumed that all their four-legged friends were safely deposited out of sight.

Today, the children were dressed in their best Sunday attire. Over to the side, several young girls, perhaps some of Menno's own daughters, scampered around, aiding the older women in service to their men. They wore their traditional navy blue-and-black smocks, now freshly laundered, with their crisp black bonnets covering everything but their faces. The younger boys, dressed in dark britches, clean shirts and straw hats, were restless and on the move but without clearly defined assignments. Perhaps their job was to stay out of the way.

This was in stark contrast to his past visits. One rainy day last spring, he and Menno, in a playful mood, were dickering over the cost of his storage shed as two of the farmer's youngsters dutifully toted pine boards and steel nails to their carpenter father. One of his toddlers, barely two years old, had clenched several steel spikes between her lips, waiting for her father to retrieve them one by one. Tell that to *your* kids, he later related to the locals down at Turnbull's.

His constituents never let an opinion go unspoken. "They raise their pigs in cleaner pens than their own kitchens," or worse, "they're carpenters, for Christ's sake…would it be too much to ask that they replace the goddamned tiles on the side of their houses? Or fix their broken windows and porches?"

His answer was always the same: a material life filled with modern goods was of no value to these transplanted Ohioans.

This was no Harrison Ford movie.

Finally, Boychuk stepped out of his Tahoe and waited for a wary and suspicious Menno to join him.

"What brings you here on this day, Brian?"

Boychuk took a deep breath and exhaled. If his hunch was right, and young Joshua was involved somehow in the violence at Remington Pond, this wasn't going to be a pleasant conversation.

"I apologize for coming today, Menno, and interrupting your service but I'm here to talk to Joshua. Can you get him out here for me?"

Immediately, Boychuk was struck by the deadened look in Menno's tobacco-colored eyes. It was as if the Amish farmer had been expecting such a request. The fact that Webster had found footprints in the vicinity of the scene was reason enough to consider Joshua as a material witness, especially since young Troyer had stayed late at that Friday night party. There had to be a connection, Boychuk thought. He just wasn't sure what.

"What's your purpose in wanting to speak with my son?" Menno asked defiantly. His eyes now resembled two narrow slits as if they were attempting to prevent light—any light—from shedding itself on the situation. The farmer would protect himself and his family from outside forces. That Menno was clearly irritated by the

interruption of their service was a given; missing now was the cama-
raderie of their past. There was more to Menno's reaction than just an
intrusion by the police on a holy day.

Boychuk described the events from the night before, and from
the previous night as well when he had witnessed Joshua at a lakeside party. He described to the elder Troyer what his investigators
had found. To the county cop, it looked as though Menno wasn't
surprised by the allegations.

"So, since we go bare-footed, you think one of mine might be
responsible, do you Sheriff? For this—" Menno paused a moment as
if he was searching for the correct English word. The sheriff helped
him out.

"—assault."

"I was thinking about it as more of an…incident."

"Clearly more than an incident, Menno. This girl was attacked,
and now she's fighting for her life and I'm hoping it doesn't become
a murder investigation."

"Joshua was here on the farm all last night."

"You know that for certain, Menno?"

"Yes, Sheriff."

"Well, I'd like to speak to him anyway."

Menno was clearly uneasy with the conversation. Shuffling his
feet nervously, he took a quick glance at the assembled flock before
returning his focus to Boychuk.

"You know we don't stand for violence," the farmer said.

"Understood, Menno."

Boychuk turned his attention away from Menno and began to
scan the Troyer farm in search of the farmer's eldest offspring. He
spotted Joshua emerging from behind their two-story farmhouse,
perhaps fifty yards away, with two others about his own age. He,
too, was dressed in church attire: a crisp dark-blue shirt with black
suspenders over a pair of black pants, and a pair of shiny black boots
that climbed half way up his shins.

Now he was engaged in what was clearly a heated discussion, though it appeared that Joshua was doing more listening than speaking. One of the young men was now wagging his finger at Joshua with obvious disdain, his voice rising. Then from behind a long table marched a young woman. Boychuk recognized her. She was a member of the Zook clan from Macassa Road. Hannah was her name, he believed. Quickly she arrived at the scene of the argument, uttered a few words and soon the situation was defused.

There was something different about Joshua today, and Boychuk noticed it immediately after the young man removed his straw hat. Missing was his traditional bowler haircut, which the sheriff had observed only two nights before. His hair was now shorn, particularly around his ears, a style that made him look more like a preppy college senior than a member of a religious sect. Was that the reason for the argument only moments before? Long hair on Amish men was a symbol of their masculinity. It was a central part of their identity.

Boychuk was momentarily stunned at the transformation. Joshua had always been a good-looking boy who went about his duties on Menno's farm without making waves. But today he was chillingly handsome. If Ria Cahill had become smitten by this man, he could understand. In the space of forty-eight hours, Joshua had become a man.

Boychuk's reaction to Joshua's changed appearance was not lost on Menno. The Amish carpenter decided to acquiesce to the sheriff's request.

"All right, Sheriff," Menno said, slowly moving toward his son. Boychuk watched as the two Troyers exchanged words while the Zook woman and the two young men stood nearby. A look of concern suddenly came over Joshua; his mouth agape, his eyes darting nervously between his father, the sheriff in their lane, and Hannah. Immediately Boychuk knew the young Amish farmer was involved in this case—somehow. He was also surprised by the look on Hannah's face. Even from this distance, there was a coolness, even anger, evident in her eyes. Had she set her sights on Joshua as a husband? Looked like it.

Returning glances to both his father and Hannah, Joshua slowly made his way towards Boychuk's Tahoe.

"My father just told me about...the English woman, Sheriff," he stammered. "I...I just don't know what to say."

"Well, you can start by telling me what you know about it, Joshua."

"Nothing...nothing!"

"Not sure I believe you, Josh. I get the impression that you might have seen the girl last night. Or even spent time with her? Is that true?"

"No...no," he stammered once again.

The sheriff then noticed Joshua's wounded lip.

"What happened there?"

"My horse..."

"Your horse did that?"

Joshua nodded.

"Your dad has told me that he's quite the ornery beast."

"That he is, Sheriff," Joshua said with a shrug.

Boychuk peered over the young Amish man's shoulders at the rest of the assembly. The men were standing in small groups of three or four, talking among themselves. The women carried platters of food towards the long tables, their eyes glued to the conversation going on between the sheriff and one of their own. He decided to soften his attack.

"You look good today, Josh," he said. "Cut your hair, I see. Where'd you get the nice trim?"

There was no answer. Boychuk continued.

"You're dressed nice, too. It looks to me you'd rather be with those friends of yours at the Pond? Maybe see the English girls again?"

"I don't know what you're talking about...sir," he replied.

"Oh, I think you do, son. Don't lie to me. We think you were with Ria on that bluff...because we found evidence." He decided to go for broke. Other than his intuition, he had nothing, yet. No clear proof that could link Joshua to the crime scene. Only a couple of footprints, but they were inconclusive. Perhaps they'd find the blanket, which had made indentations in the high grasses, and retrieve a few fibers. But most Amish garments were made of the same materials.

"Your dad says you were here all last night. But I'm not sure I can believe him either. So, let me ask you again. And again, don't lie to me! Were you and Miss Cahill together last night?"

Nervously, Joshua glanced over to the congregation on his lawn, now spellbound and silenced. He looked at his father. Then back at Hannah, and the two young men. Then back to Boychuk.

"Yes, Sheriff," he said, almost inaudibly.

EIGHTEEN

HER ARMS CROSSED tightly over her ribs, her once-enchanting face now filled with despair, Barbara Cahill gazed from the fifth floor window to the street below. It was a Sunday afternoon on a long weekend near the campus of Syracuse University and there was little activity. Not that she and Roger would be venturing outside anytime soon—unless it was to bum a smoke from one of the orderlies who congregated near the entrance. It had been nearly three years since her last cigarette, but—dammit!—she'd love one now. But she and Roger knew their fate; they would remain by their daughter's side for as long as it takes.

Eventually, over time, they'd find out who did this to their daughter but their existence now was this functional yet drab-looking hospital. These places were all the same, and Upstate Medical was no exception—a glass and concrete edifice that could be found in any mid-sized city on the eastern seaboard. But the Cahills were grateful. The medical staff had been wonderful and, so far, competent.

Barbara continued to scan the streets of Syracuse below. This city never seems to improve, she thought. It was a victim—maybe even the poster child—of the blight that rust-belt America was suffering today. There was a time, during and after the second war, that this city mattered. It was an industrial force behind the effort to destroy the Nazis. But no longer, and if it wasn't for its large public sector—the university, its vast medical complex—the city would be sunk.

Classes had already begun yet there were few signs that students or faculty were gearing up for their school year. Atop the hill stood the Carrier Dome, Syracuse's marshmallow-shaped stadium. It was empty and silent. Barbara knew that from the newspaper. On the glass coffee table in the ICU's waiting room sat the sports section of the *Post-Standard*, a sorry excuse for a newspaper if there ever was one. There was a good reason that locals labeled it the *Sub-Standard*; eight or ten pages of football coverage today and worse during basketball season but try to find a meaningful story about the Afghan war and why it was nearing its tenth year. Forget it.

Today, a loud headline told her the Orange played a road game last night, apparently trouncing the University of Akron Zips by four touchdowns, a team even more brutal than SU if that was possible. Well, any college team named the Zips *deserved* to lose. There was talk that SU might leave the Big East Conference. But who would notice if they did? You're not talking USC or Baylor or Florida State here, at least for football. Now, SU's hard courters were a different story. Theirs was a history of success. If you liked basketball.

Barbara knew the Syracuse scene well. After a couple of years at one of Pittsburgh's community colleges, where she excelled, she qualified for scholarship money and moved north, completing her degree in journalism. Though the city itself was a wasteland for real journalists, SU's Newhouse School had lived up to its imperious reputation, it being one of the top five schools of its kind in the country.

After all, Newhouse was the setting for LBJ's scandalous Gulf of Tonkin speech in August 1964, where he escalated the Vietnam War based on a lie. The North Vietnamese, as pliantly reported in the American media, had launched 'renewed' assaults on U.S. destroyers. Kennedy's successor, a big-eared, tough-talking Texan whose goal it was never to be the first president to lose a war, ordered America's warplanes to attack that day, thinking there would be a second attack. Only there was no *fucking* second attack! The military-industrial complex, as Eisenhower warned, had held the nation hostage, and over fifty thousand soldiers died. Just kids, most of them. And forty years later, another Texan in the White House launched the country into another war on a different set of lies. No more presidents from the Lone Star State, Barbara had told Hubert the other night, and he of all people seemed to agree. The country can barely survive them.

Anyway, at the age of twenty she hadn't known much about that. She entered Newhouse in 1973 when another battle was waging. This time it was a war on American democracy; a vice-president of Greek-American origin got caught with his hand in the till and re-signed in disgrace. His boss would do the same in less than a year. Transfixed on the state of the nation, she transferred to Syracuse hell-bent on becoming another Carl Bernstein. She would root out crooks and corruption everywhere.

Syracuse wasn't Columbia—few journalism schools were—but Newhouse's creds came through for her. She found a job; first in Harrisburg as a cub for the local rag, graduating in no time to the state legislature and her ambition was to land in Washington, D.C. But that was when she met her first husband, and before she knew it, they had settled in Pittsburgh and she had graduated to radio. The local NPR station was her home until she joined the steelworkers as their organizer, rabble-rouser and 'spokes chick', as she proudly de-scribed herself. Then, not long afterwards, Brad had arrived and the rest was history. Thank God she'd met Roger.

Turning away from the waiting room window, Barbara stole a glance at the love of her life, and it saddened her. More than that, she was angry. Roger, now leafing absently through a *Time* magazine, was not a well man and it obviously showed. It had all begun a couple of years ago. That was when the tremors started, the losses in con-centration and some partial paralysis. The armchair physician in her initially thought he had been stricken with Parkinson's or perhaps Alzheimer's. After all, those are the most publicized ailments for the elderly today. But then his Pittsburgh doctors told them he had contracted something more mysterious, something called *Hashimoto's Encephalopathy*, a strangely-named disease that was rarely diagnosed.

To her it sounded like some arcane malady that afflicted only Japanese emperors. First came the headaches; then more and more disorientation, even bouts of psychosis. His first doc thought he'd had a stroke. But then they came up with a disease that could be kept in check with steroids. There was no cure but it could be managed.

Jesus, though, what an ordeal. A half-smile emerged from her lips as she remembered the corticosteroid drugs Roger's youthful, British-born physician had prescribed. His response was vintage Roger: 'Look out Barry Bonds! Your home-run record isn't safe with me around!' His sense of humor had remained intact. But now this?

Just then, her distant thoughts were interrupted. Their ICU doctor arrived in the waiting room.

"Mr. and Mrs. Cahill?" Barbara abruptly turned to greet the physician. Roger dropped his magazine on the coffee table. Before them was a woman about forty-five, perhaps younger, with short coiffured Hershey-colored hair. Immediately Barbara was struck by her deep sensitive eyes, accentuated by a pair of stylish Anne Klein glasses. She exuded warmth and understanding, though her look was one of concern.

"Yes," they said in unison.

"My name is Mary-Ellen Robazza," she said. "I'm your daughter's lead physician. She'll have a team of us now, I'm afraid."

Barbara's heart sank with the news. "What can you tell us?"

The nice doctor delivered her diagnosis. Their daughter had suffered a number of injuries, the most serious of which was a crush to the back of her head.

"There's a long medical name for it, but in reality we think of it as a pulverization," she added. "This is where broken skull bones can be displaced inward, adding pressure on the brain. A second and just as serious complication could be infection."

She paused for a moment to allow her news to sink in.

"She has a number of other, relatively minor injuries which were caused by a tumbling effect to the rocks below…a couple of broken fingers, bruises and a small gash just above her right forearm."

Barbara was immediately intrigued by this news.

"As if she were trying to protect herself?" she asked.

"Possibly, Mrs. Cahill, but that's for the police to figure out. Fortunately, those rocks near the lake were likely not jagged in any way...otherwise—" Again, Dr. Robazza let her words linger a moment. Maybe she had already provided too much medical information for most parents to digest in one initial meeting. Shocked and saddened parents appear to be listening in situations like these, but fail to comprehend what was being said. It was common.

"It was fortunate for Ria that she was found as soon as she was, since she'd lost a great deal of blood. The Morgantown team did a good job in stabilizing her, but we'll have to wait and see what next steps we can take. Surgery's possible. To lift the bone fragments from the brain if they're placing pressure on it."

"Her condition, Doctor? Is she still critical?" Roger asked.

Clenching her lips, the physician simply nodded. As the head of a busy, inner-city intensive care unit, she'd seen just about every criminal element, the gunshot wounds, the knifings, the domestics that prompted scared and battered wives to use a whiskey bottle to protect themselves. She'd seen them all.

Ria Cahill's case was different.

"But I'll keep you in the loop. The next twenty-four to forty-eight hours will tell the story. We have her on a respirator and anything can happen. Unfortunately, I can't give you anything more than that right now."

Barbara's steely eyes brushed back tears. She couldn't decide whether to be grief-stricken or angry—or both.

"Can we see her," Roger asked.

"Give us another twenty minutes or so, okay? My nurses are getting her comfortable." The physician, her eyes locked on those of the concerned parents, paused briefly before adding, "Mr. and Mrs. Cahill...I would be remiss in my duties if I didn't ask you one more thing, and that is, do you know if Ria would consider the possibility of donating her organs? If her condition worsens? They'd be the greatest gift your daughter could give, if..." Her voice deadened. She knew the impact her words were having on the Cahills.

Organ donations...

Probably the two worst words in the dictionary for grieving parents.

"I'm so sorry to have to ask you this but it's my duty."

"Yes, Doctor, Ria has signed the DMV forms, I believe," Barbara answered, bidding the physician good-bye and before reaching for her husband in another tearful hug. They would need all the strength they could muster to survive this crisis. After a few moments, their silence was broken by the sound of her iPhone. Barbara reached into her purse to answer it.

"It's Brian Boychuk," she announced to her husband.

Roger watched as his wife spoke to the Morgan County cop. She became silent, obviously taking in the revelations. Thunderstruck, Barb's facial expression quickly became one of incredulity and disbelief as Boychuk told her of his discoveries.

"Okay, Sheriff," she said, her voice lower. "Thanks."

NINETEEN

RELEASING A DEEP SIGH, Menno Troyer watched as the last of the carriages departed his farm before drifting in the direction of his barn, the weight of the world on his narrow shoulders. Their spiritual service and luncheon was complete and so was their annual obligation to act as hosts. There would be no serious work today, but a farmer's responsibilities to his animals were always there.

Normally, their assemblage would have lasted well into the afternoon and perhaps the evening. They would read their passages, sing their songs and tell wonderful stories. He and his wife had been looking forward to their congregation's arrival for weeks. It was to be a time to reject temptations known as the *Hochmut*, or an overabundance of pride and arrogance, and replace them with humility, composure and reflection. In their lives, *Gelassenheit* was the collective goal of all congregations. They were not individuals. They didn't value themselves over their neighbors.

They were not like the English.

Today, however, was a different story. The arrival of the county sheriff as their service wound down was upsetting, not only to Menno and Sarah but to the raised eyebrows of Bishop Zachary Jakes. Jakes was a stork-shaped man in his early sixties with a ten-inch silvery beard the texture of steel wool. As Menno returned to the congregation, Jakes had intercepted him.

"What goes there, Troyer?" the bishop had demanded.

"A minor matter, Bishop. You and the elders have no cause for worry."

"What does the policeman want with your son?"

Menno turned his head in the direction of Boychuk and Joshua.

"There was an...incident at the Pond. My son delivered wood there the other night and the sheriff wished to speak to him about it."

The look on the bishop's face was stern.

"You make light of it, Troyer, you are dismissive but this is a serious situation for us all. We take exception to the law invading our lives. There is no such thing as a minor matter when a sheriff seeks out one of your sons for his sins."

"His sins?' Menno asked indignantly. "How do you know that Joshua has sinned? Because the English lawman arrived today? Because the sheriff wants to speak to him about an important matter? Please do not presume anything, Bishop."

"There are always consequences in situations like these, Troyer," the bishop replied.

Just then, one of the bishop's two sons had chimed in. Daniel Jakes and his brother Lucas were the young men who had engaged Joshua in a heated argument only moments before. Still single, Daniel, at twenty, was a nervous man who stood several inches shorter than Joshua and many pounds lighter. Menno had known the boy since birth and had often disapproved of his actions. A few years back, perhaps four or more, young Jakes had led a number of teens, including Joshua, down a spurious, disrespectful path of alcohol and other mayhem. Now, Menno felt the younger Jakes had become even more pious than his father.

"Why then has he cut his hair, Troyer?"

"I don't see that being any of your business, Daniel," Menno replied testily.

"It is our business when Joshua brings shame to our community!"

But Menno, his voice strong and decisive, simply walked away. He would brook no further inquiries. The congregation had demanded full disclosure, but there would be no answers. It was a family affair, and it would stay that way.

Now Menno saw his oldest son at the entrance of the hayloft above the barn doors, pitching hay to the ground. Joshua had spent nearly ten minutes with the sheriff before moving in the direction of the house, his head held low as he avoided the glaring watch of the congregation. There he changed into work clothes, donned his woven straw hat and disappeared into the barn.

"Joshua, come down here immediately," he ordered.

"I'm busy, Papa. The horses need feeding."

"The horses can wait! Come down here!"

By now, the mound of hay in front of the barn was substantial, perhaps six feet in height. Setting his pitchfork aside, Joshua jumped from the loft, landing softly in the hay, a ritual he and his siblings had done playfully many times before. Today, however, was anything but playful. He picked himself up and dusted off his clothes. Menno was clearly fuming with anger, and Joshua knew this was not going to be pleasant.

"Remove your hat!"

Joshua obeyed his father's command. His newly cropped haircut was exposed.

"Can you tell me the meaning of this," Menno said, pointing to his son's sudden, western-styled appearance.

"I cannot, Papa."

Menno was staring at the young man's hair. It clearly was trimmed neatly around the ears.

"You cannot, Joshua? Or will not?"

Once again, Joshua failed to answer his father.

"Perhaps I can explain your recent behavior better than you can. It was that English woman, wasn't it? You met with her and drank alcohol. Then you cut your hair and met with her again last night? Against my direct wishes…to end this situation immediately! Your…your…relationship, whatever it is. I should say *was*! It's over!"

Joshua didn't flinch. He had no response. But the finality in Menno's voice was striking; there was no mention or concern for the English girl's health. She was now fighting for her life in a city hospital but his father seemed more distressed about his son's future in the congregation. There were no questions—no accusations—about Joshua's role in the events of the previous night. Whether or not he had lost his temper? Whether he had hurt her? There were no such words and Joshua found that curious. Had his father not threatened just yesterday to put an end to it all?

"Answer me!" his father once again ordered.

"I have no answers, Papa."

Menno's look of frustration was unmistakable. He knew his son would be shunned from the congregation once further details of the incident at Remington Pond had surfaced. The congregation was not without rumors, gossip and innuendo. There were no modern conveniences in their homes, such as telephones or computers. But that did not matter; news like this traveled quickly throughout their community. And Joshua was news.

"Hannah Zook was not pleased with your behavior as well—"

Abruptly, Joshua interrupted his father. Now he would speak.

"I don't care what Hannah Zook thinks, Papa! I don't care what anyone thinks of me."

It was Menno's turn to glare into his son's eyes. He would deliver a stern message.

"It is time to care, Joshua! Your life is among us—not with the English. You made your choice four years ago. I offered you your freedom then, and you chose our life. You made your decision. There is no turning back. I warned you about getting involved with that English woman yesterday…"

His voice ventured away. Having said enough, Menno turned on his heels and stormed back to the farmhouse.

TWENTY

H IS EYES STRETCHING HEAVENWORD, Hubie watched
as a modest burst of fireworks ripped the skies high above
Morgantown's high school football field. Dee had him convinced
a distraction from the weekend's dreadful news would be good
medicine. He'd agreed, if only to forget that he had just turned
seventy. Was it not just recently that he'd retired from the Army?
It seemed so.

This field brought back some pleasant memories. Friday night
football. Was there anything more American than that? It had delivered him from Donna once a week, often standing by himself on the
sidelines, taking in Marauders' games when both Brian and Denny
were driving a small town high school to all-state fame. Sipping
from a thermos of black coffee to keep him warm, there was the
future sheriff making spectacular rushes, the fullback in him bar-
reling through enemy lines, setting records for rushing. Denny on
the other hand was a murderous defensive lineman, his eyes poi-
sonously seeking out his next victim, usually a hapless quarterback
from Ogdensburg or Malone or Watertown. By his senior year,
Denny had attracted the college scouts and his destiny was set. It
would be Michigan or Boise State and likely a long stint in the pros.
The scholarship was there, but that busted leg killed his hopes and
dreams and his very soul itself.

Now as he peered down those same sidelines, he noticed about
eighty or so people, old and young, seated in lawn chairs or resting
on blankets. Not far away was that family that had moved in across
the street a couple of weeks ago. They hadn't yet been introduced
but someone told him they were from Lafargeville or Chaumont or

someplace to the south. *Chaumont*! How could a word spelled like that be pronounced as 'SHMOE'. And other town names were just as puzzling; Madrid was 'MAYDRID', and Chili came out like 'CHY-LIE'. Not to mention that Charlotte was called 'SHALOTTE' for some reason. No one he knew thought to question why.

He glanced at the family once again. They were joined by another mom and dad, a couple of thirty-somethings, and together they had about five or six toddlers in tow, likely giving them a last night of freedom before the school year started in a couple of days. Jesus, how do you *feed* families that large these days? He'd had a hard enough time with Jane and Joanne thirty-five years ago and that was on his post office pittance. Only when Donna got that job selling smokes and lottery tickets at the Mobil station did they have a few extra bucks.

Actually, he was surprised to see anyone under forty around town these days, since the county's once-youthful progeny were becoming extinct. What was their future here? Economy's awful and it had been so for twenty years or more. Companies that used to make stuff—real stuff that people wanted to buy—departed in the middle of the night for China or Thailand or Mexico. Eleven bucks an hour! That was all our guys made in these plants and owners still couldn't compete. If you weren't a prison guard or a school teacher or a state trooper or a nurse or any other official sucking on the public tit you were out of luck.

Another explosion of booming sounds. Another few starbursts, and naturally the kids reacted with glee. Not exactly the Fourth of July on the Washington Mall, he thought, but not bad for Morgantown. Down the sidelines, he watched as a handful of volunteer firemen loaded the rocket-launchers with crates of explosives, likely imported from South Carolina.

Tonight, they were here to celebrate Labor Day. Soon, he and Boychuk would go duck hunting if the cop could escape his job for a few days. Joanne caught a glimpse of her father and immediately knew the source of melancholy that now spread across his jowly face. She had seen that sadness before and it was upsetting. Even before they had heard the disturbing news of Ria's assault, she and Matt decided to stay over in Morgantown an extra day. Not that she enjoyed returning to her hometown. Too many memories here, she thought. But their hectic touring schedule kept them on the road much of this past spring and summer. Now, though, she knew she had to make the time.

"She's gonna be all right, Dad," she whispered in his ear during an interval in the fireworks. Hubie turned towards his daughter. Their eyes locked a moment. "You watch and see," she assured. "She's healthy and strong and, besides, she's Barb's kid! Nobody messes with her. Reminds us of someone else we knew and loved, huh?"

"I get your drift, Jo, but I'm not so sure you'll be right on this one," he replied. "Barb's worried sick."

Joanne shook her head.

"We Schumachers are on a roll!" she said, focusing her eyes in Booker's direction for confirmation. He was wearing a brown leather bomber jacket and a crazy-horse styled cowboy hat. Noticing her smile, Matt returned the favor. Next to him was Dee, who was enraptured by the sounds and sights of a pleasant night. To Joanne's right sat Makenna. Joanne was happy that her niece had decided to spend a few days in Morgantown.

Now the young woman spoke.

It was obvious she had questions on her mind. Questions about her real mother.

"What was she like, Jo?" Makenna asked, her animated eyes now moistening. "You know, we only had those few minutes together in the store and now I've relived them over and over again. Can't tell you how ripped off I feel."

Joanne paused for a moment before answering. She too felt the same way about her twin—her only sibling—who had spent most of her adult life estranged from the family. Jane had bailed at a young age, disappearing without as much as a trace. It was only later that they knew where she had landed, their sole contact with her a brief appearance at their mother's funeral. That reunion ended more in anger than in grief. Then, unannounced, Jane had arrived in Joanne's kitchen that Thanksgiving night nearly four years ago.

"I understand, Ken," Joanne replied. "If it wasn't for...well, you know, I wouldn't have gotten to know her either. All I can tell you is that your mom was crazy...and wonderful at the same time. So smart, so curious and so ambitious. She was destined for big things, I'm sure. Maybe in politics herself."

"You mean run for office?"

Joanne nodded.

"Wouldn't have been surprised," she added. "She knew how the world was supposed to work."

Makenna listened attentively, but Joanne knew there would be further questions on her niece's mind. They sat there in silence for a moment or two. Then the younger woman spoke.

"That night, Jo—" She quickly halted her train of thought. "I'm sorry. Maybe I shouldn't bring that up again. I know it was painful for you...and probably still is. It's none of my—"

But Joanne interrupted her.

"—no, no Ken, go ahead. It is your business. You're her daughter. Ask me anything you want. I've made peace with myself about that night. Mostly..."

Makenna drew a huge breath of air and exhaled.

This was her moment.

"Did you ever think that my mom was even capable...?" she said, her voice seemingly unable of finishing her thought.

"Yes and no, Ken," Joanne said. "It's true, we could have walked out of there and never gone back. At first I thought it was just an insane, impulsive act on her part. Then as it turned out she had another motive as well."

A look of puzzlement came over Makenna.

"What do you mean, Jo? Another motive?"

Joanne took a deep breath before responding. Now she would tell the younger woman the rest of the story. "There was an *incident*..." she said as Makenna sat frozen in her chair, oblivious to the explosions of light and sound bursting in front of them. Now she was hanging on each of Joanne's words, tears streaming down her face. The best way to alleviate pain was through honesty and revelation, Joanne felt.

It was time.

Letting her news sink in, Joanne decided to lighten the situation.

"You wouldn't believe how profane she could be," she added, a smile emerging. "Loved the F-bomb more than anyone I ever knew. Don't know how many times I yelled at her to stop, and she did... for the most part."

Makenna smiled.

"I heard about some of the things she liked to say."

"A very honest woman, your mom, Ken. She said what was on her mind. You know, she never showed any remorse. Never! And in some perverse way, I admired her for that. Her favorite line was 'never say never.'"

"Your band..."

Joanne nodded, smiling.

"That was the first thing that Matt and I agreed on. You see, Ken, she gave me a new start. It was the greatest gift that I've ever received and one that I'll cherish for the rest of my life."

"No regrets...?"

"None!"

The women again sat in poignant silence, their attention returning to the show in front of them. Now the rockets were bursting in an orgasm of bright colors and boisterous sounds, the ultimate crescendo near. Soon this night would be over and Makenna would be leaving for Plattsburgh.

Just then, looking over the young woman's shoulder, she could see Boychuk arriving. He was in uniform, which meant he was still on duty on a Sunday night.

"Brian's back," Joanne said, prompting Makenna to turn abruptly.

"Even that, Jo, is still a bit strange to me," she said. "All this time I had thought my father was a State Farm agent. He's a great guy...and so is my mom and I love them both. But I wish they had told me."

As the volleys of exploding fireworks came to their predictable conclusion and silence was once again upon them, the distinctive sounds of sirens could be heard in the distance. Waving to the Schumachers, Boychuk walked briskly to where several volunteer firemen were packing up the last of the rocket launchers. Quickly, they halted their work and began to run towards their parked trucks. The sheriff then doubled back to where Hubie and the family were located.

"Hi folks," he said, his voice displaying some anxiety. "Can't stay. I have to get over to the Troyer farm. Apparently there's a fire raging there."

"Oh my God! Is their farmhouse on fire, Brian?" Dee asked, alarmed. She thought of all those children.

"Their hayfields, I believe," he replied. "But I have to run. I'll try to drop over in the morning."

He quickly turned on his heels and disappeared into the night.

TWENTY-ONE

BOYCHUK AND HIS DEPUTIES arrived at the Troyer farm to discover the fields ablaze and the family in panic. Overhead, the skies were roaring and resplendent, with flames shooting forty feet in the air. Now shouting commands in his native language, Menno ordered his brood to fill oak barrels aboard their buckboard. The children, some still dressed in dark night clothes, were pitching in, forming a bucket brigade from their well, with Rachel furiously operating the pump. Then Joshua, Elijah and Levi led Temper and Sorrel to the fields.

The Morgantown volunteers, maybe ten in total, had arrived only minutes before and were pulling their canvas hoses from two large pumper trucks they had driven from town. From his vantage point, Boychuk could see as many as fifty mounds of hay ablaze, some of the fires shooting higher than others. He knew Joshua and his brothers had harvested their crop over the past two weeks and had left it to rot in the late summer sun. And, with the likely help of some well-placed lighter fluids, it became a raging inferno.

His deputies scrambled to assist the firemen, but Boychuk knew this battle would be futile. The efforts of the family and the volunteers would be in vain. After all, Murdock Creek was far off in the distance and he doubted whether it would have been of any use after such a dry summer. A few thousand gallons from the pumpers, aided by a hundred or so buckets of well water, would not save their crop.

Boychuk was about to join his deputies when he heard sounds of footsteps from behind. He turned to see Benji Hoggarth trudging slowly up the Troyer laneway. He walked with a distinct limp, the result of a Chevy half-ton tumbling from its jack a couple of years ago, busting his left leg in three places. As usual, Molson followed loyally behind him.

"Not good, Brian," Hoggarth said, his voice emitting a guttural growl so deep he sounded as if he had been gargling with angel stone. He was dressed in work boots and dark-blue denim overalls stained heavily with grease and dirt. Under the overalls was a plaid, sleeved work shirt that might have been last laundered in July. Though only forty-one, Hoggarth could pass for a man at least five years older. He smoked and drank too much, and it obviously showed, but Boychuk knew he was a good-hearted soul. A decent guy.

"You called it in, Benj," replied the sheriff. "See anything or anybody around?"

"Naw, at least not much. I was just watchin' some re-runs from Talladega and all of a sudden this flash came from across the road. Looked out the window. Goddamnedest thing I ever saw."

"Don't suppose you saw anyone running with a torch or a jerrycan or anything like that?"

"Nope."

"No cars peeling away down Bidgood—or over there?" He pointed to a junction point about three hundred yards from where it crossed with Federal Side Road.

Hoggarth shook his head.

"Guess I was just taken in by it all, Brian. By the time I got here they were all out screamin' and hollerin'. Couldn't help them much...with this gimp leg and all. But I smelled the kerosene. No doubt in my mind they used that shit."

"Yeah, I smelled it right away too, Benj," Boychuk replied. "Betcha the sonsabitches are around here somewhere. Why light a bonfire and run away? Gotta stay and watch, right?"

Instinctively, Boychuk started scanning the countryside. The fires would burn quickly over the next twenty minutes and he would need to look around. This was a cruel act of arson; someone had a beef with the Amish, or at least this family, and his suspicions were narrowing.

He retrieved a powerful flashlight from his cruiser. Its beam could extend more than a hundred yards and immediately he pointed it at the edge of the woods in the distance, moving it slowly from one end to another. Nothing. No movement whatsoever. They likely got the hell out of there in a hurry, he thought.

"Okay, Benj, buzz me if you see anything, all right?"

"Will do, Sheriff," the man snarled, whistling for Molson to join him on his return to his trailer. "Feel sorry for old Menno and his bunch." His final word came out sounding like 'buuuunch'.

As the volunteers continued their furious work in hopes of saving some of the crop, Boychuk could see Menno in the distance. His words were incomprehensible but that didn't matter; there was a frantic, nearly hopeless sound to his voice. Between him, his family and the firemen, they had managed to douse about twenty of the blazes, seemingly forced to abandon the rest. The pumper trucks' hoses could extend only so far. At the front of the farmhouse, he saw several of the Troyer daughters sobbing. They didn't deserve any of this, Boychuk thought.

His flashlight still beaming across the fields, Boychuk walked over to one of his deputies who was aiding a fireman at the back of one of the trucks.

"Bill, keep an eye on this while I take a drive around," he said. "Maybe there's some action going on over on Federal."

"Okay, Sheriff. I know Menno's gonna want some answers, though. What do you want me to say to him?"

"There's not much you or I can say to him right now," Boychuk replied. "Give the fields as good a look as you can once the fires die down. They might've been stupid enough to leave something behind, who knows? Tell him we'll be back tomorrow."

The sheriff returned to his vehicle, put it in reverse and pulled away. He was about to make the turn on Federal Side Road when he saw a couple of tail-lights in the distance, perhaps five hundred yards away. In this part of the county, many of the roads were straight lines, a grid not unlike a checkerboard, prompting local land-owners to suspect they were carved out of barren land at the turn of the last century by some Albany bureaucrat hovering over a map with a slide-rule.

He quickly made his decision. He'd check this one out. Flicking the switch for his lights atop his roof and in the grillwork, he stepped on the gas. He couldn't make out if the vehicle ahead was a car or truck but its inhabitants had to have played a role in the hayfield fires. Either that or they were running from a DUI. Or both. Instantly, he got his answer. The car sped up and was now racing down the road at a high speed. Boychuk knew he had to close the gap soon if he was to stop this vehicle, since there were more than a few places that it could hide. There was also a stretch of gravel road up ahead and if the car continued on the same track would spray clouds of dust in its wake. The loose gravel would slow it down a bit. Or provide cover for an escape.

He glanced at his speedometer; he was now pushing fifty-five and climbing. Racing through the darkened night, passing one farmhouse after another in the distant fields, it was much more a serene setting than the carnage and violence the Troyers were now experiencing. Occasionally interrupting the fallowed fields was a heavily-forested deer tract that owners would lease out to shooters from New Jersey or Pennsylvania or points farther south. Soon hunters would arrive, all decked out in screaming orange vests, sometimes bought fresh from the shelves at Gander Mountain, and toting their Browning or Winchester bolt action rifles. They would bag their quotas, pin a tag to a doe's ear and filter into bars like Swigs or the Paddle looking for some night action. Happened every year around this time.

The vehicle ahead was now accelerating, the gap between them growing. The lights of his Tahoe pierced the solitude of the night, and now Boychuk sensed unease. He knew these roads better than anyone but feared that one or both vehicles could end in disaster. Suddenly, as expected, the headlights ahead entered the unpaved section of the back road, a cloud of dust ballooning so large that it resembled a north country blizzard in March. Visibility was close to zero. He had to close in soon or lose them entirely because there were at least two intersections ahead, not to mention numerous farm lanes and hunting paths that could provide escape routes.

A moment or two later, Boychuk's cruiser entered the gravel road and the tail-lights ahead disappeared. Immediately, he lowered his speed to accommodate the rough patch but felt his SUV starting to fishtail. Not far ahead, he remembered there was a bridge over the western end of Murdock Creek, more of a culvert actually, bordered by concrete railings. If he wasn't careful, he could wrap his cruiser around one of them.

Now his speed was under fifty, and he cleared the small bridge safely. Soon he'd re-enter another paved section of Federal and resume the chase. There was a slowly rising hill ahead and once over that he figured he would gain the upper hand. But he was wrong. His Tahoe cleared the incline but the tail-lights had disappeared. Whether the vehicle veered off on one of the side roads, or simply turned off its lights, he didn't know. But they were nowhere to be seen.

Not as much as a reflector in the night.

"Goddammit!" he exploded, banging his hands down on the steering wheel as he brought his cruiser to a stop, his halogen high beams illuminating the vacant road ahead. Switching off his blue-and-white flashers with one hand, he reached for the handset of police radio with the other. He pressed a button. His deputy answered.

"Jimmy, the bastards gave me the slip. Get your ass down to the Pond and check it out." No need for further explanation. He knew what the sheriff wanted him to do.

"Ten-four."

TWENTY-TWO

SHORTLY AFTER BREAKFAST, Hannah loaded her buggy with breads, preserves and apple cider and ordered her horse down the short, bumpy lane and away from her farm. News of the fires had travelled quickly throughout their church district and Mama announced they would help their friends, now in dire need. Hannah quickly volunteered to go. Any reason to see Joshua again was reason enough.

Wrapped in a navy blue blanket to ward off the early September chills, Hannah was thinking once again of the disturbing scene at the Troyer service yesterday. That policeman! He had arrived at their place of worship and celebration, rudely interrupting their solemn setting. He had no right to do that! Only to question Joshua about some episode over at the Pond concerning that same English girl who stopped by their roadside stand only two days before. That girl, like all the others, admired their basket work, promising to return with money but never came back. She'd heard those promises before. They were *all* the same.

Mama was right. All they do is stare at us with those eyes of theirs. Judging us, belittling us. Why would Joshua want to have anything to do with her or any of *their* lives? Their spoiled, *Satan*-loving lives?

As her buggy moved slowly up Bidgood Road and arrived in full view of the Troyer fields, Hannah saw for herself the damage the fires had done. Stacks of hay that had been drying peacefully in the weekend sun were now gone. In their place, mostly, as some were still smoldering, were dozens of charred pits. Only a few of the mounds, maybe five or six at most, had survived. In the distance, she could see

Menno and three of his younger boys armed with pitchforks, working feverishly to salvage some of the straw that had not been doused with kerosene. Near the barn, Sarah Troyer and the rest of her family were scurrying around as well, busily organizing the family's daily chores; fire or no fire, the work must get done. A look of disappointment came over her. There was no sign of Joshua, anywhere.

Whipping the reins to her horse, a few moments later she arrived in front of the Troyer farmhouse. Just then, Rachel exited the front door to greet her. At nineteen, she resembled Joshua so closely that people often asked Menno if they were born from the same egg. Rachel was an alluring young woman with light brown hair, porcelain skin and luscious hazel eyes. Throughout her teenage years, many of her English neighbors—all boys, of course—stopped often to say hello when she sold corn by the roadside with her little sisters. But when they tried to make conversation, she would shut them down. There would be no fraternizing with the English. Her future was set.

"Hello, Hannah."

"I come with food and drink for your family," the Zook girl replied. "My family shares the sorrow you have experienced during the night. A very troubling event."

"Yes..." Rachel was still reeling from the violence. She was at a loss for words.

Hannah looked back to the fields once again, and then to the barn where activity continued.

"I don't see Joshua," she said.

Rachel shook her head. There was sadness in her eyes, a look that Hannah had seen before in Joshua.

"He was gone at sunrise this morning, and we don't know where he is. Our buggy was here but he and Temper are gone. You know he rides bareback sometimes? Papa doesn't know what to believe any more but maybe Joshua has gone to the south fields to check on them." She pointed to the charred remains. "The firemen said the only fires set were here."

A look of disappointment on Hannah's face turned to anger.

"The English! It is their fault, Rachel! Today is their Labor Day. But why do they celebrate a day of labor? They don't work like we do. They're lazy! All they do is cause trouble for us!"

Rachel offered no comment, but the look on her face was sympathetic. How could she argue with her?

"It's true, isn't it?" Hannah asked.

"What is true?"

"You know what I'm talking about! That Joshua was involved with that girl at the Pond."

Immediately, Rachel became flustered. As she helped her mother feed their parishioners yesterday, she too heard the whispers and gossip about her brother's actions. But she had refused to believe the idle talk, and wasn't about to ask her parents about it. If it was true, Papa would deal with it. She saw her mother approaching the Zook buggy.

"I know nothing about that, Hannah," she replied, abruptly. "That is a matter between you and Joshua."

Hannah was momentarily surprised by Rachel's blunt answer. All along, she was certain they were allies, co-conspirators, in fact, in their attempts to land her brother as a husband. Now Hannah was not so sure.

Sarah Troyer, her dark dress now dragging through the dust under a pair of high-laced boots, arrived at Hannah's carriage. She was a stout, broad-shouldered woman who towered over her husband by four or five inches. Her most distinguishable feature was a pronounced under-bite that seemed to transform her face into a perpetual frown, perhaps warranted in that she had sired thirteen offspring—with a suspected fourteenth on the way. Not a good-looking couple, their English neighbors had gossiped, wondering aloud just how the Troyers could pop out such appealing kids, at least in the cases of Rachel and Joshua. Now, after the horrid events of the night, a look of exhaustion, even resignation, was evident.

"Hannah has brought us some food, Mama," Rachel announced.

"Thank you, Miss Zook. Please extend our gratitude to your mother and father. It has been a difficult time for us."

"What have the English police said about this?" Hannah asked. She was determined to get to the bottom of the story.

"Nothing, my dear, nothing. The sheriff was here last night with the firemen, but he has not returned. There is little they can do."

But Hannah was persistent. She was positive that the Sunday night inferno was caused by the English, and it may have been prompted by Joshua's actions. "Well, it is very clear to me," she said. "They will do anything to protect their own."

But Sarah Troyer would hear nothing of the sort.

"Young lady, it is not up to the English to care for us. We are not them. We have always taken care of ourselves, and that will continue. You and Rachel and all God's children must remember this. We are strong. We will recover. We don't need them!"

As Rachel listened attentively, Hannah chose silence. She hadn't expected a reprimand as vehement as what she had just received, especially from such an aggrieved victim as Mother Troyer. Why do we, all of us, take this abuse from the English, she wondered.

TWENTY-THREE

NOT FIVE MILES AWAY, Brian Boychuk was guiding his SUV slowly down the cedar-lined road leading to the Cahill compound when his cell phone rang. Seemed all he did was field phone calls. But he wasn't surprised. Last night, shortly after his high-speed chase, the first to call was that reporter from the *Journal*. Not twenty minutes later it was some gal from *The Watertown Daily Times* and finally, around midnight—midnight!—came a query from some journalist at the *Associated Press*, out of Albany of all places. Reporters don't own watches, apparently.

But he knew any attack of any sort on the Amish was big news, a fascinating story to the locals who basked in their quaint, pre-industrial lifestyles. Their reputation as contrarians had fed this fascination as they fought every county building code on the basis of religious freedom, even going to court to fight the 'English laws' as Menno had described them. Those battles made headlines, as did any mishap resulting in Amish misfortune. What was proliferating was the number of accidents involving the sect; just this summer, near Cooperstown, one of the locals crashed his half-ton into a buggy at night, killing a horse and injuring its driver.

Now it was Webster on the line from the crime lab and, judging by the tone of his voice, it was clear he was still irritated that his weekend plans in the mountains had been so rudely interrupted. Better get into another line of work, pal, he thought.

"Whaddaya got for me…Andrew?" Boychuk said, careful not to anger him any further.

"Well, Sheriff, a little more than yesterday but still not a whole hell of a lot," he replied. "The docs over at Hargreaves did a vaginal swab on Miss—" He paused for a moment, seeming to have forgotten Ria's last name.

"—Cahill," Boychuk answered. He was willing to make amends with the technician.

"Right…Cahill. Anyway, they did their swabs and we've confirmed that she did indeed have sex on the night of the incident. There was evidence of semen. Who she had sex with, we don't know, but we'll have the DNA type very soon. Maybe you can get a match."

Boychuk already knew the answer to that question.

"Any signs of forcible?"

"No, the kit came back negative on that. Guess she was wet and willing."

The sheriff silently swore to himself. It was bad enough the Cahill girl was in an epic battle for her life. But to have this asshole say things like that just made it worse.

"Try keeping it professional, will you?" Boychuk would steer the conversation in a new direction. "What about the fibers?"

"Now those came from some very coarse material…and we're not talking about the average picnic blanket from J.C. Penney."

"Okay. Anything else?"

"A couple of things. That clasp that that girl found—"

Boychuk interrupted him.

"My daughter, you mean?"

Somewhat castigated, Webster continued. "Right… you say she's a student at George Washington in forensics?"

"Yes, graduating soon. It's one of the best schools in the country." Why he suddenly felt he had to justify his decision to this technician, he didn't know. He was the sheriff of Morgan County and didn't need to explain his actions.

"Right," Webster replied. "Well, we would have picked it up, too, Sheriff. Anyway, we took a good look at it. Fine quality white gold. At least eighteen carats…but, of course, that doesn't establish an owner. Could've been *any* one of those kids that night."

"Let me figure that one out, Webster," Boychuk replied, reverting once again to the man's last name. Why treat this guy with kid gloves? He works for me, Boychuk thought.

"Anything else?" If Boychuk had had any patience before, it was gone.

"The footprints are still inconclusive, but we have photos, and we'll put together some models later."

"Any foot sizes, off hand?" the sheriff enquired.

"The small ones were a size eight and, judging from the narrowness of them, likely female. Probably the Cahill kid, since she wasn't wearing shoes...but we're analyzing them all. The largest one was a nine wide or a bit larger."

Webster changed the subject. "Got the call from your deputy about the fires last night. We're heading over to that Amish farm now. Obviously deliberately set, right, Sheriff?"

"Believe so. Keep me posted," he said, ending the call abruptly.

Moments later, he arrived at the entrance of the Cahill property. Labor Day had arrived with a desperate chill in the air. Gone was the stifling humidity and in its place was a cooler, grayer pattern that would likely result in rain. Mother Nature, notoriously fickle, especially in these parts, had flicked her switch.

Still behind the wheel, he gazed towards Barbara's largest cottage at the rear. Next to it was a graveled driveway where Brad's black Saab convertible sat parked. How long has that joy wagon been there, he wondered? Late last night, Jimmy had reported no signs of life here. Waiting until well past midnight, there was nary a peep; no cars, no answers at any of the doors. Nothing. Aside from a couple of motion-detecting spotlights on the storage sheds nearby, the place had been dark and abandoned.

Boychuk turned his attention to the expansive lawn that led to the water. In contrast to the weekend's celebrations, the place was calm and clean, as if the parties had never occurred. The stage where Joanne had sung a loving tribute to her father, and where Barbara delivered her toast, deliciously funny on its own, had been dismantled and taken away. Gone too were the RVs and tents; they had disappeared but not before his deputies spoke to each of their inhabitants about the events of Saturday night. At the fire pit, where a scorching inferno had raged some thirty-six hours before, only a few scarred remnants of Joshua's camp wood had survived. Give these boys a boatload of credit, he thought. They know how to build a fire. But the fun's over now.

As he stepped from his vehicle, the only sounds that Boychuk could hear were those of a gently idling motor. The Pond's waters were warmer than the air above, creating a light morning mist across the bay. A moment later, cruising near the surface, a candy-apple red bass boat arrived and immediately he recognized its driver and passenger. He watched as the twosome expertly maneuvered the boat onto its lift, where one of them flipped an electrical switch. A purring sound followed and slowly the boat rose out of the water. Then, as one gathered their requisite fishing gear, rods and pails, the other paused to relieve himself on the sandy beach.

Boychuk, his arms crossed, stood there, patiently. He'd wait for the twosome to discover his presence. Nick was the first to look up.

"Sheriff! Didn't see you standing there," he said, attempting without success to suppress a burp that seemed to come from the bottom of his intestines.

"'S'cuse me," he grinned. "Too much of Cahill's crappy coffee this morning, I guess. You know, I heard the damnedest thing the other day...that the average urination takes about fifty-one seconds. Now, who the hell stands there with a stop-watch?"

As he waited for Nick to zip up his pants, Brad was watching the sheriff closely. Better watch out, Wells; this big bohunk was not a patient man.

Boychuk, checking his watch, had heard enough.

"Well, I'm guessing coffee's not the only thing you've had today," he charged. "Not even ten o'clock and you're already wasted."

"Hey, not me, Sheriff," Brad protested.

But Boychuk was focusing his attention on Nick.

"Wells, right? Nick Wells?"

"That's right, Sheriff."

"I remember you now...from the other night. Word has it you don't care much for the Amish. That right Wells?"

Nick continued to offer up a grin. Growing more irritated by the second, Boychuk decided to push back.

"You know, Wells," he said icily, his voice rising. "My first instinct is to shove that smirking yap of yours under water for, let's say, more than fifty-one seconds. But this is your lucky day. I feel charitable. I'll resist the urge to get my boots wet."

Brad spoke up.

"Sheriff, Wells is just dealing with this in his own way."

"Doesn't appear to be too upset, Brad. Maybe I should slap a breathalyzer on both of you."

"Hey, as I said, I've just had coffee today, Sheriff," Brad repeated, attempting to defuse the situation. "What can we do for you?"

"Decided personally to pay you a visit this morning," the sheriff replied. "I know my deputies have spoken to you and all your pals about the events of the other night. But I thought I'd have a chat with you boys, myself."

Just then, a largemouth bass jumped from the fishing pail and was flailing its way across the narrow dock in search of watery freedom. Calmly but quickly, Nick retrieved a serrated knife from his hip holster and with a rapid, downward swing stabbed the flopping fish through its bulging right eye. The blow was so swift that the six-inch blade penetrated the hapless fish's head, lodging solidly in the pine wharf. There would be no escape.

Boychuk watched the scene unfold with interest. Most fishermen he knew would have reacted differently. Most would have simply retrieved the fish and returned it to the pail.

"Where you from, kid?"

"I think you already know that, Sheriff," Nick replied.

"Humor me."

"Poughkeepsie area," he said, jerking his head in the direction of the Hudson River town to the south.

"Right. Spent your summer here though, I take it?"

"That's correct, Sheriff," Nick replied.

"Got to know the Cahill kids a bit too, I understand…especially young Ria?"

"We met in Canton and started hangin' out," he replied. "Not against the law, is it?" Now it was Nick's turn to show impatience. "Where's this going, Sheriff?"

"Where am I going with this, you ask?" His fierce penetrating eyes now bore down on Nick's. "Be patient, kid. I'll tell you soon enough. But first tell me a few things. You and Ria…you boyfriend and girlfriend, that sort of thing?"

Nick was quick to answer. His cockiness re-emerged.

"Your deputy asked me all those questions yesterday."

Boychuk maintained his stare.

"I know he talked to you, but I thought I'd ask you myself."

"Guess you could say that, yeah."

"Ah, now we're getting somewhere. Like her enough that you two are planning to move in together soon? Over in Gouverneur?"

"That's the plan…or was."

"Yeah, past tense. She's kind of indisposed right now, isn't she?"

Nick remained silent.

"So, tell me, when was the last time you saw your *girlfriend*, Nick?" He deliberately emphasized the word but softened his attack somewhat, using the young man's first name for the first time.

"Saturday night by the fire. Can't remember much about that night, though. I was drunk."

"Like this morning," he retorted. "You boys are nearly out of control. But I'm mystified, Nick. Here you are at her parents' property by this fine lake. Maybe it's an opportune time to make a good impression? Especially since you and Ria, apparently, have big plans? Move in together? Maybe even get married some day?"

Now Boychuk was taunting the younger man. Sometimes an inquisition of this nature produces good information. He continued, "But I know your type. To me it looked like just another opportunity to for you to show off. To flirt with all the other girls—"

"Not true." Nick interrupted.

"No? I saw you at Mr. Schumacher's party. Making all those shooters, your shirt off, flexing your muscles. The ladies ogling you."

"I was shitfaced."

"Wrong answer, Nick," the sheriff replied. "But everyone knows that booze is famous for causing...*convenient* amnesia." Boychuk, his eyes trading glances with both of the young men, shook his head in disgust. "So what did you think of that good-looking Amish guy drinking with all your girlfriends stroking his hair?"

Nick's eyes turned poisonous, a look not lost on the sheriff.

"He was a freak show, remember?" Boychuk continued. "Your words, Wells, not mine. He showed up with his firewood and the next thing you knew he was drinking your beer and becoming the hit of the party. Hustling your girls. You remember that?"

Nick grimaced noticeably but was determined not to show weakness. He said nothing.

"But that was Friday night," the sheriff said, continuing his cross-examination. "Let's talk Saturday. Tell me about the tiff you and Ria had that night." This caught Nick off guard. Yes, he remembered that very well, even to the point at which he was dangling that fucking stone necklace in his hands. It wasn't *his* gift to Ria. That puck-chaser from Canada had given it to her, and she wore it everywhere.

"What tiff?" Nick asked.

"Don't remember it, kid?" Boychuk replied. Was it time to come down even harder? Perhaps. He returned his attention to Brad.

"Seems that your mom saw Mr. Wells here, and your sister, arguing by the fire that night. That your sister was rebuffing his advances all night." He addressed Wells again. "Now, do you remember that, Nick?"

"It might be coming back, Sheriff." He shrugged. "So what?"

It was time for Brad to speak up.

"What the hell, Nick?" he asked. "You didn't tell me anything about a fight you had with my sister!"

"Wasn't a fight, for Christ's sake!" he said, defensively. "Just a minor spat."

"So what did you spat about, as you call it?"

"Can't remember, Sheriff."

"Wasn't it that she hadn't paid you any attention all weekend?"

"No."

"No? Or maybe it was about the punch you gave young Troyer the night before? When he was leaving? That didn't go over well with her, did it?"

"I just wanted to make sure he was leaving, that's all."

"But that angered Ria quite a bit, didn't it?"

"Guess so," Nick said.

Boychuk decided to go for the jugular. His glare was so laser-like it could have melted glaciers.

"You were pissed off, too, weren't you? So pissed at her on Saturday night that you were keeping a close eye on her?"

"What are you talking about?"

"You followed her that night, didn't you?"

"No."

"You sure, Wells? Didn't you watch as she wandered off to the woodpile...not to return?"

"I never left the party."

"I don't think so, Wells. I think you watched her leave the compound and followed her up the cliff."

"Not true."

"Maybe you got into a real fight and slugged her?"

Boychuk avoided any mention of the bloody birch log. The fewer the details, the better, he decided. But Wells remained calm.

"No…and all I can say Sheriff, is if you think that's true, then prove it!"

Brad had been listening intently to the furious exchange, and decided to enter the fray. "I was at the party all night, too, Sheriff and didn't see Wells leave." Not that this was true. He was too enthralled with Natasha to notice. And liquored up, too. Besides, he had his own suspicions about Ria's attacker.

Boychuk decided to let his line of questioning about Saturday night rest. Instead, he'd focus on the events of last night.

"Where were you guys last night around ten?"

"Just cruising around, Sheriff," Brad replied. "This friggin' area's boring. Only thing going down were the fireworks. We took in those for a while, but as you know, seen 'em once…seen 'em a hundred times."

The sheriff interrupted him.

"Fireworks? Anybody see you there?"

"Maybe…maybe not, Sheriff. We stayed in the car."

"You didn't pay a visit to the Troyer farm over on Bidgood Road? You know, the place where that nice Amish kid lives? Same kid who stayed at your party the other night?"

"Nice kid?" Brad asked. "You ever see how he treats his horses? The other day we saw that asshole up and punch his horse in the snoot! Three times! Why don't you ask him if he was on the cliff?"

"Answer my question!"

"Sheriff, I don't even know where Bidgood Road is," Brad replied, still testy.

"I don't believe you. My deputy was here till after midnight last night and your car was nowhere in sight. Nobody was. Where were you guys all night?"

"Just driving around the Pond, Sheriff," Nick concluded. He was now acting as the spokesperson for the two. "Must've dozed off... slept in the car. We got up and decided to go fishing."

Boychuk returned his attention to Brad. Here was an immature young man who felt entitled to the good life. How an intelligent loving couple such as the Cahills could raise someone like Brad was a riddle. But a familiar child-rearing maxim in today's parental world was apparent: no matter how good you are to your kids—providing them every opportunity to succeed—there was still a chance they could end up as dickheads. No guarantees these days.

"So rather than driving the hundred miles or so to visit your sister in critical condition, you go fishing? Your priorities are a bit messed up, aren't they, Brad?"

"I spoke to my mom this morning. There's been no change. But I'm leaving right now for Syracuse."

"Let's take a look at your car."

"Why, Sheriff?" Brad asked.

Boychuk, however, had already summoned the two up the hill and in moments was standing at the rear of the black ragtop. The car was covered in dust. Was it the one he had chased—and lost—the night before?

"Open the trunk."

Fishing for his keys in his windbreaker, Brad did as he was told. Inside was the usual automotive gear: spare tire, jack, a few rags and the young man's toolbox. There were no specific odors, such as the smell of kerosene but another item caught his attention. It was a vinyl bag, maroon in color. He'd seen many of these before. He turned his head and locked eyes with the younger Cahill.

"Is that what I think it is, Brad?"

"Just my shotgun, Sheriff," he replied.

"I thought you told me it was in the house. Now I'm finding out that you like to drive around with it in your trunk. It's not hunting season. Won't be for some time."

"Not against the law, Sheriff," Cahill said. "I've got a license."

Boychuk eyed both men closely. He wasn't buying much of their story.

"You have a vehicle, Wells?"

"Yeah, a half-ton...but it's in the shop. Cahill here has been kind enough to chauffeur me around for a while." His smirk returned. "Nice guy that he is."

Boychuk had seen enough. He simply shook his head.

"Go see your sister in Syracuse, Brad. Become an adult for once in your life. You're long overdue." His eyes alternated between those of the two young men. "But don't stray very far." He glared at Nick. "That includes you, too, Wells."

Walking towards his truck, the door was ajar when he stopped and turned and faced them once again.

"One last question, Wells. What's your shoe size?"

The younger man told him. And with that the sheriff walked briskly to his Tahoe, started it and peeled away, spewing gravel in his wake. He had sent a message.

TWENTY-FOUR

NIGHTFALL HAD LANDED with a chilly thud across the county. Carrying a kerosene lantern, Menno was closing the barn door for the night when he heard sounds from behind. He turned his head, expecting to see Rachel or Mama arriving to help him secure the property for the night. Or Joshua. Perhaps he had returned from wherever he had gone for most of the day. He hadn't joined the family for their evening meal or prayers. He had simply removed Temper from his stall and rode off down the road.

The fires from the night before had left a damper of despair over their small tract of land. Upon hearing the news, the elders had amassed with unity and soon wagon after wagon, buggy after buggy, had arrived at the Troyer farm, laden down with staples of food and sustenance for the animals. They had arrived offering solace and support for a shaken family. Their community was strong; they would stay together in grief, much like their forbearers from an ancient land who lived lives of constant persecution.

Menno knew the fires of the night before had scared his family, especially his younger boys, Elijah and Levi, who worked the fields with their eldest brother. At their ages, they looked to Joshua for guidance, for comfort...for *assurance* that he would always be there for them.

Now the younger boys, impressionable and uncertain, were afraid. The children knew the fires hadn't ignited on their own and that Joshua's actions may have been responsible, though Mama had done her best to assuage their fears. Outwardly, she had demonstrated strength; their faith would deliver them from this evil bestowed upon their family, she had told them repeatedly throughout the day.

"We will survive" was the message the children had heard. "We will remain vigilant." Not long afterwards, however, within the confines of their privacy, Sarah too, collapsed in tears. "Our crop is destroyed," she sobbed. "Why are they doing this to us?"

But Menno was less concerned about his hayfields than with his eldest son. The family could purchase feed for his animals, and would barter with the English, offering labor in exchange for what his family required. He could replace his losses. Rather, his worry was with the elders, the bishop and the church district. Their warnings yesterday afternoon were clear and ominous. Joshua's brush with the English, especially the law, was serious. He would be banned, Menno was sure of that.

Now he turned his head in the direction of the footfalls from the rear. Mama, he called out. Are you there? Rachel? Joshua is that you? Nothing. The skies, aided by heavy cloud cover and threats of rain, had darkened quickly. Menno knew that daylight was diminishing rapidly as he prepared his farm and family for the coming winter. Now holding his lantern high in the air in an effort to illuminate the yard, he scanned the property but saw nothing. The English had their flashlights but he would never own one.

His yard became still. Since the fires, he was on edge and perhaps he was mistaken; only the winds, whistling through the hemlocks and birch beyond the rear of the barn, could be heard dominating the night. Were they playing havoc with his ears? Or was he just nervous, expectedly so.

Gently he placed his lantern on the ground in the front of the barn door, lifting an eight-foot plank and securing it across the iron hinges. If Joshua deigned to return, if his desire was to be a part of this family, he would be welcomed. But Joshua must heed his orders and resist temptation. He could rejoin the flock. But all that could wait until tomorrow, for right now he was exhausted. For now, he'd finish up here and make his way to bed with Sarah.

It happened brutally and quickly and without further warning. From behind, suddenly, he felt a pair of arms draped around the shoulders of his slight frame. Another pair of limbs focused on his short legs, tackling him heavily into the red dirt. No voices were heard, as if everything was going according to plan. He tried to turn his head to identify his intruders but was thwarted instantly, his long curly hair pulled violently backwards. These thugs wanted him to know who was in charge.

Now he felt a rope rapidly encircling his arms and feet, and as hard as he struggled, the worse it became. Before he could utter a sound of alarm, a dirty cloth was stuffed into his mouth. Instantly, Menno knew this rag had been doused at one time in some sort of cleaning fluid, perhaps even kerosene. It was making him nauseous.

Then it became totally dark, and not just because the piercing light from his lantern had been extinguished. No, some sort of kerchief was tied around his eyes and now he was seized by a wave of fear, his muffled sounds of protest disappearing into the wind. He was alone with these attackers. There would be no intervention from his family.

What came next would almost be a blur on his memory as he would tell Sarah later. The entire act had encompassed perhaps forty or fifty seconds, but the message was clear. Don't mess with us, his attackers were saying, though no words were uttered. The next sound he heard was a buzzing one, and Menno realized immediately what was happening. It was that of a battery-operated hair-cutting device, similar to the many frivolous products that filled the shelves at Turnbull's in town.

As one assailant held his body to the ground, another yanked him by his curls and began trimming his beard. It had grown ten or twelve inches since he and Sarah had married more than two decades earlier, trimming it only sporadically and only after she had joked that he was dipping it into his soup. He was an adult Amish man; his beard was a symbol of strength, honor, of masculinity. No moustache either, since hair above the lips was associated with military violence and thus forbidden.

Now, in the space of less than a minute, his beard was gone. And so were his attackers, leaving him blind-folded, tied and collapsed in the dust in front of his barn.

TWENTY-FIVE

A T MID-MORNING, Hubie pulled his Ford pick-up into a crowded underground parking garage at the Syracuse hospital. He and Dee knew this visit would be difficult for both of them, but their discomfort paled in comparison to what his sister and her husband were experiencing. Not that he and Dee hadn't suffered their share of losses in their lives. Far from it. But to have your only daughter, not yet twenty-two, desperately fighting for her life was unimaginable. They would do everything they could to help Barb and Roger through this crisis.

Their trip today to Syracuse would have been more direct had they not made a pit stop in Gouverneur, and Hillman's auto parts store. For weeks he had told himself he had needed to replace the hitch pins on his snowplow before winter set in. *Locking* hitch pins that was, since there were reports in the paper that some clowns were driving right up peoples' driveways and stealing the blades. Right out from under their noses, too. If you don't nail everything down in this economy, or in his case, buy the right locking pins, thieves will help themselves. He'd known old Art since their beer-league hockey days; he'd had a wicked slap shot that could rattle a goalie's ears and half his teeth. Hubie knew this first-hand; he was the goalie. Good thing those days are done. Hillman had fixed them up, and ten minutes later they were on their way.

Down Route 11 they went, over rolling hills and past gentle farmland and through villages with names such as Antwerp, a cousin of sorts to its more famous Belgian namesake, and an attractive hamlet called Philadelphia. Not *that* Philly, of course. But he'd guessed that some ex-Pennsylvanian had ventured further north, settled there and couldn't think of a better name. Maybe it was old Ben Franklin himself, but that was unlikely. Antwerp was an unambitious village, too, he thought; its one claim to fame being the birthplace of one Albert Woolson, he being the last man to die in the Civil War. Now talk about bad luck. If only Lee had surrendered to Grant a day earlier?

Villages like this, and hundreds like it were not uncommon, Hubie concluded, with their worn-down clapboard homes and boarded-up businesses. In one way or another, they all suffered the misery of Morgantown. Anything resembling industry had moved out long ago. A gas bar here, an antique shop there. Maybe a laundromat with hand-written signs that scribbled words like 'out of order' on half their machines. Not far away, there would be a general store with a couple of coffee booths. There, old-timers like him, long-retired and worn out like the towns themselves, could spend a few hours every day, solving the world's problems. Before making a reservation at the dirt motel.

The finest buildings, usually one-story, blonde-brick edifices, belonged to the United States Post Office—his employer of nearly thirty-five years. Of course, it was called the postal *service* now, though the service part of it was suffering. It was billions of dollars in the hole, partly because fossils like him who used to send letters were dying off. Just like newspapers. Dying a slow death in an age of the clouds. Over the years, he had heard all the snide remarks about the post office; snail mail being the most common pejorative. But can FedEx deliver a letter from Morgantown to Omaha in two days for *forty-four cents*? Not a chance. Now there was something called *Facebook*, or whatever the hell they called it. But he knew it wasn't for him. He never looked twice at Dee's computer.

"Is that where it was?" she asked as they made their way through Watertown towards the Interstate. Dee pointed to a cluster of modern storefronts that boasted a tanning salon, a Thai restaurant, a gift shop and other promising retail shops servicing the exploding presence of the military. Since the attacks, the 10th Mountain Division had become the biggest game in town, injecting millions into what was just another sleepy upstate town. Now Watertown had become surprisingly mainstream as trendy new stores that had populated only wealthier areas of the country began popping up here. Money has that effect. Attracted by gobs of Pentagon cash, brands that everyone thought would never find their way this far north suddenly discovered shoppers with pockets full of credit cards. The place was booming.

"Yeah, right there," he replied, pointing to the strip mall. "Shame they get rid of beer joints like that but I guess the land under them is worth more than anything they can make selling beer. Still, it was a rocking old barn in my day. The dance floor was nothing but peanut shells."

Dee knew all about the The Arsenal and Hubie's history there. It was the mid-sixties and the Vietnam War was escalating out of control. Bands like *Buffalo Springfield* and *Crosby, Stills, Nash & Young*—not to be outdone by the likes of *Pete Seeger* and *Barry McGuire*—were spitting out one iconic, anti-war ballad after another. It was a scene that set the stage for the rest of his life, his own 'eve of destruction,' he sometimes said.

It was where he had met Donna.

His future spouse, she of the Princess Grace-like cheekbones, was sitting provocatively at the solid oak bar. Her long legs were crossed, her long-flowing reddish-brown hair falling effortlessly down her spine. She had declared to a friend that she was there for one beer only, but that first Genesee turned into many and the next thing she knew she was pregnant with twins and living in some god-forsaken shithole called Morgantown. Her label for the town, of course. She was miserable and never failed to tell anyone who asked. But it was a life of self-inflicted misery, Hubie had concluded. He loved her and so did their girls. It didn't have to be that way.

"Let me ask you…if she hadn't arrived on our doorstep that day," he muttered as they cruised down the road, "stressed out and in trouble, would we have gotten back together?"

Immediately, Dee sensed that Hubie had moved away from the subject of his late wife. He was referring to his daughter, Jane.

"I think so, Hubert," Dee replied. "Jane and I got to know each other very well over those six or seven weeks." She paused for a beat. "She told me how much she loved receiving those holiday cards of yours. Looked forward to them, in fact, though I wished she had picked up the phone…to say hi."

"Yeah, she could have…but then again, so could I," he replied. "Takes two."

Briefly casting her attention away from the gently winding streams and verdant countryside that paralleled the Interstate, Dee glanced affectionately at her partner at the wheel. He was a good man.

"Hubert, here's the truth: the two of you came together when it mattered. And there was no doubt that she loved you."

He returned her smile before continuing their travels.

Now they had arrived at Upstate Medical and within minutes were standing at the entrance to the ICU's waiting room. Right away, they noticed Barbara and Roger sitting across from each other. Absent-mindedly, she was flipping the pages of a *Newsweek* magazine, never stopping long enough to focus on any of its articles.

Roger, on the other hand, appeared lost in thought. His hands were clasped tightly as if in prayer, though Hubie knew his brother-in-law had shunned religiosity since his teenage years growing up in Pennsylvania. Roger had rejected Catholicism, he had told him, when the parish priests arrived at school armed with flip charts demonizing Satan. How could he forget the guilt and fear the men in cloth had instilled in such young minds? After all, here was the devil incarnate, with his fire engine-red horns and matching pitchforks, threatening fire, brimstone and eternal damnation on all humankind if a single act of blasphemy was not penanced out by a Hail Mary or two. The priests had pulled out all the stops, and it was a little too much for a brainy kid like Roger to swallow.

Hubie, of course, never agreed with Roger's take on God. The warrior in him felt there had to be someone up there who made it all happen. Especially in sixty-six, when Hubie pleaded with the *Man* to deliver him from the jungles—still breathing and in one piece—and he figured *He* did.

"Hey," was all Hubie said, announcing their arrival.

Barbara, smiling faintly, dropped her magazine on the coffee table and began smothering them with hugs. The sullen-faced Roger followed suit. After a moment, Hubie asked, "What's the verdict?"

"Still critical, Hubert," Roger replied. "The doctors are keeping her in a drug-induced coma to give her a chance to survive. Dr. Robazza says she's made it through the worst, but we don't know if she'll come around. Or when..." He paused to let that thought sink in. "They don't know yet how much damage has been done."

"This is all so unbelievable, Barb," Dee said, her eyes melting.

"It is, Dee, and I for one am more than a bit pissed off," she said. "Boychuk has kept us up to date though he has little to report. Or maybe he's not telling us everything."

Hubie looked around at the empty waiting room.

"Where's Brad?" he asked.

Barb shook her head in apparent disgust.

"He told me he was coming yesterday morning, but as you can see, he's nowhere in sight. Goddamned kid of mine. You know, his hatred for hospitals is no excuse either. He is just so disrespectful."

"Not just with us, too, honey," Roger said. "With women, especially. Where he developed such misogynistic tendencies, I'll never know. I've been wracking this anemic skull of mine about his behavior for a long time."

Barb changed the subject.

"That so-called boyfriend of Ria's, too, he has to know more about this than he's been telling the sheriff. Just that look on his face, contempt for everyone. What was it that Ria saw in him?"

"I wondered the same thing, often," Dee offered.

Barbara frowned. Then she answered her own question.

"Hormones..."

TWENTY-SIX

A LIGHT MORNING MIST descended over Morgan County, transforming Menno's dusty lane into a series of deep, reddish-brown puddles. The tidiness that Boychuk and his deputy had witnessed the other day was gone. Now, the Troyer homestead had returned to the normal chaos of an Amish farm; a brood of hens, exercising a renewed sense of freedom, were racing about the yard with abandon, ignoring the family's litter of gray-spotted mongrels. Menno's toddlers, outnumbering the canines but not the fowl, stood in blank amazement, their mouths open and eyes frozen as the men in uniform made their way towards the farmhouse. An unmistakable smell of manure wafted over the property.

This morning's visit was prompted by a phone call at daybreak from a familiar voice. Benji Hoggarth was on the line, barely awake, his vocal cords paying the price of too many Mohawk Reds. He was standing next to a tearful Rachel Troyer who, under orders from Sarah, had sprinted across the road to the broken-down trailer. Benji told the sheriff's dispatcher to get the 'boys' over to the farm and fast. He had offered Rachel the use of his phone, but knew she wouldn't accept. Using any electronic device was alien to the Amish.

"Don't know what the hell happened over there, Louise," he growled to the police dispatcher, a woman he knew from Morgantown High and one who used to bowl with his sister. "Menno's kid's here and she's awful upset."

For Boychuk, the trouble that began late Saturday night with the assault on Ria Cahill and progressed to arson was now cascading out of control. He knew that he had to end it quickly or a real storm could develop, as if this wasn't a real problem, already. They arrived to find Sarah Troyer in considerable duress, muttering almost incoherently about the events of the night before. Boychuk never had much of a relationship with Menno's wife. She was always in the background, perhaps deliberately so, when he had visited the farm during better times.

Now all she could do was to direct the sheriff to her husband sitting on the front steps of the house, perhaps forty feet away. His silo-shaped straw hat was tilting downwards, his head resting in both hands as if he were in a state of catalepsy. Given the light rain, his blue overalls were tucked deeply into a pair of rubber boots that reached ambitiously to his knees. His trousers were mid-torso, held only by a single black suspender denoting a sense of humility. It differentiated his order from the more progressive sects further south and east, notably the Amish of Pennsylvania. The two officers made their way towards the frail man, and immediately witnessed a look of defeat on his frazzled face.

"Menno?"

The farmer raised his head for both cops to see the damage his attackers had dealt. Boychuk was stunned. Gone were the woolly, chestnut-red whiskers that were common among Menno and his clan. In their place were clumps of quarter-inch tufts of hair, chopped and ragged and accompanied by a couple of bloodied welts, likely caused by the blades of the electric razor. Though nothing dangerous had been used, it was a hatchet job, clear and simple, for a face that hadn't seen a blade in over twenty years.

"Are you okay?"

"Brian, I am unhurt...but not okay. This was all they did to me, but it was enough."

"Why didn't you call us last night, Menno?" Boychuk said.

Menno shrugged his shoulders in capitulation.

"I didn't want Sarah to call you *today*, Sheriff," he replied, returning to Boychuk's formal title. "What can you do now? After the fires, after all that's happened with Joshua, I didn't want to bring you here, again. But Mama insisted on sending Rachel over to Benji's..."

"Were you able to get any sort of look at them?" Boychuk asked.

Menno shook his head. "I heard a few noises before it happened... but saw nothing."

Boychuk pointed to Menno's dogs now watching the policemen with suspicion.

"They didn't kick up a fuss?"

"Ah, those hounds sleep more than they're awake," the farmer replied.

Jimmy, the deputy, chimed in.

"You say 'they'. You know for a fact that there were two guys? Maybe more?"

"Two were more than enough, don't you think?"

"I'm just glad you weren't seriously hurt," was all Boychuk could contribute. He knew how offensive this act of violence was to his Amish friend.

"I don't know who the men were last night, Sheriff, but I know who is responsible," he said with an element of sadness to his tender voice.

Boychuk acknowledged the truth in Menno's words. Joshua's actions, or more accurately, his indiscretions over the past four or five days had inflamed a number of people, two of whom he would start grilling soon. But as Makenna had said, there was very little physical evidence to link anyone to the crimes over the last forty-eight hours, and he would have to tread carefully.

The cool northerlies had picked up, turning the morning mist into a black pelting rain. Menno rose to his feet, and pulled his dark blue coat together. To Boychuk, these hand-sewn tunics with brass buttons fastened to the neck were a throwback to another era, almost like what soldiers from a ragtag Army of Northern Virginia might have worn more than a century and a half before.

"There's more," Menno said. "Come with me."

He led the county cops around the farmhouse, through the muddy, manure-strewn yard to the rear of the barn. A couple of the family dogs followed closely behind as if to protect their master from further harm. Parked for the night was one of his black buggies; it was horseless, its wooden leads resting on a tree stump. Continuing his walk to the back of the carriage, Menno pointed to its rear flap. In an instant, both cops were shocked at what they saw. Spray-painted in dark orange letters was a clear message:

KRautS!
Go Back to OHio!

"Jesus Lord Christ!" Boychuk blurted loudly, oblivious to the blasphemous words that likely offended the Amish man. But Menno remained unfazed; he'd had the morning to adjust to the new realities facing his family.

"My thoughts as well, Brian," he said with surrender. "Whoever attacked me last night also defamed my property. We're very upset by this."

Staring at the repugnant words on the back canvas of the carriage, Boychuk knew it was retribution of a hateful kind. This vendetta, which may have originated at Remington Pond, was growing. In a few moments, he'd place a call to Webster, summoning him again to the Troyer farm, though the unrelenting rain was probably washing away any possible evidence. Where Menno was jumped last night would not result in any useful clues, and Boychuk knew that. Footprints, too, would be long gone. A few rope fibers could bear fruit, but the kerosene-scented rag stuffed in Menno's mouth to silence him would be of little help. Probably a dead end, the sheriff feared.

Boychuk studied the crudely painted letters once again. There was something odd about them and he couldn't place it. Obviously, the message was sprayed in haste and in near complete darkness, since he could detect a few drips of paint dangling off the second exclamation point. But it was more than that. What the hell was it?

"Have you ever been subjected to this kind of thing before, Menno?" he enquired. "By anybody?"

Menno considered the question for a long moment before replying. He was experienced in the level of rancor aimed at him and other members of his sect.

"Brian, you know as well as I do that your people have called us many names in the past...every single day," he said, a tone of resignation and sadness evident in his voice. "We are not ignorant. We are not stupid. In your world, we don't belong, and we hear that whispered all the time."

"Menno, I didn't mean to imply—"

But the Amish farmer would finish his point.

"Come on, Sheriff," he pleaded. "Let's be honest. We have known each other a long time. I speak the truth and you know that. My people have been called many words in the past. Pigs, animals...*relics* from another time. And other things worse. Many, many times..." His train of thought came to an end. After a long pause, he knew it was pointless to continue. "Never mind, Brian. It is unimportant now. It is what you English call...irrelevant." It was Menno's turn to release a deep sigh. "Well, I have said enough for today. I have some black paint in the barn and I'll cover those words up, somehow..."

Boychuk was dumbfounded. Never had he had more compassion for a constituent, a neighbor, or a friend than he did now.

"I'm sorry, Menno," he said forlornly.

Their eyes came together one last time. The exchange ended with a simple shrug by the Amish man. There was defeat in his eyes and Boychuk knew it.

Without saying another word and shuffling through his pants pocket, the law officer removed a pen knife attached to his truck's keys and reached toward the carriage's back flaps. A portion of the painted message was still fresh in parts. With a couple of pinpoint scrapes, he expertly carved several chips from the buggy's rear cover and dropped them into an envelope from a utility bill. Then, with his BlackBerry, he snapped a picture of the message. Given the darkness created by the rain, its flash went off.

Suddenly, a bellowing voice was heard from behind, startling both cops.

"No photography!"

It was Joshua. He was standing large about ten feet away, his muscular arms crossed defiantly at his chest. Unlike his appearance on Sunday, today he was in overalls and boots not dissimilar from those of his father. Today his traditional straw hat covered his short-ened locks.

"Well, hello again Josh," Boychuk said. "Haven't seen much of you over the last couple of days."

"There will be no pictures, Sheriff," he repeated. "Please put that device away! This is our farm!"

"Sorry, Joshua, but your dad was assaulted, and now we have this," the sheriff said, pointing to the belligerent message. "This is a crime scene, like the fires the other night. Some people, it seems, aren't very fond of you Troyers."

"That may be your concern, but not ours!" he shouted.

Joshua turned towards his father for confirmation, and support. Menno again locked eyes with the sheriff.

"My son is correct, Sheriff," he declared. "There will be no more photographs. Your people took enough pictures this morning. But there will be no more. We will proceed no further."

"You realize, Menno, that this might not be the end of things here?" Boychuk said. "Things could get worse."

Menno traded looks with Joshua and the policemen, saying nothing. Boychuk continued.

"Okay, here's what I'll do. I'll put one of my guys out on the road tonight." He pointed to the rich undergrowth of brush at the edge of the Amish farmer's field. "But anyone could get through over there."

Still no response.

"And, I will need to send my investigator out here again."

"Why Sheriff?" Menno demanded.

"You know what DNA is, Menno?"

The farmer, grimacing, shook his head.

"Long story, but it helps us determine who exactly is involved in crimes. Your son here has admitted that he was with the young Cahill woman on Saturday night, and we will want to know for sure. So, we're going to ask you for a swab—"

"—no!" Joshua hissed.

"You don't even know what I'm saying."

"I don't care! I am not doing anything more in this...affair."

Now Boychuk's ire was rising. The Troyers were making this as difficult as he had imagined they would. "Interesting choice of an English word, Joshua...and accurate as well because that's exactly what we think was going on at the Pond that night."

Menno entered the discussion once again. "Have you not heard a word of what I said, Brian?" he barked. "All of your kind...you put us down. You make us feel we're beneath you."

The sheriff's first instinct was to outshout the Amish farmers. But he knew that wouldn't work. Instead, he took a more concil-iatory stance. He would need their cooperation in future days and the last thing he needed was some sort of freedom of religion stunt. These people knew how to grind justice to a halt, especially if their ways of life were threatened. Besides, there was always some liberal city lawyer ready to pro-bono them, seeking publicity.

"I am not putting you down, Menno. You either, Josh," he re-plied. "What I'm trying to do is exonerate—" He stopped himself short. English was their second language, and that might have been one large word too many. "What I'm trying to do is prove Joshua's innocence in all of this, Menno. I don't think he pushed the girl off the cliff, but we do know he was there that night, and that makes him a witness." He wouldn't use another legally concise word—accessory. Which Joshua was. An accessory.

"So, you have a choice, Joshua. You can voluntarily give us a swab of your saliva...you know, your spit?" Boychuk opened his mouth, pushed out his tongue and with his right hand made a circular motion with an imaginary Q-Tip, "or...I can arrest you under suspicion of being involved in a crime. Bring you into my office, in other words. And then I'd have a judge sign a paper ordering you to give us a sample."

He paused for a moment to let this news sink in. From the look on their faces, a combination of puzzlement and despair, he knew they didn't quite fully understand. But he continued.

"What's it gonna be, boys?"

No answer.

"Okay, I take that as a sign that you'll both cooperate," he said. "My investigators will be over later, and they'll want one of your horse blankets as well. And, oh yeah, an imprint of your bare feet, too, Josh."

"I didn't hurt that girl..." Joshua declared, his eyes nearly tearing up with emotion.

"Well, I want to help you prove that, Josh, if you're telling me the truth."

"I'm not lying, Sheriff."

Boychuk sensed Joshua was incapable of dishonesty but experience warned him to leave nothing off the table. He had faced more than his share of accomplished liars in his day.

"All right, we'll leave now," he said, returning his attention to the elder Troyer. "Trust me, Menno, it's in Joshua's best interests for him to cooperate. In the meantime, you'd better keep your eyes and ears open. This isn't good."

Moments later, Boychuk and his deputy trudged through the mud to their cruiser, the Troyer dogs following closely behind as if to escort them off the property.

"Thought I'd seen everything in the last twenty-three years, but apparently not," the sheriff mumbled as they reached their vehicle. "Time to put a tail on young Wells and his sidekick, if he's around. I'll be damned if they're not involved, somehow. Plant Bill up on the road near the Pond and have him follow them. They have to know we're watching."

"Will do, Sheriff," Jimmy replied.

Boychuk took one long last look at the Troyer farm and turned in his deputy's direction. "And I want you to take a run down to Dutchess County—the Poughkeepsie area—and do some sniffing around about this Wells kid, his family and that sort of thing. The sheriff there's a friend of mine. I'll call him and let him know you're coming. There's got to be more to Wells than he's letting on."

TWENTY-SEVEN

A N HOUR LATER and about two miles away, another Amish wagon laden with hay and pulled by a pair of muscular quarter horses, liver chestnut in color, lumbered into the Zook family farm. The rain had caused havoc to their soiled roads but that didn't prevent the giant beasts from transporting their cargo. Nor did it prevent Hannah, dressed in a dark blue smock from head to toe, from assisting her mother in their garden beside the road. The last of the sweet corn was ready for harvest, as were the green beans, zucchini and celery—always the celery. She raised her head, briefly, at the approaching wagon and then resumed her duties.

"Morning Mrs. Zook...Miss Zook," the driver high above the buckboard said in his unique dialect, tipping his straw hat. "Not a nice morning for such work, is it?"

"That it is," Hannah replied meekly, now making eye contact with the young man aboard the wagon. He was Daniel Jakes, one of the bishop's sons with whom she had spoken at the Troyer farm during church services a couple of days before. Though they were about a year apart, Daniel and his brother Lucas could pass for twins, their sunken, colorless eyes and narrow shoulders being their genetic links to similarity. Like his younger brother, Daniel's long curly locks, hidden mostly by his brimmed hat, were the color of the mud beneath his wheels. Temperamentally, too, many believed they were cloth cut from the same bolt; they exhibited a short fuse, erupting at the slightest grievance, one of which was the arrival of the police that day.

Overhearing their belligerent voices from her post at the serving tables, Hannah knew the Jakes family shared her displeasure with

Joshua's behavior. She knew there was no love lost between Joshua and this Jakes brother, the result of a long simmering feud that had started when they were teenagers. Clearly, it had progressed to this day. She knew also that Daniel was attracted to her, and to his thinking, would make a better suitor. The signals were there.

But before another word was spoken, Mary Zook interrupted the conversation.

"What is the *purpose* of your visit today, Mr. Jakes?" she asked curtly. If this young man was attempting to court her daughter, outside of their Sunday day of restful prayer, she would put an end to it.

"I am on my way to the Troyers," he announced, his senses telling him to tread carefully. "After the fires, my father wanted to help."

"Your family is very generous," Mrs. Zook said, the tone of her voice simmering but formal. Daniel took this as a signal to delve into the Troyer troubles in detail.

"Did you hear?" he asked, seeming to delight in being the appointed messenger. "There was an attack on Menno Troyer at his farm last night."

Though dismay spread quickly across the elder Zook woman's face, there were no elements of surprise in Daniel's news, since young Jakes was already too late; the Zooks were well aware of the incidents at the Troyer farm. After awakening Benji Hoggarth at his trailer, Rachel had continued her early morning travels to the Zook farm to offer the latest bit of information, hateful as it was.

Joshua had displayed such wanton and shameful actions, resulting in such despicable violence against not only his hard-working father but to the rest of the family as well. It was disgraceful, the elder Zook woman felt. Joshua was bringing shame to their order and it would not be tolerated. Daniel's father, the bishop, said as much last Sunday. How could she allow a daughter of hers to marry such a man? Perhaps Hannah should consider another suitor.

"They tied him up and shaved his beard!" an excited Jakes continued. "It had to have been the English once again."

Hannah quickly concurred.

"I agree with Daniel, Mama," she added. "The English and their ways…they don't like us. They're hateful! They don't accept—"

Her mother interrupted the young woman in mid-sentence.

"Hannah!" she bellowed. "Don't spread gossip about things that you don't know!"

"But Mama, who else would do this to the Troyers?"

"I don't know and you don't either," she replied. "We will have to wait for *their* police to determine what happened. It is not up to us."

Sitting high above his wagon, Daniel listened to the dispute between Hannah and her mother and decided to weigh in once again.

"Who else would be responsible for this attack…and those ugly words painted—in orange paint!—across one of his wagons?"

This latest revelation took the elder Zook woman by surprise.

"Of *what* do you speak, Mr. Jakes?"

"You didn't hear? The words, Mrs. Zook, that were painted on the back of their wagon," he said, repeating what the display had read, his voice rising with every new revelation. "Filthy, disgusting *English* words! They were placed there to scare them…to hurt them."

A look of gravity spread across the Zook woman's faces. Rachel had not said a word about the added atrocity.

"No, we were not told about that Daniel," Mrs. Zook finally replied, her daughter listening in silence. "Mr. Troyer is a proud man, a decent man. If we were not told about this incident he had his reasons."

"It was truly hateful," he added. "But don't you agree that they brought this on themselves?" They, meaning Joshua.

"That is for your father and the rest of the district to decide, Mr. Jakes," she replied. "I am sure the church will concur, but we wish them no further harm."

Triumphantly, Daniel felt he had scored a victory. His mission at the Zook farm was now complete, and soon he would score another;

he would deliver the hay, more a symbol of compassion than anything else for a family under siege. Either way, he would win.

"Good day, ladies," the young Jakes said, tipping his hat in respect. "Miss Zook, I do hope we can meet again under more pleasant
circumstances."

Daniel stood high in the buckboard, whipping his horses with
simple grunting sounds to perform a three-point U-turn, and soon
his wagon disappeared down the laneway and out of sight. In silence,
the Zook women returned to their duties in their garden.

Hannah was first to break the uneasy calm.

"It's truly awful what happened to the Troyers, Mama," she whispered, her voice rising in anger. "The English! They must be held
responsible for this!"

Her mother, however, was thinking differently.

"What I can't understand is why Rachel did not tell us about the
painted messages? We had to learn about this episode from Daniel."

TWENTY-EIGHT

DAYLIGHT HAD NEARLY DISAPPEARED when Brad's black Saab convertible turned off the county road and down the lane towards the Cahill camps. Thankfully the rain, combined with whipped-up winds, had come to a halt, at least temporarily since the forecast was glum. What else was new in this part of the woods?

The spin through farm country, north and then east from Syracuse with a side-trip through Lowville, had taken longer than he had expected. But that was fine with him. At Ria's suggestion last week, Natasha had parked her Toyota at home to attend the Labor Day party; today she had pleaded with Brad to take her to the hospital, a request he was quick to fulfill.

He and Natasha had been the first to arrive high above the Pond that Sunday morning, the first to make the grisly discovery. He had witnessed his sister being transported away on a stretcher, bandages filled with blood around her upper skull, staining her once glimmering, strawberry blonde hair.

As Brad entered his sister's hospital room, the events of the weekend suddenly became very real to both him and Natasha. Though tears arrived in torrents to Ria's best friend, his reaction was more muted. Of course, fresh bandages had replaced those of that ugly Sunday morning, exposing only a small circle of her appealing face. Evident also, in true clinical expediency, were tubes leading to every conceivable intravenous platform, the sight of which was hypnotic and depressing. Drip...drip...drip...on and on they went. At the other side of her bed, tilted slightly to prevent further respiratory arrest, was a bank of monitors, each recording every punctuated and programmed breath. God, he hated this.

Though they were close in age, he and his sister—his half-sister, since her father was old Roger—had never been chummy. They grew up in the Pittsburgh suburbs, Ria being the athlete, the leader, the shining star, the exemplar. He on the other hand was content to be *watching* athletes, especially if 'old Rog'—as he referred to his step-father—could finagle a couple of tickets to a Steelers game or two every fall. But he could usually be found in front of the tube every Sunday. At other times, if he wasn't hibernating in the basement of their split-level as a pre-teen at the controls of *Super Mario 64*, or trash-talking while playing *Halo* on his Xbox, or shooting Muslims, post 9/11, in *Call of Duty*, or firing up a reefer out of sight of his nagging parents, he'd disappear on fishing and hunting excursions to the nearby Alleghenies as soon as he was old enough to drive, sometimes with friends, often alone. All the while growing flaccid and lazy from puberty onward.

Of course Ria was captain of her soccer team. And the leader of her track team. And in winters, one of those over-achievers who drove through the freaken snow to the pool at 4 a.m., her aspiration being to win a spot on the U.S. Olympic squad in the 400-metre breast-stroke. Ultimately, however, her international dreams were crushed, not for lack of heart or determination, but for size. Genetics had failed her; the lithe, long-legged, muscular frame required for serious competition was never there. It became a crushing disappointment for the teenager, but she survived.

Naturally, high school had been a breeze for 'The Royal Ria', the label Brad had given her long ago. She'd had her pick of colleges, including the Ivy League. In contrast, he was lucky to qualify for one of the hapless Penn State affiliates near the city, if the word 'qualify' was the correct use of the language, his SATs sucked that bad. That he got accepted the day before classes were set to begin was only through Roger's timely intervention, he being the Carnegie-Mellon prof who had friends in high academic places. A model student Brad was not.

Entering his sister's room, Brad was relieved that he'd brought Natasha along. Immediately, she'd become a buffer between him and his mother, and a welcome one at that. He had been taking a lot of heat from the old lady about his absence from Syracuse—"even your uncle and Dee found the time to come!"—she had thundered. And "where the hell is that shithead Wells?" It was clear to Brad that his mother would not hold her opinions in check but he had tried to balance her attack by declaring that "someone had to stay behind" to clean up their property after the old dude's birthday party. Jesus Christ! What could *he* do, anyway? The docs had purposely kept Ria in a coma for her own protection. It wasn't as if she was suddenly going to wake up anytime soon and see him waiting dutifully by her side.

After his parents left his sister's hospital room, he and Natasha sat for a painful hour-and-fifteen minutes before she asked if he could give her a ride back to Lowville. Like his sister, she had been fortunate to land a job at a primary school there and was expected to greet a herd of rowdy ten-year-olds into her newly-minted fifth grade class, starting the next day. Ria was less fortunate; she would not be showing up for class anytime soon.

Lowville's a nice little place, she had said and "not that far out of your way," her large brown eyes pleading with him in a way that he found irresistible. Though the tears had wiped away her mascara and most traces of eye shadow, she was still smokin' hot, her tight faded denims and cream-colored sleeveless tank-top generously displaying her assets. Before the shit had hit the windmill, not that long ago but what seemed like ages, he'd become smitten by those Angelina lips and, of course, everything else. What guy wouldn't? That midnight stroll away from the bonfire paid good dividends.

They drove in virtual silence, each attempting to absorb the reality of Ria's tragedy, making talk so small that it was soon forgotten. Exiting I-81 at Adams Center, it had begun to rain again but that didn't stop Brad from speeding through the Black River Valley towards the Tug Hill Plateau. More what the Spanish called a 'cuesta', or ridge of sedimentary rock than a plateau, its topography was filled with towering hardwoods, its oaks and birches being the most plentiful. An anomaly, in fact since it was one of the few areas up-country that differed markedly from others in the Adirondack foothills. Brad loved the area. The deer population was abundant and, occasionally, a black bear found itself in his cross-hairs. In winter, it snowed like a bitch here too, what with all that lake effect snow coming in from the big waters to the west. That was good news for him and his power-sledding friends.

After passing a series of antique shops, the odd diner, and signs for handmade furniture along Route 177, the couple soon arrived in Lowville.

"Can you stay with me a little while, Brad," Natasha asked as they pulled up to a two-story, brown-brick building built in the late forties to house returning veterans and their war brides. "I've got some beer."

Ninety seconds later, the sound of the deadbolt attached to her apartment door barely silent, Brad had Natasha pinned against the wall, clumsily lifting her blouse over her russet brown curls, her shoulders rattling a glassed print depicting an Ausable Chasm waterfall with such force that it crashed to the carpet below, miraculously undamaged. No matter. Their pain, or at least hers, would be placed on hold for a while, the difficult visit to the hospital behind them, the memories of that horrible Saturday night assuaged. For now.

Their lips met brutally but only briefly as Brad decided there was greater treasure further south in a pair of bountiful breasts, his tongue welcoming a glorious repeat of the other night. From her purse now resting on the floor, it too a victim of circumstance, they could hear the incessant sounds of an impatient iPhone going off. Immediately, Natasha knew it was her father, the rug dealer from Rome, checking in on her as he did daily since the assault on Ria. Two rings…three…another…yet another, its ring tone echoing the high-pitched detonations of some bearded bouzouki player from a faraway paradise, maybe Santorini or a neighboring isle deep in the southern Aegean. Brad had heard this ring tone before and blamed Steve Jobs; he and his Silicon Valley pals had invented an app for just about everything. Goddammit, he now thought, can't her fuckin' old man give it a rest? What with all this noise, he couldn't concentrate, especially now that he'd become embroiled in a struggle of titanic proportions, this time the clasps of a bra that were responsible for holding up their part of the bargain.

Mercifully, the ringing stopped. Old Constantinidies or Constantinou or whatever the fuck his name was gave up and, mercifully, there was a God; his playful partner never missed a beat. Sensing his hardship, the resourceful second generation American came to his rescue and soon she had given him the gift he'd so desired, pausing momentarily to allow him his lust, her arms wrapped around his expansive shoulders, her eyes now pointed heavenward in pleasure. Then she turned her attention to his belt buckle, itself stubbornly linked atop his relaxed-fit Levi's, the waist of which had grown a peg or two over a consumptive summer. But unlike Brad, Natasha quickly overcame adversity and success was at hand. She allowed his pants to fall to the carpet, her left foot skillfully pushing the fallen picture frame aside. And so did she, collapsing to her knees, taking him fully between her lips and into another wet and welcoming chasm. She would give him what he'd wanted and then some. In time, likely minutes if she was not mistaken, her efforts would be reciprocated. It was all about maintaining equilibrium.

He had stayed for that beer, and two others and then bid her good-bye. Now after a two-hour foray through the forested foothills, he arrived back at the Pond. Where an army of party-goers once frolicked during the hot, late-summer nights only a couple of days before, a gray, almost foreboding sense of gloom had set in. Waves of whitecaps were stirring the large shallow lake into a frenzy, and from this distance he could see his bass boat taking a beating, despite its secure spot on its hoist above the melee. That tub will have to come out soon, he thought, but not before the cash tournament in two weeks. Over on the lawn, where the tent had stood, a group of plastic Adirondack chairs had overturned, strewn about like tumbleweed down the main drag of an abandoned ghost town.

Then he glanced over the stack of firewood that Joshua had delivered on Friday night, now depleted after two major bonfires over the weekend. That was the last time anyone saw his sister, ambling in the dark, pushing a wheelbarrow, before he and the Greek had made their hideous discovery hours later.

"Who the hell did that to her?" a solemn and tearful Natasha had asked him as they sipped a beer, she clothed only in a St. Lawrence T-shirt and he in his boxers. Her eyes were moistening once again. "Who the hell would want to hurt her, Brad?"

He had grimaced at the question. It was one that had consumed his every waking moment since Sunday morning, shortening an already shortened fuse.

"My bet it was that Amish bastard, Troyer," he replied. "You didn't see him when I ordered the firewood. He hauled off and slugged his horse right in the chops! Three-four times! They profess to be all fuckin' peaceful and prayerful, spewing out all that holier-than-thou bullshit, but they're just a bunch of weirdoes from the dark ages. I wouldn't put it past him!"

But Natasha shook her head.

"I don't know, Brad, I just don't think he was capable of something like that…he was so kind to us that night."

"That's because you and my sister got him wasted," he replied, his anger evident once again. "My guess is that he's a mean son of a bitch, and I'm gonna have it out with him…before this is over."

Natasha sat there in quiet contemplation, considering what Brad had said. Maybe Joshua was a mean man. Who knows? He could have lured Ria to the bluff. After all, she'd had her share of vodka shooters, too, and maybe he had demanded sex. What if he pushed her down the cliff when she wouldn't put out? If Brad knew the answers to these questions, he wasn't telling. The police? Well, they didn't share anything with her when they arrived to question her and her friends.

"What about Nick?" she said, changing her line of questioning. "Do we know that much about him? Could he have done it? He was going real psycho on her all night…that look on his face on Saturday, well, I'll never forget it. He was so pissed off!"

Now as his eyes washed over the property once again, Brad knew that he had fudged his response to Natasha. The simple answer was that he didn't know either. He'd accepted Wells' story on face value after finding him outside that tent the other morning, and still accepted it. Where he was all that night was still a mystery, likely banging hoodie girl for all he knew after his sister told him to get fucked. Never mind, he now reminded himself; Ria was in intensive care *because* of one man and one man only. Of that he was certain.

His thought process was interrupted.

From the county road high above the camps, the sounds of a diesel-driven truck could be heard rumbling noisily down the lane. He knew its source, and a moment later came confirmation. The big Chevy Avalanche, asphalt-black like Brad's foreign convertible, pulled up behind his car and a man wearing black denim jeans and cowboy boots stepped out.

"How is she?" Nick enquired. The tone of his voice was distinctly flat, his sentiment incurious, as if he was the warden of a death-row prison and was asking the technician if the deadly serum had done its job. There was no affection, no desire to hear a positive response, just a perfunctory attempt to make conversation. Like asking about the weather forecast.

Brad gazed at the man approaching. The situation was not lost on him. Instinctively, he knew that if Nick and his sister had had any sort of relationship, it was likely over. But what was the breaking point, he wondered? Was it the night that Nick took a poke at the Amish prick? Or was it the suspicion that Ria had seen Troyer again? All he knew was that it was over.

"How do you think?" was all he replied.

TWENTY-NINE

RATCHET WRENCH IN HAND, his large frame draped over
the engine of his John Deere tractor, Hubie was tightening the
last of its spark plugs when the big maroon-colored Escalade pulled
into his driveway, motoring through the peppering rain towards the
opened door of his double garage. He rose upright at the sound of the
arriving vehicle, and so too did Griz, who was sitting tranquilly by
the side. Like his master, his chocolate Lab was a tad over-indulged.
The two had a lot in common; both had turned seventy, and both
were feeling new aches and pains with each passing day.

Through the wipered glass, his sister offered a half-smile before
turning her head forty-five degrees in the direction of the empty passenger seat beside her, evidently searching for something important.
It wasn't Roger, he wasn't there. Likely her damn iPhone, Hubie
thought. Personally, he had no use for cell phones—if anyone wanted
to know where he was, they knew where to look—but if there was
ever a need for Barb to be connected to the world, as thoroughly upside down as it was, now was the time.

It had been four days since he and Dee made the trek south to
offer whatever comfort they could provide. It wasn't much, but they
felt their presence at the ICU was appreciated. What can anyone do
or say under those circumstances? The assault had been only hours
old when they had arrived, but Hubie saw the damage it had already
done to his sister and her fragile husband.

Now as she exited her SUV, dodging the rain pellets, a copy of
the *Post-Standard* acting as an umbrella, Hubie was stunned at his
sister's transformation. Gone was the woman who only days before
could have passed for many years younger, and in her place was an

imposter, exhausted, ashen-faced, even defeated. Stress-induced festoons now encircled her once-striking dark round eyes. Others simply called them sockets or bags but there was no doubt that the long vigils bedside had taken their toll.

Her hair, too, the three-quarter-length business cut that had bounced so stylishly in velvety dark-brown waves, was now different. Maybe due to this monotonous, all-too-common cascade of rain, or simply natural neglect, it looked like it needed a good wash. Either way, this was not the sister he knew. Young Ria wasn't the only casualty of the long weekend.

"Never expected to see you here today," Hubie said as she arrived to the shelter of the garage, kissing him on the cheek.

"Well, her condition is stable, which means that nothing's changed since Sunday," Barbara replied. "And I was growing stir crazy. Just had to get the hell out of there for a few hours, so I figured I'd take a run up here to see my big brother."

"Rog didn't want to leave?"

"He'd never abandon his baby…but for me it was getting to be just too much to handle."

He was about to tell her that she looked spent, but decided against it. What was the point?

"I was just going to get another beer, and you look like you could use one."

"You're reading my mind, Hubert," she replied.

They proceeded to the rear of his long garage, passing shelves filled with paint cans, tools, and other evidence of a male-only refuge. On the far wall, next to a round-shouldered refrigerator so ancient it had a chrome pull lock, was his prized gun-rack, cannonry large and small depending on the pursuit. Even as a kid, many years their junior, Barb knew that Hubert and Johnny, their estranged sibling in Illinois, had taken to the hunt. They lived, after all, so close to the Alleghenies that firing a gun was a rite of passage. If Hubert hadn't been drafted into the infantry around the time of LBJ's escalation, she was sure he would have volunteered for action. What the hell was it about men and their muskets?

Even Barb could recognize one gun from another. There was his moose rifle, a Mannlicher-Carcano, a ghoulish copy of the Italian-made job that created infamy in the space of four seconds at Dealey Plaza nearly forty-seven years before. But effective, she was told, for his trips to northern Québec and Newfoundland. Then there was the Winchester 30-30, his favorite, the one he'd take deer hunting with Boychuk and a couple of his VFW pals, that is if the sheriff could escape his duties. She spied another familiar rifle, this time it was his Remington-Lee .45, an antique he'd purchased with his earnings as a sixteen-year-old stock boy at the grocery store before flying off to Vietnam two years later.

Thank God there were no assault rifles in sight, the military-styled weapons that could fire twelve rounds in two seconds, or with clips that held *thirty* bullets or more. But she knew her brother; he'd never own one. He was a real hunter, a responsible NRA member who stored his ammunition in a safe. Once he told her that if you "miss a deer with the first eleven shells, you need a new hobby. Buy your meat at Price Chopper."

He pointed to a couple of bar stools in the corner of the garage, encouraging her to sit down. Aside from the fallen hemlock beside the river, where he liked to drop a line, this was Hubie's safe house, a destination where years ago he'd escape the travails of the domineering Donna. He'd spent hours cleaning and polishing his guns, knowing full well she'd never enter his lair.

"Was that where you kept that old double-barreled twelve-gauge?" she asked, pointing to an empty bottom rung. She asked the question but knew the answer.

"Yeah, told the cops they could keep that one. Not that I wanted the goddamned thing back, anyway, and so I've kept it empty on purpose. Besides, I like a pump for partridge now…easier to load. Holds more shells. I keep that one locked away in the house." Hubie's voice trailed off, moving in the direction of the fridge, pulling out a couple of cans of Blue Light.

Barbara snapped one open, raised it high and proposed a toast.

"Here's to Jane, the bravest woman we ever knew," she said.

"I should've blown him away myself."

"Nah, you would've gone straight to jail, Hubert, and we wouldn't have wanted that," she said.

Her eyes seemed to wander away in thought.

"I wish I had known her…as an adult, I mean. Oh, I followed her career. It was hard not to when she was on TV every day with Foley. Then when all hell broke loose and her mug was all over the news, it was too late. We would've had a lot in common."

Barbara thumb-pointed toward the house next door. "What's Jo gonna do with that old barn? It's obvious that she and 'Bruce the Boss' love what they're doing. They live in the hills now, too."

"I'm not pushing her," he shrugged. "The kid's stubborn. She'll make up her mind."

Then he moved the conversation to another level.

"You knew that Denny…" he stopped a moment in search of the right words to use but then decided differently, "…well, I just wish I had figured out what that son of a bitch was capable of."

Barbara nodded.

"Joanne told me the whole story…when she and Jane were both eighteen."

"Donna knew too, you know?" he replied. "The secrets, the deceptions. Goddammit, even in death, even after all these years, I can't find the strength to forgive her."

Barbara rolled her eyes. "How in hell did we both end up married so young?"

"Well, I got Donna knocked up, that's how."

"True…and there was no such thing as *Roe v. Wade* then."

"Are you kidding?" Hubie asked. "Donna was Catholic. She never would have considered going that route...and for that matter, me neither. Glad it never entered the equation."

"Guess so, bro...but that doesn't explain my choice in a first husband."

"What the hell was that guy's name again?"

She smiled. She had almost forgotten, too.

"*David*...the asshole's name was David! About ten years ago, I heard he moved to Hilton Head after finding some rich divorcée down in Dixie. Got remarried but no kids that I know of. Why would he? He never wanted anything to do with Brad, so I'm not surprised. To him, his kid never existed. Probably another source of my son's anger..."

Hubie nodded.

"Maybe, but what I was going to say was at least you got rid of that guy early."

"He dumped me, remember, Hubert?"

"Yeah, but I like to think that you would have seen the light and gotten the hell out. You had your education, and a new career in the works. In my case, I couldn't. Donna never thought about going back to college. We could've moved to Syracuse. She could have tried getting into med school—as a mature student. I hear it's done all the time. But I sometimes think she liked playing the victim. You know, 'woe is me' and all that? All the while painting me as the villain. All her goddamned life..."

Barbara could feel his pain. One bad decision can wreck your life. But she would close on a high note.

"But, remember, Hubert, she gave you two wonderful daughters. Don't forget that."

"You're right. But Jane, well, she should've been your daughter, not mine," he said, now grinning. "As liberal as she was."

"I would have traded you for my son..." she allowed, taking an-other deep drink of her beer. "I don't know what I'm gonna do with the kid."

Hubie shrugged.

"Not a kid anymore, Barb. Brad's twenty-four friggin' years old. It's time he figured things out for himself. Christ, when I was his age—"

"I know! Tell it to me once more! You were in Vietnam firing off your howitzers and shooting gooks as you so inelegantly put it then! I was only ten years old and yet still can remember you saying that when you'd come home on leave."

"Hey! Don't bust my balls, here!" he thundered. "And I don't say things like that, at least not anymore. I was only making a point."

Immediately, Barbara was ashamed at her outburst. That her nerves were inflamed was no reason to carve her brother a new orifice. Besides, despite their ages, she needed his strength, his resilience, his cool, placid demeanor to help her get through this ordeal.

"I'm sorry, Hubert," she said. "Didn't mean to..." She took an-other hard swig from her beer. "I need another one of these!"

"Coming up," he said, accepting her apology. "Not your fancy Chardonnays, but they get the job done." She watched in admira-tion as he made his way to the fridge. Her brother, though a man of simple tastes, was not a simple man. He had been beaten down by a difficult spouse for decades, but it never reduced his love for his girls. His words began to resonate.

"You're right," she began. "Brad's not a teenager anymore. He was such a sullen kid who preferred to be by himself...all the while Roger and I were so wrapped up in Ria and her sports. We made our mistakes. Unfortunately for Brad, everything revolved around her. Oh, we tried. And Roger tried. He'd take him to a Penguins game once in a while, but that wasn't enough. They say parents have to work hard *not* to create favorites among their kids, and I guess we failed at that."

Hubie looked at his sister with sympathy. There wasn't much more he could do but listen. But an ear was what she needed right now. That and an observation or two.

"Can't keep beating the hell outta yourself, Barb," he said. "The good thing about being twenty-four is that he has tons of time to figure it all out. But he'll have to find the magic formula by himself."

Barbara nodded in agreement. Their eyes locked for a few moments in time. She loved this guy.

"I'm worried, though," she said, finally. "Boychuk's been telling me about this Amish kid and his family and what they've been going through. Their hayfields were torched? And now some sort of late-night assault on the dad? Not sure if the sheriff is saying that Brad's involved, but he brought it up. You know, Brad finally came to the hospital the other day. Finally! But could I get anything out of him? No. And then there's that deadbeat pal of his, Wells. Wouldn't put it past that kid to do anything, including hurting my Ria..."

Her eyes moistened at the mention of her daughter. Quickly, however, she regained her composure.

"Don't know, Barb," Hubie responded. "Brian's looking into everything. Either he's keeping his powder dry for now or doesn't have a clue what happened. One thing though..."

"What?"

"Well, it seems to me that Brad's more a follower than a leader. This kid Wells, now he strikes me as the instigator—"

"—me too, Hubert," she interrupted. "Exactly what is behind those eyes of his, I'll never know."

Nodding, Hubie turned his attention back to his gun rack again before speaking. "Then again, sis, Brad has a brain. He knows right from wrong. Or *must* know the difference. Just hope he hasn't gotten himself in too deep."

Two beers led to another, and then a fourth and before they knew it, the Schumacher siblings had a good buzz on, alternating grief with gales of laughter. From the front of the garage, a rain coat draped over her shoulders, Dee arrived to find the nearly inebriated pair. So lost were brother and sister in themselves that they failed to see her standing there, grinning.

"So, this is where the party is," she announced.

Barb and Hubie looked up in unison, surprised that they were no longer alone, and burst into laughter.

"Looks like we're going to have company for dinner—and for the night," Dee said. "Either that, or I'm gonna have to confiscate someone's keys."

204

THIRTY

THE YOUNG MEN pulled into the parking lot of Swigs, a ramshackle watering hole located across the county road from Remington Pond. From the outside, the place looked as if a couple of double-wide trailers had been fastened together, end to end, its main entrance being a single glass door under a covered porch abutted to a graveled parking lot. Years ago, its pine siding had been painted a hideous shade of purple, prompting locals to believe its owner—dubbed 'Dandy Randi' for a reason—bought the paint at fire-sale prices.

Above the porch was a back-lit sign that offered chicken wings at modest prices every Thursday night. But its message was more implied than real, since several block letters had fallen down—or were stolen—and were never replaced. No matter; Swigs' patrons got the gist. They didn't spend time worrying about how the joint looked. They were more concerned that its owner retained her tenuous hold on her liquor license.

Randi, now pushing fifty, was a busty natural blonde with five marriages under her belt. She had been reprimanded more than once for selling booze to minors. A conspiracy theorist, she called it entrapment, clear and simple, and her customers had agreed. Don't the cops and state inspectors have better things to do? Besides, she said, the drinking age was a farce: how can you deny a veteran from Iraq a Miller Genuine Draft because he was only twenty?

"Don't know how you talked me into this," Brad announced as Nick found the last space in the parking lot for his monster truck. "Don't need this shit."

"Relax, ant-hill," Nick replied curtly. "What are ya gonna do? Stay cooped up in that crappy little cottage all your life? Watching one channel by rabbit ears on your old man's fifteen-year-old TV? Christ, we need this."

"All right...a couple of beers and then we can leave."

"Whiskey's in my future, too!" Nick said, his eyes now sparkling with excitement. "I'm gonna get to know a guy named 'Jim' better... Jim *Beam*, that is."

Brad shook his head. "Okay, but we'll have to take a cab back. Don't forget Inspector Gadget over there." He pointed over his shoulder in the direction of the police cruiser that had pulled up about a hundred yards away. Over the past two days, the boys had noticed the cop following their every move.

"Boychuk's trying to fuck with our heads." Brad's contempt was clear but so was his unease. "Not exactly inconspicuous."

"Who gives a shit, Cahill?" Nick replied dismissively as they made their way into the dimly-lit establishment. The packed parking lot was an accurate reflection; the place was filled with locals welcoming an early start to a fresh weekend, as if the previous Labor Day holiday wasn't enough. Like the end of the week—any week for that matter—was distinguishable from the next. Most of Randi's customers were day-laborers toiling in odd jobs, scratching for work anywhere they could find it. Like digging new leach systems or doing small-time carpentry or plumbing. Others were simply content collecting disability checks from the federal treasury.

As the young men settled on their stools, Brad could see Randi engaged in playful banter with a couple of men down the long Formica-topped bar. He recognized them; one was that dirt farmer from over on Bidgood Road. The other, a wafer-thin man about forty with coat-hanger-shaped shoulders, an ear stud and a scrawny goatee, was plowing through a plate of wings and fries. The roofing contractor got his name in the paper last week, and not in a good way. A divorced father of six, he had cooked the books to appear destitute, and was busted for food-stamp fraud. He was sipping an amber-colored O'Doul's, taking in the action behind the bar.

Dandy Randi didn't disappoint. Tonight, she was wearing a pair of tight black Wranglers and a spaghetti-strapped white top. Her hair, normally loose-fitting across her shoulders, was now tied in a librarian's bun, revealing a pair of earrings—Christian fish symbols—that danced when she strutted from one end of the bar to the other. A smart move, Brad thought; Randi knew her 'god-and-rod' clientele. Around her low-cut neckline was a thin silver chain. It was nudged strategically close to her considerable cleavage, sporting a single shiny cross that warned her patrons, men, of course, they would go straight to hell if they stared too long in one place. A bit close to the hill, if not over it, Brad felt, but a tidy parcel nonetheless. In a milfy sort of way.

"Goddamnedest things I ever heard," she said over her shoulder to the regulars as she made her way to Brad and Nick. "First, they burned their hayfields and then jumped the poor guy and shaved his beard. I heard they spray-painted his buggy too." She was now in front of them, dropping menus on the bar. "Evenin' boys, what can I get you?"

Nick was the first to speak up.

"You talkin' about that Amish farmer?"

"Yeah, someone's out to get 'em," she replied. "If it's a draft you want, I have Bud, Bud Light and Genesee. Or maybe somethin' stronger? A shot of bourbon?"

"None of that Genny crap for me. I'll take a Bud Light and a shot of Turkey, neat," Brad replied.

But Nick wasn't ready to order. His curiosity was piqued.

"So, what're the cops sayin', darlin'"? he asked.

Darlin', the kid calls me, Randi thought, a regular Romeo. But she had learned long ago to play along with horny men, no matter the age, harmless as they were, provided they were old enough. This kid qualified by at least a couple of years.

Two stools away, Benji piped in.

"Not much, other than kerosene was used," he growled. "Hell, I knew that right away. I could smell that stuff from my house. Boychuk hisself chased some vehicle the night of the fire but they lost him in their dust. Saw Menno today, too, and he looked pretty shook up. Wouldn't be surprised if he and his brood upped and moved away. That's what they do."

A clearly amused Nick peered down the bar at the farmer. "Just because of a little fire damage?"

"More than a little damage, hon, he lost nearly his entire crop," Randi added as she tapped out a draft for Brad. "You want one of these too?"

"Nah, make mine a real Bud," he said. "I'll leave that pussy shit for fat-ass here. He needs to go on a diet, anyway. And make my shot a Jim Beam." Nick returned his attention to the men a couple of stools away. "Spray paint, eh? What'd they write?"

"Called 'em names and told 'em to go back to Ohio," Benji said. "Saw it myself."

"That's where all those fuckers should go," Nick snarled. "Multiplying like rabbits. Can't drive down any road these days without runnin' over their horseshit and, 'course, one of these days, I'm gonna slam into one of 'em. Driving their wagons at night without lights. And who's this Boychuk? A trooper?"

"Sheriff," the goatee offered. "Local boy who doesn't put up with much from anyone, and from what I hear, he's not happy with what's goin' down."

"Is that so," Nick said, sipping his beer.

Brad listened to the banter in silence. He'd downed his bourbon in one gulp and signaled to Randi for another. Over the bar, resting on crudely-built shelving that was sagging down the middle, were a couple of ancient Emersons, the analogue models, each weighing about eighty pounds. One screen had the Yankees playing Baltimore, or so Brad figured as he watched the Bronx faithful, about fifty-five thousand strong, rising to their feet in ecstasy. Then the screen cut to someone by the name of Swisher rounding the bases. Guess he hit a home run to win the game in the ninth. But who gives a crap? He fished, fucked and slept, and never cared for baseball. He was from Pittsburgh after all. The Pirates never won.

The other set was tuned into one of those trivia games, boastfully called *BrainBusters*, the type where some question appeared on screen and players operating a wireless console butted heads over the satellite with stoolies everywhere. Only they used pseudonyms, never their own names.

"Groundhog Day!" Brad bellowed, answering a digitized question about the Bill Murray film where a guy lived the same day over and over. "Jesus, too friggin' easy, they better give this game another name!" Brad's outburst was loud enough for a rotund woman down the bar to glance in his direction before punching in her vote. Her thick gray hair was pinned back so tight that it couldn't be penetrated by a diamond drill bit. Offering a Texas smile in gratitude, long enough to expose only a lone pair of nicotine-stained front teeth, Brad recoiled in disgust. He returned his attention to the ball game. Now the players were greeting Swisher at home plate, grown men, millionaires all, jumping up and down like Little Leaguers in victory.

The more they talked about Troyer, the more irritated Brad was getting. His sister's face, now jaundiced and scabbed, kept haunting him. Being kept alive by a friggin' respirator while the cops were doing squat. After all, the guy was living under their nose. No secret about that.

A towel thrown over one shoulder, Randi was sipping a Diet Coke and watching Brad pumping back the booze. She seemed to be reading his mind.

"How's your sister doing?" she asked.

For a moment, Brad was taken aback by the question. But then he remembered that Ria's fall on to the rocks at Remington was big news around the community. Never mind *Facebook* in these parts, that's if any of these chumps had ever heard of it. They get their news from the bartender.

"She's alive but barely," he replied, his anger continuing to rise. "Docs tell us that she's out of immediate danger, but who knows if she'll fully recover. Might have to learn how to walk and talk again, for Christ's sake! The son of a bitch!"

"Sorry to hear that," she added. "Ria? That's her name, right?"

Brad nodded.

"I used to see her jogging down this road...training for something, I figured?"

"Yeah, she's a triathlete. Working her ass off. Was supposed to compete in Vermont next Saturday, too. Now, nobody knows if or when she'll do that again."

"Cops saying anything?"

"Nah, they're fuckin' useless!" Nick interrupted.

Randi frowned. "Hey, pal, keep the F-bombs to a minimum, okay?"

"Will do...sorry." This time he dropped the flirtatious response. From the look on Randi's face, it wasn't working anyway.

It was Benji's turn to speak up.

"Wait a minute, here," he said, turning in Nick's direction, his grisly-sounding voice growing deeper. "Didn't you just say that you never heard of Boychuk, the sheriff? He's the one investigatin' these cases. Seems you might know more about this than you're tellin' us, kid."

That set Nick off. His face flushing, he'd been busted.

"What's it to ya, old timer?"

Like Brad, Benji had been mixing beer with high test, downing shots of Wild Turkey in one swallow. Randi noticed and replaced it. Benji peered down the bar again in Nick's direction, and shook his head.

"Well, all's I'm sayin' is that you seem all too interested in everything that's gone down…especially what everyone here's talkin' about and all."

Nick continued his contempt.

"Well, *aaaall's I'm say-yun'*," he repeated in an exaggerated southern accent, "is that I woke up today to find that I'm livin' in the friggin' Bluuue Riiidge!" Nick let out another burst of laughter. It was amusement not shared by his stool buddy, Brad. Wells had a unique ability to piss people off, he thought.

"Guess the sheriff was right," Benji muttered in goatee's direction. "He knows someone like this dickhead here is behind all this shit. He qualifies."

Nick smirked once again.

"It seems the man here has a bit of the 'tude going on, don't it ant-hill?" he said derisively. "But an appropriate response for a man of his intellectual capacity, I'm thinking, would be to ask a pertinent question: do you know the difference between an idiot and a moron?"

"There's a difference?"

"Oh, yeah big fu—" Nick caught himself midstream, not wanting to anger Randi any further. "Big effing diff, my man. An idiot is a *stupid* person…" He paused for a moment of emphasis, making sure he was getting his message across, "and, generally, he's a guy with the mental equivalent of a toddler under three. On the other hand, a *moron*—" He stretched the word out for greater effect. "—is almost as stupid, but he has the mental age of a seven-to-twelve-year-old!"

He glanced at himself in the mirror and winked.

"So, old timer, where do you sit on that scale?"

It happened quickly. Randi's stools, their legs made of polished chrome and as heavy as anvils, were not easy to displace. But the one chosen by Benji crashed noisily to the floor as he lunged fist first at Nick. How he avoided Brad, his immediate seat-mate, and made it to Nick's place so rapidly was nothing short of amazing, the bartender would later tell her patrons, Benji's bum leg and all. She'd never seen him move that fast. What she also remembered were the farmer's bulbous, rage-filled eyes as he leapt toward the younger man.

Though Benji's move was forewarned in the bar mirror, Nick seemed to be a moment late and a dollar short in his defense. With a fist the size of a Florida orange, Benji landed a sucker punch to Nick's cheekbone, just below his right eye socket, knocking him off his stool and hard to the pine plank floor. In seconds, he was on top of the fallen Nick, continuing the onslaught. Benji's next blow was aimed at the younger man's nose but a pair of crossed arms rose up for protection.

"What the fuck, old man?" Nick cried. "—'ya fuckin' insane?"

His back to the floor, Nick caught a glimpse of Brad. He was an interested bystander choosing neutrality, a smile cracking his lips. Behind the bar, Randi watched as other patrons, suddenly alarmed, reacted to the noisy fracas. She had been in this business since the early eighties, even before Reagan outlawed teenage drinking, and had seen her share of beer-induced battles. Curiously, she held back this time. She would let this one take its course. Maybe old Benj would show the kid a thing or two, lippy as he was. It would be over soon with no real damage done.

With only grunts and growls coming from his tobacco-damaged throat, Benji took the lack of Randi's interference as permission to continue. He sensed that she had seen too many cops already, and unless it got totally out of hand, it would be up to him to settle this. Besides, his twenty-five years as a dirt farmer had toughened him.

He would teach the punk a lesson.

But Nick had other plans. His arms still crossed railroad-style, he was successfully warding off the farmer's further blows. There was one way, and one way *only* to end this donnybrook, he decided. Despite two shots of whiskey and as many beer chasers, Nick's youthful fitness reigned supreme. With jackhammer-like swiftness, he aimed his right kneecap in a straight line to Benji's penile package and in a second or two the battle was over.

Emitting a loud groan, the farmer rolled over hard to the floor, writhing in pain, his face contorted in instant defeat. Goatee man, his mouth filled with fries, had remained silent and inactive throughout the skirmish. Finally he left his stool to go to the aid of his friend.

"I rest my case, you fuckin' moron!" Nick exclaimed, rising to his feet, his hand nursing his facial wound. He could feel it swelling quickly, a shiner was on its way. He turned toward Brad, who was still sipping a beer at the bar. "Thanks a lot, Cahill!" he cried. "Why didn't you stop this motherfucker?"

Brad shrugged, a smile escaping his lips. "If you can't handle old Benji, who can you handle? Course it took a shot to the stones to win. That was too easy."

Randi listened to their conversation for a moment before making her decision. Wagging her finger towards the door, she barked, "You and you! Out! Now!"

She was furious, and Nick knew it.

"Call us a cab," he said, slapping a couple of twenties down on the bar as he and the bartender glared at each other.

"Keep the change...*darlin'!*"

With a suggestive wink, his glare turned into a smirk and they were gone.

Minutes later, as the sheriff's deputy watched from his cruiser, the two young men lit up a smoke under the bar's sunken porch. Soon, a taxi pulled up to the bar and with one act of final defiance, Nick cockily saluted the officer before jumping into the awaiting car. The deputy watched as the taxi sped off in the direction of their Cahill compound down the road, before pulling his Tahoe into Swigs' graveled lot and entering the bar.

"You just missed the action, Bill," Randi said, greeting the officer with a shrug. Still moaning in agony, Benji had returned to his place at the bar, his head resting uncomfortably across his arms. "But we're okay now."

"Action? What kind of action?"

"It was settled real quick," Randi replied. "We're fine."

"Something I should know about?"

"Nah," she said, glancing again at Benji. By now, goatee man had his arm around the shoulders of his friend, as if to console him in his pain. "Nothing broken, as far as I can determine."

"All right," the deputy said as he scanned the bar. "I'm more interested in those boys who just left. Assume they were pumpin' them back?"

"Well, Bill, they weren't here to play bingo," Randi replied. "But I sent 'em packing. What can I do for ya?"

"You clean their glasses or throw out their bottles yet?"

She looked at him in surprise.

But then it clicked.

"Nope. They're right here," she replied. He produced a couple of plastic bags and Randi obliged. The evidence was collected and soon he was out the door.

THIRTY-ONE

THE MORGAN COUNTY SHERIFF'S OFFICES were housed at the rear of the Court House, a handsome, clock-towered, copper-and-sandstone edifice built with the same quarry stone from Potsdam that a few Ivy League colleges chose for their campuses. Before the turn of the last century, fire had destroyed its eighty-year-old predecessor, but county fathers had learned their lesson. In true Romanesque style, the rebuilt structure was a regal replacement. Its foundation walls were made of granite five feet thick, its doors iron-clad, the walls a glazed tile. The only hardwoods used during its gay nineties construction phase was an elegant balustrade on the staircase leading to a pair of ornate, Perry Mason-like courtrooms upstairs.

County planners were determined to learn from their mistakes; there was no way that court records would be lost again. There was no way that prisoners would be released from custody, again, for a lack of said papers. As a student of the county's history, Boychuk felt his predecessors were truly visionary. For sixty thousand bucks, the august edifice instantly became the most attractive building in town. And it still was, a hundred and twenty years later.

After a relatively quiet night and a breakfast with Susan that consisted of about twelve spoken words, Boychuk arrived at the office just after seven-thirty. Other than Louise, his dispatcher, and a couple of his men gathering clipboards and other pre-patrol paraphernalia, the chief county cop was virtually alone. He was about to grab the keys to his Tahoe and join them out on the road when his deputy strolled into the office carrying his treasure, his chest bursting from under his flak jacket. This looked like good news.

The opportunity to grab a fingerprint or two from the boys might mean he could place one or both of them at the scene of the fires. Not that the prints would be admissible but that didn't matter right now. He just wanted to know. He still didn't think Brad capable of arson, not to mention an assault on the Amish farmer, but who knows? Now young Nick could be culpable. The day before, Boychuk's team, still scouring the woods behind Menno's house, had discovered a metal kerosene can hidden behind an abandoned beaver dam on Murdock Creek. This finding had held out hope. Prints lifted from the container might link one of them to the scene.

"Good work!" he beamed. An encouraging word at the right time was always good for staff morale. "Now give Webster a call and tell him you're on your way."

"Thanks, Sheriff. Will do."

"You went back to the Pond after the bar?"

"Yeah, Wells left his truck at Randi's and it's still there this morning. I double-backed to the Cahill places and the black Saab was parked beside the big house. So, I don't think they went anywhere. No doubt they saw me. Guess they didn't want to risk a DUI."

"DUI might be the least of their problems," Boychuk muttered.

"Seems there was some sort of altercation in the bar before I got there."

"What kind of altercation? A brawl?"

"No signs of a brawl but maybe a serious misunderstanding at the very least," Bill replied. "Randi was tight-lipped about it all, being as sensitive as she usually is to us being around. Benji Hoggarth didn't look too good sitting there and it wasn't because he was drunk, at least not by that time. I suspected there was some sort of disagreement."

"Think it was Wells? Or Cahill?"

"My money was on Wells," the deputy said. "When I saw them pull into the parking lot, initially, I figured they were planning a night of it. But they left all too soon. After a half an hour or so. And, Brian, just the way he saluted me before they jumped into their cab was, well, it was like he was sayin' 'up-yours-and-the –Smokey-hat-you're-wearin'."

Boychuk grimaced. It appeared that his chief suspect, make that plural right now, kept finding reasons to increase his suspicion. Earlier this morning, he had poured over Webster's preliminary report of the crimes, the few pictures he had, including a blown-up version of the buggy message, a photo that Boychuk himself had taken.

Of course, Menno wouldn't allow the technicians to take any more photos, including any close-ups of his after-dark trip to the barber. That was forbidden. The paint chips that he'd scraped from the carriage probably came from a paint can that could have been purchased at Turnbull's or Lowes or any paint store within a sixty-mile radius. Dime-a-dozen, in other words. Maybe Webster can zero in on a specific brand or chemical. There were no aerosol cans in sight when he'd ordered Brad to open his trunk the other day. Not that they couldn't have simply bought one the day after. He'd have Bill check out the stores.

"Okay, maybe you should truck on down to the Pond once again," Boychuk said. "Stay close enough to smell the bacon. Even though we don't have anything hard to go on, those guys need to know we're watching."

As Bill turned and left their office, Boychuk returned to a couple of black-and-white photographs in front of him, shots of the footprints in the earth high above the cliff. The big-footed one might have belonged to Joshua Troyer, but who owned the other indentations? Ria? Likely, but Webster said he found others. But unless he started measuring every foot size in the county, these prints might be useless.

Certainly, the vaginal swabs, processed at Hargreaves before Ria was choppered to Syracuse, had proven that intimate, likely consensual activity had taken place. Then there was the blanket. That had to be a garment similar to those used by the Amish for their horses, since the fibers Webster found in the grass were consistent with samples that came from Joshua's horse, Temper.

All and all, he felt he was building an accurate picture of what had happened that night, a night that seemed a lifetime away now, though it occurred only six nights before. Of course what he didn't know was who torched Menno's fields, or—speaking of another Remington—who shaved away his beard. Probably the same jackasses who spray-painted his buggy. But those crimes, serious as they were, couldn't measure up to the assault on Ria Cahill. She may never recover and so the question remained: who the hell swung that goddamned birch log?

Glancing out the nearby window, now being battered by a cool, driving rain that had covered the entire northeast, Boychuk realized it would be another dank, blustery day that always affected the moods, including his own, of many of his constituents. Days like this often meant trouble, particularly as fall set in. Then his thoughts returned to the artificial conversation he'd had with Susan as they refilled their coffee mugs and were out the door. They lived under the same roof, slept in the same bed but, in reality, were just roommates. As the day progressed, he'd place his daily call and, most likely, reach her voicemail. He'd tell her again that these cases were all-consuming and not to expect him for dinner. Not that it mattered; Susan had always made other plans, usually with friends or colleagues, or maybe even another lover for all he knew. That's how out of sync they were with each other. Something had to happen soon.

He was about to gather the evidence together and place it in a now-bulging file when the phone on his desk rang. Immediately, he knew its source: it was his senior deputy, Jimmy McKelvie, on the line and he was calling from Poughkeepsie. Boychuk, leaning back in his swivel chair, plopped his feet on his desk. There might be some news in this call.

"Figured I'd be hearing from you this morning," the sheriff said. "Is it pissin' down rain there too?"

"Oh, yeah, all last night and the same for today. Getting cooler as well. Summer's definitely done, Brian."

"How are things coming together?" Boychuk abruptly changed the subject. He wasn't a meteorologist. Small talk didn't interest him.

"Learning quite a bit here, I'm almost sorry to say," Jimmy said.

"Give it to me."

"Well, as you suspected, and as your Dutchess County friend told me, this Wells kid has been a shit-disturber for a long time. Misdemeanors, mainly. Some shoplifting when he was younger. Once he got picked up in Woolco with stuff he stole only minutes before at K-Mart, which wasn't very bright. Fights in school. Fights with neighbors over just about everything. You name it, young Wells was a pain in the ass. Not just at home, either. At bars, gas stations. Even at the post office!"

"Wait a minute!" Boychuk interrupted. "Wells told the Schumachers his dad was a judge. That he wanted his kid to go to law school. Maybe follow in his footsteps. Made it sound like he grew up on the right side of the tracks."

"I remember you saying that, Brian. But it appears that none of it was true. Far from it. This kid didn't exactly grow up in a Disney household."

"How so?"

"Well," Jimmy continued, "his old man was a guy who probably never set foot on a college campus, let alone a judge's chamber. More likely, he was standing in front of one."

"Jesus."

"Yeah. First visit I paid today was to his mom. She's the assistant manager at a dollar store here and, get this, she was filling birthday balloons with helium when I met up with her. Believe me, she gave me a mouthful. Seems she divorced old man Wells when Nick was a kid, and doesn't have a clue where her husband is. Skipped out on support payments years ago."

Boychuk removed his feet from his desk and sat up straight. This was important.

"Spill it!"

"Well, the first words outta her mouth were, 'what did the little bastard do now?'"

The sheriff listened with keen interest before hanging up the phone. It was coming together. No doubt about it.

THIRTY-TWO

TO INCESSANT POUNDING NOISES coming from the back door of his trailer, Benji opened his eyes and realized he had survived another night. He wasn't sure if the constant bang, bang, bang he was hearing originated from his aching cranial cavity or from the kitchen beyond the narrow hallway leading to his bedroom. Maybe both. It had been a rough night at Swigs, and not just because he'd had too many Old Milwaukees.

Raising his head above the pillow, he gazed beyond the cracks in the Venetian blinds covering his bedroom window. The yard behind his carport was cluttered with sawhorses, a rusting tractor-mower, and the shell of an eighties era Chrysler New Yorker, his first clunker and a hand-me-down from his dad. A soft blanket of mist, battleship gray to the naked eye, had covered the county for the past few days, and it remained in place this morning. The rain jarred a memory or two; the loss of his prized Buffalo Bills cap somewhere between the bar and the trailer being one of them. But he'd swear on a buckboard of Bibles that he couldn't remember how he got home, though there was nothing new about that. In all likelihood, Brookbank, the re-formed drunk, had delivered him from evil—Brookbank being his stool-mate at Randi's.

Of course, another memory quickly came to Benji's fuzzied mind. The battle he'd had with Wells at the bar. More like a skirmish and a short-lived one at that. Now it wasn't a total loss; the kid will have a tidy little shiner to nurse this morning, he was happy to recount. To Benji's chagrin, however, the only thing that Randi and her customers would remember would be the lucky strike to the gonads, rendering him just another old man suckered by a youngster playing to win. The fight over in seconds, her patrons were all too quick to return to their real mission, a jug of draft and the chicken wings special.

Then he peered at the digital clock on his dresser; it was one of those Cartex clock radios, a back-lit job with a faux-oak cover and larger than a red brick. Though it was likely accurate, the back-lit part no longer worked and it was a strain just to figure out the time. Gawwwd, it was only eight-oh-one in the friggin' morning! Who the hell is here this early? He wasn't scheduled to work today.

Slowly, he climbed into a pair of denim overalls, the same blue jeans he'd worn to the bar the night before, pulling its suspenders over bare shoulders. Then he bent his aching body down to a side table next to his bed, reaching for a Mohawk Red. No matter what happened to him during the night, his smokes were never far away. Lighting up, dragging the poisonous fumes deep into his lungs, he trudged toward the kitchen, groaning at the sight of a sink filled with dishes dirtied from two nights before. There, among the refuse was a plate that was beyond saving, displaying the caked-on remains of mac 'n cheese that he picked up at the Valero, his favorite when smothered in ketchup with a side of sausage links. Steel wool wouldn't be able to remove those stains. Might just have to turn it into a Frisbee, he thought.

He cast his eyes around the trailer. The sink wasn't the only sign of disarray; in fact, the entire single-wide could have qualified for federal disaster relief. No matter. He was a bachelor and bachelors did whatever the hell they wanted. The knocking continued. Couldn't be Brookbank at the door; Brookbank would've barged in by now.

From his position in the kitchen, Benji could see a lone figure at the door, peering through the glass. He was about to greet his visitor when the phone on the wall began to ring. "Jesus Christ, can't a guy get any rest around here?" he said aloud though, nobody, including the man at the door, could hear his curse. He turned the knob and opened the door.

"C'mon in, get outta the rain," he said, his phone now into its third and fourth rings. "Let me answer this first."

"Benj?" came the voice at the other end of the receiver.

"Yeah, it's me," he grunted, his voice halting and scratchy. "Hold on, Sheriff..." Moving his mouth away from the phone, he emitted a series of coughs that sounded as though they had originated from the bottom of both lungs. Then in one swift circling motion, he gathered a wad of spittle from the back of his throat and horked it loudly into the only space left in the sink, barely missing the dirtied stack of dishes. Knowing his visitor was watching, he turned on the tap and washed it down.

"Okay, I'm back," he said.

"Goddammit, Benj, are you all right?" Boychuk asked.

"Yeaaaah, I'm fine...but I'd be better if I didn't have to get up and answer the phone or the friggin' door!"

"You have a visitor this early?"

"Yeah, but it's okay. What's on your mind, Brian?"

"My deputy tells me that you might've been involved in some sort of free-for-all last night with Nick Wells at the bar. Is that true?"

"Yeah, but wasn't much of a fight, Brian. I landed a good one on him and he ended it real quick. Won't be able to walk straight for a week..."

"Christ! How'd it start?"

"Ah, he just pissed me off. Called me a few names...nothin' more to it than that. But I might've done a bit more damage if he hadn't done what he done."

"You gonna survive?"

"I'm all right...still, I'd like to see the prick again sometime real soon."

"Ignore the kid, Benj, leave him to me and my guys," Boychuk ordered. "You're too old for that shit, anyway. But do you think he was he looking for trouble?"

"Probably, Brian. Randi brought up the Amish stuff, the fires and all, and I caught him playin' dumb about you and your department. I kinda inferred that he knew more about Menno than he let on. Don't remember a whole helluva lot after that because I put away more than a few beers afterwards." He scratched his head and looked over at his visitor, who was standing quietly inside the door, rain dripping from his hat. Man, a couple of Tylenols would go good, now, he thought.

"What about the Cahill kid?" Boychuk asked.

"Just sat there, mostly. Didn't intervene, so's I remember."

"Okay, I'll let you go," Boychuk said. "Take care of yourself. Maybe stay away from Randi's for a while."

"Yeah, like that's gonna happen, Brian." Benji let out a throaty laugh, prompting another coughing fit. But his voice was strong enough to bid the county cop good-bye. Then he turned to his visitor, patiently waiting for the phone conversation to end.

"Joshua," he said. "What brings you here? More problems over there last night?"

"No, nothing happened, Mr. Hoggarth," he replied, his accented Pennsylvania Dutch evident. "I've come here to ask you a favor. I'll pay you back…doing anything you need me to do around your farm."

"What is it, Josh?" His curiosity was piqued. He and Menno had bartered back and forth for years, with Benji providing hay for the animals and corn seed, and even a bit of short-term cash in return for labor. But never was a request made by his eldest son.

"Can you give me a ride?" Joshua said, sheepishly. "I would like to visit a friend."

A COUPLE OF HOURS LATER, the young Amish man entered the large elevator and pushed the button for the fifth floor. This was the largest building he'd been in since the entire family boarded a Greyhound back in Millersburg bound for Morgan County. The elevator wasn't a total mystery to him; one time he'd accompanied Menno to the courthouse to pay their taxes and had ridden a lift at that time.

To avoid scrutiny, he had dressed in the clothes that he wore at Sunday services, the same day that Boychuk arrived to question him about the events at Remington Pond. He knew that hospital staff would view him differently if he was adorned in traditional Amish fare, the overalls, and the suspenders and, of course, his straw hat. No bare feet either, for obvious reasons. Today, dressed like the English, at least similar to those who were not doctors or nurses or orderlies, he could have passed for any young man from the city. That was why the receptionist downstairs, busy as she was, simply provided instructions to the fifth floor ICU.

"Does your pop know what you're doin'?" Benji had asked, as they motored southbound in the farmer's old Chevy pick-up. The older man had carried most of the conversation, limited as it was, but he'd put two and two together and come up with at least four, and maybe more. He knew the motive behind Joshua's request.

"No, he does not. I just made up my mind today."

"He's not gonna be too pleased to find ya missin' then. Knowin' old Menno as well as I do."

"That is true." Joshua was lost in thought as they rolled down I-81, the rain following them all the way to the Central Square and Cicero interchanges. Benji left it at that; there was no need to pry and, besides, he'd always liked Troyer's kid. From the moment the family arrived, when Joshua was about eleven, Benji considered him to be a respectful and hard-working youngster. So unlike the creep at Swigs the night before.

Stopping at every floor to pick up and disperse passengers, the elevator finally reached its destination. He paused for a moment to read the directional signs, before walking slowly towards a nurses' station that now appeared abandoned. Maybe they're busy elsewhere, or maybe they were in the midst of a change, he thought, since he had overheard nurses discussing their work on the ride to the fifth floor. This was good, he felt; maybe he could slip into her room undetected. Reaching the ICU, he quickly made his decision, picking the first room on the left.

Suddenly, she was there. The girl from the black convertible. She of the pine bench next to the bonfire. The beer. All the laughter… and then the kiss!

How could he ever forget that kiss?

But now…now, everything was different, and he was devastated by what he saw. Paralyzed with emotion, he found his eyes moistening, his young heart breaking, fists clenching. There was no denying the intense pain, a sense of helplessness and sorrow, even frustration. Lying in this bed, her eyes closed, her now frail frame attached to so many tubes and modern machines, he knew there was nothing he could do to alleviate her pain. He had known Ria Cahill for less than week. A week! That was all it was, but it may as well have been a lifetime for everything they had shared.

Immediately, his heart wounded and adrift, he found himself returning to another night at the Pond.

A memory….

Of that special night on the edge of her lakeside property, watching as yet another party fuelled by alcohol and loud music was reaching its zenith.

"Hello again," he had whispered as he stood between a cluster of black spruce, not far from where he'd stacked the firewood the other day. His wide-shouldered physique offered a silvery silhouette against the illumination of a lone lamp-post, perhaps twenty feet behind. Given the heat of the night, he was shirtless; only a pair of suspenders was latched to his traditional work trousers, dark blue in color.

"Oh!" Ria had recoiled at the sound of his voice, releasing both hands from the handles of the rusted wheelbarrow. "You scared me!"

A look of concern had come over him. "I—I'm sorry, Ria, I didn't mean to."

"Josh, what are you doing here?"

"I was hoping to see you again...away from your party and all your friends. I...I could not stop thinking of you. I kept seeing your face. I kept hearing your voice and remembering what you said... and I remembered our last moments today..." His words stopped as he waited for a response. It was not long in coming. It arrived in the form of a broad smile across Ria's face and, with immediate validation, he had realized he had done the right thing.

Quickly, Ria had snapped her head in the direction of the party as if she feared disclosure. The bonfire, the music and the laughter were all raging. But she sensed that no one knew where she had gone. They were alone.

"So you came to see me?"

"Yes...I was afraid you would leave and never come back."

She just stood there, silent and stunned.

"Will you take a walk with me? I know a nice spot up there," he said, pointing to the hill behind them. "Where we can have some... privacy."

Taken aback by his shocking invitation, Ria's smile had waned slightly. As she returned her gaze to the party, he noticed her brilliant blonde hair. Now it was free-flowing over a pale yellow tank-top. She was beautiful. Over her shoulder, Joshua also scanned the scene and easily spotted her brother. He had his arm around that girl, Natasha, and was smoking a long cigar. There was no sign of the other man. The one who had struck him the other night. Would he come looking for her?

Slowly, Ria turned back to face Joshua and smiled again. Extending his hand in invitation, he felt a slight moment of hesitation, though her quick blue eyes signaled a clear desire for the adventure he had offered. Her smile radiated in the flickering light of the inferno. Quickly, she made up her mind. "Yes," she had said quickly.

"Lead the way!" And in an instant, she had placed her trust in him. She *would* go with him. She *would* explore this further, and before they knew it, they were galloping up the sandy paths that paralleled the big lake, soft affectionate laughter replacing any necessity for mere words.

High above the expansive waters, its slate-like surface now yielding to a soft wind from the south, the two lovers ran. The cumulous cloud cover that blanketed the county all day was now giving way, in spots, to a full moon, providing light to an otherwise black as onyx night. Nearby, Temper stood pliantly. His leather lead was tied to a tall white birch, waiting for his owner to return him to his nightly stall. He was saddle-less, with only a dark blue blanket covering his expansive back. Spotting the giant Belgian Bay, she raced to where he was standing.

"You brought *my* horse," she had teased, reaching up to stroke Temper's long copper-colored nose. His right ear, deformed-at-birth, seemed to be winking in Ria's direction.

"Your horse?"

"Yes! I've adopted him, don't you know? He's the most beautiful animal I've ever seen!" She looked lovingly into Temper's eyes and then kissed his snout. "How are you boy? Your dad taking better care of you now?"

Joshua stood there, beaming.

"Well, Ria, you're the most beautiful *girl* I've ever seen. I knew that when we first met and I will say it to you tonight."

As she turned toward him, they locked eyes once again, this time realizing that temptation was more powerful than prudence. They both knew what was about to happen, its implications irrelevant. They cared little for their present predicament; there was no need to worry about a future, be it tomorrow or the following day or the next month.

Elegantly their lips met, tongues penetrating, their healthy, ductile bodies quivering with excitement. Joshua held Ria close as his hands caressed her hair, smothering her with kisses to her mouth and face, pausing only to discover a pair of tender earlobes with tiny diamond studs attached. Hungrily, he could not get enough of this woman, venturing into the deepest recesses of an intimacy that he had never thought possible. He was an innocent of the woods. It was all so new to him, and he loved it.

As a teen, he had had these desires before, plenty of times, not fully understanding what was happening to him until it was over. And the desires occurred often. Mostly in his bed as a teenager as he had listened to his siblings' gentle rhythms of repose. Carnal thoughts…a touch here, some gentle pressure there…and it would happen. And in unconventional places as well. Once or twice, as he drove his buckboard down a deserted county road, a girl would go by—an English girl, of course, dressed in provocative clothing—and he'd explode into a world he knew nothing about. But it had always resulted in pleasure. Later, as he grew older, he had come to realize the truth.

He had figured it out.

Now as he stared lovingly at this beautiful young woman, struggling for her life in a hospital room, he realized that she *knew* it was novel to him. She knew it was his *first* time and her instinct to take charge was irresistible. After all, she was a born teacher and Joshua would become one of her ace students. In a quick sweeping motion, she had reached for Temper's blanket, extended a gentle hand to his and led him to the soft grasses above the cliff.

She knew his desire was to accelerate. To move to a rapid conclusion. It was clear that he hadn't done anything of the sort before. So, she had led the way. She had become a calming influence, pressing two fingers to his lips in the same teasing motion she had deployed earlier in his fields. He had followed her lead, intuitively realizing that this girl knew what she was doing. Slowly, and without direct eye contact, Ria started to caress his strapping shoulders, sliding one suspender aside and then the other. Then running her hands down his tanned and muscular chest, smoothly devoid of any hair, she discovered the button to his trousers and soon he was disrobed. With a friendly nod, she signaled for him to begin undressing her, placing his hands at the base of her tank-top, granting permission to raise it over her flowing hair, careful not to dislodge the pretty necklace around her neck.

For a brief moment, Joshua had frozen with excitement. She wore *nothing* underneath and never before had he witnessed such a wonderful sight. Never before had he experienced such joy. Quickly unbuttoning her denim shorts, she allowed them to fall easily on the blanket below. In the distance, if they listened carefully, they could hear the escalating sounds of a party in full swing. Booming voices, shrieks of laughter. All to a backdrop of the music of the night. Joshua realized that Ria would have to return to the party, sometime that night. But there was no going back.

"I want you Josh," she had purred. "I've wanted you ever since we first met..." In an instant, Joshua realized what true affection was meant to be. Entering her was a discovery, a sensation like no other, and to groans of pleasure emanating from the most vivacious specimen he had ever known, they had rocked towards a blissful conclusion. It was unimaginable joy for both of them. In exhaustion, his arms became wrapped around her shoulders, her breasts pressed tightly against his silken pecs.

There they had remained, entangled, spent and satiated. Few words had been spoken until Ria offered her thoughts and now they were ingrained in his memory. "Maybe some sort of higher being could exist after all," she had whispered. "Not that I normally believe in such fairytales, Joshua, but it had to be fate, don't you think? Bringing us together tonight?"

He had agreed. It was exhilarating.

His eyes blinking furiously, his memories concluded, Joshua returned to the dreadful sight before him. Again, he was standing before Ria in her damned hospital room, his eyes filling with tears.

Another whisper, this time to himself: "I should never have left you that night, Ria," his eyes welling with tears. "I'm…I'm so sorry." Similar to her actions only days before, he kissed a pair of fore-fingers and pressed them to her forehead.

Just then, he was jolted from his quiet soliloquy by sounds coming from behind. It was a nurse, and she wasn't happy.

"Who the *hell* are you and what are you doing here?" she demanded.

Turning abruptly at her intervention, Joshua was shocked and speechless. He didn't want his memories with Ria to end this way, but knew the authorities would catch up with him soon.

About fifty-five with a moon-shaped face, a bulging waist and short peroxide hair, the nurse was now in Joshua's face, so close that he could smell an acidic mix of coffee and cigarettes on her breath. She was all business.

"I—I'm sorry, ma'am," was all he could mutter. "I'm leaving now."

The nurse's face grew more indignant, releasing a sigh like a Michelin tire losing its air.

"This is the *Intensive Care Unit!*" she bellowed with emphasis. "You cannot be in here! And you still haven't told me who you are!"

From out of nowhere came another voice. A male voice.

"It's all right, nurse," the voice said. "This young man's a close friend of the family, and I'll vouch for him."

It was Roger Cahill. The nurse's suspicious eyes darted critically from Roger to Joshua and back again to Roger. "Are you sure, Mr. Cahill? I wasn't told this morning that Ria would have any *new* visitors today."

But Roger, still haggard and drawn from a week's painful vigil, simply nodded. "He's fine. I'll handle it from here, if it's okay with you?"

"All right, but I'll have to ask both of you to leave," the heavy-set woman declared, reasserting her authority. "*Someone* has to care for the health of your daughter, and unexplained visitors don't help much!"

"I understand," he said. "You have a job to do. We'll be leaving... sorry."

His emotions still fragile from the sight of Ria in critical condition, his memories of their last night together still fresh, Joshua side-stepped around the stoutly-built nurse. It was time to leave, and soon he found himself in the hospital hallway, walking briskly towards the elevator. Roger followed in pursuit.

"Wait, young man!"

Joshua stopped, turning toward the older man with embarrassment.

"You're a Troyer, aren't you?" he asked. "Joshua, I believe?"

"Yes, sir," he replied, reverently.

Roger extended his hand in friendship, a look of compassion evident.

"I'm Roger Cahill...Ria's dad" he replied.

"Nice to meet you sir." Joshua's hand met Roger's. "I, uh, should also say thank you for saving me from that lady."

"She's just protecting her patient and for that I'm pleased."

The two men stood in awkward silence. A moment passed. Yet another. Then Roger spoke up once again.

"I know who you are...my brother-in-law, Hubert Schumacher, you know him, I believe?"

"Yes, Mr. Schumacher and I are friends. I've done some work for him in the past. He's...he's a very kind man."

Roger nodded with approval.

"Hubert says the same about you. You and my daughter have become...good friends, so we've discovered."

"Yes, sir."

"I also know, not from Ria because...well, she's still in a coma, that you and she saw each other that night at the lake."

Joshua was taken by surprise. How would her father know about their special moment together? Roger seemed to be able to read Joshua's mind.

"The police told us that you were together—"

"I didn't hurt her, Mr. Cahill!" he blurted quickly, his eyes moistening again. "I would never have hurt her."

Roger looked into Joshua's eyes. It was a look of understanding.

"The police know that, and so do I—and so does her mom. Of course, the sheriff is still trying to figure out who did it, but we're confident he will."

"I would never have hurt your daughter, Mr. Cahill," he repeated.

Roger paused a moment to absorb what Joshua was saying. He would get to the heart of the matter.

"What does Ria mean to you, Joshua?" he enquired. "After all, you two lead such...different lives. How could the two of you ever get together if—when—she recovers?" It was a painful clarification on Roger's part. There was no other option.

"I don't know the answer to that question, sir," he replied. "But what I do know is that I want very much to be with her...and I think she feels the same."

Joshua's words resonated with the older man. Like his wife, he could size up the essential character of a man. And this young man in front of him was clearly a person of integrity. His desire was to see his daughter recover fully, and if Joshua was the man she wanted, who was he to intervene? Now, Barb would be another matter. But he'd bring her around, if such an event transpired.

"All right, then."

Joshua smiled back at Roger, and in a moment he was gone.

THIRTY-THREE

A T DUSK, PRAYERS OF GRATITUDE had been shared and an evening meal delivered when Joshua entered his home. Like those of their Ohio clan, the expansive kitchen was more than a center of sustenance; it was the focal point of their faith, a symbolic place for a large familial unit to assemble at the end of yet another laborious day. It was where they came together to thank the Lord, break bread and share stories. In good times, that was. Not tonight.

One hand still clinging to the knob on the door as if he knew his welcome had worn out, Joshua immediately sensed an iciness. Their conversation would be terse. His usual corner spot, next to his mother at the long oak table, was empty, conspicuously so to the younger boys, Elijah and Levi, his wagon mates who had probed his whereabouts.

Now, as he stood nervously at the rear door of the home to the gawking glares of a dozen brothers and sisters, he could feel the tension. It had grown immeasurably in recent days, placing a heavy strain on the large family, and he knew he was to blame. Aided by the light of a half-dozen long-stemmed candles, he saw Menno anchoring the far end of the table. His father's steely eyes told the story.

Sarah had seen this look on her husband's face before. After all, they had been married for twenty-two years. Her eyes darted rapidly between her husband and her son, bearing witness to his arrival. She spoke up.

"Sit down, Joshua, I will fix you your meal," she said, rising from her seat and walking in the direction of a massive black woodstove where several large iron skillets were simmering. The stove dominated a kitchen illuminated, in addition to the candles, by four kerosene lamps, their blizzard-white rays bouncing around the room. Sarah knew she would have to intervene quickly, since she alone could heal a family now in turmoil. She alone could offer reconciliation; it was her responsibility to return the family to happier times. She was desperate.

"No!" Menno thundered. "Mother, you stay in your chair! Do not move! There will be no meals—nothing—provided to this man at this time! Not until he explains himself, and renounces his behavior."

"This *man* is our *son*, Papa," she said, continuing her voyage to the stove. "You will not issue orders to me, Menno Troyer. And I will not stand idly by and let you treat Joshua this way!"

But Menno was adamant.

"Our son, Mama, has disrespected us!" he cried. "He has shamed our family, and our community. I will no longer put up with this... in my home."

Joshua watched in trepidation as his parents quarreled in front of his siblings. Rachel, he noticed, was sitting in her usual spot on the wooden bench that paralleled the table. She was his closest ally, his friend, a soul mate of sorts and the one member of their large brood he had turned to for understanding. But her eyes offered little solace this night and immediately Joshua knew why. Rachel had felt betrayed by the love he had expressed for a woman whose name was not Zook. A secret love, no less, for an English woman. He had abandoned Hannah; now Rachel would do the same with him.

"Well?" Menno demanded, continuing his questions.

"I'm...sorry, Papa," was all Joshua could mumble.

"Sorry? Sorry? That's all you can say to us at this moment? Those are meaningless words, Joshua! All of your words this week have been so."

His mother would intervene once again. "Papa, let the boy talk!"

"Stay out of this, woman," he barked, his voice trembling with anger and vehemence. "This is between Joshua and myself."

"No, it is *not*, Papa," she said. "I will have my say when it comes to these children!" She pointed to the remainder of her offspring— twelve in total. They were staring intently at the saga unfolding in their home. Other than the baby, most offered looks of puzzlement, even fear, while others were on the cusp of tears.

"Just look at what you're doing to them!"

But Menno had already returned his focus to his eldest son, who was still clinging to the door as if he was planning an escape. Which Joshua was.

"Where were you all day, son?" he now demanded. "We needed you. But you departed early in the direction of the neighbor's house. Did you go there?"

"Yes, Papa."

"Why would you bother Mr. Hoggarth?" Menno was properly reverent of the English surrounding his farm and those in Morgantown.

But Joshua, his eyes focused on the floor boards as if in search for answers—any answers—hidden within the grain, was slow to respond. Finally, he found the courage.

"I asked him to drive me to the city," he responded. "I went to visit her…in the hospital."

A look of confirmation overcame Menno. Given Joshua's long absence, he had suspected that some such journey had taken place. But the words his son had just uttered crushed him; his struggle to keep his family from unraveling had failed. Joshua's words were more than a mere semblance of certitude; he had demanded the truth and his son had delivered. Wrapping his fingers around his chin, with only remnants of his once-proud beard remaining, he let his head drift downward in dismay. There it stayed, deeply contemplative, allowing moments to pass before his eyes again rose to meet those of his much taller son.

"You will leave the Order," he replied solemnly. Perhaps he could have formed his declaration in the form of a question but there was no rising intonation to his voice. Instead, what resulted was a somber statement of fact, one of irreversible finality. There was no turning back.

"There will be no union of the Zooks and Troyers this autumn, as we had hoped. There will be no celebrations, no joy...just this sadness. You are leaving our family and our order. This is what you are informing us tonight."

His eyes blinking furiously, Joshua was unable to focus on anyone in the room. The older children understood what their father had said and remained mute. The others, the toddlers, simply exchanged looks of total bewilderment. They also stayed silent.

"No! That is not what Joshua is saying," Sarah pleaded, now close to tears herself. "Tell me, Joshua! It cannot be true. Hannah will make a fine wife for you and together you will create a lovely family."

The young man looked sympathetically at his mother. She was the last person he had wanted to hurt. Walking to her side, he hugged her before gently placing a kiss on her left cheek.

"Mama, I'm—I'm sorry," he whispered, his voice breaking as he turned and walked out.

WITH TEARS STREAMING DOWN HIS FACE, Joshua marched toward the barn as an unrelenting September rain turned the Troyer farm yard into a reservoir of mud. He couldn't tell whether his tears were the result of the intolerable pain he had inflicted on his family or for the injured girl he had known less than a week. Maybe both, since both were reason enough to mourn. It was his actions—directly or not—that had brought everything over the past week to such a fateful fruition.

But suddenly, and without warning, a wave of joy engulfed him. It felt like a tsunami...but a good one. Yes, he had read about that disaster that had overwhelmed a poor nation on the other side of the world. Was it Indonesia? Yes, he had read about it. Strangely, as he approached the barn, it was the only comparable thing that entered his mind. This was his personal tsunami...of emotions, of relief. It was overwhelming him now. He was reborn. He had declared his independence and the frustration that he had experienced for weeks—even months—was now gone.

He felt free.

The catalyst, of course, was the introduction of Ria Cahill into his world. She would recover, he was certain of that. She was strong and determined and she would survive. They would be together. His Amish life, preordained as it was, would now be rejected. It was never his life choice and, looking back, one that he had disdained since his arrival as a child from Ohio. Now he would make his own way in the world, uncertain of his future. But he would survive; he was talented at many things. He would get a job in the English world. Maybe even achieve his high school equivalency and attend college himself, a dream he'd had since he was a youngster. It was as though a wagon, heavily laden with corn, had been lifted off his back.

Joshua made his way past the big buckboard to the rear of the barn and the stalls containing his horses. A dozen hours after he had knocked on Benji's door, it was now time to address their needs, ensure adequate water supplies, oats and hay, a labor of love if there ever was one. After what had transpired in the house, he would sleep in the loft tonight, away from his mournful mother and inquisitive siblings. His bed in the large room, which he shared with five of his brothers, would remain empty tonight, and for all future nights.

He reached the entrance to the stall where Temper was located. He knew the big horse would welcome his arrival and, true to form, he did. Now snorting cantankerously, kicking his hind legs in excitement, Temper was one member of the family that wanted him here. For a few moments, Joshua just stood there, stroking the beast's nose, playfully massaging his winking, genetically damaged ear. Acts of kindness that Ria displayed only days before.

"How are you boy?" he said, his voice loud enough for the horse to snort his approval. He was speaking English. He would need to make it in the English world and no longer would he use his mother tongue. "Miss me today? I guess I have to say I'm sorry... to you too, boy."

Suddenly, a voice thundered from the direction of the barn's entrance.

"Well, isn't that a touching sight?" the voice said. "Makes you just wanna cry, don't it *ant-hill*? Or more like puke!"

Startled, Joshua snapped his head around.

It was Nick.

Standing at the entrance of the barn, about twenty feet away, he was adorned in a black leather jacket and matching dark denim jeans, a clear contrast to his appearances at the Pond. Now instead of a fedora, a dark woolen hat, punk style, smothered his short platinum hair. Replacing the Birkenstocks were a pair of dark cowboy boots. Joshua could see that the socket around one of his eyes was a blackish-orange color.

Next to him stood Brad, he too in jeans and a dark blue windbreaker, his curly golden locks pushing out from under a Steelers cap. He was carrying a pump-action shotgun in one hand and a brown paper bag in the other, containing what Joshua figured was a pint bottle of whiskey. Instantly, Joshua knew they were inebriated.

"You are trespassing," the young Amish farmer said calmly, his eyes focused on the weapon. His first instinct was to reach for a pitchfork that had been resting against one of the barn's pillars. "You must leave at once."

A broad smirk splashed across Nick's face as Brad took another large gulp from the bottle in the paper bag.

"Hear that, Brad? Our friend here isn't exactly rolling out the welcome wagon, is he?"

"What do you want from us?" Joshua demanded.

"What's this 'us' shit, farmer?" Nick replied. "Couldn't care less about the rest of the hillbillies around here...though that sister of yours is a looker. Maybe you should've brought her to the lake the other night." He paused to give his words full effect. "Nah...we just came to see how you're doin'. Just concerned about ya, that's all."

It was Brad's turn to pipe up. He'd drop the glibness and get right to the point.

"Troyer, thought we'd find out for ourselves why you pushed my sister onto those goddamned rocks!" Belligerently, the twosome was inching toward Joshua, who was tightening his grip on his pitchfork.

The young Amish man stayed his ground. Defiant.

"I said you must leave. Now."

But Nick just ignored his order.

"What was it, farmer boy? The blonde not put out?"

Joshua glared at Nick, his venom evident. The young men were now less than ten feet apart but Nick, deciding to up the ante, had managed to position himself between Joshua and Temper. The perceptive Belgian, realizing danger, whinnied loudly as his muscled legs kicked the back of his stall.

"Or maybe she was quite willing to fuck you that night? And if that was the case, you know, that kinda *pisses* me off even more. I mean, why would Ria want to do you? Of all guys? I'm confused..." He pointed to Joshua's crotch. "Whaddaya got down there that I don't? You and that horse have something in common?"

Joshua spoke up.

"Maybe I should ask you some questions."

"Oh, you think?" Brad re-entered the mix. He was here to teach the Amish man a lesson. Though he wasn't sure how far he was willing to take this, his companion in a bag, Jim Beam, was helping him find the necessary courage.

"Yes," replied Joshua. But he would ignore Brad. Instead, he was glaring directly at Nick.

"You burned our hay, didn't you?"

Nick's smirk gradually disappeared as Joshua continued his inquisition. Deliberate, focused, his voice nearly unemotional.

"And you attacked my father too," he added. "Not hard to do, since he's a small man. No match for you. And then you painted those hate words on our carriage as well. Am I not right?"

No answer.

"But that's not the reason you are here, is it?"

Now the two intruders were glaring at Joshua. If he was afraid for his life, he was not showing it. If he felt intimidated, there was no evidence. He would level one more charge.

"You followed us, too, Ria and me, that night, didn't you Nick? To the high ground above the Pond?"

Nick had heard enough. He reached up to stroke Temper's long, brown snout but the horse, pulling on his rein, attempted to back away.

"Nice nag here, ain't he Bunker? A little feisty, I seem to remember, but has a mind of his own. Just like Troyer here." Temper, it was clear, wanted nothing to do with the man. Joshua had raised him from a foal and the horse cared little for strangers. With one exception, and that was Ria.

"Leave my barn, now!" Joshua demanded.

"Not gonna happen, farmer boy," Nick announced. "Not yet, anyway."

In a swift, roundhouse swing that Joshua failed to predict, Nick landed his right fist squarely to Temper's lower jaw. Recoiling in pain, the big Belgian reared his head back as far as his lead would allow. But he was trapped; Nick rocketed another blow to the side of the horse's head, not far from his left eye. Temper, stunned by the sudden violence, wailed again, looking to his master for answers.

Enraged, Joshua leapt into action. Dislodging the pitchfork from the dirt floor, he bolted lightning-like in Nick's direction, landing the fork's handle across Wells' upper body, thrusting Nick backwards. He groaned at the blow, but the intruder was not thwarted by Joshua's attack. With a punch as powerful as the one he had just inflicted upon the horse, Wells caught Joshua high to his left cheekbone, sending the young Amish man to the floor, his pitchfork spiraling wildly through the air before coming to a rest several yards away.

Though lighter than Wells by about twenty pounds, Joshua's dawn-to-dusk existence more than equalized the situation tonight. He was in good shape—and just as agile. He figured also the alcohol that Nick had consumed would dull his senses. Recovering quickly, he lunged at Nick mid-chest almost head first, knocking him to the hay.

"Okay, farmer, you say you don't believe in fighting," Nick said, raising himself from the floor. "But you better give it your best shot!"

"You will leave," Joshua replied, icily, "and *never* return."

Now the dukes went up and they were once again closing in on each other. Nick was the first to pounce, attempting another wild stab. But his fist sailed over a ducking Joshua, providing the Amish farmer an opening to counter attack. And attack he did, striking a blow to Nick's sternum, its force causing the intruder to gasp for air in pain. Not waiting for the man to counter attack, Joshua delivered another rapid strike to Nick's goateed chin. This stunned the invader and Joshua would attempt to finish him off. He threw a solid uppercut to Nick's jaw, sending the wounded man backwards in near free fall. The look on the trespasser was one of shock. He was losing this fight, and he knew it. Never did he believe the farmer would retaliate, let alone mount such a powerful defense.

His fists now beginning to swell with pain, Joshua was about to move in for the kill when, from out of nowhere, came the butt end of Brad's shotgun. It crashed heavily on the Amish man's skull, dropping Joshua to the hay just below the outstretched nose of Temper. Joshua's face landed with a thud, blood trickling from the back of his head.

He was out cold.

As Nick came to his feet at last, nursing his wounds, Brad stared at the motionless form that was now Joshua. Suddenly, a voice from the side entrance to the barn erupted.

"Leave my son be and leave! You hooligans!"

It was Menno and he, too, had a weapon in his hand, this time a long iron bar that he used for digging post-holes. Brandishing it like a Roman warrior, his eyes spewing hatred, Menno advanced towards the young men.

"Jesus Christ, not another one of the fuckin' rollers!" Nick was regaining some of his composure.

Brad decided to intervene. He had agreed with Wells to pay a visit to their Amish friend, maybe slap him around a bit, make sure Joshua knew they didn't agree with his romance with Ria. Now their mission was out of control. Never did he believe it would come to this.

"Come on Wells, we're done here," he said, motioning in the direction of the large barn door. "Let's get the hell out!"

But he was already too late.

From the road outside the barn arrived two sets of headlights, accompanied by the piercing blue-and-white strobes that crashed the darkness of a cool, misty night. The sheriff and his deputies had arrived.

Brad immediately froze in his place. He had thought they had given the deputy following them the slip but apparently not. Noticing his partner's paralysis, Nick took charge, grabbing the shotgun from Brad's hands.

But Menno meant business, too.

"I want you both to leave my barn!" he barked. Now only a short distance from the two young men, his iron bar jousting higher, Menno continued his approach. It was an act not lost on Nick.

"Back off old man...or I'll deal with you, too!" he said, waving the shotgun in Menno's direction. Brad, his eyes in fearful panic, knew the jig was up.

"Wells, don't do anything stupid!" Brad cried. "We're in enough shit!"

Nick's steel-gray eyes turned maniacal. The shotgun gave him the power.

"What's up with you, Cahill? Losing your nerve? You were talkin' tough just an hour ago. How you, and you alone, were going to teach farmer boy here a lesson for pushing your sister off the cliff. Even bragged about it to that Greek chick you been bangin'."

"Gimme back my gun and let's get out of here," Brad demanded.

His confidence growing, Nick was not about to budge. Suddenly, an authoritative voice from outside the barn was heard.

"Wells...Cahill?" Boychuk was now on the bullhorn installed in his truck, his voice reverberating over the property. "I know you guys are in there, and if it's trouble you want, well, you've got it!"

One of the barn's double doors began to open slowly, allowing the cruisers' high beams to spread light throughout the barn. Nick could see the silhouetted figures standing firm, the sheriff leading the way, his semiautomatic Glock cocked and ready. Jimmy, his senior deputy, stood next to him and he was armed with a pump-action shotgun. Others, Nick now thought, might be encircling the building.

"I've had it, Wells!" Brad yelled in Boychuk's direction. "Sheriff, I'm coming out."

"All right, Brad, get your ass out here, and you'd better not be carrying any weapons."

But Boychuk wasn't interested in the Cahill kid. Wells was his principal focus.

"Wells, drop the gun!" he demanded. "Take my advice. Join your buddy out here—unarmed!"

There was no response from Nick. He was keeping his eye on the elder Troyer, who was still inching toward him, his iron bar menacing. On the ground, Joshua was slowly regaining consciousness, writhing with pain.

From the barn's entrance, Boychuk's voice was heard again.

"I know *all* about you, Wells," he bellowed. "I know your whole story. How you bullshitted everybody, especially poor Ria Cahill. You told her you came from a very successful family downstate, that your daddy was a rich lawyer and judge? That's the picture you painted, wasn't it?"

He paused a moment to see if his words were having any affect. Still no response. The sheriff would raise the stakes.

"It was all a fantasy, wasn't it, Wells? You didn't tell Ria or anyone else that your old man was a deadbeat, did you? One who ran out on you and your mom a long time ago? You see, we met her yesterday in some Poughkeepsie dollar store, and she spilled the beans. Like the time she had to have you removed from the house when you were only eight?"

No answer from the man in black.

"Seems your old man slapped you around a lot before he left, too, didn't he? Especially when you threw the dog out of an upstairs window? Ria ever hear about that? Don't think so."

Finally, Nick decided to respond.

"My old lady's full of shit!"

Boychuk had heard enough. Keeping the young man occupied, with subtle eye signals towards his deputy, he motioned for Jimmy to make his way to the side entrance of the barn, the same entrance that Menno used moments before. Brad, now handcuffed and being hustled into one of the Tahoes, listened intently. He was stunned. Who the hell was this guy, anyway, he now asked himself.

"Now, where was I?" Boychuk continued. "Oh, yeah. It's an interesting little yarn, if I do say so myself. Seems your mom, a nice lady I'm told, gave up on you, putting you in a foster home. But that didn't work either, did it? Seems you had issues with other animals too. Remember the foster cat? Something about putting the 'little pissant'—your words, apparently, not mine—in the microwave? Nice move, kid! Then...then they placed you in a few group homes before you were a teenager. But one stay lasted only about a month before you were up on assault—"

"Get fucked, Boychuk!" Wells bellowed.

"Nice, Wells," the sheriff replied. "But I could go on and on and on. Conduct disorder. Antisocial behavior. We consulted a shrink and told her about you. She told us it's hard to treat. But I have a solution in mind for you—and it's called jail…"

The sheriff's words were ricocheting around the barn like ping pong balls, so much so that Nick failed to see Menno suddenly move in closer, wielding his iron post-digger like a baseball bat. The Amish man's weapon struck Nick's right shoulder hard, causing the shotgun to fire a shell in the direction of the big doors, but above Boychuk's head, blowing a hole the size of a salad plate in the barn wall. Both Temper and Sorrel reacted to the mayhem with panic, kicking their stalls and snorting loudly.

The blast prompted the sheriff to take action, swinging the doors wide open before diving to the hay strewn across the floor. His handgun was pointed squarely at Wells.

"Wells!" he yelled. "Drop that weapon, now!"

But Nick had other intentions. Twisting on his heels, he met Menno head on just as the farmer was about to strike a further blow. In a sweeping left hook, similar to the one he had used against the younger Troyer on the first night they met at Remington Pond, Nick's fist arrived at its target, the stubbled chin of the smaller man. The force of the punch sent Menno tumbling backwards, in an eerily strange slow-motion scene that could have been choreographed for the big screen by Hollywood itself.

Losing his balance, his arms flailing wildly, Menno fell squarely on the deadly, upturned teeth of Joshua's pitchfork. The sheriff watched in shock as the teeth penetrated the farmer's upper torso, his dark blue shirt now oozing a deep crimson liquid from his wounded thoracic cavity. His mouth was now agape, his lungs gasping for air. A pained and puzzled look was evident in the farmer's sad dark-green eyes as if asking, innocently, why was this happening to him and his family?

It was quick. In a matter of seconds, Menno's eyes blinked for the final time.

He was gone.

Not finished, Nick regained his balance and turning wildly in the sheriff's direction, pumped the shotgun once again and cocked it to his shoulder.

"Drop it now, Wells!" Boychuk commanded. But his words of warning arrived too late. A booming blast from Brad's shotgun resulted, its buckshot whizzing closer to the sheriff's head than the previous shell. In rapid response, Boychuk fired two shots from his handgun, with one bullet landing squarely in the young man's left shoulder and another only inches away.

He wasn't shooting to kill.

He wanted this kid alive.

It was over.

THIRTY-FOUR

IT WAS A CLEAR, CRISP DAY in the county seat, an oddity of sorts for this time of year since the Farmer's Almanac had predicted yet another gloomy November in the north country. Soon, snow would arrive from Lake Ontario in heavy layers, signaling an end of one season and the beginning of another. Or worse, Boychuk thought; freezing rain, more common now as the planet grew warmer every year, would turn these streets and highways into a treacherous mess.

Plowing through mounds of leafy refuse scattered across the road, he made a slow turn on Prospect Avenue and continued his way to the Court House, past the brown brick and clapboard edifices that were home to the town's commerce. The video rental parlor on the corner had gone under, it too a victim of broadcast conglomerates that now dispatched movies through the clouds. Fortunately, it had been replaced last month by a trendy shop called, simply, *Antiques & Things,* that sported an attractive back-lit, block-lettered sign manufactured in Rochester. No more hand-painted jobs, fortunately, like the consignment store next door, or the used-books shop next to it. On the opposite corner, where the *Morgan County Savings & Loan* offered mortgages for generations before merging with a big state bank and moving to the highway, a lively saloon had set up shop. A couple of his deputies, who should have missed a few meals, raved about the joint's Delmonicos smothered in gorgonzola sauce.

It had been three weeks since candy night, but still he saw remnants of the fall's pumpkin harvest littered across the lawns. The rotting chunks had been deposited there by youngsters who had turned the ghoulish lanterns into soccer balls. Boychuk just shrugged;

nothing much has changed in thirty years; they were just bored teenagers.

Tomorrow, Thanksgiving would arrive as well, the prospect of which caused him some dismay. He had never shared others' affinity for the family holiday. Maybe it was because his parents never encouraged such celebrations or maybe they just didn't care. Though he never got a vote, Susan always accepted an annual invitation from her sister to join her and her noisy kids to share in the holiday feast. But police work often intervened. He would arrive late, long after the *Lions* of a larger Motown suffered their predictable drubbing at the hands of just about *any* NFL rival.

Inevitably, tomorrow would be similar. Given his workload, he knew he would be late and he knew what would happen. Few words would be exchanged but Boychuk could read Susan's moods. Dutifully, but with residual resentment, she would fetch a tinfoil-wrapped plate of turkey and stuffing from the oven, along with a beer, and he would plow through dinner alone. He would crack a few jokes, talk football with a brother-in-law who had never played the game and try to make amends for his absence.

Raised on a horse ranch near Lisbon, his was an only-child existence. His mother, a gentle but troubled closet boozer, died officially from liver disease but Boychuk diagnosed it as acute loneliness. His pop, a grizzled, tough-as-nails workaholic, slumped over one day at the age of forty-nine and never woke up—only weeks before young Brian was to become a rookie cop.

Maybe it was time to pack this job in, he now thought. After all, he'd given twenty-five years of his life to police work and, maybe, it was time to do something else. But what would he do? Become a security guard somewhere? Join the state prison system? Not for him. Yet, the events of recent months didn't help matters much. He told Hubie he should have brought down Wells *before* Menno had advanced on the kid with his iron bar. Maybe Menno would be alive today, especially if he hadn't goaded Nick as he did. Naturally, the bastard had recovered nicely. But Boychuk was satisfied that Wells would do time.

Menno's funeral had been a sad affair. Only a week after Boychuk had interrupted the biweekly prayer service on the grounds of the Troyer farm, the family was forced to bring the flock together again, this time to honor one of its own. From miles around, as tradition ordained, the community arrived whether they had known Menno or not. Boychuk had instructed his deputies to direct traffic on Bidgood Road and be as unobtrusive as they could be. The Troyer family, now missing its leader, reacted with quiet dignity.

Shunning tradition that only male family members undertook such tasks, Sarah and Rachel had dressed Menno's body, clothing it in white garments and placing it in a plain pine box. Then the viewings began, three in all, open casket throughout. For most of the order, it was their first taste of the all-too-public agony that plagued the Troyer family. Yet, the focus was not on the man himself but on God. There were no eulogies, no speeches of any kind, no flowers. Bishop Jakes sang a couple of hymns, but instructed his flock that other forms of music were to be banned. Though the family would enter a year of mourning, it would never observe a formal memorial day. Nor would they make a return visit graveside, his final resting place being a lonely, weed-sowed cemetery located on a piece of high ground where Remington Pond emptied into the Oswegatchie. With Menno's spirit departing to the hereafter, their beliefs dictated a simple truism: death was more important than birth itself.

Now, as he continued his drive through an almost deserted town, Boychuk noticed other signs that the holiday was near. At a handsome two-story dormered home on the corner, he could see old Rokeby hammering steel stakes into the soil around his prized arborvitaes. The good mayor then unraveled rolls of bright orange corrugated fencing that, he prayed, would keep the damned deer from grazing this winter. At least old Neil wasn't shooting them from his back stoop like others in town. At another home next door, which was much less stately, dilapidated even, a neighbor was perched on an extension ladder installing clear plastic sheathing around his windows. He was anticipating heat losses. Winter was coming.

Boychuk's thoughts returned to another Thanksgiving in his life. How could he forget that day, nearly four years ago, when the Schumacher sisters went AWOL. Hubie, in a state of panic, his voice so breathless that Boychuk thought the old man was on the cusp of a coronary. "It's not good," Hubie had said. So set in motion a furious sequence of events that ended four days and many miles later in Lake Placid. Jane was the woman he had once loved, and he never got the chance to tell her how much, and ever since it caused him to think 'what if?'

His moment of silent reflection was interrupted by the ringing of his cell phone. He pulled into the parking lot of Turnbull's and allowed the engine in his Tahoe to idle. From this distance, he could see Darryl, the store's short, heavyset manager, taking advantage of a sun-filled day to rearrange the last of his CharBroils and Webers, now being flogged at fifty percent off. He was dumping inventory. Soon those displays would change to snow blowers, scrapers, shovels and pallets of road salt. He gazed down at his BlackBerry's screen; it was Makenna on the phone.

Her timing was always impeccable.

"Hey!" he answered quickly. "How are ya?"

"I'm great, Brian! My last paper is due today and then I'm off for five days. How are you?"

"Better now, Ken, believe me."

"You don't sound very good from this end. What's going on?"

"Just trying to sort out the Troyer mess, that's all," he replied, warily. "And still trying to figure out who hurt your cousin. I've got the Wells kid on a few serious things but I have to admit I'm still a long way away from solving the other stuff."

After the violence at the Troyer farm, Boychuk charged Wells with the attempted murder of a police officer, assault with a deadly weapon, and criminal possession. For good measure, he had added charges of trespassing and a misdemeanor count of menacing. His pal Cahill was facing trespassing, assault with deadly, and misuse of a firearm but Roger had come to his kid's rescue with a five-thousand-dollar bail bond. If Brad would plead guilty, with remorse, he might get off with probation and community service. Wells, on the other hand, would pay his dues, he was sure of that. But whether he could nail Wells on a very specific crime around Labor Day was another question.

As expected, Wells had dummied up quickly, demanding a public defender from his jail cell deep within the court house basement. There was no bail for him. His peach-fuzzed PD with a Hofstra law degree immediately discounted any ideas Boychuk might have had to lay a manslaughter charge, declaring that his client, not much younger than the lawyer himself, was simply acting in self-defense. It was "just awful" that Menno had died in the melee, the public defender had said, but that crazed, iron-bar-swinging farmer had attacked his client first. Reluctantly, the district attorney had agreed.

"Still nothing on that arson case or that beard-cutting incident?" Makenna asked.

"Just no evidence at this point...other than a gas can we found in the woods, with prints unknown," the sheriff said. "Even after we lifted a few from Wells' beer glass, after that bar fight at Swigs, we couldn't link him to it. I still suspect that he might've been on that cliff, but that's a blank too."

"I spoke to my grandfather," Makenna said. "He tells me that Ria still hasn't come out of her coma."

"No, and until she does, we won't know who hit her upside the head and pushed her on to the rocks. That's *if* she wakes up..."

"Very sad," was all Makenna could say. There was another brief pause in their conversation before she once again spoke up.

"You had a picture of that hate message on the buggy, didn't you?" she asked.

"Yeah, from my BlackBerry 'cause Menno and his boy wouldn't let Webster come out for a serious look. I also got a chip from the paint, but there's nothing there yet, either."

There was a long pause at the other end of the phone.

"Are you still there, Ken?"

"I'm here," she said. "I'm just thinking. I don't think I ever saw that photo. Just curious, since the school here—you know it works closely with federal agencies like the CIA and ATF?—is finding new ways to analyze photos. Do you still have it on your cell?"

"Sure…other guys keep pictures of their grandchildren," he said, chuckling. He was yet another parent pressuring his kid to have children. "Me? I keep stuff like this on my cell, most likely because I never get around to deleting it."

Makenna ignored the comment about children. There had been a few men in her life, including one at Clarkson, but no one serious—let alone a marriage proposal. Besides, like her birth mother, she was much too ambitious to make a commitment at the age of twenty-four.

"Why don't you email it to me—now?"

"Okay, if you think there might be something."

He placed his BlackBerry on speaker, and immediately began searching his picture files. In a matter of seconds, he was able to send the photo to her handheld device in Virginia. Simultaneously, the two were now viewing the hand-painted warning on the Troyer buggy. There it was:

$$\textit{KRautS!}$$
$$\textit{Go Back to OHio!}$$

Makenna studied the words for a few moments before speaking.

"An interesting combination of upper and lower case letters," she observed.

"That's what Webster said," Boychuk admitted. "That's penmanship these days...with cell phones and texting and Twitter, nobody physically writes anything anymore. Obviously sprayed in haste. Exclamation points to make sure Menno got the message, but nothing out of the ordinary, we thought."

"That's my overall impression, too, Brian. Not a lot here. But..."

"But?" he replied.

"I don't know, Brian, but there's something about the way he—I say *he* since Mr. Troyer believed he was assaulted by a couple of men, right?"

"Right. One held him down while the other buzzed his beard off with a battery-operated shaver."

"Well, regardless of gender, who writes letters like those a's anymore? In both lines. Think about it. You have a can of spray paint in your hand, and you have less than a minute to get the job done. If you're not opting for an upper case 'A', which is essentially a pyramid with a stroke through it, wouldn't you use the more common way of writing the lower case? The 'a' used in both lines looks very formal to me. Very odd, especially with that little tail on the lower side of the 'a'...you don't see that very often."

Boychuk studied the message once again. The small BlackBerry screen was limited in scope, but he enlarged the letters that Makenna was talking about.

"Yeah, I see what you mean, but I'm not sure if it could lead to anything," he said. "Maybe I could give Wells a can of spray paint and tell him to recreate the crime. But he's been lawyered up more than any deadbeat on *Law & Order*. Denying everything. Even his role in Menno's death. A deviant son of a—"

Makenna interjected again.

"You know, Brian, I haven't spent that much time in Morgan County but I can't help but think I've seen lettering like this before. Home-made signs, that is."

"Well, in this county, everyone and his retriever paints their own signs, Ken. They have home-based businesses, fixing lawn-mowers, small appliances—that kind of stuff. Some even play butcher, carving up deer in their back sheds."

"Guess they're common," she admitted. "Just an observation. Funny way to write, though."

He decided to change the subject.

"You've been talking with Hubie?"

"Yes, and he's as sweet as ever. That's why I was calling today. He invited me to Thanksgiving, which I think I'll do. My parents—" She hesitated a moment, reflecting on what she'd just said, continuing a delicate balancing act that had been in place since she met Boychuk nearly four years before, "are still on their cruise in the Caribbean, and for some reason, my grandfather knew that."

"I was the one who told Hubie about their cruise." Boychuk took pleasure in his revelation.

"You did?"

"Guess it sort've slipped out the last time I spoke to him."

"So, *you* were responsible for my invitation to Morgantown?" He sensed that his daughter was casting a smile in his direction.

"Perhaps…"

Now she laughed out loud.

"I should have known! Well, I told him I'd be there, and he said you'd drop over."

"I'll try my best, Ken, but either way, you and I will get together."

"Brian, you don't have to tell me, and it's none of my business, but are things not going well between you and Susan?"

It was Boychuk's turn to find a lump in his throat. Now was not the time to reveal his fate, but an answer was required.

"Not great, I'm afraid," he replied.

"I'm sorry to hear that." There was a pause in their conversation.

"Don't be Ken. It's been a long time coming."

BIDDING HIS DAUGHTER ADIEU, Boychuk gazed once again across Turnbull's parking lot, digesting the words that just came out the young woman's mouth. Not those of sympathy for the tenuous state of his union, but for her opinion about the penmanship of his perp. Makenna's instincts, her innate curiosity, will make her a force in the criminal-busting world. Yet to find one home-made sign in a forty-mile radius of the Troyer farm and *one* that resembled the message on Menno's carriage could be a daunting task. A needle in the proverbial haystack.

But it deserved another shot. He picked up his police phone and ordered Jimmy, still at the office, to make copies of the photo for every patrol vehicle under his jurisdiction, and for those at the local Troopers' barracks. Now they would be on the lookout for any sign that included the archaic, curly-Q look of the first letter in the alphabet. He still felt Wells was responsible but he would give it a shot.

First, however, he decided to pay another visit to Turnbull's and its portly manager, who was still fussing outside with his late fall displays.

"Couldn't get rid of those grills at summer prices, eh, Darryl?" he said as he stepped from his vehicle. The manager, bent over and appearing winded, looked up at the arriving sheriff and smiled.

"That's why you need to pick up one right now, Brian. I've got some great deals here. I bet one of these dandies would fit in the back of that truck of yours!"

"That assumes that I have the time to barbeque a steak once in a while, my friend," Boychuk replied. "So, don't count on me to spend any money here today. Actually, I'm here on police business."

The store manager's eyebrows arched upwards. His interest was piqued.

"You remember that case of arson and assault over at the Troyer farm that we were investigating back in September?"

Darryl nodded. "Yeah, poor man..."

"Well, then you'll remember one of my guys coming around asking about your sales of spray paint, especially when we discovered that you stock such paint? You know, the stuff that people use to paint over rust…that kind of thing?"

"One of my clerks told me about your deputy's visit," he said. "I was over in the Gouverneur store that day, I think, but I heard he was here, asking some questions."

"Yeah, the paint chip I scraped off Menno's wagon was consistent with a specific brand you sell here. It came from a can of *RustOleum* or one of those types. Not that your competitors around here don't stock it as well, but your store is the closest to the Troyer farm."

The manager nodded again, evidently remembering the episode. His store had carried those kinds of paints but not in large numbers, perhaps a few cans at best. His mind was working overtime. An idea came to him.

"You know, Brian, I had a fill-in clerk for the last couple of months, the same person that Jimmy questioned when he showed up. She said she couldn't remember selling any cans of spray paint—well, in fact, she was the type of gal who couldn't remember a lot of things, like how to count cash for one, and that's why she's not here anymore. Since Jo left a few years ago—you know, Joanne Lowry… she's using her Schumacher name again, I guess—I can't get good help. Unemployment's over twelve percent and I still can't find decent people!"

"Guess it's better to collect unemployment and bitch about not having any money," he admitted. He saw this phenomenon occurring in the quality of applications he was receiving for recruits.

Darryl continued, "But you might want to talk to my full-timer. She left on maternity leave around Labor Day, but she's back now. She might remember some such sale before that."

"She here?" Boychuk asked.

"Yup," he said, pointing to the front of the store.

"By any chance, you still have a can of that rust paint on the shelf, Darryl?"

"Probably, let's go see."

The two men entered the store, by now busy with tradesmen, their carts filled with their required wares. There were, as well, a few familiar cottagers from Remington Pond about to close their places for the season. At the side, where Darryl had set up a complimentary coffee pot and boxes of donuts coated heavily with powdered sugar, several men dressed in windbreakers, jeans and ball caps were milling about. The Fishbone Café and the post office were the most popular dens of gossip in town, but Turnbull's was a close third.

He and Darryl were walking briskly towards the paint aisle when one of the locals sipping coffee summoned him over.

"Brian, Brian! Just the guy I wanna see!" It was Whitey, a bony bearded man in his late forties. He was wearing greasy denim overalls over a pair of steel-toed work boots. He was a fixture here; a dry-waller, a trucker, a seasonal tree-pruner, and sometime wood-splitter and a guy who scrambled daily to make a buck. But it seemed to Boychuk he spent more time kibitzing at Turnbull's than on any of his day jobs. When he smiled, as he did today, evidence of crooked, cigarette-stained teeth came into full view. The man had a first name but nobody used it.

"C'mon over here a minute!"

Signaling to Darryl to put their mission on pause, Boychuk strolled towards the coffee machines. Now Whitey had an audience.

"Brian, got a good one for you today," Whitey announced exuberantly. He proceeded to tell his joke.

"D'ja hear about the young Amish boy going to the mall for the first time?" he asked. Boychuk shook his head, giving him permission to proceed.

"Okay, here goes. Seems this Amish boy and his father were in the mall for the first time and were just amazed by two shiny silver walls that could move apart and slide back together again." His eyes tilted upwards. "Hear this one?"

"Not yet, Whitey," the sheriff replied. The others stood idly by, smiling in anticipation. They had heard it before, but would enjoy it again.

"Okay, so's the kid asks his father, 'What's this, Papa?' Puzzled, the old man says, 'don't know, son...strangest thing I ever seen.' So, as the boy and his father continue to watch in amazement, this fat old broad with gray chin hairs waddles up to the moving walls and presses the button. Magically, the walls open and the fat lady walks in. Then the walls close."

Now Whitey's eyes began to sparkle. He was gearing up. "So, the Amish kid and his father watch as the numbers above the doors light up. One-two-three and so on. Then the numbers reach the end and then start falling in reverse order. Finally the silver walls open up again and out steps this gorgeous young blonde! Just beautiful!"

With a snicker, Whitey paused a brief moment. He was hoping he wouldn't blow the punch line.

"Well, the father, not taking his eyes off the young girl, tells his son, '*GO GET YOUR MOTHER!*'"

He burst into an uproarious laugh, interrupted by a long coughing spell that was alleviated only when Whitey took another sip of his coffee. Boychuk, chuckling, joined the rest of the assembled clatch in congratulations.

"D'ja like that one, Sheriff? Eh?" Whitey asked after regaining control of his damaged larynx.

"Not bad, Whitey," he said, with a laugh. "But take my advice. Don't sell your pruning shears."

Wishing them a productive day, Boychuk offered a friendly wave and before he and Darryl knew it, they were in the middle of the paint aisle. They secured the last can of paint that matched the color and texture of the hateful missive. Then, in a matter of minutes, Boychuk returned to the important business at hand, a conversation with Darryl's cashier. The new mother's name was Melissa. She was about nineteen with a sea of freckles across her round, effervescent face, and struggled to fit into her Turnbull's jacket.

She told her story.

To Boychuk's surprise and satisfaction, her grasp for details was as good as any investigator. Her memory was excellent.

Melissa would make a fine witness.

Thanking her for the information, Boychuk bounded out the door with vigor, his SUV soon lumbering down one of the side roads of his big county.

THIRTY-FIVE

A S DARKNESS SETTLED over Seward Avenue, in brisk, forty-five degree weather, the Schumacher family let out a collective roar as Joanne tossed a flaming wad of newsprint on a towering pyramid of kindling and, in an instant, a furious inferno lighted the skies like the Arctic borealis. In one brief moment, on the site of her former home, Joanne erased twenty-five years of a past that she thought was almost too despicable to forget. This wasn't just any blaze. They were there to effect closure. Her intention was to torch the memory of her septic-pumping, beer-swilling, skank-chasing, wife-abusing spouse forever.

The first item to feed the fire was a section of her house's exterior, her entire back stoop, a rotting, dangerous porch that should have been condemned a decade before. For Joanne, who often slipped on its wobbly steps as she bounded off to work at Turnbull's, it was symbolic of her marriage itself.

To Hubie's chagrin, next came his late wife's Maplewood hutch. He had argued that it was still in good condition; it could have found a home somewhere. But Joanne, stubborn as she was, was not prepared to share her nightmares with any family, as poor or needy as they might have been. The hutch still had indentations that were caused by Denny's right fist just after he sent her flying against the dining room wall. She still had nightmares of its contents—the wine glasses, cups and saucers—crashing around inside, many shattering on impact, including her mother's prized church plate. The surviving dishes could be donated, she'd conceded. But the damned hutch was going up in smoke.

However, Joanne had acceded to her father's counsel on a couple of items. One was Denny's ancient, forest-green La-Z-Boy. Something about not wanting to alert the state's environmental cops, she was told. Nor did Hubie think much of her intention to designate her husband's weighty, tubular Zenith for destruction. It was that television that had broadcast Denny's favorite show—*Friday Night Fights*—his favorite if and only if he had forsaken the Paddle or Swigs and made it home after work. Joanne gave that TV to the consignment store downtown, and if it sold, she'd donate the money to the Sally Ann.

What was especially satisfactory was watching Denny's most storied prize go up in smoke, a grotesque, full-antlered moose head that some Waddington taxidermist had stuffed after one of his successful hunting trips to Québec. She had cringed when he had brought that damn thing home, its long nostrils flaring, its sad melting eyes following her around the garage as if the beast was blaming her for its demise. That she was successful in keeping it out of the house was one of the few victories she'd had in her twenty-year marriage.

Yes, there was likely some residual value in the dwelling. But no family young or old would be moving in here, she vowed, if only to prevent them from living in a house with such a violent past. She would not foist that specter of savagery on anyone. Instead, she had asked an Amish carpenter from across the bridge—no relation to Menno Troyer—to round up five or six of his order at nine dollars an hour to demolish the six-decade-old dwelling. Her instructions were simple: haul away whatever their big buckboards could carry, but leave a few specific remnants for this night. This was no simple catharsis on her part; her house was a monument to evil and had to be razed.

Now four years to the day after the shotgun blasts rang true, Joanne arose again in her chair, downing the last few ounces of a Bud Light and smiled in the direction of the man in her life. Matt had returned from their truck with his favorite Gibson guitar, an aging Blues King that boasted an autograph by John Jorgenson, the magical gypsy jazzist, country rocker and one-time stringer for Elton John. Booker planned to strum a few bars tonight.

In the chairs next to Matt sat her dad and Dee, and next to them was Brent, who had returned home from California for the long weekend. At twenty-four, he was as tall but less broad-shouldered than his late father, while inheriting his handsome looks from his mother. Joanne's kid had done everything in his power to escape his old man's clutches, Hubie said often, in pride. When the tragic events of four years before occurred, Brent, in his youthful naiveté, had heaped the blame on his mother. That was until Jane convinced him the real victim was not his father, but Joanne. Now Brent was standing only yards from where his bedroom once stood, and his mind was racing.

On his arm was Tracy, his wife of two years. A petite Syracuse grad, Brent had followed her to the west coast when she landed a Silicon Valley engineering job. But fresh from a Cornell degree in hotel management, his job search was a short one, having been scooped up a week later by a golf resort. This night, Tracy sported a Lindsey Vonn-styled ski jacket over a pair of blue jeans. Pulled tightly around her free-flowing blonde hair was a charcoal-colored, woolen hat that resembled the Alpine skier, post-race. She had met Denny at his worst one Christmas. She would be by her husband's side on this night.

"Have to say, Mom, it's pretty weird seeing all this," he reflected.

"Yeah, my thoughts too, baby," Joanne replied. "But that's why we're all here. Finally…maybe we can all move on."

"You always said this is what you've wanted to do with the old dump," he smiled. "And for that I love you…"

Joanne returned his affection. She knew how much grief her son had been through in his short life. No kid deserved that.

Over by herself sat Makenna, her arms crossed, her eyes also transfixed on the blaze. She was seemingly lost in thought, Joanne thought. She admired her niece's strength this night. Makenna didn't have to be here but she too needed closure.

"Booker, you ready for another?" Joanne asked.

"Yep, beer me, Jo. We're not going anywhere for a while." Joanne went to the cooler to fetch her beau an O'Doul's. After nearly fifteen years of brushing his teeth with Jack Daniels, after decades of inhaling, snorting, digesting and mainlining every substance known to touring bands from Nashville to Los Angeles, Matt was clean and dry. It was either that or "goin' below ground for a long, long time," he'd said. A move to the mountains had saved his life. Meeting Joanne had enriched it.

Sitting comfortably in an Adirondack chair, now sipping her preferred Chardonnay, sat Barbara. She was wearing one of Dee's winter coats and—in honor of her daughter—a pair of bright turquoise earmuffs that she had purchased from the hospital gift shop. She and Roger had made the trip north for Thanksgiving, another respite from their ongoing nightmare. Ria was on everyone's mind, and Barbara's standard answer was "no change."

"Ken, too bad your dad couldn't make it over tonight," Barb said. "That job of his...well, does he ever sleep?"

Makenna shrugged.

"Not much. Those arson and assault cases are still haunting him, and he's still at the office. Actually, they might have a break in the case and he's waiting for a warrant. Had to send a deputy over to a cabin in Cranberry Lake to find the judge."

Joanne was inquisitive along other lines. "Is it true that he and Susan are done?"

"Yes..." Makenna replied, a look of resignation splashing across her face. She had wondered and worried whether her entry into Boychuk's world had precipitated their separation. "We had coffee this morning, and he told me. Always so sad when these things happen."

"Not surprised, though," Hubie offered. "He wasn't happy...and I don't think she was either. Never having kids was a good thing and, besides, we all knew his one true love—"

"—was Jane," Joanne interrupted. "They were high school sweethearts who didn't get past high school."

Joanne changed her train of thought.

"Oh, almost forgot to tell you, I heard from Roberto this morning," she continued. "He calls me every Thanksgiving...never misses." She was referring to the last man in her sister's life. His name was Alvarez, and he was a Manhattan lawyer that she met in Jamaica.

"How is my favorite Argentinian?" Hubie enquired. The elder Schumacher thought the handsome Hispanic was a man of integrity who had stood by both of his daughters when it mattered. Emotionally and legally.

"Still in New York, for now, but on his way to D.C.," Joanne said, glancing in Makenna's direction. "Took a leave of absence from his law firm to join your mom's old boss at the Treasury. Seems our ex-governor was so impressed with Roberto that when he was appointed Secretary he made it clear that he wanted Alvarez to head up some unit that will investigate white collar crime. That's about all I know."

"About time!" Barbara piped in.

"Oh, Jesus..." Hubie retorted. "You never give it a rest, do you?"

"Maybe when I see a few CEOs go to jail, Hubert," she said.

"Well, Alvarez is a smart guy," Hubie replied. "Honorable, too. You don't always find that in lawyers." Then he added with a grin, "Course, Foley was always a good judge of character. Asked for *my* vote, after all."

"Probably the best ballot you've ever cast," his sister retorted. Hubie just smiled and shook his head. Persistent woman, he thought.

"Roberto tells me he misses Jane so much," Joanne continued. "Says she was the sassiest, sexiest and smartest woman he ever met!"

"Brian wouldn't argue with that," Hubie ventured.

Dee entered the conversation. "Anyone new in his life?"

"Yes, apparently," Joanne replied. "It took a bit of an effort to pry it out of him—he's a very private guy—but he tells me there is a lady.

Says he has no plans to get married again, but promises me that he'll introduce her to us if it gets that far."

"Well," Hubie said, glancing affectionately at Makenna, "your dad probably knew since he was a teenager that he never really had a chance with your mom." Before his words could sink in, Joanne interrupted him.

"Jane was just too restless," she replied. "She never would have stayed in Morgantown. Too many awful memories and, besides, the world was too large for her."

"True," Hubie said. "Always felt bad for Boychuk, though. But he knows in his heart that this break with Susan is good for him. They never really clicked. He knew he had to move on, sooner or later."

An upbeat Dee intervened.

"Speaking of good, Makenna, have you told him your news?"

Joanne was the first to enquire. "What news? What's going on?"

Makenna's smile was now ear to ear.

"The FBI has accepted me into its forensic intern program," she announced, her sculptured face radiating. "I'm starting in January!"

"Oh, man, that is great news!" Hubie beamed. "Brian'll be happy to hear that. Always was *his* dream, you know, since he was a kid."

"I know," Makenna said. "Sometimes he thinks he might've missed the boat. But I won't be front-line. I'll be in the lab a long time before getting assigned to a case. Still, I am so excited. Just heard yesterday!"

"He doesn't know yet?"

"Nope, I want to surprise him tonight, if he can break away."

As hugs of congratulations abounded, Barbara sat back with wistfulness. She was hoping to see Boychuk tonight as well. She wished he would arrive with news—real news—about the one investigation that truly mattered to her. The violence that had beset the Amish was traumatic, and so unnecessary. But Ria's tragedy was the first in a chain of events, precipitating all others; if Ria had not been assaulted on that Saturday night before Labor Day, none of the events at the Amish farm would have occurred. Deep down, however, she knew that Brian may never be able to satisfy her frustrations, though her suspicions matched his. Just no proof—yet.

"It's just awful what happened to those poor Amish people," Barbara offered. "This country's made some big strides in the last twenty years but..." Her voice trailed off.

"There's always a 'but' when it comes to Barb," Roger said with a grin. He had been sitting in an upright chair beside his wife, wrapped in one of Hubie's parkas, sipping chamomile tea. Since contracting his illness, his drinking days were nearly over. A glass of Syrah, occasionally, but not much more.

"But what I'm saying is this country is racist," Barb continued. "Has been throughout history. Jefferson and Washington owned hundreds of slaves, and yet they're national treasures. Name any period over the past two hundred years and we'd find bigotry and prejudice. Even here, unfortunately, it rears its ugly head."

Hubie, who was patting Griz's large cranium gently as the loyal animal lay by his feet, decided to weigh in.

"The Amish are easy targets, that's for sure," he agreed.

"That Brad might have been part of it makes me sick," Barbara said.

"He denies all involvement, honey," Roger added, "other than joining his friend in that barn."

"I don't know what to believe from him," Barbara countered. "Answer me this: why isn't he here? He chose to go hunting, Roger. *Hunting!* And he's still talking about spending the winter in Key Largo. That says a lot about his priorities these days."

More like another means of escape, Hubie thought. Maybe the sordidness of the Troyer episode would be sufficient for Brad to flick the switch. Finally figure out how to become a responsible human being. Or maybe not.

Still mesmerized by the flames, now roaring with the fuel that once was finely lacquered furniture, Makenna decided to reenter the conversation.

"This has been wonderful for me," she said. "I look around this fire and see a family that has seen more than its share of grief. But right now, all I feel is the love. I'm so happy to have been included... thank you!" As she looked skyward to the stars, Joanne could see pearls of tears forming in Makenna's eyes.

"Your mom would be so proud of you," Joanne offered.

Watching the poignant scene unfold, his guitar prepped, Matt decided to enliven the moment.

"As someone famous might have said, *'if music be the food of love, play on!'*"

Taken by surprise, Barbara spoke up.

"That's impressive, Matt," she said. "Any man who can quote Shakespeare by a north country bonfire is a man after my own heart."

"I've loved his stuff for a long time, Barb," he replied. "You know...when I landed in California, in between all the beer joints I played in, and all the travellin' around I did, I took some courses at UCLA. Being a songwriter since I was about ten years old, I thought it would be good to learn a few things, maybe broaden my knowledge, that sort of thing. Even considered for a time landing a degree of some sort...why, I have no idea since I could never see myself with a real job, carrying a briefcase and wearing a suit!"

Joanne chimed in, chuckling. "Now that would be sight, Booker. I've never seen as much as a tie in your closet!"

"Probably never will, Jo," he laughed, pointing to a pair of black cowboy boots. "The closest thing I've owned to dress shoes are these shit-kickers. But, yeah, got over that idea damned quick. Still, I've always enjoyed a little history. The Greeks and the Romans—"

Roger interrupted. "History tells us those great empires fell not from foreign enemies but were destroyed from within," he said. "Much like our own if we don't learn to govern ourselves better."

Matt nodded with affirmation at the intelligent classics professor across from him. "English Lit, too, Rog. Any songwriter worth his spit has to read the novels by the greatest of writers, all of whom you know more about than I do. But then...I found myself immersed in Shakespeare again. For the first time since my ninth grade days back in Seneca Falls, I started reading a few of Shakespeare's tragedies. Hamlet, Macbeth, Othello, Lear—"

"—a cultured rock star!" Roger interrupted. "The esteem with which we hold for you is growing by the minute!"

Matt smiled at the compliment. "Well, we all know that his tragedies were the stories of love, war, honor, ambition, madness, revenge, treachery...in other words, what goes on in everyday life!"

Another round of chuckles.

Roger cast a glance at his wife but Barbara didn't flinch. Normally, by now, she would have interjected with more observations of her own. By the light of the fire's flickering flames, Roger could see that she appeared absent and disoriented, her mind evidently elsewhere; she was a much different creature than she had been before Labor Day. There had been dark days before, he thought. After all, she'd undergone brutal treatment for one of the most hideous of cancers. Now, however, he was reading her mind.

She was a mother.

She was facing a crisis greater than her own.

Lifted from her momentary trance, Barbara caught her husband's affectionate glances and smiled in return. This past summer, they had journeyed to the city to enjoy a few nights in Central Park, taking in several performances written by the English Bard, masterpieces from centuries before. Her tastes in the great man's writings, much like the content of their daily lives, were identical to Roger's. They were a good team.

Fine memories of Manhattan in the moonlight.

Mild evenings. Gentle breezes, summer stars...and Shakespeare. Their own version of a mid-summer's night dream.

And then she spoke.

"Thou torturest me," she muttered, in words barely audible for the family to hear.

"What did you say, Barb?" Dee asked.

"Oh, just something that came to mind. Especially with Matt mentioning Shakespeare." She paused a moment before continuing. "Just a wonderful sequence of words that just reminded me of something. Don't know why, exactly..."

"If I'm not mistaken," Booker offered, "are those words from *The Merchant of Venice?*"

Barb nodded.

Pacino's talents in the *Merchant* were the highlights of their summer. They had reveled in his powerful appearance, its relevancy arising in connection to her daughter's overwhelming love for a precious gem. And the memories of the actor's words were still reverberating through her mind.

So close to their predicament.

"Thou torturest me..." Dee repeated. The elder woman's eyes locked on Barb's as they shared a tender moment. "An interesting, even appropriate choice of words."

"Yes," Barbara added. "From the lips of Shakespeare's most famous lender, Shylock, a man in agony over the loss of his daughter. Very pertinent in my view."

The family around the fire grew silent once again, reflecting on what Barbara had said.

Finally, Hubie spoke.

"We haven't lost her, sis," he said. "She will return. She will get better. You'll see."

Barbara rose from her chair and kissed Hubie on the cheek. Never had Barbara adored her brother as much as she did now. She felt blessed, truly blessed. She had *two* wonderful men in her life, a loving, caring husband and a supportive older brother, and together they would get through this tragedy. Still, she faced a series of vexing questions: what did Ria do to deserve such pain? What did she do to merit such a horrible fate? All her beautiful daughter had done was meet a man, and for all they knew, fall in love. It was so unfair.

Now Barbara decided not to dwell on her pain. Instead, rising to her feet, she raised her glass of Chardonnay. "To my beautiful Ria! May she survive to run many more races..."

"Many, many more," Joanne replied, tipping her beer in her aunt's direction.

Deciding that a little levity was required, Booker rejoined the conversation.

"Remember Willy's words," he offered. "'*Love all, trust a few and do wrong to none*'. You know, that's kind've been the way I've been living my life these days." He turned his attention to Joanne. "At least, since I fixed that flat tire of yours up in those hills."

"And catching me singing at your piano!" she laughed.

He began to strum his Gibson. "Now, is it time for some music?"

To a chorus of approvals from the family, Booker launched a few bars of a familiar ballad. Something about being '*caught between the longing for love and the struggle for the legal tender.*' Abruptly his fingers stopped.

"As Jackson Browne would say, I'm just a '*happy idiot*'."

"Happy, yes, Booker," Joanne corrected. "Idiot, no."

"Remember this?" he asked. "This was the song that Jane bought for a quarter on the jukebox in the bar that night. Never forgot it. She said, 'C'mon Mellancamp...*let's dance!*'"

Joanne beamed at the memory.

"So, take a listen," he said, launching into the ballad from the beginning.

"**M**R. SCHUMACHER?**"

Hubie swung around in surprise. Amid the laughter and music over the ensuing half hour or so, he failed to see or hear Joshua approach from the street. Standing tall, and clutching his hat in shy deference to the assembled group, Hubie could see that Joshua's brown curly locks had begun to cover his ears once again. Gone was the clean-cut appearance that he had sported in September.

Predictably, the younger man was dressed in traditional Amish winter garments, which in Hubie's opinion, were woefully inadequate for the harsh climate that northern New York promised. In the distance was his black buggy; it was parked at the end of the driveway and led by his big Belgian Bay horse. But the Amish shunned night travel. Why would Josh be coming here so late in the evening?

Hubie rose from his chair to greet his young friend. Noticing his master on the move, Griz rose as well, dutifully ready to follow.

"What brings you here at this hour?"

"Sir...I need to talk with you."

Hubie turned towards his family. Now all eyes were glued to the young Amish man.

"Everybody?" Hubie decided to do an introduction of sorts.

"This is Joshua Troyer...a friend of mine."

As the rest of the group offered collective waves of acknowledgement, Roger's eyes met Joshua's, offering a smile in friendship. They had met before and Joshua had passed the grade. Barbara, however, looked on with benign curiosity, her eyes displaying only signs of neutrality at best. So *this* was the guy, she thought, scanning Joshua from head to toe. A nice-looking young man, she conceded, with a sensitive and sympathetic face, even caring...so unlike the other guy. But the logician in her needed to face the facts: if Ria had *not* met this Troyer man on Labor Day weekend, she would not be fighting for survival. That was Barbara's rationale tonight. Her emotions were still raw.

"Josh, let's take a walk," Hubie suggested, sensing the young man's desire for privacy. Theirs was a strong relationship, almost mirroring that of father-son, and it began well before Joshua had rescued him from his fallen tractor. But it had gelled that day, and for weeks afterwards, when the Amish man offered assistance at every turn. Later, Hubie had returned the favor; he had come to Joshua's rescue when he discovered him alone on a quiet county road outside town, attempting to repair a broken axle on his buckboard. Together they had rescued the day.

Now standing beside the tethered Temper, Joshua unloaded. It was a purging of emotions that was remarkable for its truth and clarity. Listening intently, Hubie knew he was witnessing the very essence of a young man in trouble with himself. His sobs, uncontrollable at times, were so powerful that Hubie wrapped his arms around Joshua as if he was his own offspring.

Menno had been a strict and distant man but not an unloving father, Hubie surmised. He just wanted what most fathers had wanted for their children—happiness and peace. But, for Menno, a stubborn adherence to principle and tradition—and church—had trumped all else, so much so that he hadn't realized how much pressure he had heaped on his eldest son. And Joshua had buckled under. Their terrible argument had divided his parents and saddened the family, only minutes before Menno had met his fate. And now Joshua was blaming himself.

"I should never have gotten involved with her..." the young man began, bending the older man's ears. Though Joshua's words rang true, Hubie tried in gentle and compassionate terms to say that it was acceptable for Joshua to follow his heart. That regret for a troubled past should not consume him now—and more importantly, down the road of life. After all, Hubie had some experience dealing with regret. A 'totally useless emotion,' his daughter Jane had always declared—and she was right. Now, as he held the shoulders of a trembling, grief-stricken young man, Hubie felt a rebirth of sorts. A feeling of euphoria swept over him. That he had not been there for his children when they needed him the most was true. But now, finally, he could assist a young man mourning the loss of his father. Hubie could now be the man he had always wanted to be.

"Joshua, I understand," he said after Joshua finished his thoughts. "But you only have one life. You're young...and you should take the time to think these things through. It's too soon for a decision like this...your dad has been gone only a couple of months." Hubie intentionally let his voice trail away.

"Are you sure you want to do this?"

Joshua paused before replying, the weight of the world on his broad youthful shoulders.

"Yes, sir," Joshua replied. "I am an adult. My family is important to me and I must do what is right. It is expected of me..."

THIRTY-SIX

SHORTLY AFTER NOON the next day, Boychuk and his senior deputy led a cortege of sheriff's vehicles down the rolling back roads of Morgan County towards the farm of Jonas Zook. He had heard rumblings that another Amish gathering had been planned, hastily it seemed, and now his worst suspicions were confirmed. At least thirty black carriages, their horses hitched and acquiescent, were parked in every available space leading to the Zook farmhouse. Once again, Boychuk knew he would be the usurper, the interloper, the 'English' carpetbagger.

The day was typical for November, with ominous, low-level clouds threatening not only rain but snow. Not exactly an ideal setting for an event to take place outdoors, but it was a ceremony that had to occur once a family decision had been made.

For the Zooks, however, the weather was irrelevant. This was to be a day of celebration, a *Hinglefleisch* frolic named in honor of their clucking foul, prepared in huge quantities, slaughtered, fried and served to an expected one hundred attendees. Mary Zook was clearly in charge; she was the matron of the house, placing in servitude her girls, their local friends and most of her female relatives hailing from counties far and wide.

Boychuk pulled his cruiser to the side of the road, and signaled to his deputies in the trailing vehicle to do the same. Rolling down his window, he could hear the mellifluous sounds of the elders, mostly men, singing hymns from their benches located near the opening of the barn. Young girls dressed in ground-hugging blue dresses were passing trays of food, offering a wide array of candies, fruits, cookies and cakes to the clan. Over to the side, the police officer saw a series of long tables festooned with bowls of their summer bounty: corn on the cob, fried onions, fresh baked bread and, of course, celery.

The sheriff was well versed in such Amish rituals; Menno, God rest his soul, had spoken about them with enthusiasm, likely in anticipation for such blessed events for his own children.

Menno...

His was a memory that prompted the sheriff to pause a moment in reflection. Perhaps now he could bring some justice to his late friend and his troubled family.

Casting his eyes around the gaggle of invited guests, Boychuk spotted the bride. There was Hannah, resplendent in her finest full-length dress, a dark navy in color, of course, and complete with her best black bonnet. The man in him figured Hannah would make *any* Amish man a good wife. It would be her responsibility to darn the quilts, till the gardens, bake the pies and breads, and sell baskets by the road. All while giving birth to as many new members of their labor pool as she could over the next twenty years.

The sheriff gazed again across the property. The older women, made frumpy from years of near-annual childbirth and their affinity for sweets, were organized and orderly. Waiting for instructions from Mary were the nubile nieces and daughters who had yet to take the plunge. In this mix, Hannah stood out. Wearing the broadest of smiles, she was giggling with one of her friends. She was happy.

Then Boychuk spotted the bridegroom. He, too, stood apart; his buttoned down suit was crisp as lettuce, his boots polished a midnight black and covering his growing locks was a new straw hat. He was clean-shaven, as expected, though that would change now that he would become a married man.

As the ceremony was about to commence, Boychuk raised his hand again in the direction of his deputies' vehicles. Wait, was the message. Now Bishop Jakes, alone at the front of the barn, stood stoic at a lectern as the prospective bride and groom emerged together. They were followed to the front by their side sitters, or as the English would say, groomsmen and bridesmaids. The service was surprisingly brief, perhaps only a couple of minutes long and, immediately, family and friends surrounded the newly married couple, offering their best wishes.

Though distance prevented him from hearing the spoken words, Boychuk knew the bishop was engaging his flock. He knew their presence today would be reviled. There was no getting around it, however. He had a job to do and he'd do it. Nodding in Jimmy's direction and releasing a huge breath of air, he placed his Tahoe in drive and soon passed the buggies, the tethered animals and their youthful attendants, stopping just short of the wedding party. From the passenger seat of his SUV, he retrieved his flat-brimmed hat, a symbol of authority if there ever was one, and placed it on his head.

Unlike his relationship with Menno Troyer, Boychuk was unfamiliar with the Zook family, with little or no interaction with Jonas himself. They had exchanged waves occasionally from across the cornfields or by the edge of the road as he had passed by the family's farm, smiling as the slim-shouldered man with the carrot-blonde beard went about his daily work. But Boychuk could not say he knew the patriarch of the clan.

Today, that would change.

In an instant, the arrival of the police vehicles began to alarm the assembly, a look of concern enveloping their faces. Revelers who moments ago had hugged and congratulated the newlyweds, smiling, joking and laughing, stopped in their tracks as the uniformed cops arrived at the place of festivities.

Boychuk walked conspicuously towards Joshua and his new bride. There was no sign of Menno's widow; she was likely helping Mary Zook in the preparation of the noon meal. But the groom's sister was there; Rachel was among the attendants, and so were her younger siblings. Feelings of guilt overcame the sheriff. This family had seen enough tragedy this year, but he was hoping that his actions today would alleviate some of their pain.

"Joshua...*Mrs. Troyer*, let me be the first to congratulate you," he declared sincerely but without emotion. "My deputies and I wish you a very happy life together."

"Thank you, Sheriff," Joshua replied meekly.

Jonas Zook was the first to intervene in Boychuk's path.

"Sheriff, can we help you?" The arrival of the police on this day of all days had twisted his face into contortion. It was filled with anguish.

"I apologize for our presence here today, Jonas," he declared.

"Then what is your business?" Jonas was growing indignant, as Boychuk knew he would. The Amish farmer's eyes became cold and venomous, his anger steadily building. "This is my daughter's wedding day! Whatever your mission, couldn't it have waited until tomorrow?"

"Again, I apologize, Jonas, but we're here to speak with a couple of your guests," Boychuk said, scrutinizing the assembly.

"Who?" Jonas demanded.

The sheriff spotted his first target near the serving tables. He was a man standing next to his brother. He was shorter than Joshua by at least three inches and less well-built. The sheriff had seen both before, around town and in their fields, but had never spoken to them. As the commotion gathered force, others attending the nuptials moved in, providing a semi-circle of support. These people stuck by each other. Violators of their traditions were not welcome.

"Daniel Jakes?" the sheriff asked.

"Yes, I am him," said Daniel. His brother Lucas, a near twin in appearance but about sixteen months his junior, was now shuffling about in trepidation. Both wore frowns of fear, a look that did not go unnoticed by the sheriff and his entourage.

"Well, Daniel Jakes, I have a warrant for your arrest in connection with the assault and battery on Menno Troyer in September. I am also placing you under arrest for the crime of arson and the burning of Mr. Troyer's hayfields the night before the attack."

The congregation let out a collective gasp, and began muttering amongst themselves. Instantly, Boychuk felt out of place. It was as if he had just parachuted into a Anabaptist Bavarian village during the sixteenth century. In seconds, his deputy had the stunned young man in custody, reading him his Miranda rights to deaf, and likely incomprehensible, ears.

Jonas Zook was in shock, his mouth agape, his nearly coal-black eyes glaring at the English invaders. The lanky bishop, who moments before was clearly in charge, was also visibly furious. Nothing in the lives of these older men had prepared them for this.

"W-w-what is the meaning of this, Sheriff?" a stuttering Jonas cried. "How can you say that young Jakes here is responsible for those events?"

Boychuk, twenty-five years a cop, was ready for such a confrontation. He would go on the offensive and nail the guilty parties right here and now.

"Perhaps you should address that question to the bishop's son, Jonas," he replied. He fixed his eyes on young Jakes, now in handcuffs.

"What's your story, Daniel?" he began. "Why did you burn Menno's hay that night...only to return the following night to commit even worse acts? Attacking him. Cutting off his beard? Terrifying his family by spray-painting his carriage?"

Dumbfounded, Daniel would make one last attempt at denial.

"I-I, uh, didn't do it!" He looked into Jonas's eyes for compassion, but there was none. The elder Zook knew the police were a cautious lot; they wouldn't risk such charges if they didn't have evidence.

By now, the bride herself was nearly apoplectic with grief. Hannah's eyes darted back and forth between her father, her new husband and the sheriff. Joshua himself was listening to the conversations, but stood silent.

"I don't understand," she cried. "On my wedding day! Daniel, is this true? Did you do those things?"

Ignoring the rapidly growing emotional scene, Boychuk knew he would have to stick to his plan.

"Daniel, we know you were responsible for the fires and the attacks. Earlier this morning, we were able to put it all together. The spray paint you used on the back of Menno's buggy, the message you wrote, telling the Troyers to leave the area was the same paint we found in your barn."

Daniel was now stuttering in disbelief and denial.

"I did nothing of this sort, Sheriff!"

But Boychuk continued with his indictment.

"On the contrary, Daniel, you gave yourself away. The lettering you used in your hateful message was the proof. It is identical to the sign right outside your farm, advertising that you have '*Sheds For Sale*'. The letters you used are identical to those used in that word— *Kraut*—that was painted on Menno's buggy. Not a very nice word to call one of your own, was it Daniel? Coming from us—the *English* as you would say—is bad enough. But from you?"

The younger Jakes said nothing.

Boychuk took his silence as permission to continue.

"The electric razor too, the one you used on poor Menno's beard? Now I asked myself, why would Amish like you want to buy such a razor? But then I found out why, since we have a witness, a cashier at Turnbull's who'll testify that you bought it—and the spray paint—at her store just before the attacks. We have it all."

"No…" Daniel muttered in his defense.

"Afraid so," Boychuk replied. "And not a smart move, Dan. It was just a matter of time until we would figure this out."

Boychuk would go one step further. Though forensics had yet to link the fingerprints found on the gas can near the Troyer farm to the can of spray paint, he was confident that they too would prove the kid's guilt.

"You know, the one thing I'm not sure of, Daniel, is why? Why'd you do it, Daniel? What did you have against Menno and his family?"

The sheriff guessed right. He wagered that Daniel would cave under his interrogation, and he did. His eyes filling with rage, his hands rattling the stainless steel cuffs now locked around his wrists, Daniel exploded.

"Menno and Joshua were *shaming* us!" he bellowed. "Joshua became involved with that English woman. He had *relations* with that woman!"

Daniel's eyes were now locked on the bridegroom's, his competition for Hannah's attention. His nemesis.

He continued, "At the same time, he was preparing for marriage to my Hannah—"

Hannah interrupted.

"My Hannah? Well, that was never—"

"Yes, Hannah, it was I who wanted you for my wife—not that man!" he hissed, nodding in Joshua's direction. "He doesn't want you!"

It was Joshua's turn to interject.

"That's not true..." he said without conviction. Glancing again at Joshua, Boychuk could see some anger growing in his eyes as well. For a fleeting moment, he thought Joshua would lunge at Jakes in retribution. But the newly-married man kept his peace.

"Now, you weren't alone those nights, were you Dan?" Boychuk said, returning to his investigation. "Who was with you?" The sheriff shifted his attention to Lucas, who was standing mute throughout the bitter exchange. "It was you, wasn't it Lucas? You held Menno down that night, didn't you? While Daniel shaved Menno's beard? I'm right, aren't I?"

Awestruck at the charges, Lucas remained silent.

"Well, Lucas? You were there that night too, right?"

There was a pause as all eyes were focused on the younger Jakes man. Finally, his fearful eyes darting back and forth from those of the bishop's and others, Lucas nodded.

It was true.

Hannah, growing more distraught, her eyes welling, could not believe what was occurring. This was her special day. She had finally landed Joshua Troyer. It was preordained, he was hers and hers alone—but now her wedding day was in tatters. She pleaded with her father to make things right.

"Papa, this can't be true," she wailed. "Tell me it isn't happening."

Now it was the bishop's turn to speak.

"This is outrageous, Sheriff!" he roared. "I don't believe a word of it! You and your English law cannot come to our community and spew your lies!"

"Your boys here, Bishop, say differently," Boychuk replied. Signaling to Jimmy to arrest the second Jakes boy, now his attack would deepen. The young men would not act on their own volition. They required leadership.

"I'm curious, Bishop, about your role in all of this. Your boys here—" He paused a moment to let it sink in. "—wouldn't do anything on their own, would they? I'm thinking they alone wouldn't be that upset about Joshua and his dalliances with the English girl, now would they? No, it's my opinion that your boys needed direction."

His arms crossed tightly in defense, the reverend knew where the sheriff's questioning was going.

"Absolute falsehoods!" Jakes bellowed, his voice thundering in indignation. A gust of wind appeared, causing his long stringy beard to flutter wildly.

"What was it, Bishop?" Boychuk demanded. "What was your motive? Revenge? Against poor Menno...for blowing the whistle on your boys a few years ago? When my deputies caught them drinking? You blamed that on Menno, didn't you? Or what about those episodes of sex with a minor? Menno told me about that, too. But there wasn't much we could do about it. But he knew your boys were the instigators. Right?"

"These are outrageous lies, Sheriff!" The bishop scanned the assembled group, now in complete shock, their heads bowing in shame.

"Am I incorrect, Bishop?" Boychuk continued his accusations. He was building his palisade of evidence in front of the religious man's flock. He would go out on a limb, and use shock value to get to the truth. He believed that old man Jakes was a cultist who held disproportionate authority—in the extreme—over a close-knit community built on the sanctity of trust.

Not the first episode, either. There was word leaking out of one Ohio police precinct that another 'bishop' had sanctioned brutal violence, ordering his young brethren—sons and nephews—to beat those of his kind who disobeyed him. Worse, there was talk that the demonic religio had ordered married women to have sex with him.

To cleanse them of their sins...

All motivated, ostensibly, by religious differences—if not hedonistic desires.

Was Bishop Jakes such a man? Was he a latter day Branch Davidian? Like the wackos from Waco, but on a smaller scale? Or worse, a Charles Manson? Maybe, Boychuk now thought. Perhaps today he had stymied crimes yet to occur.

The sheriff's eyes scanned the assembly again. He knew his charges had stunned this group, especially on such a holy day. The looks on their faces said it all. They were attempting to digest the news. The English had always imposed their rules and their laws. They had flaunted their wanton ways upon their young, with their terrible temptations. But never would they have believed that their own kind would rise up and order physical attacks on a fellow member of their sect.

Joshua had sinned; that was true. He had disgraced his community. But he had shown remorse and had done his penance. He had asked for Hannah's hand in marriage, an act that welcomed him back to the fold. It was now up to their God to make the final judgment.

But Boychuk knew he had to close the deal on the Troyer case—now.

"You heaped the blame on Menno, didn't you, Bishop?" Boychuk said, his voice rising for effect. "First, for wanting to expose your boys and their fun with booze and sex? And now, for allowing his son—Joshua—to fall for an English girl? Am I right?"

Daniel was listening intently to the sheriff's new accusations. Now he too exploded in anger.

"Papa, tell him!" he screamed. "Tell him that you ordered Lucas and me to do those things to the Troyers!"

But the bishop would brook no further candor from his son.

"Stille junge!" Though the bishop blustered in his own tongue, Boychuk understood the meaning of what the elder Jakes was saying. He was shutting the kid up. He glanced over to another deputy standing nearby.

"Cuff the old man," he said. "And Mirandize him, too."

THIRTY-SEVEN

HEAVY, WET SNOW began to swirl throughout Morgan County as night fell, and soon accumulations of six inches were reported. Fortunately, the bitter chills of late November were sufficient to prevent an onslaught of ice rain, and for that Joshua was thankful. Temper and Sorel could navigate in snow without hardship. But ice was another matter.

Tonight was his wedding night. After the carriages had departed the Zook farm, their inhabitants still reeling from the mid-day arrests, Joshua busied himself with the task of delivering his new bride to their new home. Generously, Menno had set aside a small amount of cash for the purpose of helping his oldest son, and his bride-to-be—any *Amish* bride that was—settle their own property.

Their community of carpenters had offered to gather in huge numbers and build them a home on a vacant piece of property. But Joshua deemed it wiser to find a farm that already had a suitable dwelling, and fortunately, in October, an eight-acre parcel with a small barn and a two-story home became available about two miles down Federal Side Road. It was expected that Joshua would follow in Menno's footsteps. He and his new wife would procreate, quickly.

Hannah seemed to rebound quickly from the mayhem earlier in the day. Too quickly, in Joshua's opinion. The flock had split their emotions between anger and dismay but, almost magically, Hannah's mood transformed to one of elation, her tears of anger and grief turning into a look of frozen determination. Abruptly, she took charge, announcing loudly that the day's celebrations were over and it was time for everyone to leave. With frenetic, near hysterical energy, she had bounded from table to table to begin the clean-up. It was over, she said, regardless of what the Zooks had wanted for the rest of the day. It was time for everyone to leave. To many in attendance who were still in shock, it had bordered on rudeness. Uncharitable behavior, in fact.

Together they had travelled in the new carriage, another gift from his late father, to their new home. In anticipation for their first meal alone, Hannah had brought a basket containing several chicken dinners from the wedding feast, complete with mashed potatoes, gravy, salads, two pieces of apple pie and jelly rolls. Her new table, and its accompanying hutch, was festooned with two crystal vases—not for flowers as the English would have done as she told Joshua—but for a dozen or so large stalks of leafy green celery. It represented happiness. True happiness!

Now as he placed his horses in their stalls, Joshua couldn't escape the sense of sadness that had enveloped him. He knew he should have been content. He knew he should be enjoying a newfound peace of mind because, in his heart, he was doing the right thing. After all, he had told his father so; at dawn, breaking with Amish custom, he had visited his father's grave high above Remington Pond. There, briefly, he had wept again. There he had begged for Menno's forgiveness, declaring that he would finally make him proud.

But as he gazed into Temper's large sympathetic eyes, stroking his chestnut mane, all Joshua could see was her. *It was Ria.* They were together again on the bluffs above the Pond's dark, shallow waters, the foothills of the majestic Adirondacks looming large in the September moonlight. It was as clear a vision as he had ever had in his life for there she was again, her long flowing blonde hair cascading down a perfect spine, a pair of quick blue eyes lovingly teasing his own. Damn, he cursed. Why had he done this to himself? Why had he ventured so close to the big lake? Especially since he had avoided it every day for the past two months. But now he realized there would be no escaping what had happened. There would be no respite. The memories were just too strong.

Exhaling deeply, his tasks complete, Joshua trudged through the driving snow toward his new home, if he could call it that. He could have done better, he thought. In another life, he could have designed a stunning home of his own. One with sweeping porches and elegant dormers, like those of his native Ohio.

Instead, he had settled on this aging edifice. His future was set. With most of its window panes cracked and now covered with plastic sheathing to deter the bitter winds, Joshua realized that he had to turn this decrepit house into a home, erasing all evidence that English families once occupied the place. That meant removing its electrical outlets, disconnecting overhead lamps and ridding the place of a decades-old, oil-burning furnace. Now that he had dug a new latrine about fifty feet from the house, any and all signs of indoor plumbing would disappear as well. It would be an Amish home, now.

Yet there was much more to do. He had uprooted the worn and spotted carpeting that once covered his wooden floors but the pine planks would require several coats of linseed oil. Their living room was large, but furnished sparsely, with only a couple of straight-back chairs, a bench, a side table and a hutch filling the space. Though he was grateful to the community for their generous donations for making their connubial residence comfortable, his new home was still a drafty old dump and Joshua vowed to make it a decent place to live. They would not exist in squalor.

Entering the kitchen and removing his galoshes, Joshua could hear Hannah in their bedroom. The door was ajar and she was humming a hymn from the ceremony earlier that day. She had wanted to recreate that sense of rapture she had felt when they repeated their vows.

Inside the room, she had removed her wedding attire and had donned a floor-length nightgown that was tight to her chin. Of course, she would happily remove her garments for Joshua, giddy at the thought of bedding the one true love of her life. She had won! She had succeeded in marrying the most eligible man in their community, and what a prize! For he was the strongest young man anywhere, and easily the handsomest creature she had ever laid eyes on.

Her dream had come true.

"Hannah, I'm back from the horses," Joshua called out, returning his voice to his native tongue. It was unavoidable.

Standing in front of her antique bedside dresser, yet another donation from one of the folk, Hannah saw her reflection in the mirror and smiled. Two long candles, one on each side of the framed Maplewood mirror, illuminated her image, revealing a pale fleshy face and round dark eyes. Locks of long wavy brindle-colored hair flowed across her ample bosom.

Joshua has never seen my hair, she thought.

But he will like it. He will be pleased.

Slowly she released the top button of her nightgown, followed by another...and yet another. She was determined to make herself as beautiful as she could for her man, for her Joshua. She was equally determined to make him forget about that damned woman! That venal person! She frowned at the thought and instantly reprimanded herself, offering a quiet prayer to God asking for forgiveness. She would do her penance. But God, she told *Him* often, that *evil* English woman had almost ruined her life!

Staring longingly into the mirror, she became mesmerized by the beauty and clarity of the object in front of her. Slowly and from around her neck came a loose-fitting necklace arrangement. *Her* necklace was unlike any of those fancy, expensive English ones. Not at all like those decadent pieces of shame that she had seen in the window of Algar's, the jewelry store in town.

No, this one is more befitting for me and *my* new husband!

A simple, even innocuous, piece of string but very appropriate for the large sparkling stone that she acquired one night.

She smiled. Beautifully encased in silver, it was not exactly green...and not blue, either.

The foolish English called it 'turquoise.'

She had defeated her nemesis.

"You would have made a terrible wife!" Hannah whispered aloud. "So wrapped up in your vile English ways. You deserved your fate. For your sins."

Removing the necklace and placing it secretly beneath a few undergarments in her top drawer, she heard the door to the bedroom open behind her.

Smiling, she turned in Joshua's direction.

"I am ready for you, my dear husband..."

B UBBLING WITH JOY, Barbara Cahill bear-hugged her happy husband of nearly twenty-five years before reaching into her purse for her iPhone. Now she was galloping down the hall towards a waiting room by the windows where she knew she'd find better cell service.

Slipping and sliding on the cold terrazzo floors, bouncing off a housekeeping cart filled with toilet paper, towels and cleansers, she almost bowled over a group of orderlies still upset at the idea of having to work another Thanksgiving weekend.

But she didn't care!

Well, she did...since the staff at Upstate Medical had been so kind to her and Roger over the past two months. She vowed to apologize for this maniacally crazy mom shit!

Later!

Right now she had an important call to make and nothing—nothing!—was going stop her. Finally, as she reached the 'Parental Misery Center', as she had dubbed it, she took a quick look out at the condensed cloud cover that had blanketed the city. It had started snowing last night upon their return from Morgantown, and hadn't stopped.

Syracuse, she thought. Weather always sucks!

But right now, she couldn't care less. Right now she was in love with this wonderful town, its hospital, the doctors, the nurses—everyone and everything, even its goddamned weather!

She consulted her cellphone in hand—and was thrilled. Four bars! Even in this weather. Isn't life grand? Immediately, she punched in a ten-digit cell number that she had come to know by memory. How could she forget it?

Be there, she pleaded as she heard one ring....and then a second...and now a third. Be there!

Finally, a response!

"Boychuk," came the simple reply.

"Brian! Barb Cahill here!"

Instantly, he sensed the energy in her voice.

"Barb...sorry I missed you at your brother's place yesterday."

"No problem, but I think we'll be seeing you soon!"

"Where are you? Back at UMC?"

"Yes, Brian! And I've got news—wonderful *fucking* news! Oops, pardon my Irish."

"What? What's going on?"

"Brian, you're the first one I had to call! I think you should drop everything there, hop in that big truck of yours and get down here right away."

"Why? Why? Is Ria okay?"

"Better than okay, Brian! Better than anything in the world right now! A few minutes ago, Ria opened her eyes!"

"Wow! That is great news!"

"Yes!" she replied. "And for the first time in months, too! And guess what?"

"What?"

"She's talking!"

ABOUT THE AUTHOR

R.M. Doyon has been a journalist, speechwriter, public relations executive and author for more than three decades. His first novel, *Upcountry*, was published to rave reviews in October, 2010. He and his wife, Shelley, split their time between the shores of the St. Lawrence River and the California desert.

Made in the USA
Middletown, DE
06 July 2015